THE RUBY RING

Tyndale's Battle for an English Bible

A Novel

by

Karen Rees

To Kathy and Dick,

May you always value the Bible and the Truth it proclaims.

Karen Rees

CROSSLINK
PUBLISHING

The Ruby Ring

Ɗ CrossLink Publishing
Ɋ www.crosslinkpublishing.com

ISBN 978-1-936746-46-0

CONTENTS

CHAPTER 1 – JUNE, 1515

"This time, Owen, do you think my lady mother's babe will be born alive?" asked the child riding straddle-legged behind the youth on the ancient white charger as they crossed the summer meadow.

The question tensed Owen Alton's back and tolled in his head like a funeral bell. He twisted in the saddle to glance at Jane Horne. She was sucking the end of one dark braid. Her dusky gaze clung to his face in hopeful expectation.

"Don't chew your hair."

His order carried the authority of long acquaintance and five years seniority in age. Jane spat out the wet mass and tossed it over her thin shoulder.

Owen turned his head and nagging thoughts back toward Wynnfield Hall. Beyond the distant border of oak and ash that edged the meadow, the manor's red-brick chimneys stood tall against an azure sky. Those chimneys had been a welcome sight indeed when, as a dirt-streaked, tearful and lost little boy of six, he had paid his first visit. Lady Eleanor, Jane's mother, had taken him up in her lap and cuddled him. Mistress Alton, for all her mother love, would never have risked soiling her gown.

Now those same chimneys, piercing the steep shingle roofs, were worrisome reminders of the apprehensions of the day. Earlier he had walked over from his grandparents' manor eager to tell Lady Eleanor and her chaplain, Sir Joseph, that he was entering Cambridge in the autumn to study for the priesthood. Instead, on his arrival, he had learned that she lay groaning behind one of her bright mullioned windows. Once again she was gambling her life to bear a son to her second husband, fat kindly Sir Harry.

I should have spent these last hours praying with Sir Joseph, Owen fretted, remembering his sister dead in childbirth a year ago. That's where my duty lies now that I've decided to be a priest. But he sent me off with Jane. A service, he called it. And a priest also serves.

Mary, Mother of God, have mercy on Lady Eleanor. Whatever she has been, protect her now. Grant her this child, alive and healthy.

Jane broke into his prayer.

"Owen, what do you think?"

A flash of annoyance tightened his mouth. Why must she be so insistent? If she craved assurance, so did he. But honesty denied complete confidence.

"It's in our Lord's hands."

"That's what Sir Joseph says when he doesn't know the answer." Jane sighed. "I would so like someone to play with. If Lucy lived with us rather than in London, I could play with her little boys. I am their step-aunt, you know. Sometimes I play with the cook's daughter. But having my very own brother or sister...."

Bored by Jane's musing, Owen's attention strayed. The string of fish they had spent the afternoon catching flopped wetly against his leg as the old horse plodded across the wide meadow. When they passed one tall clump of flowered grass, a cloud of yellow butterflies spiraled into the air and surrounded them briefly with a restless swirl of borrowed sun.

The charger, apparently sensing the nearness of his home stable, lifted his ears and quickened his pace. Owen settled more firmly in his seat. Near the meadow's edge, the horse broke into a thudding gallop. They charged through the rim of trees, swept past the barrel-chested bailiff, Howard Willcotte, and scattered a small flock of hens scratching for bugs in the stable yard.

Owen reined to a stop before the open stable door. The bailiff came puffing up, clutching his flat brown cap on his russet head. He swung Jane down and accepted the fish. Owen handed the reins to the stableboy.

"You best take Mistress Jane to the house," Willcotte said, his voice tight. "She was wanted earlier."

Owen looked across Jane's head at Willcotte's weathered face and small, rust-colored eyes.

"Is something amiss?" He mouthed the words softly.

Willcotte rubbed his long upper lip with a forefinger.

"You'll know soon enough," he said, moisture gathering in his eyes.

Owen's stomach chilled. Grabbing Jane's hand, he hurried through the half-timbered gatehouse and across the base-court toward the brick manor house glowing a warm rose in the afternoon sun. He glanced up at the solar window. It was thrown open to welcome the scented summer air ... or to let a soul depart.

Inside the hall, golden fingers of sunshine stretched down from the high narrow windows to ladder the rush-covered floor. Finding no one, they wordlessly traversed the long room: sunlight and shadow, sunlight and shadow. The vivid image of a miracle play Owen had seen in London leaped to mind, angels ascending Jacob's ladder to heaven.

But people went to purgatory.

They put the dais behind them and entered the blue parlor. This room also was empty. Around them, the house was silent, too silent.

Jane's fingers tightened on Owen's hand. With no one to direct him elsewhere, he climbed the wooden stairs with her to the private bedchambers above. Their leather slippers whispered harshly as they crossed the passage room and stopped outside the partially opened solar door. Owen hesitated. He glanced down at Jane, uncertain whether to knock or enter unbidden.

Before he could decide, his ears caught the weak, high-pitched mewing of a newborn babe. Jane's apprehensive expression was swept away by a flood of joy.

"It's the babe!"

She shoved the heavy door wide and dragged Owen through. At the solar's near end, the midwife was wrapping a red-faced mite in a length of white cloth. Owen looked toward the other end of the room. Between one heartbeat and the next, even as Jane began to slide her hand free, his eyes focused on the three people around the bed.

Sir Harry sat slumped on a stool, tears winding through the hills and valleys of his chins. The family chaplain, Sir Joseph, stood at his shoulder, gray head bowed, lips moving in silent prayer. From the bed's foot, Lucy Horne Terrell peered around at them. Her eyes were red-rimmed, her heavy, pug-nosed face blotchy. Owen caught frantically at Jane's slipping fingers.

"No, Jane. Wait."

His voice was a strangled whisper. Jane glanced up with a questioning look. He nodded toward the bed, resplendent with scarlet embroidered hangings, where Lady Eleanor lay so quietly under the blue damask coverlet. Death had closed her cornflower-blue eyes, blanched her soft cheek and left her as remote as a carved and painted angel in St. Thomas church roof. It had yet to dim the honey-gold hair pouring across her pillow.

Now I can't tell her of my decision. The thought seared Owen's mind and brought burning tears to his eyes. Sir Joseph was wrong. I should have been praying in the chapel. He dropped Jane's hand and fled the room.

Freed from Owen's restraint, Jane edged toward the frighteningly still figure of her mother. Behind her, she heard the babe wailing.

Surely Mama was sleeping. Soon she would waken and hold out a welcoming hand. The babe was always the one to die. Not Mama. Not Mama.

Jane crept forward, straining for any sight of movement from the bed. She tried to speak but her throat was filled with pricking thorns. Only when Lucy's stout arms fastened around her was she aware of her stepsister. She struggled fiercely, desperate to reach her mother. Lucy's grip held. Abruptly, she stopped resisting. With a sob, Jane collapsed against Lucy and allowed herself to be carried from the bedchamber.

Three hours later Jane was sitting on a bench with her stepfather listening to his mild wheezing and sucking her braid end. Around them, black mourning draped the blue parlor's plaster walls and enveloped them in premature night.

With a weight in her chest as heavy as an anvil, Jane watched the door. Lucy would come through it when she had finished laying out Mama in their small chapel. Jane herself had once buried a sweet furry kitten. Mama had given her a velvet scrap for a shroud. Would Lucy be as tender?

At last the door opened and Lucy appeared. She crossed the floor, her feet crunching the rushes, and stopped in front of Sir Harry.

"It's done, Father." Her voice, usually boisterous, was muted.

Sir Harry nodded his bald head and his jowls trembled. His once solid mountain of flesh now resembled a pile of limp dough.

"The requiem mass will be tomorrow afternoon," Lucy said gently. "I've given orders for the funeral banquet and sent word to the neighbors. Should I write to Lady Eleanor's relatives? And her first husband's family?"

Her stepfather straightened abruptly as if someone had rammed a stave up his back.

"No! They deserted her. They never sought amends all these years. They've no claim on her. Only me. I cared for her then. I'll care for her now."

The red-faced, mewing mite that had cost Lady Eleanor her life lived only a week after Jane saw her mother laid in the floor of St. Sebastian church in Hensford town three miles away. She alone had tears for this fresh loss. Indeed, apart from herself, the whole household seemed to forget the tiny child almost before his grave was filled.

"Must you go back to London, Lucy?"

Jane was perched on a stool in the accounts room watching Lucy at the writing table struggling to compose a letter to her husband.

Lucy paused.

"I told you I'd stay until September. That is, if George can come in August." She wiped an ink-stained hand across her brow and left a smudge. "If I'd had a tutor as good as your chaplain when I was young, I'd be a scholar now." Her broad face split in a grin. "No, I wouldn't. I'd have run off from lessons every chance I got."

"I mean," Jane said, "couldn't you stay after September. Couldn't you stay for always?"

"And what would become of our wine business? I had enough of being poor when I was your age."

"You wouldn't be poor. You'd have Wynnfield."

"Wynnfield was your mother's, not my father's. It's your inheritance."

"You can have it if you'll stay."

"You say that today. It'll be different when you start thinking about marriage and dowries. Hush, now, and let me finish. I need George to bring his aunt. She can order the household 'til you're of an age to manage it yourself."

8

Lucy's completed letter, although somewhat ink-smeared and filled with truly creative spellings, produced the desired results. When George rode in through the gatehouse after Lammas, Dame Edith Terrell rode, straight-backed, at his side.

At Lucy's nudge, Jane stepped forward in the courtyard and dropped a nervous curtsy to her guest. As she came clumsily out of it, she caught a whiff of lavender from Dame Edith's black gown. The purple flower's scent had been her mother's favorite. Jane's throat closed so she was unable to voice the expected welcome. Dame Edith, smiling down at her, seemed not to mind.

When September arrived, Jane wistfully watched Lucy gather her family and servants to return to London. Just before their horses carried them out of sight beyond the curve of the red-berried hawthorn hedge, Lucy turned to wave. Jane, standing with Dame Edith near the gatehouse, dutifully lifted her arm in reply. They were gone.

Jane felt a light hand settle on her shoulder, then Dame Edith began to turn her gently but firmly toward the house.

"Sir Joseph is expecting you for lessons, child. And, this afternoon, you must start learning to embroider."

The prolonged visit of Lucy's lively boys had dulled Jane's first sharp grief. With the passing of time and the full routine Dame Edith set, she gradually adjusted to her losses. Losses three times over, though she only realized it later when she waited in vain for Owen Alton to visit.

He came once the summer after her twelfth birthday to see the chaplain. Jane sat listening to them carry on a spirited conversation in which she could take no part. They spoke in Latin. After Owen left with hardly a word for her, she insisted that Sir Joseph teach her the language. She worked diligently and made good progress. The chaplain died the autumn she was fifteen. She wrote to Owen, in Latin, telling him of the old priest's passing. He never replied.

Far away on the Continent in that year of 1521 the German monk Martin Luther continued to stir up conflict which blew across the Channel with cloth from Antwerp. His heretical pamphlets found a ready audience among the questioning and questionable elements in London and the universities.

From Winchester, good King Henry penned such a brilliant denunciation of the monk that Pope Leo X honored him with the title 'Defender of the Faith'. That same year, the new defender commissioned Thomas More, the ablest intellect in England, to refute the heretic's dogma and complete Luther's overthrow.

The year passed. Jane, marking her sixteenth birthday, gave little thought to the battles being waged for the souls of men. In the spring, Dame Edith received word that a near cousin had died in a hunting accident. His young widow needed her services. She packed her chests, handed the household keys to Jane and departed. Although

Jane missed the older woman's decorous society, she felt no qualms in becoming the chatelaine of the manor. Dame Edith had trained her well.

Occupied with her narrow busy life at Wynnfield, Jane continued to hear whispers of heresy. To her, they had no more substance than the dawn mist. She had more pressing concerns. The year of 1523 had arrived. In a few short months, she would be seventeen. Despite Lucy's prodding, her stepfather was making no move to secure a husband for her.

CHAPTER 2 – JANUARY, 1523

Owen clutched his woolen traveling cloak more closely against the fitful rain that was fast turning to spitting sleet. Despite fur-lined gloves, he had little feeling left in the hand gripping the reins of the rattleboned nag carrying him through the raw January night.

The miserable weather and calamitous event that had necessitated this wretched journey were beyond his control. But he was a fool to have bypassed his grandparents' manor. Although with them dead he would have found small welcome, by now he would have found shelter. Nostalgia alone was drawing him on the extra mile-and-a-half to Wynnfield Hall.

The pale moonlight that had accompanied him for the last few hours was gone now, blotted out by clouds. He peered through the blackness of the winter-dead woods and listened. The rustle of sleet against bare branches, his horse's wheezing and the thud of iron shoes on the frozen track were the only sounds.

The breeze dropped abruptly. Off to his left he sensed the sheltering denseness of a towering thicket. A moment later Owen rounded the curve of hawthorn hedge that guarded the approach to Wynnfield Hall. Ahead, the solid black of a gatehouse rose to meet the hazy black of the sky. Off to the right a dog barked.

Owen reined up before the closed stable and dismounted stiffly. Leaving his drooping horse, he stumped on icy feet through the gatehouse and across the base-court toward the house and its welcoming lighted windows. He ignored the stinging of his fist as he beat upon the thick oak door. It opened at last. A blue-liveried manservant peered at him across a flickering candle stub. Owen mumbled his name. The servant waved him in.

His sodden cloak flapped about his legs as he followed the circle of candlelight the length of the darkened great hall toward the family's chambers. When he stepped with the servant into the bright warmth of the paneled winter parlor, Owen knew he'd been right to ride the extra distance.

To the left of the crackling fire, Sir Harry and the bailiff, Howard Willcotte, were bent over a chess game. To the right of the fireplace, between dark polished cabinet and jewel-bright tapestry, a young woman in a wine gown worked at a spinning wheel.

Owen peeled off his gloves as the servant announced his arrival. Sir Harry shifted around on his stool, his fat wrinkled face blossoming with surprise. He heaved himself up and waddled across the room, hands outstretched in welcome.

"Owen Alton. Where'd you spring from? Or is it Brother Owen?"

"Not yet."

"Here, take that wet cloak off before you catch a chill. It's devilish weather."

13

Owen clinched his jaw to keep his teeth from clacking and fumbled with the fastenings. The servant took his cloak and spread it to dry over a chest near the fire.

"I left my horse by the stable. He isn't much of a mount." Owen shifted, uncomfortably aware of the sting of saddle-galls. "I'm not much of a rider."

"Howard will see he's stabled," Sir Harry said. "Get to the fire. You look half frozen."

As the bailiff left, Owen gratefully crossed to the lively blaze and stretched his hands to the heat. Almost immediately, his chilblains began to sting. He moved away to a more comfortable distance and turned to toast his back. Only then did he notice that the woman had left her spinning and was giving orders to the servant. From his novitiate, he had learned numerous tricks of seeing, and dismissing, women as mere bundles of clothing taking up space. But this time his attention was caught. This tall slender maid seemed familiar.

She must have felt his quizzical gaze for she cast him a warm smile. He answered with an impersonal nod and turned back to Sir Harry.

"I'd meant to be further toward London. Then the weather worsened. I should have stopped at Stoke Hall, but -."

"Nonsense. You did right to come on. A cold welcome you'd have had with the manor nearly closed. How long has it been? Two, three years?"

"More like six."

"That long?" Sir Harry cast Owen a perplexed look.

"It's been four-and-a-half years, Father." The maid joined them. "Owen visited the summer you bought the spotted deer-hound."

"Oh, yes." Sir Harry's look cleared.

He began regaling Owen with tales of his dogs. His stories went unheeded. Owen was staring at Jane.

On the rare occasions when he'd thought of her at all, he'd always pictured her as a child. Except for her eyes, delicately lidded and as dark as a night sky, a rather plain child. He was startled to see how she'd changed. Although she didn't have her mother's striking beauty, his disinterested look found her quieter features pleasing. She must resemble her father. He pushed the thought away.

Owen was abruptly aware that he was staring. He felt his face heat and quickly switched his attention back to Sir Harry and the dog stories.

"You can see the pups in the morning," Sir Harry was saying.

"I need to leave at first light. My parents are expecting me in London."

"No trouble, I hope."

"My brother Walter has died." *And with his death he's destroyed my life.*

Jane's murmur of sympathy was drowned in Sir Harry's exclamation of dismay.

"Both your brothers dead. How grievous for your parents. What did he die of?"

Owen's mouth tightened. He saw again the bitter words of his mother's letter ordering him home. 'That whore gave him more for his twenty pence than he sought.'

"He caught a fever."

Owen was saved further questions by the arrival of a servant with his meal. The aroma of venison stew joined the odors of damp woolens and candle wax and set his mouth to running water. Having departed Cambridge hurriedly, he'd eaten nothing since his breakfast of goat's milk and rye bread. He was all at once ravenous.

"So many deaths. It seems but yesterday I lost Eleanor."

Jane moved from supervising the table setting to lay a hand on Sir Harry's velvet sleeve.

"It's late, Father. Remember you're sitting with Master Willcotte in the manor court tomorrow."

"You're right. It'll be a tiring day." He yawned widely, his chins compressing into fat pink rings. "You see how she cares for me," he said to Owen. "I don't know what I'd do without her."

Jane sat at the table idly twisting the ruby ring that had been her mother's and watching with satisfaction as Owen dipped into the stew. Her stepfather had retired, and she had dismissed the servants. For the first time in years she had Owen to herself.

Although she grieved for him over the reason behind his arrival, as Dame Edith would have said, the rain that wets the laundry, waters the garden. The joy that had overwhelmed her when he'd walked through her door, which his initial cold response had pierced, was hers again, restored by his look of astonishment that said he'd not recognized the woman she'd become.

She studied him as he ate in silent concentration. Already a man on his last visit, he'd changed little. The intervening years had merely added a man's width to his medium height and further maturity to his square-jawed face. Even his sacking-brown hair, damp from the rain, lapped his ears in the familiar way.

As she mused, the small sounds drowned out by Owen's arrival reasserted themselves. Once again she heard blown sleet brushing the glazed windows. On the mantel, the lantern clock ticked away the hour. Hungry flames whispered secrets to the chimney. A log, shifting in the coals, snapped with a shower of sparking gold.

The tranquility enveloping her must have touched Owen also. The strain in his face lessened and his tense mouth relaxed. His dexterous fingers dealt more gently with the bread end as he tore off a bite. He sopped gravy from his plate and tucked the morsel into his mouth. After a sip of mulled wine, he lifted his slate-gray eyes and smiled.

"It's peaceful here. Just as I remembered. I'm sorry I didn't recognize you. You've changed."

"Everyone changes."

"And everything." His eyebrows dipped. "But by whose hand? Our Lord's or the devil's?"

His words shattered the tranquility and chilled her. She watched, bewildered, as he came to his feet and began to prowl the room. If only she dared go to him, take his hand and offer whatever comfort he needed.

Owen stopped to stare down at the chessboard.

"Have you ever wondered how a pawn feels?"

"I'm not good at chess."

He glanced about the room, his expression growing wistful.

"I used to bring my troubles here to your mother and Sir Joseph. They seem such small ones now." He fell silent for a moment. "I never answered your letter about his death."

"It doesn't matter." Determined to bring back a happier mood, she added, "I hope you noticed I wrote in Latin."

"I did. Whatever prompted you to learn?"

Too many silent years had passed between them for her to answer with complete candor.

"It seemed the thing to do at the time. My choice of books has widened."

Owen dropped the chess piece he'd been fingering and eyed her. His face inexplicably brightened. He returned to his seat.

"I've a Latin book you might enjoy. I'll leave it for you to read."

"All right. And when you return to Cambridge, you can stop to see if I've finished."

His brightness faded. He flattened a bread crumb with his forefinger.

"I probably won't be returning."

"Have you finished your studies then and are ready to take holy orders?"

"I doubt I'll be ordained. Not now. Not ever."

"But what of the priesthood?"

"What, indeed. I've been struggling with that question for the last year. To have it answered like this."

He pushed up from the table and resumed his pacing.

"Whatever are you saying?"

Owen halted at the fireplace.

"You never met my brothers, did you. When Clement drowned, my mother thought it a simple thing for me to change to the law. After all, she'd lost her lawyer son. Only because of my father...." He cut the sentence off. "Never mind the details. Now both my brothers are dead. My parents have no other sons for the business."

"No. They couldn't ask that," Jane said, coming to her feet. "Not to give up your dream. They couldn't be so unfair."

Owen began jabbing the poker into the glowing embers, rearranging the fire. In the awkward silence Jane studied him, unable to fathom his compliance. After tossing a fresh log on the flames, he dropped the poker and dusted his hands. He crossed the room to stop in front of her, his mouth stern.

"I'm the one being unfair. And not completely honest. The truth is ... had Walter not died I still couldn't take my vows. When I'm ordained I'll kneel." He dropped to one knee before her and caught her hands flat between his. "I'll put my hands between the bishop's like this and swear on peril of my soul to absolute obedience."

He thrust her hands away as if they were the live coals he'd stirred and rose to his feet again.

"I can't swear. In all clear conscience, I can't. I no longer agree with the Church. How can I give it absolute obedience?"

Jane gaped at him in consternation. Had his brother's death and his parents impending decision unhinged his mind?

"But, you ... you can't stop believing."

"Of course I haven't. I've merely clarified what I believe."

His answer made no sense.

He returned to his pacing.

"Do you know I've not had one course of scripture in nearly seven years of study? Before I'm deemed fit to open the mysteries of the Bible, I must first master music, astrology and geometry. My logic classes don't teach me how to discover the truth, just how to debate." He halted, his fists clinching. "What of my soul? And the souls of the poor folk under my care where I a priest? Am I to win their way to heaven by my power of argument? Small wonder people are taking interest in Luther's writings. If the Church won't meet their needs, they'll seek those who will."

At mention of Luther, she sagged with relief. Owen was not beset by madness. Luther was real as were his ideas. The devil's ideas! Her knees buckled and she sat abruptly. Owen continued to prowl the room, her gaze following him.

"If not a priest, what are you?"

"I want to know the scriptures. The Church certainly doesn't teach them. The clergy are as ignorant as the people they lead. William would have even peasants familiar with the Bible."

"William?"

"Sir William Tyndale." He halted and his look brightened. "He's a priest, a brilliant scholar. He came up from Oxford a few years ago. I've been studying with him."

"Does this Tyndale accept the Church's teachings? Or has he forsworn his oath?"

"I've never thought to ask. He did accept Lutheran tracts from me. I can't ask him now. He's gone to Bristol." He shrugged and returned to stand by the table. "Whatever his answer, it's too late. I've too many doubts and Walter's dead." He cast her a wry smile. "I could become a Lollard preacher. They take no vows."

Jane jumped to her feet and grabbed his arm.

"And they get burned at the stake. I'll not see that happen to you."

He brushed her concern aside.

"That Latin book I mentioned. I'll leave it with you. Promise to read it?"

The abrupt change of subject left her floundering.

"What is it?"

"Erasmus's New Testament." He gave a humorless laugh. "Don't look so worried. The Church allows it. You only get sent to the stake for reading English scriptures."

Owen departed at the first hint of sulky dawn. His bony mount carried him down the frozen track and out of sight behind the black tangle of hawthorn hedge. Beyond, the naked trees reached their sleet-crusted limbs toward the dirty underside of cloud cover. By the gatehouse, Jane shivered in the damp cold. She cast one last pensive look down the empty path then hurried back to the warmth of the house.

In her room, her cloak hung on a peg, she hugged the small hot fire. Her look strayed to the book laid on the mantel the previous night. Gingerly she picked it up. For the hundredth time she regretted having accepted it. She wasn't so much afraid of the Church as of the book itself. It, and that priest, had caused a disturbing change in Owen. What might it do to her?

After last night, she felt closer to him than ever before. At the same time, he had become a stranger. Also, she was frightened for him. If he should even hint to others about the thoughts he'd shared so freely with her....

She studied the book's worn cover for a moment then crossed to a nearby chest and shoved it to the bottom. She would keep her promise to Owen. She would read his book. But she had not promised when she would read it.

Owen was chilled to his joints by the time London's sprawl appeared on the drab horizon, its tiled roofs pierced by a hundred steeples. St. Paul's Cathedral towered over them all like a queen over her ladies. The late-afternoon gloom was slipping into early night when he rode through Bishopsgate and into the courtyard of the Three Rings Inn where he was to leave his hired mount. From there he set off stiff-gaited toward Bucklersbury Lane.

The chest balanced on his shoulder sat one book lighter than it had the previous day. He hoped that Jane had started on the testament by now. Sharing with her a part of the truth he'd found shone as the one flicker of hope in his disintegrating world.

The icy wind whipped at Owen along Threadneedle Street and across Poultry until he escaped it up his own narrower lane. A dozen paces brought him home.

Normally the substantial premises would be doing a brisk trade at this time of day with housewives and kitchen boys hurrying to purchase a pot of honey or sack of salt before closing. Now they bustled past toward other grocer shops. Their steps slackened briefly as they tossed curious, sympathetic glances at the shuttered windows and padlocked door, at the black strips of mourning fluttering on the shop front and on the closed courtyard gate beyond.

Owen stopped at the gate and lifted a gloved fist. Half-a-minute later the peephole revealed the gatekeeper's grizzled, toothless face. Wood scraped metal, the heavy latch lifted and the gate cracked open. He slipped through.

The long cobbled courtyard stretched silently before him, empty of the usual bustle of men, carts and sumpter horses. The gray stone warehouse to his left, like the shop, stood shuttered and locked. Even the half-timbered house, old wing above the shop and warehouse, new wing across the end of the yard, appeared devoid of life. Three stories of windows stared out across the yard like black hooded eyes. Only in the hall windows directly above the warehouse did a gloomy light show. Shifting his chest, Owen trudged across the yard and climbed the outside staircase.

As he pushed open the hall door, the wind swirled in with him. Candle flames flinched and the black mourning cloths curtaining the walls from ceiling to floor stirred restlessly. The numerous tapers burning in their wooden chandeliers should have sufficiently brightened the room and given its careful order an air of welcome. Instead, the somber drapes reduced their valiant efforts to feeble islands of light floating in a sea of melancholy.

Finding no one in the hall, Owen continued up the stairs to the bedchambers, turning automatically toward the one that, when at home, he had shared with his brothers. He twisted the latch and pushed open the door. Once again draped mourning met him. But, unlike the courtyard and hall, this chill room was not empty. On the bed beneath a row of flickering candles, a body lay wrapped neatly and with finality in a white linen shroud.

Why wasn't Walter already in his grave?

Owen backed out and pulled the door shut with a fumbling hand. He sleeved moisture from his eyes, turned and collided with one of the maids. She was a dumpy, pockmarked woman, her graying hair neatly tucked into a white cap.

"Master Owen. You've come. Your mother wants to see you."

"I need to wash first." He glanced down at his travel-stained garments and saw Walter's corpse. He swallowed. "Is the west chamber empty? Good. Would you fetch a jug of hot water?"

The maid started on her way. Owen plucked at her sleeve, halting her.

"When will the funeral be?"

She threw him a guarded look.

"Don't know, Master Owen."

She ducked her head and shuffled off.

A short while later, dressed in clean brown hose and a tan doublet, Owen tapped on his parents' chamber door. The door jerked open and he was facing his father. One look at Humphrey Alton's square face, now florid with rage, told Owen that he was walking into the middle of an argument between his parents.

His father glared up at him across the threshold.

"Don't stand there like a simpleton. Come in!"

Owen stiffened but did as ordered. He watched his father stump about the bedchamber, throwing tight looks at his seated wife. Clearly his father's normally sanguine temper had been tried too far.

Owen glanced uneasily at his mother. Catherine Alton, in a black brocade gown, sat at her dressing table combing her long silver-blond hair. She was an attractive woman, her almost-smooth skin belying her age. Only in the discontented hardness of her blue-violet eyes and set of her mouth could the effect of the years be clearly seen.

"I want my son buried. But for your stubbornness he'd already be in his grave."

Humphrey kicked a stool out of his way.

"And that thieving priest would be eight pounds richer. I won't pay that much."

"What choice do we have? Leave him where he is?"

"But eight pounds! That's twice what I pay a servant for a whole year. He'd have it for a day. Why must we forever be paying gluttonous churchmen? Taxes, tithes, masses, burial fees. And it doesn't stop when we're dead. That greedy priest spouting purgatory to your father robbed us of half his estate. We won't pay." He shook a blunt finger at her. "Not one farthing. I'll see him in court first."

Catherine's naturally pale face blanched. She rose to her feet. Standing, she topped her husband by an inch.

"And lose everything like friend Humme's wife did? What's left to her now? Her husband murdered in prison. His possessions confiscated by the Church. All over a burial fee. You'll pay that fee. And masses for my son. He'll need them."

Humphrey's jaw jutted.

"He was a good son."

"He was what you made him."

"What do you mean by that?"

"You know. But for you, he'd be alive today. You killed him!"

Owen gasped.

As his mother advanced, his father retreated to the foot of the bed.

"He worshiped you. What example did you set? How many bastards have you fathered? Any pretty face or honeyed tongue turns your head. He copied you. Now he's dead. You killed my son." She raised her fists and lashed out. "Murderer!"

Making no effort to protect himself, Humphrey backed against the carved bedpost, face distorted.

Even as Owen sprang forward to pull his mother away, she began wailing. He pushed her down onto the chest at the end of the bed. She continued to wail.

Owen straightened, his breath coming roughly, and forced himself to look across at his trembling father. He took a cautious step, reached out to him.

"Father...."

Humphrey shuddered and shrank away. With a deep animal groan, he rushed out of the room.

The following morning Walter's funeral procession assembled in the courtyard to walk to St. Mildred's. The slush from yesterday's brief thaw had, overnight, turned into ice that crunched underfoot. The hired musicians had their heads together trying to tune their cold pipes and lutes. Pallbearers waited beside the coffin, its black-draped lid adorned with yew and rosemary. A fellow strode about the yard handing evergreen branches to the mourners. Owen accepted one. The smoky, wintergreen scent of death filled his nostrils.

He joined his parents directly behind the casket. His mother stood between himself and his father, her gloved fingers slipping over her silver rosary, her lips moving in prayer. She remained stiff and withdrawn, every detail of face and apparel correct. Owen looked past her to where his father huddled in a fur-lined ebony gown, his face an expressionless mask. Their eyes met briefly. Humphrey's lips narrowed and he turned away. Despair swept through Owen.

Why must his mother always make him a rebuke to his father? She had long flaunted his choice of a religious vocation as if it were an atonement for Humphrey's infidelities. Now she'd made him a witness to her hysterical accusations. Would his father ever forgive him for being there?

Owen's despondent thoughts were interrupted when the funeral procession began to form behind him. Frederick Steiner, Humphrey's minor partner, limped up on his wooden peg accompanied by his short, round-faced wife. They took their places just behind his parents. Friends and members of the grocers guild came next. Since Humphrey was a well-liked man, the numbers were so large that the line was forced to curve back on itself. At the tail and nearly even with the coffin's stand, the Alton employees gathered, whispering and stomping their feet against the biting cold. Owen glanced incuriously across.

One young man returned his look with the usual insolent stare. Owen's attention sharpened. He had forgotten Dick Bolt. Though he had not seen Dick for several years, he could never mistake him. Apart from the hazel eyes and crooked nose, viewing Dick was like looking into a mirror. His mother's accusation reverberated in Owen's head. He also wondered how many other bastards walked the London streets bearing those particular features. The familiar embarrassed fascination gripped him. He casually shifted his eyes away, affronted but not surprised that Dick had joined the procession with not a sign of mourning about him.

Owen wakened to the shouts of men and clatter of cart wheels on cobblestones below his west-chamber window. He pulled his bedding over his cold nose and burrowed deeper into the warmth of the feather mattress. If only he could recapture that limbo state of sleep that blotted out troubles.

It was too late. Steely cold light gave shape to the frosted window, Walter's funeral was over, and soon his parents would turn their thoughts to his future. What that future held was largely beyond his control. At least he could be master of himself.

Owen sucked a lung full of chill air, flung back the covers and leaped onto the cold floor. Hopping from one bare foot to the other, he pulled on his shirt, hose and doublet.

A short while later, washed and combed, he hurried down the stairs to the warmth of the dining parlor. Striding through the hall, he was relieved to find that the black tunnel had been restored to a neat room of bright embroidered cushions on red-painted chests and polished oak cabinets against white plastered walls.

The mourning had also disappeared from the dining parlor. Nothing now muted the soft gleam of silver plate in cupboards and on the sideboard or dulled the morning light slanting through the windows. When Owen entered, his mother, still clad in black, stood fingering her rosary by the bow window that overlooked her back garden. She glanced up.

"So you've wakened at last." She waved a hand toward the manchet bread and yellow cheese on the linen tablecloth. "Eat now. Your father will be along shortly to talk to you."

Owen tensed at her settled tone. Had his future already been decided? Mechanically he poured himself a cup of goat's milk from the green pottery pitcher. This was none of that blue, watered-down stuff sold from sour buckets. This came warm from a goat that was led around every morning and milked directly into the containers of the first housewives to catch its owner.

Owen was chewing a bite of bread when his father stumped in. Judging from his father's mottled jowls and puffy eyes, he had slept badly. He stopped at the far end of the table, his feet planted wide.

"When you've finished, report to Frederick in the warehouse. He'll be teaching you the business. I haven't the time."

Owen stiffened. He swallowed, but the bread refused to go down. Or was it anger that lumped in his throat? Until she spoke at his elbow, he wasn't aware that his mother had left the window.

"I'm sorry, Owen." He saw her glance briefly at his glowering father. "We're both sorry. Your father and I discussed it last night. You're needed here. Before, when we had...." She halted briefly, then, "The situation has changed. I'm sure you understand. The Church can always find other priests. We don't have another son."

Sweeping rage robbed Owen of speech. Under the table, his fists clinched until his forearms ached. Almost seven years of work.

All ended with a simple 'I'm sorry'. As if his life's dream was nothing more than a broken toy, easily replaced.

"I'll need my books and clothes." He was barely able to push the words out.

"The hired help can fetch them," his father said. "You're needed here. It's time you made something useful of yourself."

On that brutal evaluation his father stalked out. Owen's mother touched his hair lightly.

"You'll make a fine merchant."

Then she, too, departed.

He was alone. His breathing was loud, uneven. He brought his fist down on the table with a crash that set the pewter dishes clattering. He had known this would happen. He'd even told Jane as much. It was illogical to feel such rage. Since conscience prevented ordination, why not turn his hand to his father's business?

It was the way his parents had made their decision. They had never attempted to understand or even acknowledge the force that drove him. Now they dictated that he should be a grocer. The flowers dead in the garden below would revive with the spring and blossom again. What of the fire that burned within him? What would become of him when spring again bloomed?

CHAPTER 3 – WINTER-SPRING, 1523

The man assigned to teach Owen the business had sailed into London forty years earlier aboard a crippled Prussian grain ship. The merchantman limped up the Thames, its main mast a storm-splintered stub. The snapped spar had changed the lives of three German sailors. Two had been buried at sea. The third was carried to the monks at St. Anthony's hospital, London. The monks saved Frederick Steiner's life. They couldn't save his mangled right leg. He hobbled out on a wooden peg, his days as a sailor ended. Unable to find work in a foreign port, he survived until winter on the monks' dole and begging. The first snow found him huddled against the stone buttresses of All Hallows Barking parish church, his belly shrunk almost to his backbone, accepting that he must return home or die.

On his way to the Steelyard to plead for passage from the German merchants, Frederick passed a tiny grocer's shop, its goods artfully displayed on the fold-out counter. He stopped, mouth watering, at the sight of the enormous meat pie in the square hand of the short, cheery shopkeeper. The young grocer looked Frederick up and down. Taking out his knife, he halved the pie and handed one piece to the gaunt, shivering sailor. Thus did Frederick Steiner and Humphrey Alton begin their partnership.

At first Frederick worked for food and a second straw mat on the floor of the little back room. Humphrey, all his deceased hawker father's savings invested in his venture, could offer nothing more. The unusual partnership prospered from the beginning. Humphrey, a box giving him height at the counter, used his comely face and easy banter to sell maidservants and artisans' wives more than they had planned to buy. Frederick kept the store stocked and balanced the books.

The advent of Henry VII brought new peace and prosperity to England and provided the female populace with fatter purses to carry to Humphrey's store. Moving to a larger shop and wider clientele, Humphrey voiced the desire to replace their straw pallets with a goose feather mattress. Frederick, hand tight on the purse, refused. Time enough for soft beds, he said, when they had soft women to put in them.

Soon Humphrey found such a woman, a barmaid at the Two Bulls. Frederick offered to lodge elsewhere if Humphrey wished to wed. No, Humphrey said, he wanted better than a barmaid to establish his line.

The years passed, the coffers gradually filled and Humphrey changed mistresses several times. Frederick meticulously recorded Humphrey's expenditures on his lemans, his frugal German soul bemoaning every coin.

The day came when the coffers overflowed. At the same time property on Bucklersbury Lane came up for sale. Standing in the courtyard, the partners knew this move could take Humphrey from a hawker's son and petty grocer to a merchant of wealth and repute. With superstitious care, Frederick triple-checked the books. A month after the place became Humphrey's, along with a hefty debt, he galloped off to court a rich wife, leaving Frederick to tend the store.

Catherine Stoke had been a pert and spoiled child when Humphrey first met her prosperous yeoman father on his yearly trip to Stourbridge Fair. Although fourteen years his junior, Humphrey had never quite dismissed her. She was fifteen, naively romantic, ambitious and still spoiled when Humphrey, always an expert salesman, set about selling himself to his prospective in-laws. A brief, intense courtship gained Humphrey a wife: beautiful, gently brought up and her father's sole heir. He signed the marriage contract with satisfaction.

The bride's arrival in London kindled increasing dissatisfaction in her. From Humphrey's tales, Catherine had envisioned herself as the wife of a merchant prince, exchanging hospitality with nobility. Instead, she found her new home over a warehouse, the rooms not even as grand as those she'd left, and her handsome dowry spent on moneylenders.

A far more serious disillusionment came when she caught her husband of two months with one of the maids. If they'd had time to grow into love, she might have cried and he might have felt remorse and mended his ways. As events fell out, the timing was bad. Tired of her complaints and stung by her unexpectedly sharp tongue, he stormed out. When he reappeared, she turned a cold, proud exterior to him, seeing him for less than he was where previously she had seen him for more. The love she might one day have given him went instead to her children. He continued to squander his on barmaids. She ran his house well, acted the responsible mother and never again hired a pretty maid.

In time, Frederick also married, choosing an industrious seamstress. She failed to bear a child for his old age, but she saved a goodly penny making their garments. On Frederick's wedding day, Humphrey presented him with a cottage beyond the city wall though the gift delayed by two years the new wing Catherine wanted for her growing family.

And it was to Frederick that Humphrey took nine-year-old Dick Bolt some years later when the lad's mother ran off with a passing soldier. He'd handed Dick to Frederick to raise just as now he sent Owen to him to learn the business.

Owen liked Frederick. As a small child riding the tall German's broad shoulder, he had felt himself among the clouds. When slightly older, he trailed after Frederick, proudly imitating his limp, until the day Humphrey saw him and knocked him halfway across the room. Only later did Owen realize that his father thought he had been mocking Frederick.

Frederick, with his hobble and careful manner, seemed to prefer Owen's quieter, more studious ways to that of his older rowdier brothers. With Owen alone, he spoke his native tongue and expressed delight when Owen absorbed the second language with ease.

Now, as Owen side-stepped a string of winter-shaggy sumpter horses in the busy courtyard, he snapped at them in German and glared at the panniers slung across their backs which were being loaded with merchandise for grocers in towns north of London. He halted at the warehouse door. An intense desire to turn and flee back to Cambridge flooded over him. But to what purpose? By his own hand, he had shut that door. He had only this door now. Setting his jaw, he stepped through into the dusky interior.

The mingled fragrances of half-a-hundred spices and herbs filled Owen's nostrils and created an atmosphere headier than an Easter-decorated cathedral. Sage and fennel, ginger, cumin and cloves, nutmeg, galingale root and cinnamon vied for shelf space with syrup of Genoa, madder and white Castile soap. Larger produce sat in neat piles on the floor: boxes of raisins or dates, sacks of grain, peas and lentils, bags of bay salt and fine table salt, kegs of honey and cheap liquid black soap. All these and much more filled the storehouse with their presence and the chill air with their scents.

Looking for Frederick, Owen strode down the center aisle. The orderly sacks of coarse produce, the short deep shelves jutting from the walls, all created the vague resemblance of the pillars and bays of some crude church.

This was the only cathedral in which he'd ever officiate.

The jeering thought dogged Owen all the way to the accounts room, tucked between warehouse and street-fronting shop. Frederick was at the table, bald head bent over a large record book. Owen stalked in.

"I've come as ordered."

Frederick looked up. Under his beetling brow, his hazel eyes lighted and a smile crinkled his lined face. He carefully wiped his quill on an inky rag before laying it aside. He motioned Owen to a stool.

"A merchant I am to make of you, your father said."

"So I've been told."

Frederick studied him. The smile was replaced by a look of understanding.

"Sometimes life is that way. When I was younger than you, from the monks' school away for adventure I ran to be a sailor. Now I'm a merchant. When I lost this," he tapped his stump, "for me, the world ended. But I was wrong. A merchant's life is better. The beds are softer. You will find a new life. We'll start here in the accounts book."

Owen knew that Frederick spoke the truth about one thing. He would have to build a new life. When, a week later, his belongings arrived from Cambridge, they brought with them one link with the old. Between the pages of a book, the friend who had shared his bare lodgings had tucked the name and address of a London bookseller secretly dealing in Lutheran tracts.

"Owen with the figures is quick," Frederick reported to Humphrey some weeks later as the two sat in the accounts room making out an order for spices from the Continent. "He writes a neat hand."

"He should with all that tutelage in him." Humphrey knew he sounded short-tempered. But he had good cause. What he'd had to suffer recently was enough to sour milk.

"A good worker he is," Frederic continued. "A fine son you've reared yourself."

"I had little hand in that. If I had, he might have turned out more human. I should have put a stop to this priest business years ago." Humphrey shoved the inventory book away, all the irritations of the last fortnight roiling to the surface. "But Catherine was set on Owen entering the Church. Her tongue can strip bark off a tree. For peace, I let her have her way. Besides, I still had two other sons. Now what've I got? A single son with no more life than a milksop." He began to pace. "He's so sober-faced. Do you know what he does of an evening? He reads. A fortnight ago he asked for a few shillings. I thought he wanted new hose. Or to go out with friends. Instead, he comes home with a Latin testament."

Humphrey took another angry turn about the room.

"He and Catherine make a grand pair. Her with her black weeds and eternal masses and him with his books and long looks. All we lack is a priest to ring the Sanctus bell." He kicked the stool from his path. "Last night I had friends over for a dice game. Catherine was outraged that we'd play in a house of mourning. You'd think I'd pissed on the bishop during holy communion. When I called Owen to join us, he said he didn't gamble. In front of my friends. He's no right to act holier."

"I won't gamble."

"But you're a pinchpenny."

"Perhaps Owen also is. I know how little to him you gave for living in Cambridge."

"Even more reason to learn the game. Walter did and never lacked money. He never acted better. He looked up to me, wanted to be like me." Humphrey winced at a memory still raw. "I miss him. In the evenings, with you gone home, I've no one to talk to. Walter and I had such good times together. I didn't want him to die." Frederick's figure blurred. "I warned him about bedding common whores. I'm not to blame that he didn't heed."

Fredrick pulled himself up and crossed the floor, his peg clunking with every other step, to drop a hand on Humphrey's shoulder. The weight was comforting.

"Don't grieve yourself so. Always Walter was headstrong and into mischief. Remember the Christmas pudding in which he put the alum? For a week, like this everyone looked," he said sucking in his lined cheeks. "And the time he turned mice loose in the maids' room followed by a cat. The screeching and howling I still can hear."

The knot in Humphrey's chest began to loosen, and he felt a smile coming.

"Remember when he climbed the canon's orchard wall," he said, "stole his prize apples and left a dead snake in the tree? I beat him for that one. I laughed myself double after. If only I could have seen the canon's face. No doubt he missed the humor. Why must churchmen disavow merriment along with the rest? That's Owen's problem. He doesn't know how to laugh." He picked up his stool. "Leaving him with Catherine every evening isn't helping. He's my son, too. Time I did something about it. I know." He plunked the seat down. "We'll take Owen out tonight. Show him what he's missing."

Frederick nodded.

"But no gambling and no whores."

"Oh, all right. At least not yet."

As the withering winds of February warmed into March, Owen struggled to learn the business. Keeping accounts, writing orders, waiting on customers and manhandling deliveries from the Continent gradually became familiar routine. In those first difficult weeks two developments brightened his dull days.

He gained a friend in the bookseller who kept Lutheran writings secreted in his bedchamber. That procured him inclusion in the lively discussions among the bookseller's like-minded customers, reminiscent of the debates at the White Horse Tavern in Cambridge.

Owen always departed from these private gatherings with a lighter step and a renewed hope that he would find a way to serve God.

The other activity, surprisingly, was the time spent with his father and Frederick. From occasional meals at prestigious inns, Owen progressed to attending guild meetings and other gatherings with the two men. He also discovered that his father shared his delight in watching spring arrive. Most Sunday afternoons they strolled out to the fields beyond London to see what changes the week had brought to the swelling buds on hawthorn, elm and horse chestnut.

One Sunday near All Fools Day, they were returning through Bishopsgate.

"Is the little shop where you started business still there?" Owen asked.

Listening to his father and Frederick reminisce at their shared weekly meals had sparked his curiosity.

Humphrey threw him a surprised look.

A short while later his father halted at the head of an alley and pointed at a tiny shop squeezed between two equally minute ones, its worn wooden shutter now closed and locked.

"I'd forgotten how small it was." His voice was tender.

Owen stared at the shop in amazement.

"Why, Father, I had no idea you'd accomplished so much."

Humphrey glanced up; the lines at his eye-corners crinkled in pleasure.

"No one's ever asked to see the old shop. Not even Walter."

They continued on their way. His father strolled along the Sunday-quiet streets, face lit by a smile.

"Frederick's right. You have been working hard. Don't think I haven't noticed. And I'm pleased. You're quieter than Walter, but you think more. That's not bad. Walter and I had great times together. You and I can, too. I see that now. I've spent a lifetime building the business. Making my dream come true. Someday it'll all be yours."

But it isn't my dream. Owen caught the words back barely in time.

As they ambled toward home he grew more despondent with each step. What of his own vocation? How could he fulfill his vow to serve God, a vow no less real for being spoken only in his heart? To what important undertaking could he turn his hand?

After talking with Jane Horne in the winter parlor, he had thought he'd found a mission. If he could study scriptures with others as William Tyndale had with him, that would be worthwhile work. What had come of it? Nothing. Jane remained some thirty miles distant. Neither of his parents had any interest in his Latin Testament. Was he doomed to spend his life trapped in his father's dream? Must he forever sell sugar loaves to faceless customers while others led the fight to bring God's truth to England?

Weighed down with frustrations, Owen scarcely noticed when they reached Bucklersbury Lane. He and his father arrived at the courtyard gate physically only a foot apart. He was bitterly aware that, in mind and heart, they were as distant as York and Bristol.

One April Saturday afternoon Humphrey and Owen caught a boat across to Southwark to see a troupe of players on a makeshift stage set up in the Red Stag Inn yard. The boisterous performance soon had the audience whistling and laughing, Owen and his father with them. As they left, his father threw an arm across his shoulder and steered him toward a tavern with a paint-chipped picture of a mermaid hanging over the door.

Once inside, Owen stared dubiously around the taproom. Long, cross-grained tables, cheap wooden bowls and floors littered with gnawed bones held out none of the welcome he'd grown accustomed to in the other taverns he'd frequented with his father. Even the light reaching through the unglazed windows seemed dingy.

Humphrey called an order to the stout, bronze-haired barmaid then settled at a table still cluttered with the remains of a meal. He waved Owen to a stool.

Rose, as his father had addressed her, filled two metal-rimmed wooden tygs from the cask behind her and came toward them, weaving her bulk between the tables with all the ponderous slowness of a passenger barge moving up the Thames. She deposited the drinks on the cleaner side, pulled a dirty rag from her apron and cleared gnawed bones and spilt ale with a single practiced sweep. She shoved their tygs at them then settled across from Owen, leaned thick forearms on the table, and eyed him with interest.

Humphrey cast her a slight smile.

"My son Owen. He's been away."

The answering smile that cracked Rose's painted face seemed conspiratorial. She peered into the dark recesses at the back.

"You, May, come here."

The trumpeted order brought immediate results. A curly-haired woman, her face also put on from a paint pot, appeared at Rose's elbow. Owen struggled not to stare at her breasts bulging over the low edge of her red kirtle.

"Master Alton's son," Rose said.

May, reeking of musk, squeezed in next to Owen. Her skin had a tired look, like a much-used but infrequently washed linen sheet.

"By the by," Rose said, turning back to his father, "I ain't seen Walter for some time."

Humphrey's jovial look shriveled.

"He caught something from a girl at the Three Foxes. I lost him a few months ago."

"I'm sure sorry, Master Alton. He was a good boy. And generous. They ain't got a decent house over there. That'd never happen here."

Owen's stomach went cold, his face and the rest of his body hot. Had his father brought him to a brothel? He felt a hand sliding up his leg. It kindled a different heat in his loins. He jerked round to gape at May.

"Would ya like to see the upstairs, Master Owen?"

For a moment, he couldn't move.

Get out of here!

He banged the tyg down, stood abruptly and stumbled back, away from the hand.

"I'll see you at home, Father."

"Sit down," Humphrey said, his face darkening.

"Here's for the ale."

He fumbled for a coin. It slipped from his fingers, hit the table with a clink and rolled off the edge. Ignoring the two startled women and the blood pounding in his ears, Owen fled.

He was still standing in the street, hot with embarrassment, fighting anger and bitter disappointment, when his father burst through the tavern door. Humphrey grabbed Owen by one arm and jerked him around.

"What do you mean walking out like that?"

"There's nothing inside for me," Owen said, struggling to keep his tone neutral.

"You've no right to act holier."

"I'm not trying to. I simply don't want that kind of life."

"Why not? It's good enough for me. It was good enough for Walter."

"It killed him."

His father's face changed from scarlet to the color of porridge.

"You're as sanctimonious as your mother. Go on." He shoved Owen away. "Go home. I want no priests about me."

"Father...."

"Leave me alone."

Humphrey turned and headed for another gaudily painted establishment. Owen watched helplessly as his father disappeared inside.

Owen looked up from his merchandise list when Humphrey strode into the accounts room a week later. Since the disastrous trip to the Mermaid Tavern, his father had hardly spoken to him. They dealt with each other now as polite strangers.

Humphrey scrutinized Owen with the same look he wore when judging merchandise samples.

"You're to accompany Frederick to Bristol after St. Mark's Day."

Owen fingers tightened on his quill. So his father had been serious about not having a priest in his house.

"What am I to do?"

"Just be there. I'm considering a partnership with a grocer, a Master Bench."

"Bristol's so far."

"It's the port for the Atlantic. When someone finds a western route to Japan, Bristol will get the trade. Twenty-five-years-ago I sent six pounds with John Cabot when he tried. My money sank with his ships. Someday, somebody will succeed. When they do, I intend to have a part."

"How much are we investing this time?"

"I'm not sure yet. But, this time, it'll stay on land. Frederick will handle the negotiations. You be civil to the family, including the daughter. Bench dotes on her." Humphrey ran a critical look over Owen's worn green hose and russet doublet. "You'll need new clothes. I've already given orders to the tailor. Be there at one o'clock."

Inspiration struck. Perhaps something good could be gotten out of this rejection. He spoke quickly before his father could leave.

"When the Bristol business is done, could I stay a few days to visit friends?"

Humphrey shrugged.

"All right. But no longer. When you return, I'm sending you to Stoke Hall to check the accounts and make the place ready for your mother's summer visit."

When Owen left the tailors some hours later, he headed for John Long's bookshop near St. Paul's churchyard. The small establishment boasted only one customer when Owen stopped in. This particular client, a poor scholar by the look of his gown, occupied the bench provided for patrons paying to read by the hour and had his nose deep in a worn copy of Chaucer's tales.

At sight of Owen, the lanky bookseller handed the charge of the shop to his son. He led Owen up steep steps to the chamber overhead. Once inside and with the latch dropped against unannounced entry, John Long faced him.

"What of Luther's will you have this time?"

"One copy each of the last two pamphlets. I'm traveling to Bristol in a fortnight and want them for a friend."

"Bristol?" In between dark brow and bobbing Adams apple, Long's expression grew speculative. "I've an order of tracts for Bristol. Would you deliver them?"

"Don't you have a regular carrier?"

"I did. He was stopped by churchmen on his last trip and barely escaped with his life. Now I don't dare use him even in Essex and East Anglia."

Owen digested this information. From the first he'd known that Luther's tracts, forbidden by Church and outlawed by State, were of necessity smuggled into and around England. He'd never before given much thought to the details, or the dangers. To become a smuggler himself.... Fear prickled between his shoulder blades and blew cold in the pit of his stomach. Another emotion triumphed over the fear. Purpose. The door he'd banged hopelessly against all winter had suddenly sprung open.

"I'll do it. When I return, I'll be going north almost to Cambridge. If you should need something delivered there...."

Owen left the bookshop as exuberant as an apprentice on holiday. After Bristol and the later trip toward Newmarket and Cambridge, he might become a regular carrier. Frederick had mentioned sending him out as a buyer, calling on farmers and smaller traders that provided much of the locally produced merchandise his father handled. Those trips would take him to the very areas John Long had mentioned. Also, with his trip to Stoke Hall, he could see how Jane Horne was progressing with his Latin Testament.

As he passed, he tossed a coin and a cheery word to a filthy beggar child. The future shown bright as the new risen sun ... provided the churchmen didn't catch him.

CHAPTER 4 – MAY, 1523

T
he trip to Bristol took slightly over four days. The first day, trotting along the well-trampled road beside Frederick, Owen's thoughts were held captive by the bundle of tracts secreted beneath two suits of new clothing in the small leather chest bouncing behind his saddle. Expecting churchmen any moment, he tensed at every approaching traveler. Fortunately, Frederick, also a poor horseman, was too taken up with his uncomfortable seat to notice Owen's nervous preoccupation. Waking from their first night in an inn, he realized that the greatest hazard of the last twenty-four hours had come from the fleas in the inn's straw mattress. From that point, he was better able to remain calm whenever they met fellow travelers.

The journey passed uneventfully. Dodging patches of rain, he and Frederick jogged across the flat green plains and forests of the Midlands. As they reached the rolling, wooded Cotswolds, the gray cloud blanket thinned. A bright May sun broke through to welcome them to Bristol. They trotted out of the forest and reined up to study the small city before them. Nestled in the convergence of the Frome and Avon Rivers and backed by emerald hills, Bristol lay secure behind its thick turreted walls.

Entering the massive city gate, they asked their way to King Street of an egg hawker. Owen noticed, as they passed along, that the streets were less crowded and odorous than London's. They veered at High Street and, as directed, rode down toward the Avon, bristling with the masts of ships riding at anchor in its tidal waters. At St. Nicholas church they turned again and shortly arrived at Master Bench's courtyard.

The familiar bustle of carts welcomed them as they dismounted. Owen elected to hold the horses while Frederick limped toward the warehouse in search of Master Bench. As he waited, he surveyed the Bristol grocer's three-storied home with casual curiosity. A gray tile roof topped pale yellow half-timbered walls. Pots of sweet william, rosemary and marigold brightened windows in the upper floors. Beyond the flurry of courtyard traffic, a row of apple trees, their boughs laden with bloom, half-hid a newly greening kitchen garden. All bespoke a pleasing prosperity and homeliness.

Owen was watching two men unload a cart of wood when Frederick emerged from the warehouse with a stout gray-haired man in a dark damask gown and black velvet cap. Master Bench, for so he must be, carried with him the same air of comfortable affluence as did his property.

As Frederick made the introductions, the grocer's broad face beamed with welcome even as his sharp hazel eyes inspected Owen.

"My wife and daughter are calling on a friend," Master Bench said as he led Owen into the house. "You'll have time to remove the travel stains before they return."

A short while later, a gray-clad maid appeared at his chamber door. The Bench family were awaiting him in the hall. Owen locked his chest and tucked the key away. He didn't want some over-zealous servant stumbling onto the Lutheran tracts.

He entered the hall to find his hostess and her daughter seated by the bow window. As he approached, Mistress Bench looked up from her embroidery frame. Her button nose twitched as if she were sniffing the air. Agnes, her buxom shape tightly encased in a rose gown, left off fondling the silky ears of her tiny brown lap dog to cast him a demure look.

As Master Bench introduced his family, Owen recalled his father's orders. He bent over his hostess's thick hand with all the gallantry he could muster. Mistress Bench responded with a parrot imitation of her husband's earlier radiant welcome. In her turn, Agnes, blushing and dimpling, set her pet aside to drop a deep curtsy.

The dainty dog trotted over to Owen and lifted huge brown eyes. His tiny pink tongue lolled between sharp little teeth in a doggy smile. The next moment he sank his teeth into Owen's ankle.

Pandemonium erupted. Bellowing like a mad bull, Master Bench lunged at the little beast. His wife shrieked and jumped. The embroidery frame crashed to the floor. Agnes screamed. Releasing Owen, the dog dashed under a bench against the paneled wall. Agnes charged after, her bright skirts flying. She plopped down before the seat, reached under and hauled the animal out. She lifted him till they were eye to eye.

"You naughty, naughty Poopsie. To bite the lovely gentleman. Shame on you." She gave him a shake. "Apologize immediately."

Frederick, having arrived in time to see the attack, bent to peer at Owen's punctured hose and bleeding ankle. He straightened, his face suitably serious, his eyes dancing.

"You will live."

Agnes carried the captured creature to Owen.

"Lick his hand to show him you're sorry," she said, eying the dog. She looked up at Owen, her cheeks pink. "Put out your hand."

Owen, smarting at the pain in his ankle and trying to conceal his anger, had no desire to prolong the situation with a canine apology. However, no one sought his opinion.

Reluctantly he extended his hand sure the little beast would sink his teeth into it as well. The dog appeared to be considering the possibility. Fortunately, he must have rejected the idea. He gave Owen's hand a drooling swipe. His victorious mistress immediately whisked him out of the room.

Owen next faced fervent apologies from his host and hostess. He at last escaped to his chamber where he washed and salved the wound and changed his torn hose. When he regained the hall, Agnes, minus the dog, was waiting.

"You poor, poor man. Here, let me fetch a stool for your ankle. It must hurt dreadfully. Would you like a cushion?"

Feeling as foolish as he had with the dog hanging on him, he allowed her to prop his foot on a stool. Agnes flashed him the same triumphant look she'd given her penitent dog then rejoined her mother at the righted embroidery frame.

For the next hour, Owen attempted to make conversation with the Bench family while Frederick silently looked on. During one uncomfortable pause, Owen noticed a book's spine behind the latticed cabinet door.

"Is that a book I see?"

"Agnes," Master Bench said, "fetch the book."

Agnes bounced to her feet and a moment later presented the volume to Owen.

He leafed through the Hours of the Blessed Virgin, displaying an interest in the collection of prayers, devotions and superstitious stories that he was far from feeling.

"Do you read, Agnes?"

She shook her head, chestnut curls springing about her face.

"Oh, no. Father says a woman has quite enough to do managing a household."

So much for that.

"I've never visited Bristol before. I'd like to see some of its sights."

"Agnes can show you tomorrow," Master Bench said. "Accompanied by her mother, of course."

Discussion of Bristol carried them until the evening meal. Afterward, Agnes entertained them on the virginal. When the brief concert ended, Owen praised her lavishly, bringing dimples and blushes to her round face and setting her parents glowing with pride. That night, ankle throbbing, he wearily settled into bed. Had his father witnessed his performance, he could not help but be pleased. If only Frederick would hurry with the negotiations so they could be on their way.

The following morning Owen and Agnes set off with Mistress Bench in close attendance. He dutifully admired half-a-dozen churches, Temple Cross and High Cross, the guild hall and the market house in the center of Wine Street. At each, Agnes named the building then looked up expectantly as if presenting a piece of her own handiwork for Owen's approval. He arrived back at the Bench home in the late morning with the two women and a head that some blacksmith was using for an anvil. At least the morning's efforts had located the bookshop where he was to deliver Long's Lutheran tracts.

After the meal, Master Bench insisted on showing Owen the business which, he explained proudly, had belonged to his family for three generations. The inspection ended in the yard where the grocer discoursed on his Spanish trade and the future of sugar and Bristol soap. When Frederick stumped up Owen breathed a silent prayer of thanks.

Master Bench cast Frederick a broad smile.

"Well, Master Steiner, I'm satisfied we can come to agreeable terms." He clapped Owen on the back. "Very satisfied." Then, to Owen, "I'll not keep you longer. Doubtless Agnes has other sights to show you."

With a second broad smile, he left. Owen's forced grin sank into a grimace.

"The idea you don't like?" Frederick asked quietly in German.

"I'd rather do penance," Owen said in the same tongue. "At least Father will be pleased that he's gained his partnership."

"What of the terms has he told you?"

Owen cast his mind back to the brief conversation in the accounts room.

"Nothing, actually. He said you'd handle the details. I was to be pleasant to the family."

Frederick's beetling brow puckered. He glanced around at the busy yard.

"We must talk, I think. But not here. Come."

Puzzled by Frederick's tone, Owen followed him down Back Street, out a city gate and past a row of small thatched cottages. Before them lay a tree-speckled water meadow sloping gently away to the Avon. The meadow contained two munching goats and a small boy sprawled lazily in the new grass. Owen heard a blackbird trilling at the river's marshy edge. On a hill across the Avon to the left, St. Mary

Redcliff parish church lifted her lacy spire to the blue sky. Far off to the right, beyond the converging River Frome, the massive limestone abbey church of St. Augustine sat solidly amidst chapter house, monastery and encircling band of fields and orchards. The warm May breeze, heavy with the scent of flowers and odors of mud and marsh grasses, played about them as they started across the meadow.

Thought the scene was tranquil, Owen's misgivings grew as he followed Frederick. They halted under a giant elm halfway down the slope. He leaned back against the rough trunk.

"What didn't Father tell me?"

"With the Bench maid you are to wed."

Owen jerked upright, speechless with shock. Frederick continued.

"For several years this joining of businesses and families your father has been planning. Walter was to have been the one. Now it must be you."

"That's impossible. I won't wed her."

"Why not? A good dowry she has. And the heir she also is. Her training to keep the house is good. A fine wife she will make and a soft one in bed, I think."

Infuriated, Owen paced the elm's shade pool. Beneath his anger, fear swelled. Why must they keep pressing him into something he wasn't?

"Should I need a housekeeper, I'll hire one. As for my bed ... I'd rather sleep alone."

Frederick studied him with an uncertain look.

"You would have been a priest," he said at last, his tone one of reluctant reverence. "Is it that God has marked you, that, in your heart, you are celibate?"

Owen stripped a new leaf from a low branch and began wadding it up. His face, and his loins, heated at the memory of the whore's hand creeping up his leg.

"I've been given no time. When Father looks at me he sees Walter. When he isn't seeing Walter, he sees a priest. I'm not the one and I can't be the other. So what am I? You advised me to make a new life. I'm trying to." His thoughts jumped to the smuggled tracts. "But I need time. At the moment, I feel too unsettled to consider a wife."

"Taking a wife is very settling. It is not as if tomorrow you must wed. First there is the contract to complete. And the betrothal and time for sewing the wedding clothes. And for the wedding itself to prepare."

"Now or later," Owen said, throwing the mangled leaf away, "I won't marry Agnes. She's not got two thoughts in her head to rub together. And her little dog is vicious." He saw Frederick's mouth twitch. "Think what you will. I'm serious. I won't have her."

"Your father will not be pleased. He this marriage wants."

So I'm to disappoint him again.

A more immediate problem occurred to him.

"I can't remain now, letting the Benches think I've agreed. I'll explain and move to an inn."

"Nein! We must stay, at least till the morrow. And to the Benches you will say nothing. It is for your father to explain."

Owen hesitated. His father might continue with the marriage plans despite his objections. Informing Master Bench now would counter that. It would also humiliate Agnes to her face and certainly anger Frederick. He dared not do it. He badly needed his moderating influence. Whatever happened, his father could hardly drag him to the altar.

"All right. I'll let Father handle the refusal. But we leave first thing tomorrow."

"At least we will the sooner see our own beds."

"I'm not riding back with you. I'm visiting a friend in the area."

"Then, your father about the trip will ask me."

"Tell him what you will. But don't give him cause to think I'll change my mind. I won't."

After taking their leave of the Benches, Owen and Frederick rode together until they passed through the city gate leading to the London road. There Owen made his second farewell and watched Frederick jog away in the early-morning traffic. For the first time since he'd left Cambridge four months ago, he was his own master. He felt as free as a soaring swallow.

Owen reined his horse around and stopped at the first inn he saw. There he stabled his mount and changed from gray jerkin to his black one in case he found himself on the same street with the Benches. He then set off for the bookseller's shop.

Once he reached the narrow street, he relaxed. The Benches had existed happily for ten years with only one book. It was unlikely he'd meet them here.

The two reading stools inside the open door, which had been occupied yesterday as he'd passed with Agnes, were empty today. The shop's only inhabitant, a heavyset young man with pale-red hair, lounged behind the counter. He looked up when Owen entered.

"I'm seeking Master Cole."

"You've found him."

Owen quietly repeated the words that the London bookseller had had him memorize. Cole pulled a volume off the shelf behind and opened it on the counter.

"Show interest in the book should we be interrupted." Softly, "What do you bring?"

"Pamphlets from Germany."

"What's become of my regular carrier?"

"He met churchmen on the road."

Cole started.

"Did he escape?"

61

Owen departed to return three hours later as directed with the bundle of pamphlets secreted in his clothing. This time the bookseller had a single customer. A pimply-faced youth sat on a reading stool following his finger down a page of print. Without comment, Cole waved Owen into the back. Before quitting the store, he shook the reader to attention and pointed to a long stick leaning in the corner.

"Bang the ceiling if I'm needed."

The youth nodded and returned to his book.

"He comes in every Saturday regular as the bells," Cole said.

Cole clambered up a ladder into an attic room. After Owen scrambled through, Cole dropped the trap door and fastened it. He took Owen's package and waved him to a seat on the narrow bed. Cole settled down at the small table wedged in a corner and shuffled through the pamphlets. The tiny living space and sparse furnishings reminded Owen of his stark Cambridge quarters. That had been a different world.

Soon the bookseller gathered the writings and crossed to the wall where limp garments hung from pegs. He fiddled with a peg, removed a board and deposited the tracts on shallow shelves.

"I've got customers who will welcome these," he said, replacing the board. "Where do you go from here?"

"Back to London."

"I might have something for you to carry. How soon do you leave?"

"Not for a day or so. I've a friend here, a priest. He's employed by Sir John Walsh of Little Sodbury. I'm told it's somewhere north."

Cole's look sharpened.

"What's your friend's name?"

"Sir William Tyndale."

"Did you know that, two months ago, he was brought before the Chancellor on heresy charges?" Cole said as he settled down on the bed beside Owen.

"That's ridiculous."

"They say he defended himself well. He got off with only a strict warning this time."

"This time?"

"The church officials who accused him will try again. I've heard them in the ale houses railing against Tyndale. Sooner or later they'll have him."

"Why should they be so strongly against William? He's no agitator."

"No? He's certainly stirred up trouble here."

"Is he still in Sir John's employ?"

"Yes. Likely that's why he received only a warning. The Walshes have influence. But even Sir John can't protect him forever."

"I want to see him. Can you tell me how to get to Little Sodbury?"

"Tyndale may save you a trip. Most Saturday afternoons he comes in to preach on St. Austin's green. He's a fair speaker and previously drew good crowds. More recently, people are growing afraid to attend. I used to hear him myself. Now I can't risk being marked by the churchmen."

Rapping underfoot interrupted them.

"I must have a customer." Cole bent to release the trap door. Before he lifted it, he looked up. "Regarding you carrying for me. I'll be walking out Frome gate right after early mass tomorrow. If you're willing, be at the gate. Don't approach me; just follow at a distance. If you're meeting Tyndale today, I can't afford to be seen with you tomorrow."

When Owen left the bookseller, his nose led him to a collection of cookshops. After filling his belly, he set off toward the Augustinian abbey and St. Austin's green. The green, spreading between abbey-yard wall and Brandon Hill, appeared a popular place with the citizenry. Chatting maidservants, children playing tag across the grass and rowdy apprentices prowling in groups dotted the area. Owen, searching among them for a certain slight form, noticed a knot of people near a chestnut tree on the far side of the field. He set off.

Coming up to the gathering, Owen smiled. He'd found William. Dressed in a drab woolen gown, the priest was using a rock for a platform as he expounded scriptures in his usual lively style. William's roaming look locked with Owen's. His plain face lit with glad astonishment even as his tongue rolled smoothly on. Owen surveyed his friend. He'd not changed at all since Cambridge. But that couldn't be true. William must have changed. At Cambridge he'd never been accused of heresy.

Owen's thoughts were interrupted when several apprentices pushed past him to the front of the gathering. The crowd shifted to accommodate the newcomers. As Owen shifted with it, his eyes lit on a sharp-nosed man at the furthest fringe of listeners. The man returned Owen's look then leaned down and whispered to his companion, a dumpy man with a pox-scarred face. Owen studied the two from his eye corner. They appeared as interested in the listeners as they were in the preacher.

When William ended his sermon, the motley crowd left quickly. The only ones to linger were a servant girl with a live goose under her arm, Owen and the two watchful strangers. The girl exchanged a private word with the priest. Owen waited impatiently to greet William. The girl departed at last. William crossed to him, face alight and hands outstretched in welcome.

"It is you."

The two men, on the verge of leaving, stopped to study Owen anew. William caught their inquiring looks and released Owen's hand.

"I must bid farewell to my most faithful listeners." He turned. "Gentlemen. How good of you to come. I hope to see you tomorrow also."

The sharp-nosed man gave William a sour look. He stalked off, his companion trotting after. Owen's look followed them.

"Who were those two?"

"Nobody of importance. Tell me, what brings you so far from Cambridge?"

"I've left the university."

As he strolled around Austin's green with William, Owen poured out all the disappointments, frustrations and indecision of the last months. Not since the night with Jane Horne had he talked so freely.

"I lie awake at night thinking that, if Walter hadn't died, I'd be preparing for my ordination. Of course that's an illusion. I can't be ordained, not with the doubts I have."

He recalled the question Jane had put to him in that long-ago conversation.

"How did you manage to take your vows?"

They halted momentarily as a handful of screaming children chased a cur across their path.

"I didn't have your doubts. I was such an unworldly man. People say I still am, My doubts came later when I studied the scriptures. For good or ill, I'm a priest for life. Only now I realize my obedience must be first to God and then to the Church."

"I want to serve God, too. I can't now. I'm a merchant juggling money and merchandise and trying to avoid getting an unwanted wife."

"Perhaps you can't preach God's truth from the pulpit. What man can nowadays?" William's tone was unexpectedly bitter. "This smuggling is important. Luther's ideas are making people face the corruption in the Church. Until evil is recognized, how can it be removed? Be patient. God will give you a task when he's ready."

Something about his tone caused Owen to peer at him. He was looking at the abbey.

"Those two men earlier, they're churchmen," William said, ambling on. "They're waiting for me to speak heresy they can carry to the Chancellor."

"I heard you were charged. But why?"

"Because my employer spreads a lavish table, and likes lively discussion. The churchmen he invited decided to impress him by arguing scripture with me. They thought to eat me along with the pork pies and legs of mutton. They found me not nearly so appetizing."

Owen grinned at the picture William painted. His smile faded as he remembered the outcome.

"Wouldn't you have been wiser to have trod more softly?"

"And allow them to distort the truth? I spoke gently and only what could be found clearly in scripture. They charged me with heresy. More than anything, that shows the Church's corruption."

"I've never heard you speak so passionately."

William's eyes lost some of their fire, but his mouth remained resolute.

"You're not the only one struggling to find your way. Little Sodbury is far removed from the university atmosphere. This last year I've seen how corrupt the Church has become. In these months, God has showed me the only way to restore its purity. The scriptures in English must be available to everyone. The plowboy in the field needs to know the scriptures as thoroughly as the highest abbot in the land."

Owen had heard innumerable debates on this issue at Cambridge.

"You would give it to them?"

"Yes."

The intentionality of his answer halted Owen.

"I was only speaking in abstract."

"I'm not. If God spares my life, I'll translate the scriptures and see them printed in English."

Dumbfounded, Owen stared at his companion. The priest's face burned with conviction from his high, wide brow to his narrow chin.

"But how? And where? You can't. The Church would never permit it. And without permission, it would be your death."

He stopped, left breathless by the first glimmer of a vision. Not his small one of smuggling tracts to Bristol, to Cambridge, to Newmarket. This far surpassed the accomplishments of John Wycliffe who had bequeathed only a few expensive, laboriously hand-copied English Bibles. This vision was capable of transforming the hearts of multitudes, of reaching down the decades to alter the world.

"Can I help?"

"Pray for me. I've decided to go to London. I'll not be safe here much longer. I've heard the new bishop, Cuthbert Tonstall, is liberal minded. If I can gain his permission and a place in his household while I translate, I'll be protected."

"And if he refuses?"

A shadow crossed William's spare face.

"Pray that he doesn't."

As early-morning worshipers emerged from mass, Owen loitered near Frome gate consuming a meat pie. He popped the last juicy bite into his mouth as the red-headed bookseller strode past. Licking the gravy from his fingers, Owen casually set out after him. Cole passed a string of cottages hugging the road, then took the left track that led over a stony hill and into the royal forest north of Bristol. When Owen crested the hill, he found Cole waiting for him. The bookseller glanced about as if to assure himself that they were alone. Satisfied, he pushed through the tangle of bushes bordering the road and into the dew-wet forest beyond, Owen close on his heels. They made a wide arch back toward Bristol and ended behind a woodcutter's waddle-and-daub hut which Owen vaguely recalled passing earlier.

He was about to question Cole on his excessive caution when the bookseller knocked on the low back door. It opened, Cole bent his head and stepped through. Owen followed. Once inside, he was abruptly aware that the dim interior was filled with silent people. He looked about. At least a dozen rough-garbed men and half that many women sat or squatted about the room.

Bodies shifted and legs drew up. Cole and Owen squeezed through to a corner. The bookseller dropped to his haunches on the hard-packed dirt floor and braced his back against the whitewashed wall. Owen settled beside him. Several of the room's occupants cast curious, guarded glances at him.

"What is this?" Owen whispered.

"Lollard meeting," came Cole's soft reply.

Astonishment tingled through him even as a whisper rippled over the assembly. All heads turned toward the low entry.

A tall, wiry man with a dark, ugly face sidled in. His buff tunic and black hose were even more worn than the garments of the rest of the gathering. Nevertheless, this obviously was the man they awaited. Someone immediately relinquished a stool and passed it over the company's heads. The newcomer squeezed it in beside the fireplace. He stretched his arms above the crouching people and offered up a prayer. His muted nasal voice carried clearly to every corner. When he finished, he bent onto the stool and began to exhort his fellows from the scriptures.

In the distance, the chiming Bristol bells called laggards to prime. The listeners in the small, stuffy room paid no heed. They merely leaned closer, calloused hands slack in their laps, lips parted, their weathered faces drinking up the message like parched fields drink rain.

Owen squatted, his feet growing numb, intent on the Lollard preacher's words. For him, this mean, crowded, secretive service stood in stark contrast to the mass: beautifully housed in spacious cathedrals, rich in solemnity and steeped in a thousand years of tradition. The early Christians must have gathered thus to hear St. Paul, meeting in dark and hidden places, in peril for their very lives. A rush of emotion swept through him.

The meeting ended much later with a benediction and a collective sigh. People stood cautiously on cramped feet. Owen straightened to lean against the wall until his circulation returned. The rest of the assembly milled around, speaking in low voices and casting oblique glances at him. Otherwise, they ignored him.

"We'd best go," Cole said.

As Owen followed the bookseller back out into the bright morning light, he felt as if he were stepping through time. He glanced at the sun. Cole had given him a morning he would not soon forget.

But he must meet William in a few hours. Also, he'd not yet been told what he was to carry or where it must be delivered.

Rather than retracing their steps, Cole led Owen deeper into the forest. Growing restive, he was on the verge of questioning when they broke out into a rock-strewn clearing. Cole crossed to a weathered limestone outcrop, took a seat and sleeved perspiration from his brow.

"It's hot today."

"I thought you wanted my help."

"We shouldn't have to wait long."

"What are we waiting for?"

"You'll know soon."

Obviously he was saying no more. Owen glanced at the climbing sun. With a shrug, he curbed his impatience and settled down on a second rock. The breeze whispered among the newly green branches while insects rasped from the dappled shade of a larch. In a nearby beech tree, a wren began to sing. Back the way they'd come, Owen heard the rustle of something large moving through the forest. Cole squinted in the direction of the sound. A dark shape appeared in the shadow of a sturdy oak. For a heart's beat, the figure remained motionless, like a stag alert for danger. Cole lifted a beckoning hand. The Lollard preacher stepped into the sunlight.

He crossed the clearing and stopped in front of Owen.

"The peddler," Cole said by way of introduction.

"It's my occupation." The newcomer folded himself down on a third stone. "So you're the new carrier." The peddler's deep-set eyes bored into Owen. "Exactly what happened to the old one?"

"John Long didn't say. Merely that the churchmen almost caught him and he's in hiding."

"When did this happen?"

"A good three weeks ago, at least. Perhaps longer."

The peddler exchanged a sober look with Cole. He turned back to Owen.

"Did Long mention the carrier's younger brother?"

"No."

"How did you come to know Long?"

As the sun inched higher beyond the treetops, the peddler questioned Owen about himself, his dealings with the London bookseller, even about William Tyndale.

Cole must have a very loose tongue.

Irked, Owen gave a carefully edited version of his recent visit with the priest. Only an instinctive awareness that something important lay behind the questions kept him answering.

At last the peddler fell silent. He looked past Owen to Cole. The bookseller nodded slightly. The peddler faced Owen again.

"The carrier you replaced wasn't the only one the churchmen found out. I was in Oxford a fortnight ago. Another carrier, younger brother to our Bristol one, was waylaid by churchmen. He was killed.

Until you arrived, we thought it an isolated mishap. Now we know otherwise. Something is wrong in London. Until we learn how the churchmen got their information, we're all in danger. I'm going into hiding. I've been tried for heresy before. I'll end at the stake if I'm caught again."

"What of me?" Owen said, a light sweat breaking out on his skin.

"We want you to carry a warning to Long's contacts among my people."

"Won't that be dangerous?"

"For them or for you?"

Owen felt his face heat. The peddler continued.

"This was your first trip. It's unlikely the churchmen will be on to you yet. In waging war, there's always a risk."

The peddler was right. He'd chosen to serve God this way. He must become inured to the danger.

"Give me the names and places."

"One last matter. When you reach London, don't approach Long immediately. If the Church is onto him, we don't want you caught in the same trap. Contact a man in Coleman Street first. He should know if it's safe."

CHAPTER 5 – MAY TO JUNE, 1523

Begrimed by travel and aching in every muscle, Owen trotted into London early Saturday evening. Since the previous Monday, he had delivered four warnings between Bristol and London. One had taken him almost to Oxford. He'd slept where night caught him, three times in wayside inns, once in a peasant's hut and once in the guests' dormitory of a small monastery an easy day's ride from London.

Entering the sprawling city as the sun slid down its church spires, his mind moved sluggishly from events of the past week to the need for news of John Long. Not until he reached Bucklersbury Lane did he remember why he'd been sent to Bristol. *Agnes Bench.* He groaned.

In the courtyard, he climbed stiffly from the saddle and handed the reins to the gatekeeper. Wearily he hefted the clothing chest to his shoulder and dragged toward the hall. Owen opened the door and collided with his father. Humphrey was garbed resplendently in black satin doublet, mink-trimmed jerkin and a silver collar. His father drew back and surveyed him with a narrow look.

"It's time you returned. Frederick said you don't fancy the Bench girl."

Owen waited, too dull to handle a discussion now. His father continued.

"Judging from Frederick's report, I think her quite suitable."

"Father, I -" he began, dragging up strength.

"I've no time now. I'm late for a guild meeting. Tell me your complaints after you return from Stoke Hall. You're to leave day after tomorrow." He wrinkled his nose. "You need a wash."

With that last order, he departed. Owen stumbled up to his chamber, a mumbled prayer of thanks on his lips. He dropped the chest, shoved the door closed and fell across his bed. The next thing he knew he was being shaken. He opened bleary eyes to find a servant bending over him.

"Master Owen, wake up. You've slept through Sunday morning mass."

Four hours later, luxuriously clean and full fed, Owen set off for Coleman Street. He located the peddler's friend with ease. Another hour of anxious waiting in the Lollard's stuffy attic chamber brought an agitated John Long.

"I know I shouldn't speak ill of the dead," the bookseller said, his Adam's apple bobbing as he hunched on the bench beside Owen, "but the youth was a fool. And so was I. I should never have let him carry for me. He almost brought us all to ruin. He bragged about the smuggling to a maid and she told her priest."

"How did you find out?"

"When the young idiot was killed, the priest pressed her for more information. Fortunately she knew little. But she did know how to find his brother. He had to flee to the Continent. My second carrier lost his nerve and has quit. It's a wonder we aren't all sitting in the bishop's prison."

Owen glanced out the unglazed dormer window at the lengthening shadows. His thoughts jumped to his impending departure for Stoke Hall that conflicted with his need to deliver the peddler's remaining messages.

"If you'll give me the hire money for the horse," the Lollard said after Owen explained his dilemma, "I'll deliver the message for Colchester. I've friends there."

Long nodded and turned back to Owen.

"You can still tell those around Cambridge and Newmarket. I'll find a way to get word to Cole and the peddler. You'd best not carry writings this trip. I'm in no mood to have you caught. I want at least one carrier left from this debacle."

Owen, too weary to lift the reins, let his tired brown mare pick her slow way along the narrow track to Stoke Hall. In little more than a fortnight, he'd spent twelve days in the saddle. The last warning had been delivered, and journey's end lay just ahead. His duty done, fatigue rolled over him in a mighty wave. Tomorrow would bring keen satisfaction at a job well done, hope at the possibilities opening for him and anticipation of studying the scriptures with Jane Horne. Now all he longed for was twenty-four hours of uninterrupted sleep.

"You haven't even opened the Testament, have you?" Owen said.

Jane's needle halted. He'd arrived without warning a short while ago as she sat in the garden mending her stepfather's linen shirt. She shifted uncomfortably and looked up at him. His lank sacking-brown hair was straggling well over his ears. He needed a haircut. Her heart began beating foolishly. She definitely preferred a merchant's trim to a priest's tonsure.

"I intended to read it," she said, recalling the book buried deep in her chest. "When you were here in January you talked so strangely." She pulled at a loose stitch. "With your brother so recently gone, I doubt you knew what you were saying. You were talking heresy."

He slipped onto the bench beside her, his expression intent.

"I don't recall everything I said. But I spoke the truth. If you had only read the Testament, you would have seen for yourself."

Jane looked away toward the high, honeysuckle-draped wall that provided this quiet, sweet-scented corner. Since that cold January night, Owen had been often in her thoughts. Of all that had passed between them, one fact had gradually eclipsed all others. He now was not to be a priest. Why, then, she wondered with unexpected anger, must he still sound like one?

"It's no matter. I'll release you from your promise."

Jane, hearing the disappointment in his tone, relented.

"No. I'll keep my promise. When next you come, I'll have started your book."

"I'll come tomorrow."

Owen, on horseback, emerged from the forest trail beside the stream that meandered between woods and meadow. He spotted a familiar splash of yellow in an oak tree on the meadow side. The yellow splash must have seen him for she waved an arm. With a smile, he set his mount into the shade-dappled water. He gained the other bank and tied his horse to a low branch beside Jane's.

They had met almost daily during the last fortnight, sometimes at Wynnfield, sometimes here at the forest edge. The afternoons never contained enough hours for all they found to talk of. One day he accepted an invitation to go hawking with her stepfather. His first awkward attempts at handling the bird brought much laughter. Three times during the first week he stayed for a meal until, unexpectedly, Sir Harry asked if he were never fed at Stoke Hall. After that, they met elsewhere and at other times. Owen didn't care what excuse Jane gave for meeting him each day. All that mattered was that she did. He stood now, hands on hips, watching her as she lay along the thick branch and peered into a thrush's nest.

"There are four of them." She laughed. "Just listen to them. They think I'm their mother."

After a last look, she shifted carefully toward the cleft of the tree. Owen sprang forward and guided her slipper to a foothold.

"When you were small, I seemed always to be fetching you out of trees," he said, catching her round the waist and helping her to the ground.

He remained behind her, his hands still around her waist, her rose scent heady in his nostrils. Today he could have told Frederick with certainty that he had no wish to remain celibate.

"You were as good as a brother to me."

The words hit Owen like icy water. Abruptly he stepped back and flung himself down on the stream bank. He didn't want to be her brother. Even less he wanted her to see him as a priest. That she did had been made blatantly clear the previous day. The memory tormented him.

They'd been strolling in the orchard, talking as usual. He was telling her of William Tyndale's plan to translate the scriptures and his own eagerness to help in some way. As he talked, he realized for the first time how much he needed her to understand what he'd found and share it with him. Jane had halted under a mulberry tree and examined a low branch.

"You still seem more a priest than a merchant," she said bluntly, cutting him off in mid-sentence.

His step, and heart, faltered. Fear robbed him of a ready reply - fear that, should he attempt to take her in his arms and be a man with her while she saw him as a priest, she would shrink away in revulsion. He'd mumbled something about change coming slowly. For all his education, he felt as ignorant about courting a maid as the most backward pleasant.

Reliving yesterday's frustrations, Owen plucked a fallen twig from the grass and began breaking it into pieces. Overhead the young thrushes burst into sound again as their mother flashed in. Owen threw his broken twig into the stream. The pieces spun away.

"I'll be returning to London in the morning."

Jane picked a stray buttercup from the thin edge of the meadow and tucked it behind her ear.

"How shall we spend our last hour?" she asked brightly, settling at the base of the oak.

"I've been wondering how you're coming with your reading."

"My reading?" Her smile faltered. "I'm well into the first gospel."

"Do you see what I mean? The Church doesn't hold true to the scriptures."

"I think people see what they want to see. Take Father and Howard Willcotte. They're forever arguing over which makes the best fodder, broad beans or black. I can't see the difference. The animals do equally well on either. What's the benefit in proving one right and the other wrong?"

"You're talking of crops. I'm speaking of truth and lies." Owen stood, too frustrated to remain seated. "When Walter died, my parents paid for masses to shorten his time in purgatory. The Church knows scripture doesn't teach that. Why do they accept the money?"

"Your parents received comfort for their payment, didn't they?"

"Don't you see? The comfort was based on a lie."

"I only know one thing." Jane rose and shook out her skirts. "If the Church is wrong and you're right, that makes you a merchant rather than a priest. But whether the Church is right or you, how will my life change?"

Owen stared wordlessly at her. She continued, her tone resentful.

"Would you have me lie? To claim understanding just to please you?"

"No. Never that. I'm sorry. I'm being unfair. Why should you realize in a few weeks what it took me months to grasp." His shoulders slumped. "I'd best see you home and bid Sir Harry farewell."

Owen helped her mount, his disappointment keeping his touch brief, impersonal. Strained silence accompanied them to the manor house. They left their horses at the stable and were crossing the base-court when Sir Harry came out of the house.

"Owen wanted to bid you farewell," Jane said to her stepfather when they reached the porch. She turned to Owen. "I'll change my gown and join you shortly."

Leaving Owen and her stepfather in the hall, Jane climbed the stairs to her chamber. Fighting tears, she changed her old kirtle for her Tudor-green gown.

She couldn't say when she'd changed from loving Owen to being in love with him. Perhaps the conversion had begun on that January night. She was sure of only one fact. When he'd ridden back to Stoke Hall after his first visit a fortnight ago, he'd carried her heart with him. She had hugged her secret to herself, a secret too new and precious to undergo public scrutiny, and rejoiced that Owen would be nearby for at least a fortnight. Time enough to win him from his priest's ways.

How quickly the days had flown, taking her confidence with them. The fortnight was over. His behavior today was no different from when they'd walked in the orchard and she'd accused him of still being a priest. She'd prayed that he would deny it. He hadn't. Today, all he wanted was to discuss scriptures. Yet, at times, she thought she saw something in his eyes. Why didn't he speak?

Her maid was tying her sleeve points when she happened to glance out the window. Owen stood in the base-court with her stepfather. The stableboy was bringing his horse. Surely he wasn't leaving without a word of parting!

Jane flew down the stairs, through the hall and out to the base-court. Owen was setting foot to stirrup. He must have heard her rushing feet for he pulled back and turned.

"Here she is, after all," Sir Harry said, his fat face perturbed. "Now you can make your farewells in person."

Owen looked uncertainly from Sir Harry to Jane.

"I intended to ask Owen to stay for a meal," Jane said quickly.

"I would -." Owen began.

"Nonsense." Sir Harry cut in. "Owen has too much to do at Stoke Hall to waste time here waiting to be fed."

Jane could think of no other excuse to delay him. Under the watchful eye of her stepfather, she bade Owen good-bye. She had to stand mute as he rode out through the gatehouse. She couldn't let him go like this.

"Owen, wait!"

She jerked up her skirts and heedlessly ran after him. Owen swung from the saddle. Acutely aware of her stepfather, Jane halted an arm's length away.

"When will I ... we ... see you again?"

"I don't know. I'll return as soon as I can."

"I'll read your testament."

The intensity of his look lifted her heart. He stepped back into the saddle and set his horse in motion. Just before the hawthorn bushes blocked him from view, he turned and waved.

Slowly she made her way back to her frowning stepfather.

"You acted unseemly, daughter."

"I'm sorry. Owen and I had quarreled. I wished to crave his pardon."

"Nevertheless, your behavior was improper."

"Yes, Father."

With Owen gone, Jane's life resembled a wheel that had lost its hub. Household routine gave shape to her days but couldn't supply the core. Only he could do that. Who knew when he would return? All she had was his book. This time she didn't bury it away. Each night upon retiring, she drew the candle close and read a while. When Owen came again he would find her diligent.

If Jane had not been blinded by her loneliness, she might have noticed that something was afoot. Twice when she thought her stepfather out with his hawk, she discovered him in the accounts room penning letters.

Sir Harry was a worried man. He had observed the growing affection between Jane and Owen with increasing unease. He knew it must be stopped. He'd been a fool to ignore his daughter Lucy two years ago when she'd urged him to make a match for Jane. Fortunately it wasn't too late.

One cloudy day near the end of June, Jane met her stepfather as she left the dairy house. He was beaming.

"I've something to show you."

She returned his smile and followed him into the house. In the accounts room, Sir Harry lowered his bulk behind the writing table. He picked up a letter from the clutter of papers and waved it at her.

"Lucy is coming. And bringing my grandnephew. You remember Francis Grady."

Jane felt her smile falter. Francis's colorless, bony face floated up from memory. He'd been fourteen and she eleven the single time Sir Harry decided to spend the Christmas season in London with Lucy. Francis was judged old enough to join the late-night festivities. She was sent to bed.

Later she sneaked out with Bess, the cook's young daughter who was acting as her personal maid, to steal glimpses of the celebrations in the hall below. Francis caught them standing hand in hand in their nightdresses. Despite his embarrassment, he stood his ground long enough to rebuke her for appearing in public in such attire and in the company of servants. He seemed even more horrified by her second offense than her first. He obviously tattled for they had received a scolding in the morning. She had not seen him since and was glad of it.

"I remember Francis."

"Good, good." Sir Harry gave the letter a smug look. "The Christmas we visited London, my nephew and I discussed a match between you two. I've delayed it, not liking the idea of you leaving me. Recently I thought, why can't Francis live here with us? My nephew has other sons for his tanner's business. I wrote to him and he agrees. Isn't that wonderful, Jane? Francis is coming for a visit first. The betrothal will be in London after Lammas and the wedding at Nativity. Then we'll come back here to live, you and Francis and I."

"Why wasn't I told?"

"But you were. I mean ... you have been ... now." Sir Harry was enthusiastic.

"I don't like Francis."

"You were children when you last met. Lucy writes that he's a fine young man. I have her letter somewhere." He rummaged through the clutter. "Here it is. Read for yourself."

Her stepfather shoved a paper toward her. She took it with a trembling hand and bent her head. The words were an incomprehensible blur. Jane dropped it back on the table, fighting panic. She again saw Owen's departing look. The memory gave her courage.

"Father, I ... I want to wed Owen."

The trembling words seemed to echo off the plastered walls and checkered tile floor. Before her eyes, her stepfather's mass of flesh became a mountain of rock.

"No. Your marriage is already settled. Has been for years."

"Father, please."

"The Altons are commoners, hardly better than peasants and hucksters. Your mother was a lady."

"What are the Gradys? Tanners and skinners."

Sir Harry's face darkened.

"Francis's grandmother was my sister. He has her blood."

"Your sister married below her station. Why can't I?"

"She could do no better without a dowry. You have Wynnfield."

"What do you have against Owen apart from his lack of good blood? He'll inherit Stoke Hall and his father's business."

"He would have been a priest."

"He's not a priest now."

"Perhaps in his heart he remains one."

Jane's own heart trembled at her stepfather's words. Had she read into Owen's parting look what she had wanted to see there? She pushed her doubts away lest they show on her face.

"His parents will expect him to marry. Knowing him as I do, I could make him a better wife than any other."

"He's not my concern. You are. Francis will make you a good husband. I can't say the same of Owen."

"You think he won't do a husband's duty toward me? Why not ask him."

"Enough!" Sir Harry struggled to his feet, his face purple. "I'll not have a chit of a girl telling me how to handle my affairs. I've a mind to lock you in your room."

Jane stood also and gripped the table edge for support.

"Lock me up. Beat me if you wish. Only please don't make me wed Francis."

Despite her defiance, her knees shook so violently the keys hanging from her girdle clinked. That and Sir Harry's heavy breathing were the only sounds in the room. Gradually his high color lessened and he sank back into his chair. His chin settled into the fatty rings of his neck as if he were considering. He cast her a shifting look.

"Mistress Alton is at Stoke Hall. I could put the suggestion to her."

Jane was around the table in an instant and wrapping her arms around him.

"Oh, thank you, Father. Thank you."

"Leave off strangling me," Sir Harry said gruffly.

When Jane released him, he eyed her gravely.

"What if she rejects the idea?"

"Why should she? With Wynnfield as my dowry -."

"But if she should, would you agree to wed Francis?"

"If I can't marry Owen, it matters little who I have for my husband."

"I'll call on her in the morning."

After Jane floated out, Sir Harry sat brooding, trying to ease his conscience. Ironically, had he decided to lock her up, he'd have been obliged to first request the key. And who would have managed the house? Ten years ago he would have had the energy. But not now. Not with his heart pounding erratically in his chest. Dishonorable as it was, he'd been forced to use her ignorance. But it was for her own good.

Because of that, he, a knight of noble ancestry, must demean himself and go like a beggar to a mere yeoman's daughter, to the very one who had grievously insulted Eleanor. He had little choice. Only by humbling himself to that woman could he carry back her rejection. He must see Jane safely married to Francis. He felt old and tired.

With fearful eagerness Jane watched her stepfather ride off to Stoke Hall the following morning. Unable to concentrate on household duties, she settled in the winter parlor with her embroidery. Half-a-dozen times, imagining the sound of a horse, she flew to the window. The long shadows in the base-court had shrunk to half their size before Sir Harry rode in through the gatehouse.

Standing at the window, heart pounding and palms wet, Jane watched him dismount and hand his horse to the stableboy. Two minutes more would bring the answer that would define the rest of her life.

Her legs carried her through the blue parlor and across the dais as far as the main table. There she faltered. Hands gripping the low back of a carved oak chair, she waited as her stepfather came slowly up the hall. He stopped before her; his face filled with sympathy.

"I'm sorry. Mistress Alton said they've already chosen a wife for Owen. The daughter of a Bristol grocer. He's met the girl. The marriage settlement is agreed upon. From the sound of it, his betrothal should come even before yours."

Jane received the news in stark silence. Out of the fragments of her shattered dream, she grasped one knife-sharp splinter. Owen had come to her almost straight from the Bristol maid. He was to marry and he'd not even had the courtesy to tell her. The hard, bitter thought blocked tears. Carefully she loosened her desperate grip.

"Thank you for asking."

She turned away and started for the blue-parlor stairs.

"Francis will make a good husband. You'll see."

Once around the stair curve, Jane jerked up her skirts and fled the rest of the way to her chamber. She slipped the bolt home with trembling fingers, turned and threw herself against the heavy carved bedpost. Its hard edges dug painfully into her cheek. The hurting without was nothing compared to the agony within.

They'd already found a wife for him, and he didn't even tell me.

She buried her face in the gold damask bed-hangings and wept.

Lowering skies marked the day of Francis's arrival and mirrored Jane's mood. Having given final instructions to the servants, she wandered restlessly about seeking some incomplete task to give occupation to her thoughts. She discovered nothing. All principal rooms had long since been prepared and smelt pleasantly of fresh rushes and herbs. Tall candles sprouted from sconces and wooden chandeliers. The renewed brilliance of silver plate in the hall and parlors barely outshone the glow of cabinets and sideboards that bespoke hours of polishing. Freshly beaten carpets draping side tables and newly stitched cushions on chests and benches scattered a jewel box of colors about the house. Crisp linens covered the beds. In the kitchen, preparations for an elaborate meal were well underway.

Standing in the blue parlor, Jane knew that Wynnfield Hall looked fair enough for a king's visit. Her stepfather should be well satisfied. For him alone, she had driven the servants and herself these last weeks. She cared little what impression Francis formed. Caring had died with Mistress Alton's reply. Blocking Owen from her thoughts and burying his testament deep within her chest, she had docilely agreed to all her stepfather's suggestions regarding Francis's visit. By noon, nothing remained but to watch the rain and shiver in the seeping damp. Head pounding and knotted stomach revolting at food, she retired to her chamber, stripped off her gown and climbed into bed. Surprisingly, she slept.

When she awoke, the sky seemed a little less gray and the rain had stopped. Her head, though thick as a wool sack, no longer throbbed. The painted-enamel clock on the mantel said it was time to dress. As she plunged cold hands into the hot water Bess brought, Jane wondered if the maidservant remembered when Francis had caught them in their nightdresses. She didn't ask. Their close friendship had of necessity been remolded into a less intimate relationship the moment Jane had taken the household keys from Dame Edith's hand. No longer did they play hare and hound through the orchard trees or whisper secrets or share a bed. Soon Bess would have a new bed mate. She and Dickon the carter were to be wed at Michaelmas.

And I'll be wed by Epiphany. She pushed the thought away.

On impulse, because she badly needed to feel bright, she brushed aside the black brocade gown selected earlier in favor of her yellow satin one. Bess was making the final adjustments to gown and hood when a dog barked. Jane's stomach knotted.

"Are they coming?"

Bess scurried to the window.

"I think so." Her head cocked. "If the rain will hold off a bit longer...."

Jane quickly plucked her ruby ring from her jewelry box and twisted it on.

"We must be in the hall."

Originally Sir Harry had planned to welcome their guests in the base-court. The rain had canceled that. Jane hurried down the stairs expecting to see the blue-liveried servants forming an orderly row near the main door in the screen that separated hall from entry. Instead, they were milling about while Sir Harry shouted random orders from their midst. He caught sight of Jane.

"Quickly, daughter. They're dismounting in the base-court. The rain has stopped. We can meet them outside."

He grabbed Jane's wrist and pulled her through the screen into the passage. The servants crowded after. Even as Jane stepped onto the covered porch, the rapidly darkening sky opened in a drum-roll of thunder. Rain began pelting down. Their guests, caught in the very act of dismounting, dashed for cover. Across her stepfather's thick shoulder, Jane glimpsed a dozen sprinting figures, arms flailing, gowns flying, legs pumping. Lucy, mouth agape, led the charge through the cloudburst, a herd of servants, sons and welcoming Wynnfield dogs close on her heels. Dragging her younger son in one hand and clutching up her bulky skirts with the other, she bore down on them like a cow on the loose.

Retreating before the onslaught, Jane and Sir Harry collided with their own servants rushing for the courtyard. Before they could be turned, Lucy and her following burst in. The swirling press poured into the great hall sweeping Jane with it like a hapless blossom on the crest of a flood.

In the hall they circled, caps askew, clothes bespattered, feet and hosen muddied. They shouted and laughed and sucked air while the dogs danced excitedly about the edges.

"Francis insisted ... on stopping at the village ... to tidy himself," Lucy gasped as she clung to her father's arm, dampening his Tudor-green doublet. "He wanted to look his best ... when we got here. Little good it's done." She ended with a shout of laughter.

The uproar gradually subsided. The Wynnfield house staff carried off Lucy's servants, sons and tutor to their chambers. Of the sixteen people who had been seething about, three remained. There should have been four. Francis was missing.

"We had him when we arrived," Lucy said, looking around.

Jane, standing to one side, her head pounding anew, heard voices in the entry. Francis stepped through the screen. Lucy had been wrong to assume his toilet in Hensey village had been for nothing. Neither on lavender satin doublet, blue velvet jerkin or white silk shirt nor even on his elegant mulberry hose were there any dark spots of rain or mud. From his flat plumed cap to the slashed toes of his beribboned shoes, he was completely unspoiled.

"Francis," Lucy said in amazement, "you're not even damp."

Francis casually dropped a coarse hand onto the silver dagger haft sticking from his embroidered sash.

"If you'd waited for the rain to slacken ... and come across under a covering...." An elaborate shrug completed his sentence.

So it was for a tanner's son aping his betters that I've scrubbed Wynnfield from attic to kitchen.

Trailing Francis were his manservant and Bess's carter, Dickon, who had been set to helping with the horses. Both were stripped to their shirts. Their wet garments and the dripping doublets that draped their arms said clearly how Francis had been sheltered as he picked his way across.

95

"Jane?" Lucy glanced around. "Come meet Francis."

Jane, uncomfortably aware of her mud-splattered gown, reluctantly left the shelter of her stepfather's wide back. She dropped a graceful curtsy, an apology ready on her lips. She saw Francis's eyes widen as they swept over the ruin of her dress. His mouth thinned and two spots of red appeared on his bony cheeks. Jane straightened again, her head high. He would have no apology from her.

"Whatever happened to your dress?" Lucy asked.

"A dog shook on me." Turning back to Francis, "We've made your chamber ready."

She looked for a servant to show him the way. Whereas a short time before they were everywhere, now not a single one was at hand. Only Dickon Carter remained, his mobile face puckered in a silent whistle, his eyes bright with curiosity.

"Dickon, show Master Grady to the orchard chamber then find Bess and send her to mine."

The brown-faced youth grinned and pulled his cap at Francis.

"This way, your lordship."

Jane knew she should rebuke Dickon for his impudent humor. She didn't. Francis looked too pleased.

Alone in her chamber, Jane jerked the points of her sleeves loose and stripped off the yellow gown. Flinging the dress over a chest, she gave vent to a brief storm of angry tears before Bess could arrive.

Some time later Jane grimly surveyed herself in the silver mirror that Bess held. The black hood and gown made her appear older, and quite proper. Francis should approve.

Jane had guessed correctly. When she appeared for the evening meal, her future husband's face registered satisfaction. Sitting between Francis and her stepfather at the high table, she forced herself to relax. No doubt the earlier unpleasantness had stemmed from the confusion of the arrival and from nervousness, both hers and his. He seemed easy enough now as he heaped lavish praise on the meal. He gazed about the hall with evident pleasure. Jane, following his look, attempted to see the brightly painted hammer-beam ceiling, the huge brick fireplace, the silver-filled cupboards, the brilliant arras cloth on the near wall through his eyes.

"I wish my grandmother Constance had lived to see me come to my rightful place."

His words grated like sand between Jane's teeth.

"Father's older sister?"

"Yes. She lived in manors even grander than this. When I was a child, she used to tell me tales of her youth. The grand lords and ladies, the tournaments, the knights who begged to wear her colors. Did you know she was almost a lady-in-waiting for the queen? If she hadn't been taken ill just when Her Grace was picking someone, I'm sure Grandmother would have been chosen."

"She must have found it hard having to wed a tanner's son after that."

If Francis detected sarcasm, he gave no sign.

"I'll never understand how she could have lowered herself." He switched his gaze from the hall to Jane. He smiled again. "My friends envy me for gaining a wife of noble blood." He lifted his silver goblet and leaned close. "To your health, my lady."

His breath smelled sour. She casually tucked her chin and began sopping up gravy with a bread scrap.

"No doubt our life here seems much quieter than London," Jane said before he could launch into any more extravagant gallantry.

Francis's brows drew down over his beak of a nose as he looked at the servants enjoying their meal below.

"Your life can be disagreeably noisy. In London it's not fashionable to eat with the servants."

The following morning, Francis followed Sir Harry into the accounts room. When they rejoined Jane at noon, her stepfather's face was tired but beaming.

"Didn't I tell you? This grandnephew of mine will make you a fine husband. He's already looking into the running of Wynnfield. My brain is too old for all his questions. I told him to ask Howard."

"Jane," Francis said as they strolled in the garden several days later, "the bailiff knows more of Wynnfield's management than Sir Harry does. That bothers me. We could easily be cheated."

"Master Willcotte wouldn't do such a thing."

Francis's expression tightened. It hadn't taken her long to learn that this particular look meant that he was affronted.

"He's only a servant."

Jane stopped between periwinkles and daisies. She had let many of Francis's petty criticisms or ignorant observations pass without comment for the sake of their future. This slur could not go unchallenged.

"Howard Willcotte has been bailiff here since before I was born. He is far more than paid help. He is a loyal and valued member of my household, almost like family."

"How can you, of all people, say such a thing?"

"Why me, of all people?"

"Because your father, your real father, was nobility."

"Is that so important?"

"Of course. Your true father's ancestors were intimate with kings. Have you never given it thought?"

"Not as much as you, it appears."

"Haven't you asked Sir Harry?"

"I did once. Father put me off. I think my question hurt him."

"Nonsense. Your emotions are too tender."

A sudden worry halted Jane. She laid her hand on Francis's arm. The oval ruby in her ring glowed heart-red against his dark sleeve.

"Don't question Father about them." Then, though it rankled, "Please?"

Francis smiled and covered her hand with his, smothering the ruby.

"I've no need. I learned enough from people in London. The Radcotts could trace their ancestry back to the Normans who arrived with William the Conqueror. Your grandfather had estates scattered over much of northern England. Unfortunately, they were entailed in the male line. Your father was the last. He died in an affair of honor. If you'd been a boy, you would have inherited it all. As it was, when your grandfather died, everything went to the king."

"If I'd been a boy, you wouldn't be here."

"You shouldn't joke about such things, Jane. And, in the future, don't allow the servants to overstep the bounds."

Jane swallowed indignation.

"Yes, Francis."

Jane sat in a secluded corner of the garden listening to the breeze whisper in the honeysuckle and basking in solitude. She'd had little enough recently with Francis always at her elbow. Tomorrow would be Lammas, the day they would leave for London. She had come to say 'good-bye'. When next she sat here she'd be betrothed.

The honeysuckle would still be wafting its sweet scent over this corner, but her life would be changed. During the course of his visit she had become almost resigned to marrying Francis. Their union might even be reasonably successful. If only he weren't so unsure of his dignity. She'd not dared laugh at his clumsy attempts at hawking the way she had at Owen's.

The sound of footsteps interrupted her thoughts. Francis's voice shattered the silence.

"Jane, what are you doing out here? Shouldn't you be overseeing Bess with your packing?"

Jane stiffened. To assure him her maid could pack without oversight would be futile.

"We finished this morning."

She kept her face averted in the hope that he would go away. Instead, Francis bent onto the low wall beside her and reached for her hand.

"I know the wedding's been set for Nativity. The truth is, I don't want to wait that long. If we spoke to our parents, they might let us marry at Michaelmas."

Jane kept her head lowered. She was surprised yet again by evidence of his growing affection. It seemed strange because she felt nothing for him. No, she corrected herself, he wasn't fond of her. He was fond of the person he insisted she must be. That was the difference. She was trapped, forever to be someone else.

"If we moved the wedding forward," she said gently, "don't you think people might believe we were acting in indecent haste?"

"You may be right. Christmas seems so far away."

Jane casually freed her hand and stood to leave.

"The time will come soon enough."

CHAPTER 6 – JUNE TO AUGUST, 1523

Two days after bidding Jane an awkward farewell, Owen rode into London. His return brought the expected confrontation with his father. A lengthy argument in the parlor accomplished nothing. Owen remained firm in his refusal to wed Agnes Bench.

"I've spent my life building the business," Humphrey shouted, red-faced. "I'll not see it die because you're disinclined to marry and carry on my name."

"I'm not refusing to wed. I'm only refusing Agnes. I want someone I can talk to."

Thinking of Jane, Owen almost blurted out her name. He caught himself in time. His relationship with her was still too delicate to chance his father's heavy-handed interference should he like the idea. Later, when he himself was more sure....

"Talk. You don't marry for talk. You marry to produce children, to advance the family. What do I tell Master Bench? That his daughter's got to have talking lessons before my son will take her?"

Humphrey halted in his pacing to glare at him. Owen met his father's look with silence.

"Frederick thinks you should learn the business more thoroughly before being distracted by a wife. I'll give you the summer. Walter would have wed her at Lammas. You have until Michaelmas."

When Owen left Jane, he'd expected to be returning soon to buy produce for resale from the area farmers. June passed, and July. He traveled into East Anglia several times, secretly carrying literature for John Long as well. Never once did Frederick send him remotely near Wynnfield Hall. During the long weeks he wrote half-a-dozen letters to Jane. He tore them all up. He had to see her face when he asked her to marry him. During those weeks his father made no further mention of Agnes Bench. Owen didn't deceive himself. The autumn would bring another and more serious conflict.

August arrived. Humphrey rode off to join Owen's mother at Stoke Hall. From there, he would journey to Stourbridge fair where merchants from all over England and the Continent gathered to trade. Before he left, he instructed Owen to ride up with the pack train of goods bound for the fair. Owen's hopes soared. The trip would take him to within a few miles of Jane.

The day after Humphrey's departure, William Tyndale arrived at Bucklersbury Lane. Owen insisted he lodge with him while he waited for an interview with Bishop Tonstall. No doubt he would be accepted into the Bishop's household before Humphrey returned. Once there, William could translate the scriptures into English in safety.

A week passed. The Bishop still hadn't replied to William's request to call on him. Owen swallowed his last bite of breakfast and rose from the table. He looked across at William. The priest sat with a Greek dictionary propped against a bowl of plumbs, studying while he ate.

"I'm going to open now. See you at noon."

William nodded absently.

Owen twisted the key in the padlock that secured the narrow side door of the warehouse. He stepped through and paused to inhale the heady fragrances. Pale morning light reached soft fingers past him into the dark interior. He liked the early morning hush before the warehouse woke to another day. One of the cats wrapped itself around his leg. He bent to scratch gently behind its ears before unbarring the big doors and running them back along the walls. The cat's yellow pupils narrowed.

Owen was shoving the second door on its track when Frederick stumped into the courtyard with Dick Bolt. He watched them approach. Frederick made a comment and Dick burst out laughing. Owen frowned. Dick always had a pleasant word for Frederick. He was politeness itself with customers, calling them by name, inquiring after their families, saving items from recent shipments which they had wished for when stocks were low. He paid Owen's father unfailing respect.

It's only with me that he's so surly.

The two men entered the warehouse. Frederick returned Owen's greeting with a cheerful reply. Dick gave a sullen nod to the space above Owen's left shoulder then disappeared through the shop's back entrance.

"Why can't he give me a civil word?" Owen asked Frederick.

"He's a good man. Here his life has not been easy."

"Why does he stay?"

"His father is here."

"I know. But for his hazel eyes and broken nose, he could nearly pass for me."

"His nose was a present from your brothers. Dick was twelve. Almost the poor lad they killed."

"I'd forgotten."

"Your father whipped your brothers. He said to them that here Dick was to work. That Dick also is his son, he did not say. Because of your mother, never will he say that."

"If he would, Dick might not hate me so."

"Your brothers he hated. You...? I do not know. Dick, also, I think does not know."

Owen stepped briskly down Bucklersbury Lane, a new Lutheran tract jammed up his sleeve. He cut through the grocer's shop, taking the shortest route to the warehouse. The shop was empty of customers. Even Dick was absent.

He strode past the shelves of merchandise just as Dick rushed in from the opposite direction. They collided. The tract in Owen's sleeve fluttered to the floor before he could catch it. Dick, mumbling a hollow apology, dove for the writing even as Owen grabbed for it. Dick reached it first. He came slowly to his feet, scanning the tract clenched tightly in his hand.

"I'll have that," Owen said.

Dick looked up with a crafty smile.

"I certainly wouldn't."

Owen plucked the damning thing from Dick's now slack hold. He silently berated himself for his carelessness. What Dick might do with his newly acquired knowledge Owen dared not consider.

Owen closed with lightning speed the following evening, checking the wooden shutters, barring the big warehouse doors and snapping the heavy padlock shut on the smaller one. Finished, he sped across the courtyard and into the house. He took the main stairs two at a bound. William had been summoned by Bishop Tonstall that afternoon. Owen chafed to know the outcome.

He found William sprawled on his narrow bed, hands locked behind his head, staring at the plaster ceiling.

"Well?" Owen perched on a stool. "Did you get a place in his household? Is he going to let you translate the scriptures?"

"No."

The word dropped like a stone. Owen stared at him incredulously.

"But why? What reason did he give for refusing?"

"Reason?" William swung his feet to the floor, crossed to the small table and picked up his Greek New Testament. "He gave no reason. He didn't even mention my request to translate.

"I'd waited in the anteroom over an hour. When I eventually saw him, he was dictating letters. My request had to be inserted between paragraphs. Of no more important than a footnote." William thrust the book back onto the table. "You should have seen him. All decked out in silks and satins and wearing six rings. I counted them. He had a gold chain set with huge emeralds around his neck. And jewels as big as the end of my thumb on his shoes. I couldn't believe it ... jewels on his shoes. Our Lord hadn't even a bed to call his own."

"Didn't he say anything else, anything at all?"

"He said he was confident I'd find service elsewhere in London." William slumped back onto his bed. "He began dictating again, and I found myself back in the anteroom with the other supplicants. I didn't even have time to collect my wits. I stayed more than two hours. I thought the first interview must have been a horrible mistake, that I'd be sent for again. Eventually a clerk came out. He shouted that the Bishop would see no more today. Everyone left. So did I."

"Couldn't you get permission from another bishop?"

"Which one?" William's voice was ripe with disgust. "Longland? Have you forgotten that, two years ago, he had hundreds of Lollards arrested? Not Fisher ... not after the sermon he preached when Luther's writings were burned here in London. No, Owen. There isn't a bishop in all England who would grant me permission."

"I'll also need two kegs of table salt, six sacks of bay salt, one crock each of raisins and prunes and four dozen bars of Castile soap. Lady Hallenbrooke insists on it, you know."

Owen, helping in the store, added the items to Lord Hallenbrooke's order. Three days had passed since William's disastrous interview with Bishop Tonstall. The priest had spent them closeted in his chamber or roaming London. If only he could be with William. Rather he was trapped here taking orders as if nothing else mattered.

Lord Hallenbrooke sniffed about the place, peering into sacks, boxes and barrels like a hound that had lost the scent.

"God's eyes, it's hot." He wiped a velvet sleeve across his freckled face. "I was all for returning to Waring Hall Immediately the King disbanded Parliament. Lady Hallenbrooke refused. She has gowns to be finished and necklaces on order."

He stopped, drew his brow down in concentration and ticked off on his fingers.

"Two boxes of pepper. Treacle of Genoa, five kegs." His gaze dropped to the crock beside him. "And two pounds of these hard sweets."

Owen dipped his quill into the inkpot.

"Are you married?" Lord Hallenbrooke asked. "You're not? Well, don't. All they do is spend money. This trip to London has left me a poor man. Between my wife's trifles and Wolsey and his Parliament.... Blast that man. What right does he have to raise our taxes to pay for his French war? It's not helping me."

The nobleman broke off as Dick entered from the back with a sack of dried peas. He watched Dick plunk the load down. He turned to Owen.

"Your brother?"

Owen shot a glance at Dick bent over the lentils.

"Yes."

Lord Hallenbrooke made one final circuit of the shop. He gave directions for delivery, popped a hard sweet in his mouth and departed. Owen added the delivery instructions to the order. Finished, he wiped the quill and laid it with the order sheet on the counter. He looked up to find Dick staring at him in bewilderment.

"Why did you tell him we were brothers?"

"Because we are."

Dick's expression closed. Insolence returned.

"So we're brothers. What do you expect me to do? Go down on my knees in gratitude?"

Owen's temper flared.

"Stop blaming me for your birth. And get this order filled. I'm going out."

"When I married, besides the dowry and wedding banquet, your mother gave me three new gowns, two pairs of leather shoes and a whole chest of linens," Lucy said as she steered Jane along the street toward the dressmakers. "I'm determined that your wedding will be even grander."

Jane felt too lackluster to respond. Lucy grabbed her arm and stopped in the busy thoroughfare. A baker's lad carrying a load of fragrant loaves had to sidestep abruptly. He went past them with a rude word. Lucy peered at Jane.

"Are you ill?"

"It's just...." Jane said. "I've not been sleeping well recently."

As Lucy opened her mouth to comment, Jane heard Owen's voice. He was calling her name. Her heart stopped. Lucy looked back through the crowded street.

Owen, walking off his anger at Dick, only noticed the two women, one round as a wine tun, the other taller and slim, when they stopped. Though he couldn't believe his good fortune, he recognized Jane immediately. He'd seen her slender shape too often in his dreams to be mistaken. He sprinted off, dodging through the crowds.

"Jane! Jane Horne."

He saw Lucy look around. Jane remained motionless, face averted. Only when he reached them did she slowly turn toward him.

"Why, it's Owen Alton," Lucy said.

Jane opened her lips then close them again. Her eyes were dark pools in her pale face.

"You should have told me you were coming to London," Owen said.

"I thought you were in Bristol." Jane's voice was low and hard-edged. "No doubt your betrothed is missing you."

"My betrothed? I've got no betrothed."

Jane went white to her lips.

"They told me you had. A maid in Bristol."

Owen, seeing her stricken look, knew something was dreadfully wrong.

"My parents do want me to wed a maid there. I won't have her." He swallowed. "Jane, are you staying with Lucy? May I call on you this evening? I've something to ask you."

"Can't you see she's ill?" Lucy said. "Come along, Jane. The dressmaker is just a few steps further. She'll have a seat and a cup of wine."

Lucy caught Jane's arm and began pulling her away. Owen moved quickly to block them.

"May I come?"

Jane's eyes swam with tears.

"I doubt you should call," Lucy said, clearly impatient. "My cousin might take it amiss."

"Your cousin?"

"Yes. Francis Grady. He and Jane are to be betrothed."

A sword plunged straight into Owen's heart.

"But I wanted to wed you."

Jane's face flooded with life. Now her tears were dew on a rose.

"Yes."

She stepped out of Lucy's grasp and reached her hand to him. He caught it between his two. Beneath his jerkin his heart was thudding so hard it shook his ribcage.

"We've got to talk."

Her hand tight in his, he hurried Jane away up the street. Behind them he heard Lucy calling.

"Jane. Come back. You can't go. You're to wed Francis."

The afternoon sun had sunk too low for its bright rays to penetrate Lucy's street by the time Owen returned with Jane. Reluctantly they dragged through the premature dusk. Ahead of them, a snail-paced cart clattered along, piled high with hogsheads of Gascony wine bound for the cellar of one of the vintners lining the way. Owen welcomed the delay. For two hours, wandering among London's fields, they had held the world at bay, safe and inviolate from the storm to come. Now, ahead, he could see the gilt winged horse flying over George Terrell's vintner shop. Sir Harry waited in the home above. The storm was about to break.

Jane twined her trembling fingers more tightly in Owen's as she gave him a brave smile. He answered in kind. Despite his show of confidence, he wasn't deluding himself. They would be waging an almost hopeless battle. To refuse a marriage from the first, as he had done, was hard enough. To withdraw agreement a mere week before the betrothal, when every detail had been settled, was unheard of. The pressure on Jane would be tremendous, not only from Sir Harry and Lucy but from the Gradys as well. Whatever their personal feelings for Jane, they would be violently opposed to having Wynnfield Manor drop like a ripe plum into someone else's pocket. Regardless of the difficulties, Owen could not let Jane go. Her heart was his. He would fight for her hand. To his advantage, he had both the London business and Stoke Hall behind him. He could outbid Francis.

They found Sir Harry dozing in Lucy's overly furnished parlor, his balding head lolling against a chair back. Lucy sat nearby at her embroidery frame. She looked up when they entered; her features hardened. She pressed one thick finger to her lips and nodded toward her father.

"He's asleep. You can explain your shameless behavior when he wakes."

"You needn't whisper," Sir Henry said.

He opened his eyes and straightening in his seat. Owen saw him look at Jane. His right hand began to quiver on the chair arm. He moved it to his lap and covered it with his left. Lucy shoved her embroidery frame roughly aside and heaved herself to her feet.

"Father, lock her in her chamber. She's acted disgracefully."

Owen, keeping his hold on Jane's fingers, spoke over Lucy's protests.

"Sir Harry, I want to offer for Jane. If you'll examine my financial prospects -."

"Jane's marriage is already decided," Sir Harry said, settling more solidly into his chair like a knight bracing for combat.

Jane released Owen's hand and approached her stepfather.

"You know I agreed to wed Francis only because I thought Owen was marrying elsewhere."

"And so he is." To Owen, "Or have your parents changed their minds?"

"No, Sir Harry. But from the first I've told them I won't have the maid."

"You show yourself not only disobedient but disrespectful. Your parents have every right to pick a wife for you."

"My parents could never find a better wife than Jane."

"You aren't my concern," Sir Harry said. "My grandnephew will make the best husband for her."

Jane dropped to her knees and clutched her stepfather's thick hand.

"Father, please. Francis won't make me happy."

Sir Harry's expression softened.

"There are many kinds of happiness, daughter. You can't deny his interest in the management of Wynnfield. Or that he's proud of you before his friends."

Jane's head went up and she squared her shoulders.

"Do you know why Francis is so interested in Wynnfield's management? He thinks Master Willcotte is cheating us. He wants to know how. As for his friends, of course he's proud of me. I'm the last of the noble house of Radcott."

Owen saw Sir Harry's lips press into a thick line as he studied Jane in the stretching silence. Abruptly he had a suspicion of what was going through Sir Harry's mind. Choosing his words with all the care of a combatant choosing his weapon, he spoke into the tension.

"Sir Harry, I know you want what's best for Jane. So do I. I believe I can provide for her better than your grandnephew could. I know her too well not to understand how best to protect her interests. Can you say the same of Francis Grady?"

Sir Harry turned shrewd eyes on Owen.

"Sometimes ignorance itself is protection."

He had guessed correctly. This was the heart of the matter. Owen breathed a quick prayer before continuing.

"But can ignorance be relied upon? I would have said that knowledge and acceptance are more trustworthy."

Sir Harry's heavy face grew reflective. Owen felt sweat break out as he waited for a response.

"I've nothing against you directly," Sir Harry said at last. "Nor do I deny Jane cares for you. Left to yourself, you might take proper care of her. But you can't answer for your parents."

Owen's mind was as sharp as a sword point.

"But if they accepted her, what then would you have to fear?"

"Let them accept her first."

"If they would? If my father were to approach you about a match, would you give your consent?"

Owen heard Jane stir and Lucy gasp. He dared not shift his attention from Sir Harry.

"Your father?" The old knight's faded-blue eyes narrowed. "Not just your father. Let your mother also ask Jane's hand for you. Only then will I consider the request."

Owen flinched inwardly. Just as he'd seen victory within his grasp, his sword had struck armor and glanced off.

Joyfully, Jane threw her arms around her stepfather's neck.

"Oh, Father. Thank you, thank you."

"Father!" Lucy cried, aghast. "You can't break the marriage agreement. What of our honor?"

Sir Harry pulled Jane's arms away and held her off.

"Don't thank me yet. Just because I haven't the heart to beat you into marrying Francis doesn't mean you'll wed Owen." He swung on Lucy. "I'm not breaking my promise. I'm postponing the betrothal. It's unlikely the Altons will give their approval. They already have a wife for Owen. Once Jane sees this, she'll be more ready to accept Francis. Or would you seriously have me beat her into submission? Her own mother told me to allow you a voice in who you married."

"What will you tell the Gradys?" Lucy asked.

"The truth. Jane prefers someone else." He struggled out of his chair and started for the door, Lucy trailing. "They must decide what story to give their friends."

"May I call on Jane this evening?" Owen asked quickly as Lucy and her father halted by the entry.

Sir Harry swung round, his face red with sudden rage.

"You may not! You've caused enough trouble in this household already. Jane and I will be leaving for home in the morning. Until then she'll see no one but Francis, should he call. Go now."

Sir Harry jerked the door open. In the brief moment the two by the entry had their attention averted, Owen caught Jane's hand to his lips. He pressed a kiss into her palm.

"I'll be at Stourbridge fair," he murmured.

Jane's shining eyes spoke her answer.

Lucy, clearly determined to see that he left, followed Owen out. Sir Harry closed the door after them. He leaned his forehead against it. When, several hours earlier, Lucy had come rushing in crying that Jane

118

had run off with Owen, for one terrifying moment he'd taken her literally. A vision of a wedding being performed even as Lucy gasped out her story swam alarmingly before his eyes. Then reason returned. Jane was too well brought up. She would come begging to wed Owen as she had pleaded at Wynnfield Hall. That time he'd made a pretense of conceding to her wishes. What was he to do this time?

Before he could decide, Jane had returned. But it was a different Jane. The quiet, pale, dutiful girl of the past two months had disappeared like some shadow figure. In her place stood a maid vibrantly alive and glowing as bright as a candle flame. Seeing the change in her, he had been even more fearfully uncertain. If only Eleanor were here.

He turned from the door. Jane stood by a small table, hand enfolding closed hand as if guarding something precious. He waddled across the room to her.

"In the end, child, he'll bring you pain."

"I love him, Father, and he loves me. How could he cause me hurt?"

"I pray God you never have reason to learn."

With Bess's help, Jane happily packed her chests while her stepfather called on the Gradys. Lucy could collect her two half-stitched gowns from the dressmakers and send them on. Sir Harry returned barely in time for the evening meal, his step and face despondent. Jane wisely asked no questions, not even whether Francis planned to call. He didn't come. That night, for the first time in weeks, she fell asleep with a smile on her lips.

Across the city, Owen didn't find sleep so easily won. He tossed restlessly between the linen sheets, reliving the day. He gave fervent thanks for Dick and the brief, heated quarrel that had sent him stalking from the shop. But for his half-brother, he would never have met Jane. He could forgive Dick anything now.

Magnanimity toward Dick deteriorated into misgivings about the future. How would he gain his mother's permission? Her pride guaranteed her refusal. He must find a way to change her mind, and soon. How long would Sir Harry delay Jane's betrothal? He also was unsure of his father's reaction. At least he could pray and hope.

That glimmer of hope did little to quiet Owen's mind. A guilty worry kept sleep at bay. Everything had happened too quickly today. So much had been left unsaid. Above all, he should have told Jane about his smuggling activities. Would she have committed herself to him if she'd known? In fairness to her, she must be given the choice. Pray God her decision would remain the same. He would tell her at the fair. He wanted no walls between them. He desired her heart and her body. He wanted her mind as well.

Owen rolled over. At last he slept.

"Father," Owen said, dry mouthed, across the table corner, "I want to marry Jane Horne."

He and his father were taking their first meal together at a Stourbridge-fair cookshop. This being slack time, only a handful of eaters hunched over the rough trestle tables beneath the bright awnings.

Humphrey grunted in surprise and dropped a half-eaten pigeon onto his trencher.

"And I thought your priest's training had made you too delicate. Jane Horne, of all people." He burst out laughing.

Owen stiffened with indignation. He had stopped at Stoke Hall yesterday in a vain attempt to gain his mother's approval. Despite her icy refusal, she'd not treated his request with derision.

"I'm glad to have given you amusement." He started to rise.

"Don't be an ass." Humphrey grabbed his sleeve. "I'm not laughing at you. Not exactly. You took me by surprise."

Owen sat down again. His father was studying him.

"When you refused Agnes Bench, I was furious. I thought.... Never mind what I thought. I'm glad to know you've at last got an itch for a woman. Makes you more human. What dowry does she have?"

"She inherited Wynnfield Manor from her mother." Owen watched his father's eyes light and almost saw the figures calculating in his head.

"She's worth more than the Bench partnership. And she has it now. I wouldn't have to worry that Bench might give a third of his wealth to the Church as your grandfather Stoke did."

Humphrey tore a pigeon wing free and chewed the bones clean. Stomach knotting, Owen waited for his father's decision.

"All right. If she can be had."

His muscles went slack. He told his father of the meeting in London, of Sir Harry's condition, of his fruitless attempt to gain his mother's permission.

"Clearly you're resolved to have her," Humphrey said with amused admiration. "Why did your mother refuse?"

"You know." Owen was unable to keep the bitterness from his voice.

Humphrey's face darkened.

"I'm the last one to help you there. The wench sounds like a lot of trouble. We can have the Bench maid at a word."

"I want Jane Horne."

"At least the girl had property. Is she as determined for the match as you?"

Owen's thoughts jumped to Jane's ignorance of his smuggling.

"I'll know soon enough."

CHAPTER 7 – SEPTEMBER, 1523 TO MAY, 1524

J ane came instantly awake. Beyond the half-drawn bed curtains, the corners of her chamber still held the last dark fragments of night. She hopped out of bed and, shivering in the early-autumn chill, padded to the window. Outside, pale dawn filtered into the base-court. Already the manor was stirring to life. As she watched, two men strode across the court toward the gatehouse.

The door opened behind her. Bess bustled in with a pitcher of steaming water. Jane washed energetically and pulled on chemise, kirtle and gown. As soon as Bess had bound up her hair, she left the maidservant to pack the last of her toiletries in the small chest and fairly skipped down to the blue parlor to breakfast with her stepfather. Even as she ate, she knew Dickon Carter would be loading their chests onto the pack horse.

A full three weeks of impatient waiting had passed since Owen had tucked the farewell kiss into her palm. Now the waiting was ended. Today she would see him.

Midmorning had arrived before Jane, riding ahead of her party, spotted the bright flags fluttering above the fairgrounds. She glanced back through the other fair goers thronging the road to check on her companions. Howard Willcotte was in the lead. Sir Harry trotted along after him, his manservant riding at his elbow. Dickon and the pack horse, with Bess riding pillion, brought up the rear. When their small company had set off in the dew-wet dawn, three days spent at the fair with Owen had seemed a heavenly eternity to Jane. Now the hours were shrinking with the shadows. She resented even the loss of a minute. She threw another impatient glance over her shoulder at her dawdling company. If only they would ride faster.

An hour later, having tidied herself in the small guest chamber of her stepfather's old Cambridge friend and paid her social obligations to their host, she was free to speed her way to the fair. Dickon, Bess and Howard Willcotte had already departed.

Leaving the town behind, Jane skimmed lightly over fields of beaten stubble, all that remained of crops hurriedly harvested to make way for the springing tent city. In past years, she had spent hours wandering happily along makeshift streets overflowing with Italian silks, delicate glassware, luxurious Russian furs, and a vast array of ribbons and laces, fancy cakes and other fairings, stopping now and again to watch a dancing bear or a gaudily clad juggler. This year, like a bee lining for its hive, Jane made straight for grocers' row and Owen.

Owen was leaning over the narrow counter showing a sample of raisins to a stout woman in a mustard gown when Jane spotted him. Her heart fluttered. She hovered at the far edge of the counter waiting to catch Owen's attention. As the customer laid out her coins, he looked up and saw her. A smile broke across his face. Owen threw a quick word to his workmate, ducked under the counter and straightened up in front of her. Their fingers twined.

Jane looked around at the boisterous sprawl of the fair, consciously noticing it for the first time. Where would they ever find a private corner? Owen appeared more confident. He guided her through the maze of temporary streets, past the makeshift stables at the fairground's far edge and across a narrow strip of open field toward dense oak woods. The oat stubble standing stiffly unbroken said that few people had come this way. Owen led her through the rim of underbrush and low tree branches into the woods. A few steps more and they came out onto a deer trail. He pulled her into his arms. Time stopped. Her heart sang as she eagerly returned his kisses.

"You smell like a gillyflower," he murmured. "I know a good place where we can talk."

With a secret smile, he started along the narrow, winding path. Their feet made scarcely a sound on the dark ground, soft-padded with rotting leaves. A few minutes' walk brought them to a twisted old chestnut, close-crowded by elm and ash. In ancient times the once supple sapling had been bent down by some calamity. The persistent chestnut had survived and eventually reached toward the sky again but in a grotesque, tortured way. It crouched ahead of them now, in appearance more a mountain of living brushwood than a stately tree.

The trail swung around the tangle and dipped into the bed of a meandering stream. Owen carefully handed Jane down the steep bank onto a grassy lip that only a heavy rain would cover. Now she could move dry shod almost to the middle. She glanced about.

"How did you know where to come?"

"I've been here before."

"For business or pleasure?"

"Strictly business."

He came to stand beside her near the rippling water.

"I've told my parents I want to wed you."

"I know. Your father came a week ago. Father says your mother must come as well. I'd hoped...."

Her voice broke. The grievous disappointment she'd fought for the last week formed a hard lump in her throat.

"She wants the girl in Bristol. She'll be forced to change her mind eventually. Promise you'll not wed Francis before she does?"

"I'd never do that. Is she pretty?"

"As pretty as Francis, I expect."

With a smile, Jane relaxed against Owen. She tucked her head onto his shoulder, loving the feel of him and the warm security of his embrace. She determinedly pushed all worries over the future from her mind. Now was all that mattered. Above her head, Owen broke the silence.

"I've something to tell you ... something I should have told you before we spoke to Sir Harry in London. But everything happened so fast."

"Mmmm?"

She was thistledown floating above the treetops. How could she possibly still feel the ground beneath her feet?

"I'm involved in smuggling Lutheran literature."

Owen's words slammed her to earth. She tensed and leaned back in his arms to stare at him.

"What? What did you say?"

"I'm helping to smuggle Lutheran writings."

Jane broke free and moved away. She stood looking at him.

"Do you mean you've passed a few pamphlets to someone? Hearing Lucy, half of London could be guilty of that."

"I've passed more than a few. I'm a distributor for all sorts of writings smuggled in from the Continent. I deliver them to Colchester, other places, at fairs like this. Fairs are perfect places." Owen's face became animated. "Between my father's business and my own, my time is getting quite full."

"I'm flattered you've any left for me."

His eager look faded and he reached out to her. She stepped back. His hand dropped.

"When I had to give up the priesthood, I felt as if I'd lost my purpose, my soul. I wanted to show people the truth. Instead, I was showing them soap and salt and peas. Then God handed me this opportunity. I couldn't turn my back on it."

"I see."

She did, all too clearly. He called it an opportunity. She should have remembered that, for him, the priesthood had been more than an occupation. With that avenue closed, how quickly he'd found another to fill this special need.

I wanted to be the one to fill your needs.

"What you're doing is against the law. Doesn't that bother you?"

"Not as much as I'm bothered that William Tyndale wasn't given permission to translate. The Church has no right to deny people the scriptures. My disobedience toward their laws is nothing compared to their disobedience toward God."

"It's also against the king's law."

"Then the king shares their guilt."

The disgust in Owen's voice frightened her. She watched as he moved restlessly about the grassy lip.

"Surely given the right translator, the right time -."

"William is an excellent translator. As for the right time.... It's always the right time."

"What you're doing is dangerous. If you're caught...."

"I don't intend to be caught."

His answer was lightly said but something in his eyes belied his tone.

"And if you are?"

"Regardless of what individual bishops do on occasion, Wolsey sets the tune for the Church in England. He's guilty of many sins, but not of heretic hunting."

Jane stared blindly across the stream. Around them birds twittered in the branches and a fish slapped the water. Owen continued.

"I've told you because you've a right to know. I can't tell you more. I'm risking my life with you. I've no right to endanger those I work with."

Jane shivered in the noonday heat. If she should lose him....

"Promise you'll take every care. And Father must never know. He would absolutely refuse to let us wed."

"You do still want to marry me?" Owen's voice was all at once thick.

"Oh, yes." His face blurred before her eyes. She reached out. "But you make me afraid."

He caught her hands and pulled her close.

"I don't want to lose you. I can't lose this opportunity either."

"I understand," she whispered, burying her face against his neck, accepting his caresses. He had become as unyielding as the ground beneath her feet. "It's all right. I don't mind."

A short while later, once again surrounded with the fair's noisy traffic, Jane and Owen parted. Owen strode off toward grocers' row while Jane, her stomach rumbling, set out for the cookshops. She halted abruptly. Owen had likely spent his mealtime with her and would now go hungry until evening. She swung around and sped after him to ask if she could bring him a meat pie. She spotted him just as an ugly dark man in rough garb caught his sleeve. Rather than shaking the fellow's hand off as she expected, Owen paused to exchange a brief word with him.

Jane stopped in the busy track. Why did she sense something odd in that quick exchange? She scolded herself. Owen's admission of smuggling had unsettled her. She could give many reasons why someone would speak to Owen at the fair and all of them innocent.

The following morning, Jane set out with Bess and Dickon to make the purchases Wynnfield Hall would need for the winter. She carried a list ranging from ink and paper to straining cloths, spices and embroidery floss. She ended at Owen's stall. There she bought four sacks of bay salt for the Michaelmas butchering and received Owen's promise to stroll about the fair with her in the afternoon when business slackened.

Her marketing completed, Jane wandered around the fair alone. She saw Dickon and Bess pass hand in hand. Seeing her maidservant's glowing face, Jane felt a stab of envy for the girl's untroubled marriage arrangements. Not for Bess the concern over social status and dowries. She was untouched by business or family ties which must be made more secure. Their union would be no more complicated than moving Bess's few belongings from her parents' two rooms over the kitchen to Dickon's single room above the cart house with a stop at the village church in between.

Jane sighed. If only she and Owen could wed soon. Once she was his wife, she could draw him away from this dangerous smuggling and make him more content with a merchant's life.

She paused to watch a contortionist tie himself into knots even a snake might envy. Beyond the spectators she spotted Owen striding past. As she gazed after him, wishing she were at his side, she realized that the ugly dark man of yesterday was following close behind. Curious, she slipped out of the crowd and started after. Owen appeared to be making for the temporary stables at the edge of the fairgrounds. In another moment, he disappeared around the rear corner of the horse enclosure. The dark man was hard on his heels.

She hurried toward the same corner and peered cautiously around it just as Owen and the dark man disappeared together into the woods. Without hesitation, she crossed the strip of stubbly field and quietly pushed through the underbrush onto the deer trail. She paused in the dimness, her ears straining to catch the sound of men. All she heard was the rasp of insects and her own uneven breathing. Abruptly, instinctively, she knew where Owen was going. She also knew why. Standing in the stream bed yesterday he'd claimed to have done business there. Only one business required such a private meeting place.

Cautiously she slipped down the path, heart thumping, her breath catching at every turn. Yesterday the distance to the old chestnut had seemed far. Today she found herself facing the tangled tree before she knew it. The thick bushy growth blocked her view of the stream. It didn't entirely muffle the sound of men's voices. Slowly, quietly, Jane lifted branches and crept inch by inch through the wall of brush into the hollow black interior of the deformed tree. Her slippers made scarcely a sound on the spongy rotten leaves, the collection of decades, as she ducked under the bent tree trunk and came up on the side overlooking the stream. With infinite care, she shifted branchlets aside.

Five men stood in a knot beside the rippling water. As she expected, Owen and the dark man from the fair were there. She gasped when a third man moved into view. Howard Willcotte. What did her bailiff have to do with Owen's smuggling? The fourth man had a gentle, lined face and a head of white hair that shone like silver in the sunlight. Only the face of the fifth man, a huge, black-bearded giant in a brown jerkin, remained obscured.

The five talked for some time, their words distorted by the rush of the stream. Of a sudden, the tableau began to shift. The giant briefly dropped a hand onto Owen's shoulder. Hunching his massive shoulders, he turned away and clambered up the far bank to disappear into the woods. The silver-haired man followed him. The meeting was over. The remaining three were already coming her way. They would pass within two feet of her hiding place.

Her muscles bunched. Dropping to a crouch, she scrambled under the twisted trunk and into the tree's hollow center. She could hear indistinct voices as they drew closer. The branches that had shielded her stirred as if Owen and his companions were using them for handholds as they clambered up the steep bank. She was fervently thankful that her gown was dark. Ten more thudding heartbeats and their voices were fading.

For some time after silence returned, Jane remained in her hiding place, afraid to stir, only vaguely aware of the wood ants stinging her ankles. She struggled out at last and tiptoed hurriedly back along the path. Her ears were pricked for sounds of men ahead, lest, in her haste, she should run into them. She checked at the edge of the wood. Seeing no sign of Owen or the other two in the field or by the horse enclosure, she broke from cover and fled back to the noise and happy unconcern of the fair.

A few minutes later she was standing safely in the midst of a crowd. Before her, a juggler in blue-and-red striped hose was keeping three apples and a wooden trencher in the air. She brushed leaf mold from her skirt and ran shaky fingers over her head feeling for telltale twigs. She couldn't say what had prompted her to follow Owen. If he should learn she'd spied on him, he would likely be angry. Already she was ashamed of her behavior. She had little choice. She would have to keep it from him.

When Owen had left for the fair William Tyndale had been so disheartened that, when he returned home a month later, he fully expected to find the priest removed to some obscure country post. Instead, he discovered William had taken up residence with Humphrey Monmouth, one of London's wealthy cloth merchants.

"Master Monmouth has provided me with more than a place at his table," William said nodding toward the three Sunday-afternoon visitors carrying on a lively discussion at the other end of the long paneled hall in which he and Owen sat. "He's given me a window to the world. His guests discuss all manner of topics. They're more alert to current happenings than those who dined at Sir John's table." The priest's voice dropped. "Listening to them, I believe many would welcome an English Bible. If only I can find a way."

Owen glanced around. No one was close enough to overhear. He still dropped his voice to match William's.

"You're continuing with your plan? without Church approval you'll be courting death."

"I've no wish to become a martyr. Still, there must be a way...."

Dick Bolt arrived at work the following morning with his left eye swollen nearly shut, a dark bruise staining his jaw and his upper lip split. Owen, facing him in the dim warehouse, frowned.

"I tripped," Dick said defiantly. He gingerly touched his damaged face with a raw-knuckled hand. Beneath his challenge, he wore smug satisfaction. Obviously the person Dick had tripped over had fared far worse.

Why today, of all days, with Father away and Frederick at home with a stomach complaint?

"You're in no shape to wait on customers," Owen said. "I'll handle the store. You unpack that load of spices."

Dick shrugged and stalked off.

The day dragged by with frequent showers and little trade. Owen spent the afternoon restocking shelves in the shop. He was balanced precariously on the edge of a large barrel shifting merchandise to a top shelf when the street door banged open, bringing with it the sound of rain and flying feet. Before Owen could turn, a hand grabbed the bottom of his doublet and yanked.

"Dick! Come down this instant."

Owen had no time to explain that he wasn't Dick. He came down to land on his back with a thud. He lay gasping for breath and trying to focus on his assailant. The girl, garbed in blue servant's livery, was small and freckled, with hair the color of burnished copper. At the moment, the expression on her pert face was changing from extreme anger to acute embarrassment.

"I thought you was Dick Bolt."

Owen groaned and struggled to sit up. Dick, sticking his head in from the back, reared up in surprise.

"Nan. What are you doing here?"

Nan spun, her wet skirt tail slapping Owen across the face. Fairly hopping in restored ire, she advanced on Dick.

"So you did it." She shook a finger up at him. "You can't deny it. Just look at your face."

Dick, a full head taller, retreated before her. Even after they disappeared from sight Owen could hear their every word. Grinning at the tongue lashing Dick was receiving, Owen cautiously picked himself up off the floor. Now Dick's voice was gaining volume.

"I warned him. He won't be putting his hands on you again."

"He was just testin'. I can handle him."

"So can I. My way. He won't be doing any more testing."

"And how will I explain to the mistress?"

"Why should you explain? You aren't the one with the busted-up face."

Nan's laugh exploded.

"He did look pretty funny waitin' on the master this morning." Her tone sharpened again. "In future stay out of my affairs. I already got three brothers to come to my aid. I ain't needin' a fourth."

"I've no intention of being the fourth."

A pregnant silence fell. Their voices resumed at a much reduced level. Strain as he might, Owen caught nothing more. He rubbed his sore back. He'd likely have bruises in the morning.

Witnessing a part of Dick's private life was gratifying. They had worked together for over half-a-year. Though Dick's sullenness was mostly a thing of the past, he continued to ignore all Owen's attempts at friendship. The face Dick turned to him now was frequently guarded and watchful. At times it was blatantly crafty. Always it was impersonal.

The word 'brother' had never again passed between them. Neither did Dick mention the damning Lutheran pamphlet that had slipped from Owen's sleeve. Owen didn't delude himself. Dick hadn't forgotten either incident. The two words 'brother' and 'heretic' lay between them like creatures unborn, growing in the blackness of the womb. When one or the other burst forth, which side of Dick would respond? Would it be the clever calculating merchant or the hotheaded and personable young man whispering with a girl in the warehouse? More to the point, what danger would it bring to Owen?

The street door jerked open a second time. Humphrey Alton, his dark gown dripping, sloshed into the shop. Owen, aware of the two in the back, sprang up and greeted his father loudly.

"Father, you've returned. How was your trip from Stoke Hall?"

"Are you blind? Look at me. The horse threw a shoe. I had to walk the last mile in the rain. I should have come with your mother when the weather was good." He glanced around. "Where's Dick?"

"He's working in the back."

Humphrey pushed past Owen, in no temper for further delay. Owen let his father go. He would receive fair payment for his tumble if Dick and his girl were caught.

A moment later Owen heard his father growl at Dick. Dick's reply, as always, was respectful and almost warm. Their voices faded as they moved deeper into the warehouse. When all was silent again, Nan popped from the back, raced through the store and out the door without a glance for Owen.

Owen sat in his chamber on All Hallows eve and stared at the blank paper on the writing desk before him. Jane's last two unanswered letters lay at his elbow. What should he write? He certainly couldn't tell her of his recent smuggling trips or of William's abiding hope to produce an English Bible. Even if such topics were safe to put on paper, she wouldn't wish to hear of them. At the fair she'd told him she understood his need to serve God. He knew she didn't. That lack of accord was an obstacle between them. If longing and prayers could have broken down the barrier, it would have been destroyed long ago. His one consolation lay in the knowledge that she was reading his Latin Testament. Surely she would soon come to understanding.

In the meantime, he would write of other things. She would enjoy hearing he'd taken part in the Lord Mayor's show with his father and the rest of the grocers' guild. Almost he could see the interest lighting her dark eyes as he described the glittering procession of magnificently decorated barges accompanying the Lord Mayor's silver-oared vessel to Westminster to receive the King's approval of his election. After writing for some time Owen concluded with words of devotion. He promised, if possible, to see her at Nativity.

As the ink dried, he glanced over what he'd penned. It contained so little of real importance. If only he could write all that his heart held. He folded the heavy paper and sealed it with a red blob of wax.

Half-a-week later Jane eagerly broke that same seal in the privacy of her chamber. Her mouth grew tender as she read Owen's letter. After a rapt second reading, she ran her fingers over the neat script as if to touch the writer. Her joyful heart sang. He might come at Nativity.

Her reverie was interrupted by a rap on her door. A maidservant stuck her white-capped head around the door edge.

"Mistress, there's a peddler in the hall. He asks shelter for the night and to show his wares."

Permission given, the maid disappeared. Jane returned to the letter. She savored it a third time before tucking it away in her chest.

On her way across the passage room, she looked through the inner window into the hall below. The peddler was busily arranging his goods on a hastily erected trestle table. Jane's head craned forward in astonishment. It was Owen's ugly dark acquaintance from Stourbridge fair.

So this is what smugglers did as a side occupation.

Having recently attended the fair, Jane had thought to leave perusal of the peddler's goods to the servants alone. Now she changed her mind. She entered the hall with what she hoped was an indifferent expression and glanced over the ribbons and laces, purses and caps, pieces of lawn, girdles, combs and pewter pots. The peddler stood respectfully to one side, his deep-set eyes alert for any flicker of interest that could mean a sale. She lay a mirror aside.

"Do you have any books?"

Jane watched with carefully concealed amusement as the peddler rummaged in his pack. He held out a copy of 'The Hours of the Blessed Virgin'.

"Have you nothing more?"

"No, mistress. If you tell me what you want, I could bring it next trip."

What would he do if she asked for a Lutheran tract?

"Perhaps another time."

"With your permission, mistress, I'll show my goods to the servants."

As Jane left, she wondered how soon Howard Willcotte would find his way in to view the peddler's goods.

Owen, hurrying on his way to see William Tyndale, pulled his fur-lined gown closer against the chill January wind. He had returned from Wynnfield Hall a week earlier. Apart from the time needed to deliver literature in Cambridge and Newmarket, he'd spent Twelfthtide with Jane.

Regardless of the joy of being with her, his visit had been rife with tension. Sir Harry, for all his surface politeness, had treated him like an interloper. Jane was to have wed Francis Grady at this season. Little wonder that Sir Harry had so resented his presence. Jane had developed an almost morbid concern for her stepfather's health. She feared that he'd fall ill and, faced with death, demand that she wed Francis immediately.

For his own part, Owen's commitment to his private business had been an unspoken source of strain between them. When, at the fair, she had claimed to be afraid, he'd not taken her seriously. Now he was beginning to. Should Dick Bolt denounce him as a heretic, he would be found guilty and forfeit both life and property. If he and Jane were married, that would include Wynnfield Manor. Jane had good reason to be afraid. He could destroy her.

If only she believed as he did and the worst happened, he would at least have her understanding. That she didn't put a completely different cast on the situation. He'd been unable to keep back the words that had claimed her last summer at their chance meeting in London. He had even less strength to give her up now. Not that she showed any desire for him to do so. When she had twined her arms about his neck and kissed him farewell, almost her last words had been of her longing to be his wife. Yet if she didn't come to believe as he did, could he, in all fairness, ask her to risk everything for his belief alone?

Owen pushed the disturbing thoughts aside as he leaned into the freezing wind. Only one more street and he'd be at Master Monmouth's house. His grip tightened on the book tucked securely inside his gown.

"Luther's New Testament."

William's long face lit with reverent awe as he held the book. Owen hitched his stool nearer the earthen pot of glowing coals that provided a suggestion of warmth in the cold solitude of William's small chamber. The crackling fire in the hall below would have warmed him better, but this book could only be shown in private.

"I got it from a friend in the Steelyard," Owen said. "His family lives near Worms."

"If only I knew German. You do, don't you? Is Brother Luther a good translator?"

"Fairly good, from what I can tell. I'm not a Greek scholar like you. I had to compare it with Erasmus's Latin Testament."

Owen watched William leaf through the book, his gaze devouring the clean, uniform lines of print. When he looked up, his face was ablaze with determination.

"With God's help I will do this for England though every churchman here stand in my way." He laid the book on his small table. "Teach me German."

William's German lessons were interrupted during Lent when Owen's father became ill. Humphrey's walk through the rain after Stourbridge fair had left him with a stubborn cough that had come and gone several times over the intervening months. After eating the Lenten diet for a fortnight, the cough returned. This time it was accompanied by a low fever. Catherine made coltsfoot decoctions, applied linseed poultices to her husband's chest and fed him onion gruel. Scold as she might, she could not keep him in bed. The business needed his attention. In desperation, she sent for the physician. He recommended Humphrey resume eating the more nourishing foods allowed to children and invalids. Humphrey flatly refused. As if to balance sins committed during the year, he'd always kept a most stringent Lent. He wouldn't deviate now.

Owen was caught up in the crisis. No word of his could persuade his father to remain abed or his mother to curb her peevish comments. He could only spend additional time with the business in the hope that his father would take more rest.

Lent ended at last. With red meat and warmer weather, Humphrey's health improved. Owen's mother, seemingly vexed that her dire threats hadn't been vindicated, grudgingly took herself off to mass to offer thanks. Owen penned a long overdue letter to Jane and then paid a visit on William Tyndale.

William was unusually animated as he and Owen settled in a quiet corner of Master Monmouth's hall.

"I'll soon discover how good a tutor you are. I'm leaving for Germany at month's end." Though William lowered his voice, it still rang with exhilaration. "I'm going to translate the New Testament, print it and see it smuggled into England."

Owen thrilled at the thought.

"It sounds so simple ... and safe. At least safer than doing it in England. But how will you cover the costs? And get the testaments in? Once they're here, I can help distribute them."

"I hoped you'd offer. As for the money.... Have you ever heard of the Christian Brethren?"

"I suspect most of what I pass on is smuggled in by them."

"I've met one of them. He knows of my hope. Last Wednesday he assured me the Brethren would help finance the printing. They'll also ship the books in from Antwerp."

"How will you get them from the printers to Antwerp?"

William gave him an unconcerned smile.

"Likely most of a year will be spent on translating and printing. Our Lord will surely provide a solution by then."

In the next few weeks, Owen spent hours studying the problem. He was grateful for all he'd learned in the last year about transporting goods. He questioned everyone he dared. What roads led to Antwerp?

Through which German states did they pass? Which states were for Luther and which for the Church? What was barge transport like on the rivers? Where were shipments likely to be checked by local officials? When and where were the main fairs held?

As he gathered the scraps of information, he tried to fit them into a comprehensive picture. So many gaps remained. It would be so much easier if he himself could travel the roads and rivers. If only he could put his life here aside for a year, even half a year, and take it up again on his return.

That was impossible. And in that lay the crux of his mounting frustration. This opportunity to help William could prove to be the most important of his life. But, if he went, he'd return to find Jane wed to Francis Grady. Sir Harry had delayed this long only because of Jane's resistance and the fact that Owen was undisputed heir to his parents' wealth. His father would never allow him a six-month sojourn in Germany. If he left without permission, he might well be disinherited. At the very least, his Lutheran leanings would come out. Either eventuality would end his hopes to wed Jane. All her determination would not prevent a marriage with Francis at that point.

Owen was grateful for the sickle moon high over sleeping London as he accompanied William and Master Greene of the Christian Brethren down to the Thames. The moon's watery light showed them the way without picking them out. In a distant street, the night watch called the hour.

They reached the steps and stopped. The wet scent of the river floating in on the night breeze filled Owen's nostrils. All decent folk were abed, their windows shuttered and their doors bolted. Only rogues and the night watch roamed abroad at this hour. And priests who were departing for the Continent without permission.

On this late April night, William was becoming a fugitive. By slipping out of England secretly and without the king's approval, it was hoped the churchmen would be longer in finding his trail. For all their light talk of Germany being safe, from the arrival of the first Testaments into England, William would be a hunted man. He could expect nothing but the stake if he were caught.

The merchant ship which would carry him to Hamburg was a dark shadow in midstream. The creak and groan of rigging alone proved its substance. In a few hours, it would weigh anchor and begin its journey to the ocean. A small boat waited at the foot of the steps, barely discernible in the shadows, ready to carry William to his ship. Owen could hear the river lapping the boat's sides. A moment later William came softly down the steps. He touched Owen's arm lightly in a silent farewell. They had already said all the important things. The less talk now the better. Voices carried far over water.

The boatman caught the step edge to hold his small craft steady. William clambered aboard. Awkwardly he settled his thin frame onto his seat. Would he suffer from seasickness? The way he grabbed the boat's sides when it lifted and fell with a wave was not encouraging. Owen handed the two chests across to be settled at the priest's feet. They made a pitiably small amount to carry into a lifetime of self-imposed exile.

The boatman bent to his oars.

"God speed you, William."

The boat swung into the current. An overwhelming sense of loss swept Owen. He should be going with William. He leaped down the last steps into the lapping waves, his hand outstretched to call the boat back. A cloud slipped over the moon and plunged the river into blackness. Slowly the cloud drifted past. The inky darkness lighted fractionally. Owen strained to see. The boat was gone, swallowed up in the sable shadows of the river. He stood alone, his hand reaching out into emptiness. He fisted it and let it fall. But for the cloud....

CHAPTER 8 – JUNE, 1524

"Master Owen, your father wants you in the dining parlor."

Owen nodded to the maidservant hovering in the office door. He marked his place in the column of figures he was adding, holding the total in his head.

"You're to come straight away."

Narrowing his eyes, Owen attempted to see the total. It was gone. He glared at the numbers he'd have to refigure. He laid his quill aside and stretched up, easing the stiffness between his shoulder blades. He left the warehouse and made for the outside stairs to the hall, dodging a laden cart on the way. Just over a month had passed since William had sailed. Master Greene should soon receive word that he'd reached Wittenburg safely.

"What is it, Father? Mother, what's wrong?"

Owen looked apprehensively from his mother sitting stiffly at the window overlooking the garden to his father standing grim-faced beside the dining table. Humphrey was tapping a folded paper against the linen tablecloth.

"Your mother was tidying your belongings. She found this."

Humphrey jammed the paper at Owen.

Even as he reached for the sheet, he recognized it. His muscles tightened. That very morning he'd slipped the Lutheran tract between two of Jane's most recent letters deep in one of his chests. Only someone purposely searching would have discovered it. Owen swung to face his mother.

"You've no right to make free with my personal papers."

Catherine opened her mouth but Humphrey cut her off.

"That's not the issue. This tract is. What was it doing there?"

"I was reading it."

"Well, burn it. And any others you've got secreted away. I'll have none of that in this house. We're good Christians here. You're to have nothing more to do with these heretic ideas. I want your word."

Owen sucked in his breath.

"I'm sorry, Father. I can't do that."

"Don't be an idiot. Of course you can. Just give me your word and that's an end to it."

"You don't understand. There's truth in this pamphlet. Here, read it for yourself."

He thrust the paper at his father. Humphrey knocked his hand away.

"Truth?! Since when has an Englishman had to look to a German monk for truth. Especially an excommunicated one who's slandered our good King."

"He's also been accused of slandering the Pope. Doesn't that bother you too?"

"The Pope isn't English."

"Enough." His mother swept across the floor to stand beside his father. "You speak of truth. Here's another. If you persist, you'll endanger not only yourself but us as well."

"And my business." Humphrey tore the pamphlet from Owen's fingers and crumpled it in his fist. "Swear to have no further dealings with these German heresies."

"I believe in these teachings."

"Then you're a heretic as well." He stared at Owen as if he were looking at the devil himself. Then he spun on his wife, his face livid. "This is all your doing. First he'd be a priest and now.... What kind of unnatural child have you borne me?!"

Catherine shrank under his attack.

"He's as much your son as he is mine."

"Not if he's become a heretic." Humphrey rounded on Owen again. "Do you hear me? I'll not have any son of mine endangering everything I've spent a lifetime building. Foreswear this whole business or get out."

The room rocked. What he'd feared for months was happening.

"You can't mean that, husband." Catherine flung herself on Humphrey. "He's our son. Our last son."

"Your last son, madam," Humphrey said, jerking free. "I still have another."

Catherine's face turned the color of wet ash. She opened her mouth, but all her slack lips produced was a gurgle.

"Well, what will it be? Will you swear or be turned out of my house?"

Owen tried to speak but words wouldn't come. Through the open parlor windows he could hear the scrape of boxes and the banter of men unloading merchandise in the courtyard. The sounds seemed far away. The long column of figures waited in the office. Oh, Jane, I'm being given no option. He found his voice at last.

"I'll start packing."

Owen's arms were piled with clothing when his chamber door burst open. His mother rushed in. She snatched up the garments and frantically pushed them back on their pegs. His green doublet fell to the floor in a crumpled heap. In a frenzy, his mother spun to face him.

"You must stop this folly now. You can't leave. I won't permit it. I won't see Dick Bolt taking my son's place. Your father's already sent for him." She grabbed his arm and tried to drag him to the door. "You've got to make peace with your father."

Owen tore his arm free but she continued to cling to him.

"You want to hurt me." She was trembling. "It's because I refused you permission to wed. I'll withdraw my objections. She can

151

be yours within the week. Only go to your father now, before it's too late."

He thrust his mother violently away. She staggered and caught the doorjam. He stared at her, hating her for what she'd just done.

"It's already too late. I've a job to do."

"Owen, you must -."

He shoved his mother out the door and bolted it against her. Covering his ears with his hands, he tried to block out her hysterical cries. When at last they ceased, he shuddered. He leaned to retrieve his doublet from the floor, but his hand shook too much to grip it.

Owen stared blankly at the disordered heap of clothing on his bed. One chest sat open on the floor. Another balanced on a stool. Deciding what to take and what to leave was more than he could handle. He felt utterly weary. If only he could curl up in bed, pull the covers over his head and shut out the world.

Someone was pounding on his locked door.

"Open up." Dick's voice was urgent, demanding. "Let me in."

Owen fumbled with the bolt. When he lifted the latch, Dick almost tumbled in. He checked and gaped at the empty clothes pegs, the pile of belongings on the bed, the open chests.

Leaning against the closed door, Owen watched his half-brother.

"He said I'm to take your place. That I'm the only son he has left." Dick's voice broke. "I've waited all my life to hear him call me 'son'. But to have it come like this. I almost threw the word back in his face."

"Why didn't you?"

"I am his son. It's time everyone accepted that."

Owen resumed packing. He added the bundle of Jane's letters to the smaller chest. The next moment he took them out to stare at them with a mind curiously empty. He returned them to the chest.

"He said you had a Lutheran tract," Dick said. Then, defensively, "I didn't tell him."

Owen looked up. He'd forgotten Dick's presence.

"My mother found it. Why didn't you tell? You've known all this time."

"I would have if you'd been like your brothers. They thought me a cuckoo in their nest. But I've a right same as they. If caring matters, I've a stronger claim on the business. I love it more than either of them did, certainly more than you. When Father dies, if you'd tried to cut me out of a share, I'd have used that tract against you. You can be sure of that."

"It'll all be yours now."

He picked up his gray doublet, folded it then dropped it into the chest. He added a second garment.

"You're making a jumble," Dick said gruffly, elbowing Owen to one side. "Tell me what you're taking."

Owen sank onto a stool. His hands dropped listlessly between his knees.

"I won't need much where I'm going."

Dick looked around, his expression hopeful.

"You have a place to go?"

"Yes." Surely Master Greene would help him get to Germany.

"I'd take everything. What you don't need you can sell. The extra monies may come in useful."

"I've got to ride up to Essex first."

"That maid you wanted to marry?"

Owen winced. He slammed the door on that line of thought and dredged up another to fill the void.

"What about you? Are you going to wed that red-headed fighting hen, or wait for Father to send you to Agnes Bench?"

An embarrassed grin broke across Dick's face.

"I don't know. I've not had time to think."

Dick turned back to his task. Soon he dropped the lid on the second chest. The remainder of Owen's possessions waited in a neat pile on the bed.

"I'll find a basket for these." Dick looked sideways at Owen. "I never imagined.... If you waited a few days, he might change his mind."

"I thought you wanted the business."

"I do. I'd have found great pleasure fighting you for it. There's no joy in getting it like this."

"Even if Father did change his mind, I know now I can't stay. I've something that must be done on the Continent."

"Is it worth giving up so much?"

"If, in the future, you hear that an English Testament has come to London, you'll know it was."

Dick's eyes widened. He whistled softly under his breath.

"If that's your job, you'll certainly be safer gone."

He glanced around as if searching for something more to pack. There was nothing.

"Well, that's it, then." He stood kneading his knuckles.

"Could you tell Frederick I didn't get the accounts finished? Be kind to my mother." His voice failed. He thrust out his hand uncertainly.

Dick looked down at the extended palm. He brushed it aside and threw his arms around Owen.

Jubilantly Jane paced the pleasance with Owen's latest letter in her hand. A clump of bright pansy faces smiled at her from the flower bed, while in the orchard, a blackbird trilled joyfully. The sweet summer breeze caressed her cheek and set the sweetbriar leaves dancing with delight at the good news.

The letter, delivered while she and her father had been calling on friends in Hensford, could not have contained better news. William Tyndale was gone. Owen wrote that he'd accepted a position far from London. Jane's spirits soared higher than the bird song. From the first, the priest had been a constant reminder and drag on Owen back to the life he'd first chosen, a life which excluded her. Now that danger was past.

The conviction, growing since Twelfthtide, firmed into a granite-hard decision. Bess, wedded at Michaelmas, was already three months gone with child. She, on the other hand, seemed no nearer being a wife than she'd been last August.

Jane reread Owen's letter promising to come soon. When he did, she knew exactly what she would say. They should marry now. She was past her eighteenth birthday. Surely among Owen's acquaintances there was a priest who would consent to hear their vows. Once they were wed, they'd find a way to make peace with their respective parents. In the meantime they'd be together.

The pleasance door creaked on its hinges. She turned and saw Owen step through.

With a glad cry, Jane flew down the path and into his arms. He clasped her tightly, his rough cheek pressed against her smooth brow. His body was as taut as a drawn bow. He began to tremble. Jane wrapped her arms more closely about him. Gradually his shaking ceased and his grip slackened. She peered into his haggard face.

"Owen, what is it? What's wrong?"

Pulling her down beside him on the nearest bench, he took her hands in his.

"I'm leaving for the Continent. It wasn't safe to tell you in a letter. William's gone to Germany to produce an English Testament. I'll help smuggle it into England."

Goose-flesh raised over Jane's skin.

"For how long?"

"A year? Probably longer."

Her heart nearly failed. Instinctively she tightened her hold on his fingers.

"Let's find a priest to wed us now."

"It's too late." Haltingly Owen told her of the clash with his father. "I've hardly more than the clothes on my back. Even the horse that brought me is borrowed. I knew I should have gone with William. I didn't because of what I'd lose. Now I've got nothing."

"You still have me."

Owen released her hands and stood. With growing alarm she watched him move away.

"Your father would never permit us to wed now."

"I'll marry you without permission. Wynnfield can provide our needs. If you must go, I'll go with you."

"I may be little better than a fugitive. I'll not make you one as well."

With a herculean effort, Jane held herself erect as she stared at him.

"I've always been more yours than you've been mine."

"Do you think I wanted us to end this way? Leaving you is tearing me in half."

"You can do it, though. You've got something better. Your God and your precious Tyndale. I could almost hate them both."

Owen caught her arms in a tight grip.

"Don't say that. Promise me."

Jane pulled loose and backed away.

"By what right do you demand promises of me now?"

His shoulders slumped and silence fell over the pleasance. In the orchard even the blackbird was quiet. The light breeze ruffled his lank hair, stirred the sweetbriar leaves and sent a letter fluttering into the marigolds. Owen took a step toward the pleasance door.

"Wait!" She couldn't let him leave with nothing but harsh words. She would never see him again. "How will you live on the Continent?"

"I'll manage."

Jane looked down at her ring. The ruby glowed as red as a bleeding heart. She tore at her finger, wrenching off the ornament.

"Take this. Sell it if...."

"But it was your mother's."

"Will you refuse me even in this?"

Owen reached out and, without touching her, plucked the ring from her fingers.

She watched him follow the path to the pleasance door without a backward glance. The hinges protested as it shut behind him. The sound cut through Jane like a knife. Dazed, she lifted her hand and saw blood trickling down her finger. In tearing off the ring she'd scraped her knuckle. She lifted the wound to her lips. The blood had a sickening taste.

She sank down onto the bench and began to weep.

The afternoon shadows were an hour longer when Sir Harry came down the stairs from his nap. The bailiff met him in the parlor, folded paper in hand. The blood pounded in his ears as he read Owen's note. He crumpled it in his fist and set out to find Jane. Sir Harry searched house, outbuildings, pleasance and even orchard to no effect. Returning past the private chapel, he opened the door and glanced in.

When Eleanor was alive, the room at the far end of the family wing saw daily use. As well as hearing mass, she had come morning and evening to light candles before St. Mary of Magdalene and the Blessed Virgin. His wife's devotions were not curtailed even by the wandering artist who, for a winter's lodging and a handful of coins, filled the plastered west wall with bright Bible scenes.

When the family chaplain died, the chapel, though kept in good order, had fallen into disuse. Nowadays, he and Jane rode the three miles to Hensford town to worship where his father and grandfather had worshiped. Sir Harry had only that excuse for not finding her earlier.

She was huddled on a padded bench before the altar, the beaten gold crucifix glowing dimly beyond her head.

Jane's tears were spent by the time she heard her stepfather's heavy tread and wheezing breath coming down the side aisle. Another moment and he was patting her clumsily on the shoulder.

"He's not worth the tears."

Jane kept her chin tucked.

"You spoke to him?"

"No." Sir Harry lowered himself onto the bench beside her. "The churl left a note with Howard."

At mention of the bailiff, Jane's jaw set. Of course Owen would tell Willcotte farewell. The thought gave her the strength of anger. Her stepfather was talking.

"... didn't have the courage to give a proper explanation. Listen." Sir Harry smoothed the wrinkled paper across his huge knee. "... 'had a disagreement with my parents and have decided to go to the Continent.'" He wadded the paper up anew. "I've a mind to demand the reason from Humphrey Alton."

Jane stiffened. Even now her every instinct was to protect Owen.

"What does it matter? He's gone. I want to hear no more of Altons."

"You're right, of course. Put the whole affair behind you. I knew he'd bring nothing but sorrow. He wasn't like other men. He wanted to be a priest and was denied. It made him unstable. You're well free of him. In time you'll see I'm right."

He patted her shoulder. Gradually his look brightened.

"I'll write to Francis's father -."

"No! Do you think I could face Francis now?"

To Jane's relief, he said no more.

After Jane retired, Sir Harry stumped off to the accounts room. He settled at the table and reached for a sheet of writing paper. He felt weighted down with age and worries. Summer flourished all around him. But soon winter would return. He had felt his age too much during the last one. His heart had pounded in his chest more often than ever before. He must see Jane wed before autumn. That way, whatever came, he would have fulfilled his vow to Eleanor. Jane would outlive her present grief. Whether she came to love Francis or not, a babe at her breast would bring joy to her heart. He pulled the candle closer, dipped quill into ink and began to write.

In the days following Owen's departure, Jane would have crawled into some dark corner with her grief if she'd been allowed. She was not. The household keys jingled from her girdle. At the very least, servants must be supervised and meals ordered. She also knew her stepfather watched her covertly. For his sake, and because her pride would not let the bailiff witness her unhappiness, she made a determined effort to hide her sorrow. True to his word, her stepfather made no more mention of the Altons. Therefore, to hear the name from a maidservant was a shock.

"Mistress Alton is here. She wishes to speak with you."

Jane, brewing lavender water in the still-house, froze in the middle of her stirring. She lifted the long-handled spoon from the pot of steeping blooms. Quickly she laid it on the table before the servant noticed her trembling hand.

"Show her to the blue parlor."

Jane braced her shoulders and walked into the blue parlor. A handsome woman, pale-haired and black-gowned, turned with a rustle of satin skirts. Jane's heart lurched. This stranger's face held the shape of Owen's eyes and his mouth when he was stern. Her heart settled again. It also contained something definitely not Owen, an element cold and hard but weak beneath, like ice undermined by the spring thaw. She stopped a cart's length from her guest. This was the woman who had kept her and Owen apart until it was too late.

"You wished to see me?"

Mistress Alton settled into a chair like a queen expecting to hold sway in a court not her own. She dropped her riding gloves onto the small table at her elbow, linked her fingers in her lap and looked Jane looked up and down.

"Somehow, I'd expected someone ... less ... ordinary." She paused momentarily. "Why did Owen leave?"

"You're his mother, and you don't know?"

A faint flush stained Mistress Alton's cheek.

"I thought it was because I wouldn't let him wed you. So I gave my permission. He went anyway."

Pride alone held Jane steady as she absorbed this new blow.

"Tell me why my son left."

For one brief moment Owen looked out of his mother's face and rung the answer from her.

"This Lutheran business had become his whole life, as being a priest had been before."

Mistress Alton's expression grew haughty.

"He was going to be a priest because I planned it."

Jane stared at her.

Mother and son were so alike. Neither would entertain an idea that was contrary to what they deemed right.

"He turned his hand to the business without protest," Mistress Alton said firmly.

"Owen found what he believed was a truer way to serve."

"Are you saying he took this German heresy seriously? No person in his right mind would.... Why, the Church has stood since St.

Peter. It controls a quarter of England's lands. These heretics have nothing. Only a fool would think they can stand against Rome."

Jane bristled.

"Owen is no fool. As for his seriousness? You've as much proof of that as I."

The silence stretched taut between them. Mistress Alton stood and reached for her gloves.

"Thank you for your time."

The words were said to the empty space beside Jane. She started toward the door. Jane stepped in her way.

"Why did you refuse permission?"

Mistress Alton's face changed as if a shutter had fallen. She drew on her gloves, working the soft leather carefully over her fingers. Only when the last finger was smoothed did she speak.

"After thirty years I'd had enough of bastards."

It took a moment for the implication to hit. Jane sucked for breath but her lungs refused to fill. She had the same terrifying sensation that she'd had as a child when she'd tumbled into the icy horse pond. Her lungs filled at last.

"You think that I...."

Mistress Alton looked at her curiously.

"They haven't told you?"

"Please go."

Her chin sunk in introspection, Jane perched on a stool at the foot of her stepfather's bed waiting for him to awaken from his nap. His wheezing snort snapped her head up. His eyes opened. She rushed to bend over him.

"Mistress Alton called." Despite her agitation, she noticed her stepfather start. "She said.... She thinks I'm a ... that Lionel Radcott wasn't my father."

Jane peered at her stepfather, waiting for the shocked surprise, the angry indignant denial. Instead, he shrank back into the white bolster, one hand clutching the gathered neck of his shirt, his expression stricken. She squeezed her eyes shut. She didn't want to know. It was too late. She opened her eyes again. Her stepfather was sitting up, his quivering jowls flushed with anger.

"She's talking nonsense. Catherine Alton is a sharp-tongued tale-bearer."

Jane paid no heed to his belated outburst. She crossed her arms tightly, holding herself together. Sir Harry's blustering protests petered out. She spoke into the silence.

"Why didn't you tell me? Why did I have to hear it from her?"

Tears gathered in his eyes. He dabbed them away with his sleeve ruffle.

"I never wanted you to know, to have your mother's memory dishonored."

"Who was my father?"

"I don't know. No one does. Only your mother." He fell silent for a long moment. "She told me that she'd never before been unfaithful to her husband. The man had come like a memory out of her past and was gone again as quickly."

Her stepfather swung his heavy legs over to sit on the edge of the bed, his chin sunk into his fat neck. After a time he continued.

"She might never have been found out if her husband hadn't died. He was killed in a drunken quarrel the very day he returned from a long journey. When Eleanor was found to be with child two months later, the Radcotts knew it couldn't be his. They tried to discover the man. When they failed, they allowed her to leave on condition she made no claim on them for her unborn child. Her own family cast her off. Your mother fled here, away from everyone who knew her."

"How did Mistress Alton find out?"

"She had a relative in the Radcott employ."

"So everyone knew but me."

"No. Whatever her other faults, Catherine Alton's no talebearer. She told me only because she knew of my feelings for your mother. She thought to warn me against marrying a...." Her stepfather bit the sentence off.

For a long moment all Jane heard was his heavy breathing. He looked up at her.

"Your mother never gave me cause to worry. She was five months gone with child when I first saw her. The Blessed Virgin herself couldn't have been more beautiful. I'd ridden over to meet the new neighbor and see the manor house being built. I'd not thought to remarry after Lucy's mother died. Then I saw Eleanor. She was standing there in the cold November wind discussing doorways with Howard Willcotte and the master mason, clutching an old blue cloak over her womb, shielding what lay there.

"Despite my feelings, I lacked the courage to approach her. What of value could I offer such a noble lady?

"Then Catherine Alton came with her warning. It gave me hope that I did have something, my name and my protection for her unborn child. I had watched your mother too often, her hand spread protectively over her womb, not to suspect her fear. If she died in childbirth, who would care for her babe?

"We were wed a fortnight before you were born. When her time came and her fear was the greatest, she told me the ruby ring she had was to be yours. It had belonged to your father. I had you christened 'Jane' after my mother's mother."

Jane looked down in bewilderment at the finger which still bore the feel of a ring ... the ring she had torn off a week before for Owen's sake. Her father's ring.

"Did Owen know?"

"Yes."

The house slept as Jane sat at her dressing table braiding her long hair for bed. In corners and behind chests the darkness waited for her to snuff her candle and free it.

She stopped, pulled the taper near and reached for her silver mirror. Peering into it, she studied her features as she would a stranger's. She saw a slender face, dark hair and brows, delicately-lidded, almost-black eyes set a hair's breadth too close on either side of a straight, blunt-tipped nose. Hers was a reasonably pretty face, even a lovely one if Owen were to be believed. But she was not breathtakingly beautiful, not golden like her mother, not blue-eyed. She looked deep into the mirror attempting to see past her woman's visage to the man who had stamped it.

Abruptly she slammed the mirror down. Her breath roughened with anger. She felt betrayed. Betrayed by her stepfather, by the mother who that day had become a stranger, most of all by that shadowy man who had given her a face but no name. Despite that, she experienced no anguish. Anguish was Owen walking away and shutting the door between them.

The Tuesday before St. John's eve Sir Harry called Jane into the accounts room.

"I've heard from Francis's parents about the wedding. Hear me out," he said when she started to protest. "You can't withdraw from life simply because it's dealt ill with you. I'm too old to wait longer.

The wedding will take place by August. Whether here or in London and the date I'll leave to you. But it will take place."

Jane bowed her head. In his own way, her stepfather was right. A different thought lifted it again.

"Do Francis and his parents know of my birth?"

"No, thank God."

"Francis, at least, must be told."

"I think not."

"He believes my father was Lionel Radcott. He's proud of it. We mustn't deceive him."

"Who will it hurt? You'll make him a good wife. His knowing won't change that."

"But Father –."

"No, Jane. I've not protected your mother's name all these years to have you bring it into disrepute now. Neither before nor after your marriage are you to tell Francis anything."

Jane tossed restlessly, the pillows hot under her head. Waking earlier and feeling stifled within the inky darkness of the curtained bed, she had yanked the near drape open. Now, the first hint of midsummer dawn was outlining the room's furnishings. Her body ached with weariness but her troubled thoughts would not still. Her stepfather had said the wedding must be by Lammas. Then, let it be at Lammas, here at Wynnfield, as unpretentious as Francis would allow.

Pray God he never discovered the truth. Owen had known, yet had wanted her. Longing for him burned through her, driving her from her bed. All that remained of him were a handful of letters and his Latin testament.

On impulse she crossed to her chest and pulled the book out. Perhaps, here, she would find something of Owen. She settled beside a window, drew the tail of her nightdress over her toes and, turning the book to catch the soft, spreading light, began to read.

CHAPTER 9 – JULY, 1524 TO JANUARY, 1525

They brought Sir Harry's body home in a cart. The old knight, having paused in the sheep run to speak with the shepherd, had suddenly clutched his chest. Before Willcotte could question, Sir Harry toppled headfirst from his horse. The bailiff flung himself off his mount and rushed to his fallen master. With great effort he rolled the mountainous body over. Pressing his ear against the flabby chest, he listened for a heartbeat. Nothing. Willcotte straightened and glanced at the bandy-legged sheep man.

"Help me lift him onto his horse."

The gaping herder remained motionless. Only his bearded lips moved, muttering prayers.

"Now!" Willcotte barked.

The man reluctantly moved closer. With the shepherd catching up Sir Harry's legs and Willcotte gripping the fat shoulders, they struggled to lift the body. The old knight's loose, ponderous form defeated their every endeavor. They would get a firm grip on one part of him only to have other parts slip from their grasp. After a few minutes of breath-robbing exertion, Willcotte let the body sag gently to the ground. Sir Harry's vacant face came to rest in a clump of daisies.

Willcotte moved away, drawing the shepherd along by the arm.

"I'll fetch a cart. You stay with him."

The shepherd twisted to peer at the head in the flowers. He crossed himself again, his eyes big. Willcotte tightened his hold on the man's scrawny arm.

"See you guard well."

Leading Sir Harry's horse, Willcotte galloped for the manor house. If only he could have stayed and sent the shepherd for the cart. But, had he done so, the idiot would likely have broadcast news of Sir Harry's death like seed corn and had the manor in an uproar. Mistress Jane must not hear in so callous a way. She had grown wan these last weeks grieving for Owen Alton. He dreaded adding further sorrow. At least Sir Harry hadn't suffered. He must tell her that.

When he arrived at the stable yard, he sent one servant for the Hensford priest and three others off with the cart. He would easily overtake the slow vehicle before it reached its unhappy destination. First he must break the news to the young mistress.

As he'd expected Willcotte passed the cart. He topped the low rise and scanned the pasture below. A dirty white blanket of sheep grazed their way across the mead. He saw neither the shepherd nor the round heap that had been Sir Harry. He twisted in the saddle. The cart was closing on him. He kneed his horse down into the flock. Scattering the shuffling animals before him, he eventually located the body. He knelt beside Sir Harry, silently asked forgiveness for not remembering better where his master lay. Around them, the sheep munched steadily on.

Two of the candles in the private chapel guttered, throwing fitful light across the carefully laid-out body of Sir Harry Horne, knight. Jane, seated near the bier, seemed unaware when Willcotte rose to replenish them. He took his seat again and glanced at Jane. Her stark, dry-eyed stare frightened him now just as it had when he had broken the news of Sir Harry's death. If only she would cry.

He shifted uncomfortably on the padded bench grown hard. His weary thoughts shifted as well, reviewing the details for the morning. The coffin lay ready in the shadows. Mourning draped the house. Musicians had been hired to lead the funeral procession. The cook was even now preparing the funeral banquet. The priest would hold the requiem in Hensford, though of what use the mass would be....

Willcotte looked at Jane again. Tomorrow would be a difficult day for her. How he wished Lucy Terrell could be here to share the burden. She wouldn't even receive his hastily-penned message until the day after. Had Sir Harry died in winter they could have waited for her. Already, in this hot July weather, the body was beginning to swell.

He was glad Jane would marry soon. She needed someone to care for her. Personally, he didn't think much of Francis Grady. He did wish she'd lie down. He'd try again to get her to rest when these candles burned lower.

Jane remained staring down at her stepfather's coffin in the floor of St. Sebastian church after the last mourner had filed out. Five generations of Hornes had found their final rest here. The wealthiest lay in a marble sarcophagus in the chancel. By her stepfather's time, the Horne fortunes had so declined that they rated no better than a hole in the side-aisle floor halfway down the nave. Sir Harry had laid his two wives there with space between for himself. Eleanor's money had enabled him to screen off that portion of the aisle so the graves remained relatively untrodden.

Jane stood beside the pile of pale-red soil next to Sir Harry's open tomb. She purposely blotted out thought. She must not disturb that part of her which had frozen yesterday at Master Willcotte's announcement. A frozen limb begins to hurt only as it thaws. She glanced down at the words chiseled on her mother's ledger. Faithful Wife. With those two little words, her stepfather had covered his wife's shame and held her up in honor for all generations to come. To the end he'd been the loyal knight. Now he was dead.

The shell enclosing her heart shattered. She stumbled around with tear-blind eyes and collided with the brightly painted parclose. Dropping her forehead against the screen, she began to sob.

Lucy arrived two days later. Francis was with her. Under different circumstances, Jane would have been embarrassed having to face him. Sorrow left no room.

"George wanted to come," Lucy said tearfully after embracing Jane in the hall. "His gout is bothering him again. At least Francis was able to."

Jane looked past Lucy to her future husband.

"As your intended, it was my duty. I believe in fulfilling one's responsibilities."

Obviously he hadn't forgiven her for preferring another. Would he ever?

The voice of the Hensford priest rebounded off the plaster walls of the single, ill-furnished parlor at Horne Hall, the main subject of Sir Harry's will. The old manor house, consisting of little more than the hall and a few small rooms at either end, had not been a place of residence for the Horne family since the completion of Wynnfield Hall. Although brought into good repair in recent years, no rushes carpeted the black-and-white tile floor nor were the yellow walls draped with cloths to block drafts or mute the echo of the priest's words.

He finished reading Sir Harry's will. Horne Hall and its adjoining acres went to Lucy. He laid the document aside and swept the room with a mournful eye. His somber gaze bypassed Francis and Howard Willcotte to settle on Lucy. He cleared his throat.

"Mistress Terrell, as you've heard, your father left ten pounds for the cure of his soul. A suitable amount ... if he'd died in bed with a priest at his side."

Jane tensed. Beside her, Lucy stirred. The priest continued.

"As cure of Sir Harry's soul I must remind you that he died unshriven."

Lucy clutched Jane's hand.

"What can we do?"

"The church has need of a new font. Let one be bought and engraved with his name and the words 'Pray for Me'. What better way to balance his unrepented sins than him being the holder, so to speak, of the holy water that blesses and purifies." The priest turned his attention to Jane. "A bit of land to cover the cost of more masses would not be ill-advised. Perhaps one of the fields nearest Hensford?"

Jane looked down at Lucy's thick hand gripping hers. She struggled to order her thoughts. Her heart had shrunk at the priest's pronouncement against her stepfather. But, with her next trembling breath, Owen's condemnation of masses for his brother's soul sounded in her mind. Payment for comfort based on a lie. Then, too, she had read a story in his testament which no priest had ever told her. The blessed Lord Jesus himself had told the thief on the cross, 'Today you will be with me in paradise.'

Whom was she to believe? Jane wrestled in vain with the question. Only when Francis dropped a hand onto her shoulder did she realize he'd left his stool.

"My great uncle was a pious man. I doubt he had many sins that needed forgiveness. The font should be more than adequate to cover them." He turned to Lucy. "Naturally Jane and I will pay half the cost. That's the least we can do."

Jane tensed.

The least is all he wants to do.

The business finished, Lucy stood. Jane slipped from under Francis's hand and wandered to the window. Outside, their horses were cropping the grass at the edge of the courtyard. Behind her, people began taking their leave. Lucy left with Willcotte for a quick survey of her inheritance. The priest started back to Hensford no doubt to order his font. Jane remained with her back to the room and Francis.

All at once she was glad her stepfather was dead. He could no longer be hurt. Whether she believed or not, she would have given the field to honor his memory. She couldn't give him obedience.

She turned to face Francis.

"You must know something before we wed."

Francis, reaching for the pitcher of cowslip wine, paused with a questioning look.

"I recently learned that I'm a...." Her lips wouldn't frame the word. "Lionel Radcott wasn't my father."

"What do you mean Lionel Radcott wasn't your father?"

"Just that." This time the word came. "I'm a bastard."

The pitcher slammed down.

"You're making sport of me."

"Father told me over a month ago."

Francis's complexion blanched.

"Who else knows?"

"I think some of our neighbors. A few people in London."

"Do my parents know?"

"No."

"Well, don't tell them!" Francis lifted the pitcher. Its lip rattled against the edge of his goblet. He gulped the drink down. "If my friends were to find out, I'd be a jesting stock. They warned me something must be wrong with you."

Jane fought against welling anger. His shock was speaking and must be forgiven. Her whole life with him hung in the balance. She mustn't allow a sharp word from her to tip it wrongly. She sat, picked up a limp green pillow and began twisting the worn fringe as she watched Francis. Gradually his color returned. He poured himself a second cup of wine.

"Who was your father?"

"My mother never said." She cocked her head, watching him. "Perhaps one of her servants?"

The expression that swept his face tipped the balance. Jane flung the cushion aside. She would never share her bed with any man who could look at her like that.

Riding back to Wynnfield at Francis's side, Jane made no effort to ease the tension. Fortunately, Lucy was engrossed in discussing plans with Willcotte for a new wing on Horne Hall.

They passed the hawthorn bushes. Wynnfield Hall lay before them, glowing a warm rose in the late-afternoon sun, its roofs and spiraling chimney stacks touched with silver. Jane glanced at Francis. He was gazing with longing at the house. She dismounted and handed her horse to the stableboy. Francis hurried after as Jane strode across the base-court. He caught her arm. She looked up coolly. Flushing, he dropped his hand.

"Perhaps I've been hasty. We could still marry. No one need ever know. You can't run a manor by yourself."

"My bailiff is quite competent. You can tell your London friends something was wrong with me after all."

Before Francis could find his tongue, Jane linked arms with Lucy and accompanied her into the house.

Lucy sat open-mouthed in Jane's chamber listening to her terse explanation for the wedding's cancellation.

"So that's why she married Father. I've wondered all these years." Lucy colored. "You've never been eighteen, fat and dowerless. Knowing as surely as the sun rises that no man would offer for you. Father's prospects were hardly better." Lucy pulled her handkerchief out and blew her nose. "I'm glad she received value from the marriage. She gave us so much."

"You don't mind?"

"Mind?" Lucy jammed the handkerchief into the neck of her gown and came to her feet. "Of course I do. It tells me something about your mother I don't like knowing." She peered out the window. "The sky is clouding up. We'll have rain before morning." She turned back. "It doesn't have to cost you the marriage. Francis will recover, especially with Wynnfield to sweeten him."

"No, Lucy. If we were to wed, all his life he'd go in dread that his friends would find me out." Jane pressed her lips together momentarily. "Or that I'd do what my mother did."

Lucy dropped onto a chest, her legs in an unladylike sprawl.

"Why, by everything sensible, did Father want Francis to know?"

Jane's hand stilled on the damask bed curtain she was fingering.

"He didn't want it. I decided...."

Lucy's eyes popped.

"You decided? You purposely disregarded Father's wishes. And him barely in his grave. You used to be such a sweet, biddable girl. I don't know what's happened to you."

"I wanted to be fair to Francis."

"Fair!" Lucy surged to her feet. "When have you ever been fair to Francis? Certainly not last summer. Throwing him aside for a would-be priest within days of your betrothal. Keeping him hanging all these months. Now you've done it again. Don't talk to me of 'fair'. You've clearly forgotten the meaning of the word. You've used Francis very ill."

Lucy departed, her anger unabated. Jane sank down onto the edge of the bed. Lucy was right. She had treated Francis badly. Nonetheless, telling him had been right. If only she could cry and wash some of the pain from her lacerated heart. For the moment she had exhausted her supply of tears.

After an overnight shower, the early-morning sun winked through treetops and crusted the grass with sparkling water jewels. At the gatehouse, Lucy gave Jane a quick farewell hug. Mounting the block, she set her foot into the stirrup. Francis, already astride, was clearly as restive as his horse to be away. He only allowed Lucy time to take the reins before spurring his horse down the muddy trail toward London.

Jane gripped her hands together as she watched them disappear behind the dripping hawthorn hedge. She had wanted this. Why, then, was she filled with panic? She almost cried out that she would accept the marriage, only they must not leave her here alone.

Four months ago her life had been interwoven with bright rainbow hues of happiness. Now all that remained was a ragged remnant in muted shades of gray and grim black. Owen had gone, leaving her unfit to love another. His book had robbed her of the comfortable security of the familiar faith. Her stepfather's shade walked the rooms of Wynnfield with a reproachful look. The face in her mirror bore no name. She had brought undeserved hurt to Francis. In Lucy's eyes she measured badly.

Jane scrubbed roughly at her streaming tears. Reluctantly she started toward the manor house, guilt and ghosts her only companions.

In the weeks that followed, Jane threw herself unsparingly into the work of the manor. When she wasn't occupied with household duties or accounts, she was at Willcotte's side overseeing the harvest, dealing with tenants and preparing for the approaching winter. By her own hand she'd isolated herself. Now she must fill that isolation with activity or have it filled with recriminations.

Jane virtually withdrew from the outside world. When Stourbridge fair opened, she sent the cook's wife and Willcotte in her place to make the necessary purchases. She had no interest in riding over to see the new wing of Horne Hall under construction. But for the fines she would have incurred, she would have absented herself from weekly mass at Hensford. The new baptismal font graced the chancel there. Although she had readily paid her share of the cost, the font was an unwelcome reminder of all she was trying to forget.

As the autumn evenings lengthened, she took to dawdling over her meals in the great hall. The cheerful noise of the servants at meat held the black-winged night thoughts at bay. Often she fell into bed with a prayer of thanks that one more day had passed with no new misfortune. Jane dared not consider how she would survive the enforced idleness of winter. When Lucy wrote at St. Andrew's tide inviting her to share Christmas with them in London, Willcotte urged her to go. In the end she declined. The contemplated pleasure of seeing Lucy was outweighed by the awkwardness of facing Francis. According to the letter, he was marrying a skinner's daughter at Twelfthtide. He would find her presence most unwelcome, especially at this time.

With grim determination she prepared for Nativity at Wynnfield. The house was decorated, Christmas foods cooked and a huge Yule log dragged in. With an empty heart, Jane admired the decorations, nibbled the delicacies, presented the servants with presents and watched the Yule log being slowly consumed. She cried when she received gifts from Lucy. She cried so easily these days.

The year of 1525 blew in with a piercing icy breath from across the Cambridgeshire fens. The wind's freezing fingers rattled tree limbs and probed each crack and loose-fitting window. It shrieked and whistled and twirled snow on its tail. The sheep huddled close in their barns while the household hunched near roaring fires. Ice coated the inside of Jane's chamber windows and hardened in her water pitcher. After three days, the wind departed with a sigh. Dry snow, finer than wheaten flour, was left frosting trees and piled against walls and in hedgerows. The leaden sky lightened and a pale sun appeared.

Willcotte trotted off to Horne Hall to learn how they'd fared during the storm. Jane watched him go, bundled to his ears, his horse's iron shoes ringing on the frozen ground. Restlessness roiled up within her. She couldn't bear being confined to the manor house one moment longer.

A short while later, dressed in her warmest woolen gown and fur-lined cloak, she brushed aside the stable lad's concern and set foot in stirrup. Once through the woods and past the clump of cottages that was Hensey village, Jane tucked her cloak more closely and gave the bay his head. The horse, restive from lack of exercise, broke into a gallop. When they neared a side road, she pulled hard on the reins, turning him from the track the bailiff had taken. The road must be hers alone.

The bay thundered down the narrow trail through the forest, Jane clinging to his back. The whipping wind tore her breath away and stung her eyes to tears. She merely tucked her chin deeper into her hood. Soon they broke from the narrow trail onto a wider and less familiar one.

Blinded by the wind, Jane failed to see the bit of boggy road, slick now with ice, until she was upon it. Too late she jerked the reins. Her horse hit the ice and went down. She struck the iron-hard road and rolled.

She came to a stop on the verge, her cloak tangled about her. The world of black naked trees spun in a dizzying arch above her head. Gradually, the forest slowed to a halt. When she made a weak effort to push herself up, sharp pain shot through her right arm. She fell back with a gasp. The pain subsided to a dull ache. Utterly weary, her eyelids drooped as the deadly cold began seeping through her clothing.

The stark tangled forest lay about her, silent and lifeless. She was alone on a deserted frozen road in a desolate frozen world. Alone. She had no one now. No one would miss her if she were gone. How easy it would be to close her eyes and let sleep take her. Never again would she waken to emptiness and failure. Misfortune dogged her every step. She couldn't even manage so small a thing as a ride.

Oh, Lord Jesus, help me.

A tear formed and slipped past her ear leaving a cold trail of moisture. She began to cry. Somewhere beyond her head, she heard the bay snort softly. The small familiar sound broke the awful stillness and stirred her drifting mind to awareness. She'd forgotten her horse. Had he been hurt? Had her failure condemned him as well?

Mindful of her sprained arm, she managed to turn. The bay stood, head drooping, flanks streaked with sweat. But he stood. She must see to her horse.

She struggled to her feet. Cradling her injured limb, she hobbled toward her mount. He limped to meet her, blowing clouds of white vapor. She caught up the dragging reins and smoothed a hand down his neck.

Jane glanced around. She had ridden so far. When Willcotte returned, he would eventually send people to search for her. Hours could pass before she was found. She must find shelter. She looked up and down the track. Memory stirred. Once, last fall, she'd come this way with the bailiff. They had stopped at a cottage to water the horses.

Had she passed it? No. Nothing but emptiness lay behind her. Her only hope lay ahead.

Leading the horse, Jane plodded up the road toward the place where it bent out of sight in the black, silent wood. Her left hand stiffened around the reins and lost feeling. Gradually the long curve fell behind. She caught a faint scent of wood smoke on the air. In the distance, the dark woods gave way to a plowed field. Heartened, Jane trudged on. Another field appeared and then the remembered cottage, thick-shagged with thatch, its chimney sending up a thin gray trail.

As she approached, she searched for the name of the tall, immaculate, deep-bosomed woman who lived here. Elizabeth. That was what the bailiff had called her. Elizabeth, wife of Jack the weaver.

Jane turned off the track into the cottage yard. A large brown dog bounded out of a shed, barking excitedly. She halted, warily eying the animal. The cottage door opened and a black-bearded giant stepped out. Something stirred in Jane's mind.

"Master Weaver, I'm Jane Horne from Wynnfield Hall." Her stiff lips slurred the words badly. "My horse slipped on a patch of ice and injured his knee."

Jack Weaver looked at the horse and then back to her.

"Will you go in where it's warm, Mistress? I'll see to your mount."

Gratefully she stepped into the cozy dimness of the neat cottage. The yellow-haired woman of Jane's memory left her spinning wheel and came forward with a flustered smile.

"You must be chilled to the bone," Elizabeth Weaver said after hearing Jane's explanation. "Here, sit you down by the fire and rest your arm. I'll fetch a hot drink. I'm feared we're fresh out of mulled wine."

As she talked, she set a stool for Jane near the blazing hearth and dipped a long-handled ladle into the simmering pot slung there. Had she not been shivering, Jane would have smiled at Elizabeth's innocent airs. For all its sturdily-made furnishings and bright painted walls, she doubted this household ever saw any drink better than homemade ale.

Jane gladly took the wooden cup of thin soup Elizabeth handed her. Her teeth rattled against the metal rim as she sipped the scalding liquid. The broth, tasting of turnips and rabbit, was as warming as any mulled wine could hope to be.

While Elizabeth refilled her cup, Jane noticed two blond heads peeking around the loom that dominated the other end of the room. The little boy and his younger sister gazed at her in solemn shyness.

"My children," Elizabeth said with evident pride.

The door swung open bringing a gush of winter and Jack Weaver. His head nearly brushed the ceiling beams.

"Your horse has a bad knee. I put him in the barn with mine and rubbed him down."

"Thank you. Could you stable him until he can travel? I'll pay you well."

"I'll need extra hay."

"Of course. Also, could I borrow your horse to get home? I'll send him back with the hay."

"I'll fetch you home and get the hay myself. It's best not to be out alone in this weather."

Master Weaver is right, Jane concluded miserably as she bumped along behind the giant on his plow horse. And now to be brought home like an irresponsible child.

The stableboy was scanning the road when Jack's horse plodded around the hawthorn curve and reined up at the stable. Once dismounted, Jane, swallowing embarrassment, explained and gave orders concerning the hay. After thanking Jack, she hurried toward the warmth of the manor house. At the gatehouse she glanced back. Jack was turning to follow the stable hand.

Something about the way he moved, hunching his massive shoulders, his black-bearded face not quite visible, stopped Jane short. The vague nagging feeling of having met him before returned with renewed force. She saw again the image of five men at a stream. She had identified Owen, Willcotte and the peddler from the fair. She hadn't recognized the white-haired man nor the black-bearded giant who had hunched his shoulders as he departed, his face never clearly in view. She knew now. That man had been Jack Weaver.

CHAPTER 10 – APRIL TO JULY, 1525

One blustery day in early April Jane was working on the ledger when the bailiff walked into the accounts room. He closed the door behind him.

"We'll be having guests tonight, Mistress. The shire constable and his men. I left them about two miles back. They have a prisoner."

"A prisoner?"

"That peddler. The one who comes occasionally with laces and ribbons."

Jane's breath caught. Owen's peddler!

"Do you know the charges against him?"

"He was caught with heretical writings."

"Why are they coming here? Aren't you afraid?"

Willcotte's facial muscles twitched.

"I invited them."

Why had it seemed so important to pretend ignorance of his dealing with Owen and the peddler?

"I saw you by the stream at Stourbridge fair with Owen, Jack Weaver, the peddler and that white-haired man. I know you were all somehow involved with Owen's smuggling."

Willcotte's small eyes widened.

"He never told us."

"He didn't know. He'd not wanted...." She stopped. It no longer mattered what Owen had wanted. "Why did you invite them?"

His finger began stroking his lip. Jane twisted the goose quill, waiting. His finger dropped.

"The peddler's already been tried for heresy. Last time he recanted. You know the law. This time he'll be sent to the stake."

"Then why invite them?" A frightening new thought occurred to her. "You want to help him escape."

"He's not a criminal, Mistress. Not like a thief or a murderer."

"How will you do it?"

Willcotte was silent for so long Jane wondered if he would answer.

"If he were locked in the smokehouse," he said. "It's out of sight of the hall. I thought to slip out and free him."

"Won't the constable set a guard?"

"Any watch would be on the outside. If I can find a way that won't rouse them, they'll think he escaped on his own." He glanced impatiently at the door. "I've got to find a way out before the constable comes."

Jane stared at him, her mouth dry, her breathing uneven. She had to stop him. The constable must depart in the morning none the wiser, the peddler still safely in chains. He would be tried and burned at the stake ... burned for doing what Owen had been doing.

"Wait." Jane found herself on her feet. "I'm coming with you."

The smokehouse, standing alone behind the row of kitchen offices, was a small, steep-roofed, waddle-and-daub structure. The sweet-pungent odors of ash smoke and last winter's hams filled Jane's nostrils as she peered through the door to watch Willcotte examine the dim interior. The light falling across her shoulder revealed sooty walls and iron meat-hooks dangling from blackened roof joists. The only other light came in through narrow cracks around the log wedges filling the draft holes that were notched into the hard earthen floor along the walls.

Jane glanced around apprehensively. This place could easily serve as a prison. The walls were six inches of hard-packed clay with a core of close woven willow saplings. The same willow webbing stretched across the roof beams, providing an anchor for the thick thatch.

The bailiff stepped back into the sunlight. Jane trailed as he circled the building, scrutinizing the exterior. One of the hounds lying against the back wall stretched up and followed them. Willcotte stopped to eye the low iron door through which fresh logs could be fed to the fire within. He shook his head.

"The constable's no fool. He'll secure this door. We've got to find a way that will pass notice."

"But how? The peddler isn't a mouse."

Willcotte's face lit.

"Not a mouse. A mole."

He was away, striding for the main door. When Jane reached the entry, he was inside on his knees slinging the wedges away from the draft holes. After he'd moved the last wedge, three bright strips of light lay along the base of the walls. The final hole remained dark.

"Watch that one."

He was gone again, hurrying out the door. Jane, puzzled, focused on the dark spot and waited. All at once light broke through. Immediately it dimmed and Willcotte's arm reached through almost to his shoulder.

"I see you."

Willcotte's voice came through the gap.

"Come round."

When Jane reached Willcotte, he was squatting on his haunches, chuckling softly.

"The hounds have dug here most of a foot. All that's needed is to move a few inches of dirt. I can have him out in no time, slick as an eel."

The dogs left off nosing about and trotted away toward the road. Willcotte came to his feet.

"Our guests are arriving."

Jane was standing on the manor-house porch when the constable and his four mounted men-at-arms rode in through the gatehouse. The peddler stumbled along behind, pulled by a lead tied to his manacled wrists. One side of his face was dark with caked blood and dirt. When he was permitted to stop, he collapsed like an empty sack. For one chill moment Jane saw Owen lying there. She slammed her mind shut against the picture. She must behave normally with the approaching constable.

Jane graciously greeted the stocky man with the tired face and shrewd eyes, offering him a guest chamber and his men straw pallets in a room above the gatehouse. Willcotte had advised her to separate him from his men and to put both far from the peddler.

"You can lodge your prisoner in the smokehouse."

"He'll be safe enough chained to one of my men for the night," the constable said.

Jane drew herself up stiffly, fighting panic at the potential ruin of their plan. She had no time to consider how quickly the bailiff's plan had become hers also.

"I'll have no heretic sleeping under my roof."

"Can the place be secured?"

"You may judge for yourself," Jane said, releasing her breath slowly. "My bailiff will show you the way."

At meal's end, Jane bade the constable good night and watched him leave with Willcotte. She looked with satisfaction at the heap of gnawed pigeon bones surrounding her guest's plate. He'd also helped himself to a fair amount of bread, cheese and lamb pasty. Willcotte had said to feed their visitors well since full-fed men sleep more soundly. That being the case, the constable should sleep like a bear in winter.

Half-an-hour later Willcotte came to her in the winter parlor. Two months ago she'd taken up chess. Now, most evenings, they played for a time or she read to him. Tonight the chess game sat neglected in the corner, its armies holding a truce across the checkered squares. She laid her book aside.

"Are our guests settled?"

Willcotte nodded.

"Will there be a guard?"

"On three-hour shifts. They ate well and are anxious for their beds. They'll be careless."

Some of her tension eased.

"When will you try?"

"During the second shift. I need food from the larder. The peddler must hide till Jack and I can move him."

Jane slipped the key from her ring and handed it across. She followed it with a fist-sized bundle tied in a cloth scrap.

"Ointment for his wounds and a bit of money to help him on his way." Then, because this was a night for secrets, she asked the question she had carried for months. "Do you ever hear from Owen Alton?"

"No, Mistress."

Jane saw Willcotte's cautious, concerned eyes examining her. She turned her face into the shadow. He must not read whatever might be written there of dull hurt and muted longing. She reached for a candle.

"I'll keep vigil in my chamber."

"When he's safely away, I'll slip the key under your door."

Neither mentioned what they would do if the escape failed.

Jane awoke from her vigil with a start. A bright strip of moonlight lay across her blanketed knees. She had purposely left her bed curtains wide and had remained sitting, her back against her pillows, to prevent sleep. It had still caught her. She peered at the bottom of the door searching for the larder key. The floor was empty.

Her breath caught. The watch had been alert, the escape had failed, and Willcotte had been discovered. Then reason returned. The moon's position said that the bailiff would only now be making his attempt.

Jane slipped out of bed and padded barefoot to the window. The moon's dangerous light illuminated the courtyard like day. By contrast, the shadowy corners were as black as the bottom of a well. Was Willcotte even now slipping from one shadow to another toward the smokehouse? She watched a bank of deep-blue clouds drift across the sky. They reached the moon's bright face; the world dimmed. Time crept by.

The cloud bank was almost past. Shadows began to form once more. Another moment and light would again flood the earth. In the stable yard a dog barked, one quick burst of sound.

Jane's attention locked on the gatehouse. She waited, hardly breathing. Her ears strained for more barking, for shouts and the sound of running feet. Any moment she would see men rushing out. She peered through the window, her every sense strained to the fullest, waiting. Silence. Louder than all the tolling bells of London. Silence.

Jane wiped her clammy palms against her white nightdress. Two more large clouds drifted past the moon. Three smaller ones followed. The moon hung like a round white cheese over the black trees beyond the gatehouse.

A stealthy footstep outside her door and the faint scrape of metal on wood caused her to turn her head. There, protruding from under the door edge, was a black shape. Almost unbelieving, she rose and sidled across the floor. The larder key. Unexpectedly her legs folded. She squatted on the floor, her hand tight around the key. It was smooth and cool and hard against her palm. The deed was done.

The following morning Jane entered the hall to find the constable in a high temper. Willcotte, standing by grave and regretful, enlightened his mistress. The prisoner had escaped.

The constable, rising soon after first light, had made straight for the smokehouse. He found the place padlocked, his guard asleep and his captive flown. All that remained was a meat hook, an enlarged draft hole and an empty wooden trencher. Clearly the heretic had dug his way out with the hook, silenced the dogs with his supper and had fled.

Over the next hour the constable led his men on a thorough search of all out-buildings and into the nearby woods, but without success. Midmorning saw them take their leave. Jane, watching from the winter-parlor window, waited only until she was sure they were gone before she hurried to the smokehouse to see the hole. Already Willcotte was there giving orders to fill it. It seemed such a small, shallow depression. But the peddler had not been a heavy man.

Exhilaration flooded her. She looked up at Willcotte. He must have read her expression aright, for the corners of his mouth twitched, and his eyes held the same innocent expression they had when he checkmated her king. As she started back to the hall, he fell in beside her. Once they were well away from listening ears, Willcottet spoke quietly.

"The peddler asked me to thank you."

"How will you get his shackles off?"

"It's already done. I borrowed tools from the smithy and broke the locks before I left him."

"Who is he?"

"A Lollard preacher."

They had reached the front entrance. Jane stopped by the porch and searched his face.

"Are you a Lollard also?"

Willcotte nodded.

"What made you one?"

He pulled on his long upper lip.

"My father was one and his father before him. Our way is more true than the Church. Also, I want my scriptures in English."

"But you go to mass," she chided gently.

"I'd be fined if I didn't. The village priest can't know what's in my mind."

"What about Jack and his wife?"

"Jack wants to know more than the Church will tell him. Elizabeth cares for nothing but her house. Some have the desire and some don't. I've never understood why. Mistress, do you have the desire?"

Jane looked away. This was the question she'd been avoiding for weeks. She met Willcotte's eyes again.

"Yes."

A fortnight from the day that Jane had watched the constable ride out through the gatehouse, she saw Jack Weaver ride in. Ostensibly he came to ask about buying wool for his loom. In reality he brought Willcotte word that the peddler was safely away to Wales, helped by the white-haired Lollard in Newmarket.

The bailiff quietly shared the news with Jane that evening as they sat at meat in the hall. Later, when they were alone in the winter parlor, rather than turning to chess or another tale from Chaucer, Jane diffidently brought out her Latin New Testament. When she explained what it was, Willcotte's face lit as if heaven's gates had sprung open before his eyes. With night stealing in around them, Jane began to translate.

From that day, whenever time allowed and no passing travelers shared their evening, Jane read the scriptures to the bailiff and they discussed them. At first her translations were clumsy. As summer advanced, her mind quickened and her words flowed more smoothly. Often Willcotte would beg her to repeat a passage, mouthing the words after her with intense concentration.

One such evening, early in July, Jane translated a passage for the third time. The bailiff crashed fist into palm.

"Ah! I can't remember."

"There's no need. I can always read it again."

The bailiff glanced uneasily at her.

"I'm not remembering for myself alone. It's also for Jack."

"For Jack!" She almost dropped the book.

"When you started reading, I had to share the passages with him, at least what I could remember. But I can't keep them in mind well enough." He hesitated. "Jack wants me to write them down as you read. I told him 'no', that you've done enough already."

Jane sat in shocked silence. When it had only been the two of them, she'd given little thought to the risk. Translating had seemed such an innocent act. For the first time, the wider implications hit.

"No, you mustn't write them down. It would be too dangerous."

A week passed before Jack came. Jane knew he would and dreaded his arrival. She was in the milk larder counting cheeses when the maid brought word. She went limp with unexpected relief. The waiting was ended.

"Show him to the accounts room."

Whatever else the coming interview demanded, it required privacy. The servant bobbed a curtsy and disappeared. Jane crossed the base-court slowly.

She'd not spoken to Jack since that winter day. He should have seemed a stranger. He didn't. He'd known Owen, had helped in the peddler's escape, was an intimate of Willcotte's. Most importantly, he'd been a part of the bleak January day that had marked a turning for her. On that empty road she'd faced the loss of all those she had loved and trusted, faced her own failure. Her life had been stripped to a raw and bleeding core, her soul laid bare. Then she had taken the horse's reins and stumbled on. Somehow, looking back on that day, Jane knew that she'd not been alone after all. God had been there with her. He had not failed her.

Through the hard, lonely months which followed, that thin thread, that indisputable fact, had held her as firmly as an anchor chain.

She had stumbled on that day and met Jack. Though she'd only spoken to him once, he was no stranger. If he had been, or if Willcotte had been here rather than at Horne Hall preparing for Lucy's arrival, she would feel more capable of facing the huge weaver waiting in the accounts room.

Jane entered the room and took a seat behind the table. Only then did she look up at her unwelcome visitor. She should have remained standing. He towered over her, robbing her of command.

"Please be seated, Master Weaver."

Jack folded himself onto a stool, his knees jutting up before him. Even reduced to half his height, he remained an intimidating mass.

"Mistress," he began humbly, twisting his cap in his great hairy hands, "Howard told me not to bother you. You mustn't blame him. Please, Mistress. Let him put the scriptures down when you read."

"I'd be breaking the law and putting us all in peril."

"I'd take great care."

"As the peddler did? He almost ended at the stake."

"He knew the risk. What he had was worth it. Give me the scriptures, Mistress. I swear to you, if I end at the stake, I'll bring you no harm."

"Don't you understand? I'd be responsible."

"No. You'll only be to blame if you deny me what you have. That's how the Church acts."

"What of your family? If you're caught with English translations, what will become of them?"

"What will become of them left to the Church's ignorance? They need the truth."

Jane caught her lips in her teeth to stop their unexpected trembling. He sounded like Owen. In that moment, to her horror, Jack slipped to his knees, his hands locked in entreaty.

"Mistress, I beg of you. Give me the translations."

"All right. But your blood is on your own head."

During the next days, by candlelight in her chamber or behind the locked accounts-room door, Jane fulfilled her promise. Slowly the stack of papers grew. Her quill scratched its way along, setting into English passages that could bring death when they were meant to bring life.

When, a week later, she handed Willcotte the sheaf of pages tied with a leather thong, he expressed contrition. Jane brushed his apology aside. The thing was done. Now she wanted to push the whole affair, and its potential for disaster, from her mind.

"Jack must be satisfied with these. I'll do no more."

CHAPTER 11 – AUGUST TO OCTOBER, 1525

"George should be pleased with what you've achieved," Jane said as she trailed Lucy across the private dining parlor in Horne Hall's new wing.

"I hope he's pleased enough to allow me additional furniture." Lucy ushered Jane through the connecting door into the old parlor. "With four new bedchambers and a second parlor I need more."

Jane stopped to look at the picture of a formal garden, bright with birds, flowers and gaily garbed courtiers, which adorned one wall.

"I especially like your arras cloth."

"I had to have it." Lucy's expression grew tender. "I first saw George in a garden just like that, sporting with a friend. The wrestler nearest the rose trellis reminds me of him before he started going bald. He was so handsome."

Jane had not realized until now how hungry she was for family talk after the long difficult year. She rejoiced that Lucy would be near until after Michaelmas.

"I was taken with him from that very moment," Lucy said. "I wasn't the only one. Your mother gave me the bigger dowry. George saw he'd do better with me and a new wine trade than that high-nosed miss his family favored. We've showed them. His sister, or even his older brother, haven't done as well." Lucy swung her attention from the arras cloth to Jane. "I owe your mother so much. I'm going to repay the debt by seeing you married. I know at least two London men who would make suitable husbands."

"I doubt the Church would approve of my having two husbands."

"Be serious. You're already nineteen-and-a-half. If you delay much longer, you'll be left with nothing but widowers."

"You were twenty-one when you married."

"I'd no dowry until then and George was a year younger. With Wynnfield Hall, you could have anyone you want. Come to London and let me introduce you."

"How? As your bastard stepsister?"

"We'll say you're my half-sister."

"What of Francis?"

"He was too proud to tell the truth. He said that Father's death turned your thoughts to a religious vocation. He can't change his story now." Lucy studied Jane. "I've sometimes wondered. Have you developed a vocation?"

Images of the peddler and the roll of translated scriptures flashed across Jane's mind.

"Hardly."

"Why, then, do you insist on burying yourself here as your mother did? I used to think she had a vocation and your birth interrupted it. She never set foot farther afield than Hensford the whole time she and Father were married. Now I think she was hiding, or perhaps doing penance. At least she had a husband and child in her seclusion. Merely because that would-be priest proved faithless -."

"I'll not be a debt paid to my mother's account," Jane said, unwilling to have Owen talked of. "I'll marry when I find someone I want."

"I hope that time comes soon. You've become as prickly as a hedgehog." Lucy took on a smug look. "If you won't come to London, it's coming to you. At least part of it. Sybil is bringing them."

"Sybil?"

"George's niece. Her mother sent her to us so I can find the wench a suitable husband. She's the type I hated when I was making the rounds. Sweet as honey to the men, vinegar to anything in skirts. She has half the eligible London males trailing her like hounds after a bitch. She's riding up with George and the boys, and bringing friends. No doubt mostly men. She thinks you're my age. I'd love to see you steal her admirers."

A few days later Jane set out for Horne Hall to meet Sybil and her entourage. She was in no mood to be exhibited, but Lucy would be furious if she didn't appear. She arrived to find everyone absent except Lucy who was sitting in the old parlor embroidering a picture of St. Francis and the animals.

"George's sister claims their grandmother embroidered one as big as a bed," Lucy said arching her wide back. "I think she made the whole story up for spite."

Jane relaxed onto a nearby bench.

"Where is everyone?"

"George and the boys are with the harvest. Sybil is riding with her friends. She brought six, four men and two women. Of the girls, one is already betrothed. The other is plain as a post." Lucy threaded a new strand of green onto her needle. "You'll even the numbers a little. Did you fetch that book? Good. Read to me. I'm desperate for a diversion from this infernal stitching."

Laughing voices heralded Sybil's return. Jane lowered the copy of Chaucer. She bit her lips quickly to brighten them as the boisterous group streamed into the parlor. She dismissed the four young men with scarcely a glance. Equally she ignored the rabbit-faced girl trailing in the rear. Curious, she glanced from the voluptuous, stylishly gowned girl with the lively black eyes and raven hair to the delicate, yellow-haired maid with the rosebud mouth. Lucy beckoned to the yellow-haired girl.

"Sybil, this is my half-sister, Jane Horne."

Sybil's blue eyes narrowed. She came forward, trailing men. Her bright smile never faltered.

"Should I call you 'Aunt Jane'?"

Lucy snorted.

"Certainly not. Jane is scarcely older than you."

"How stupid of me. Appearances can be so deceptive."

One of the men snickered. Jane felt her face heat.

Score one for Sybil.

"Jane hoped to ride with you," Lucy lied. "Unfortunately, affairs on her manor delayed her." Two of the men looked more closely at Jane. Lucy continued. "She's been reading to me, in English of course. Unlike Jane, I don't understand Latin."

"I never bothered to learn to read," Sybil said. "I've heard it makes one squint. But, truly, I'm impressed."

"My brother would be also." The words came from the black-haired girl who'd stopped by a card table. "He can't abide an ignorant woman."

Sybil's rosebud mouth straightened into a short, angry line. Before she could answer, the other girl turned to Lucy.

"Mistress Terrell, you may have to drive me away with a stick when it's time to leave. All this fresh air. If you could market it in London, you'd come away with a fortune."

Cecily Denzil was the girl's name. Already Jane liked her if for no other reason than that she'd put Sybil's nose out of place.

Introductions complete, Sybil cast Jane a dour look and herded her men away for a dice game. One elusive young man seemed willing to remain if Jane had given him the slightest encouragement. She immediately joined the rabbit-faced girl in admiring Lucy's needlework. After a time he drifted off to the dice game. Only then did Jane desert her companions in favor of Cecily, who was playing a game of solitaire at the card table.

When the game finished, Cecily swept the cards up with a gratified expression.

"Did you win?" Jane asked.

"I always win. I cheat."

Jane laughed.

"I'll remember that."

Cecily leaned close, eyes bright and dimple flashing.

"Do you truly read Latin?"

Jane nodded, her face warm.

"Richard probably would be impressed. Father certainly would. He's been after me for years to learn to read anything. I've absolutely refused. You've no idea what expectations people have once you learn."

"Is Richard your brother?"

"Yes. Sybil wanted him to come too." She glanced at the noisy group around the dicing table. "I've no idea where she'd have put him. He refused. He has that much sense, at least. I'd have refused as well but London in August is so boring."

"Is your betrothed joining you later?"

"Hugh? Oh, no. He'd never leave his beloved law office for a frolic in the country. His idea of enjoyment is a heated debate with

Father and Richard over some obscure point of law which hasn't concerned anyone since Henry II. Lawyers are the bane of my life."

Much as Jane had enjoyed Cecily, she welcomed a reason to absent herself from the activities of Lucy's other guests. August was harvest time, one of the busiest months of the year. Riding back from the far barley field on a sweltering afternoon a few days later, Jane couldn't resist the tempting coolness of the stream half hidden by larch and willow. She was standing in a patch of shade-dappled water, skirts tucked into girdle, silken ripples washing around her bare legs, when her horse nickered. It was answered by a second animal.

Startled, she splashed around. Cecily, on horseback, was watching from the bank. Jane peered past her with trepidation. If Sybil should catch her thus.... The meadow beyond was wonderfully empty.

"Is that water as inviting as it looks?"

"Yes."

Cecily dismounted and began stripping off shoes and hose. She stepped boldly from the grassy bank and waded out into the current, her green damask skirts held well away from the water.

"This is marvelous. Have you ever tried it with nothing on?"

Jane felt her face burn.

"And get caught by one of the shepherds? How did you find me?"

"Your sister gave me directions and one of your outdoor servants sent me off this way. Is Wynnfield Manor actually yours?"

Jane nodded.

"My mother owned a goldsmith shop when she was alive," Cecily said. "When Father's especially upset with me, he says I'm like her. I hope he's right."

"Who owns the shop now?"

"My brothers, Richard and Nicholas. Richard will likely sell his half to Nicholas. He's studying at Lincoln's Inn and is determined to be a lawyer."

Cecily began wading to and fro. She halted in a shady pool of deeper water beside the drooping branches of a willow. For a time the only sounds to be heard in the drowsy afternoon were the soft rush of the current, the rasp of insects and the breeze whispering in the treetops.

Cecily shrieked. Her scream was so sudden and so sharp that a thrush in the nearby ash flashed away.

Arms flailing, she lunged headlong through the water, skirts dragging about her pumping legs. She hiked the wet fabric up and splashed her frantic way toward the nearest low bank. Once there, she leaped for the safety of the grass. She stood quivering, white-faced, gasping for breath. Lifting a trembling finger, she pointed toward the dark pool she had so hastily and ungracefully left.

"Something's in there. It felt my leg."

Jane, witnessing Cecily's flight with astonishment, was all at once enlightened. She set her teeth into her lips and opened her eyes wide in a bid to contain welling laughter.

"Probably just a fish."

The words were her undoing. Laughter gushed out and could not be stemmed. Half-blinded by tears, Jane staggered to the bank and collapsed in convulsions at Cecily's feet.

The fast-growing friendship between Jane and Cecily succeeded where all Lucy's urging had failed. Before Cecily left with George and the other guests after Holy Cross Day, Jane had agreed to winter in London. She would return with Lucy after Michaelmas. She only hesitated at the thought of living with Sybil.

A week before their departure Lucy received a message from George.

"Something must be wrong," she said to Jane who had arrived for a brief visit. "Why else would he write when we'll be seeing him so soon?"

Lucy broke the seal and unfolded the letter. As she read, her face took on a most peculiar expression, at the same time shock, disgust and smug satisfaction.

"Wellll. Sybil's done it at last." She wagged the letter at Jane. "George caught her lifting her skirts to an admirer. He threw the young man out and gave the wench a good caning. She's currently locked in her room awaiting her mother." Lucy glanced at the letter again. "I need to leave for London right away. Most likely his sister will blame us for her darling's fall from grace. I'll not have her browbeating George."

"Perhaps I'd better cancel my visit."

"Sybil isn't ruining your winter. You can come later. I'll write once something is settled."

The Michaelmas daisies had bloomed and faded for another year before Jane heard from Lucy. Her letter, when it arrived, was short and to the point. Sybil was wed and removed from London. Cecily had come asking after Jane. Lucy would expect her by the third week in October.

Jane sat in the winter parlor facing Howard Willcotte across the chessboard. In her chamber above, four small leather chests waited for an early departure in the morning. The late autumn evening was passing as had so many others. The fire crackled in the fireplace. The Tudor clock on the mantle ticked away to bedtime. Yet this night was different. It marked both an end and a beginning.

Jane pulled her thoughts back to the game and shifted her bishop. Willcotte raised a questioning eyebrow. He moved his knight and checkmated her king.

"I'll work on my game in London," she said.

"Your concentration is lacking."

"I know." She sighed. "London seems a world away. I'm almost afraid to go. But I have to. Lucy's right. I've got to make some changes."

"Jack Weaver asked me to bid you 'God speed'."

"See that he takes care while I'm gone. He owes me that." She stood. "I've something for you."

Fetching a roll of paper from the accounts room, she handed it to the bailiff.

"I translated some of your favorite passages."

Only recently had she realized how much she would miss this unassuming man. Over the last months he'd become a dear friend and adviser.

"I've something for you also." Willcotte pulled a bit of folded paper from his purse. "This is a Lollard in Coleman Street. Should you need help, or have news you can't put in a letter the regular way, show him this note. He'll get word to me."

"I'm not going to London to involve myself with more Lollards."

"You're not the same person who traveled there before. I'll rest easier if you have his name."

Willcotte came to his feet and stirred the coals in the fireplace, banking them for morning. Laying the fire iron aside, his finger went to his lip. Tonight was the last time they would talk face-to-face for five months. Jane knew he had something on his mind. She remained at the chess table, toying with the pieces, waiting.

"When I was young, not even as old as you, the Church brought a persecution against the Lollards. Fear can do horrible things to people, can make them do terrible things to each other. I saw husbands turn against wives, wives against their menfolk. Children informed on their own parents. The Church officials let our terror do their work for them. When it was over, I left that place."

He faced Jane in the flickering candlelight.

"I know Mistress Lucy wants to find you a husband. Have a care who you accept."

CHAPTER 12 – OCTOBER TO NOVEMBER, 1525

S pires thick against the sky welcomed Jane to London. She was actually here. Following Dickon Carter, she trotted past the ribbon of houses and gardens bordering Spitalfield. On the previous visit for her betrothal, she'd been too despondent to take interest in anything.

Now her gaze roamed in all directions. As she rode through Bishopsgate, she tossed a coin to a beggar child. She craned her neck to better admire the richly painted inns they were passing and almost tangled herself in a string of sumpter horses loaded with wool bags. She was halted again near St. Anthony's Hospital. A small scholar, noisily pursuing a pig that had been rooting in a rubbish pile, dashed beneath her horse's neck. Skirting the Stocks Market bustle, Jane and Dickon turned into Walbrook Street. Here the raw stench of hides coming from the skinners' quarters sent her hurrying on, hand over her nose. As they passed shops bulging with honey, pitch, wax, ropes and a dozen different types of dried fish, the air improved slightly. Eventually they turned onto the Vintry, that section of Thames Street where the wine merchants lived.

As Lucy's green courtyard-gate came in sight, they fell behind a lumbering cart piled high with kegs of Madeira. They and the vehicle halted before George Terrell's shop. George's older son, a beefy thirteen-year-old with Lucy's pug nose, loped out. He caught sight of Jane, waved and shouted for his father. Having raised the call, he joined an employee in manhandling the delivery to the huge vaulted cellar.

George appeared, his broad face beaming. He swung Jane to the ground as easily as he moved wine barrels. Somewhere overhead she heard her name being called. Tipping her head back she spotted Lucy hanging out of a window. With happy disregard for propriety, Lucy shouted that Jane should come up.

Leaving George and Dickon to see to her mount and clothing chests, Jane squeezed past the cart and into the Terrells's courtyard. The name 'courtyard' was too grand for the wide cobbled walk between the house and boundary wall. The space was further reduced by rows of potted plants, now little more than dying leaves, ranged along the walk.

Jane ran up the outside stairs to the first-floor dwelling. Coming into the hall from the crisp cold, she found the long paneled room, overfull with tables, benches, chairs and chests, to be hot and stuffy. As if to make up for her impoverished early years, Lucy crowded her home with every comfort. Given time and enough money from George, Jane was certain she would do the same with Horne Hall.

"I'm here," Jane said to Lucy.

"And barely soon enough. I've found another young man I want you to meet. A draper's son."

Before Jane could answer, Dickon and a Terrell manservant appeared with her chests. Lucy led the way to the bedchamber on the floor above.

"Sybil had it before," she said. "I made sure the servants gave it a thorough airing and changed the linens."

Compared to the hall, this room with its bed, dressing table and single large chest seemed almost empty. Dickon and the manservant deposited her chests along one wall and departed. Jane began to unpack.

"Let your maid do that," Lucy said.

"I didn't bring Bess. She has a child."

"You can't go about London without a personal servant. It isn't done."

Jane lifted out her wine kirtle and shook it free of wrinkles before laying it carefully in the large chest. Her thoughts jumped to the Latin Testament tucked at the bottom. She must keep that one locked. She wanted no one stumbling across the book. Owen had assured her the Church permitted its reading. She'd see for herself.

"You can borrow one of my servants," Lucy said. "You also need a gown made in the latest style. You want to look your best. I thought to invite the young men, one a week."

"I came to London to see Cecily Denzil, not to find a husband. Also I want to hear a decent sermon. The village priest is barely literate."

"Since when have you been interested in sermons? You'd do better to think of your future."

"Don't stare so," Cecily said. "Everyone will think you're just arrived from the country."

"But I have," Jane said as she stood with Cecily in the middle of St. Paul's Cathedral. She craned her neck, her gaze drawn upwards by the slender ribs of gray stone which converged in the vaulted ceiling floating a hundred and thirty feet above.

Her gaze drifted lower and she revolved slowly. The high Norman nave with its twin rows of strong stone pillars and heavy round arches stretched far to the west, a great chiseled canyon ending in three separate pairs of tall wooden doors heavy with locks, bolts and bars of iron. To the east, the richly carved rood screen was merely the introduction to the Gothic splendor of the choir, the gilded high altar and the brilliantly jeweled rose window. Off to the north and south, the shorter transepts lay like the outstretched arms of a crucified Savior. This largest of all England's cathedrals was a memorial to the faith of countless numbers who had labored throughout two centuries, turning their skills with wood and stone into a visible prayer to God.

All their efforts of devotion couldn't move them one whit closer to heaven.

Jane's high-lifted adoration plummeted to earth, to the dressed-stone floors worn uneven by the thousands of feet that had trodden them, back to the hundreds that trod them now.

All around her rose shouts and laughter and heated debates. Raucous-voiced image and taper sellers hawked their wares from stalls set up between the heavy stone pillars. Velvet-robed merchants did business in the shadow of the north-transept's great cross. Rude-tongued students and apprentices used 'Paul's Walk' as a short cut between Carter Lane and Paternoster Row. City wits strolled the aisles exchanging news of the day. A hoard of scriveners plied their trade for illiterate customers, fitting small tables into whatever space remained.

"If the Lord Jesus could see this place," Jane said.

"Hmmmm?" Cecily looked up.

"Christ drove the moneychangers from the temple with a scourge when they turned it into a place of business like this."

"You've no appreciation for Church commerce. Come on, let's walk around outside while we wait for Richard and Hugh."

Jane followed without further comment. She must guard her tongue. She'd sounded like a Lollard.

"I'm looking forward to meeting Hugh and your family," she said as they passed out the great west doors.

Cecily's response was drowned by chiming bells. When the peals dimmed, she glanced at the clock in the right tower.

"They're going to be late. Probably they have their heads in a law book and have forgotten we're going to the theater."

"They're not late yet," Jane said.

"Don't you ever get impatient? I do. All the time. And not just for people. I want something exciting to happen, something more than getting another dress or marrying Hugh. I want something big, something that will change my whole life."

Looking at Cecily, Jane felt a hundred years older.

"Someday something will happen. Only it may not be what you want. You'll wish, then, you'd put more value on what you'd had before."

"Are you speaking from experience?" Cecily's eyes brightened with curiosity.

Inwardly Jane drew back. Much as she liked Cecily, she had no wish to share the past with her.

"Of course," she said lightly. "And experience says we'll soon be interrupted. So tell me quickly what these buildings are." She waved a hand at the structures framing St. Paul's west entrance.

"That's the Bishop of London's palace. The tower here with the clock and bells is Lollard's Tower. And that's St. Gregory's church beyond."

Jane peered up at the old stone stronghold.

"Why is it called Lollard's Tower?"

"The Bishop keeps heretics locked up there."

Jane shivered.

"Does he have prisoners now?"

"Who knows."

Cecily turned away to scan the crowds streaming into the churchyard. Jane was left to stare up at the somber building.

"Here they are at last."

Jane turned away from the grim structure and collided with a man's black velvet shoulder. As she stepped clumsily away, a strong steadying hand caught her elbow. She looked up into the most beautiful dark-blue eyes she'd ever seen.

"Jane Horne, my brother Richard."

I see why Sybil wanted him.

Jane felt heat flood her face. She dropped her gaze and gently freed her arm from Richard's grasp.

"And this is Hugh Peterman."

Hugh limped forward on a clubfoot. In spite of Cecily's comments, Jane had expected to see someone younger and more stylishly dressed than this stoop-shouldered man with thinning brown hair.

"Jane thinks we should take scourges and drive the hawkers from Paul's Walk," Cecily told the two men.

"Cecily!" Jane said, caught between laughter and embarrassment. At least now she could be excused if her face was red when she again looked at Richard.

"I prevented her. I'm a true daughter of the Church."

Richard cocked a dark eyebrow.

"Cardinal Wolsey would be glad to know. You didn't sound so loyal when we came with Father to hear Bishop Fisher preach against Luther at the book burning. What was it you said?" He glanced around and dropped his voice. "Something about Wolsey being an over-dressed sausage who'd dragged all London out to hear Fisher rail against a poor German monk. Don't you remember, Hugh? I've never seen Father so angry. I think he even scared you, Cecily. I know he did me."

"You know I didn't mean a word of it." Cecily clung to Hugh's arm, her dimple flashing. "I was out of sorts. Someone in the crowd had left a muddy footprint on the hem of my new gown." She turned to Jane. "The day was so exciting. I'd never seen that many peers, bishops and foreign dignitaries in my life. And all decked out in gold and jewels. I still recall thinking that, had we been the ones to provide their trinkets, we'd have made a fortune."

"Cecily was a child at the time," Hugh said to Jane.

Cecily bristled and dropped his arm.

"I was thirteen. At that age were you a child?"

"I was never allowed to be a child at any age. Whatever you were then," Hugh continued with a smile, "today you're a beautiful young woman who is going to be late for the theater."

If Hugh intended to distract Cecily, he succeeded. Another minute saw them striding as quickly as Hugh's uneven step would allow toward Fish Street and the inn where the production was to be held. It seemed only natural that Richard should fall into step with Jane.

"I'm sorry if the shopkeepers in Paul's Walk distressed you," he said.

"It's just ... they seemed out of place," Jane said, not daring to look at him.

"We Londoners are accustomed to seeing them. I'd never thought how they might strike a visitor." He touched her arm with light fingers, guiding her around a puddle. "I hope you won't think ill of us because of it."

"Oh, no." Jane glanced up at Richard. His clean-shaven cheek was pink. She felt her own face warm and, alarmed, quickly looked away. She was not ready to risk her heart again.

Jane watched the comedy unfold on the rough stage, determined to disregard the man at her side. By play's end she'd almost succeeded. She claimed Cecily for the walk to the Denzil home, leaving Richard to follow with Hugh. When they reached West Cheap, Hugh excused himself and limped away. Jane found Richard at her elbow. Three abreast, they ambled past goldsmith-shop windows glowing with plate and trinkets of all description. At Guthran Lane, Cecily stopped.

"Lilies and a unicorn," she said pointing to a sign of a garlanded unicorn prancing on a heraldry-blue background hanging over a shop's half-timbered front. "That's all we have left of the Denzil coat of arms." With that cryptic remark she reached for the latch. "Come meet my brother Nicholas."

Two heads were bent close over an engraved ewer when Jane entered. The stout man in the mulberry gown was obviously a customer. The other was an older, shorter, brown-haired version of Richard. While Nicholas completed his sale, Jane browsed among the gold and silver utensils, the casket boxes and enameled clocks, the plate and jewelry. She heard Nicholas bid farewell to his customer. A moment later he was approaching her.

"May I show you something, Mistress?"

"She's not here to buy," Cecily said. "She's my friend Jane Horne. But, should she want anything, I'll see we get her trade. Jane, what do you think of these?"

Cecily pulled out a tray lined with black velvet and filled with an assortment of gold necklaces.

"They're beautiful. Especially this one," Jane said, lifting the chain.

The necklace, set at intervals with pearls, had a cluster of pearl flowers accented with green enameled leaves dangling from the center.

"Richard designed that."

"You did?" Jane met Richard's eyes for the first time since they had left the play.

Richard nodded.

She carefully returned the necklace to its place. Had Richard not been the creator, she would have bought it. The thought of wearing something of his was inexplicably too personal.

"By the way, Richard," Nicholas said, "I've a new customer, a nobleman, who wants a christening cup. Could you do a few sketches by week's end?"

"Sorry. I've got too much to cover in my studies before Father returns."

"I only need a couple. He's a lavish spender so gaining his business is important."

"So are my studies."

"Why let Father turn you into a second-rate attorney when you could become the best goldsmith in London?"

Jane saw Richard's eyes spark fire.

"I made the decision to be a lawyer."

"Father had nothing to do with it?"

"Of course he was pleased."

"I'll say he was," Nicholas said. "He smiled for a whole hour."

"Why must you keep harping at me? You'd think I wanted to be a cutpurse."

"I'll stop harping when you come back to the shop. You're an artist. Grandfather Smith trained us both. He knew."

"I'm going to be a lawyer, Nicholas. A good one like Father. I'm sorry to have disappointed you. I'd please everyone if I could."

Richard nodded to Jane then stalked out a rear door.

"He may be willing to let his skill be wasted," Nicholas said to Cecily. "I'm not."

"You wouldn't object to the money he'd bring you either. You're as bad as Father. Why can't you both leave him alone?"

"If Father hadn't taken that lawsuit for Lord Danbury - ."

"It's still his life. Come on, Jane. I'm tired of this conversation. Let's go upstairs."

Jane, an uncomfortable witness to this private squabble, was more than willing. Cecily whisked her through the rear door and across the workshop, a place of furnace heat and tool-cluttered workbenches, of acid odors and half-raised bowls that glowed warmly in the hands of the journeyman.

They put the workshop behind them, crossed a small entry room and climbed wide wooden stairs. At the top Jane found herself on a roomy landing with a dining parlor to the left and a hall to the right. Facing her was another set of stairs continuing on to an upper story. Cecily turned right into the hall.

Because the Denzil home was larger than the Terrell's and in a wealthier section, Jane expected to find their hall equally comfortable. She was taken aback at sight of it. The room, though bigger than Lucy's, was monkish in its plainness. The few cushions on benches and settles were faded and worn, the paneled walls bare of adornment. Even the pots of flowers that would normally have added color were fading with the autumn. The only bright spot in the whole drab room was a gilded harpsichord in a far corner.

Cecily, her face clouded, dropped onto a bench.

"I'm sorry about that." She gathered her skirts so Jane could sit beside her. "Nicholas is right, though. Richard wasn't meant to be a lawyer."

"Why did he decide to be one?"

"To please Father. He's not bound by the oath." She must have read Jane's unspoken perplexity. "We used to own five manors. Or rather Grandfather Denzil did. He was a nobleman under Richard Plantagenet. So you see, half my blood is as good as yours. After King Richard was killed, Grandfather lost it all, title, manors, everything, because he wouldn't swear loyalty to Henry Tudor. On his deathbed he made Father swear never to seek service with the Tudors.

"Father's kept that oath. He doesn't care who the king is as long as he has the law. He also doesn't mind living like this." She glanced around the bare hall with a wry look. "It's the loss of position he resents. I saw his face when he arrived home after Lord Danbury's case. Father won the case, of course, and Lord Danbury kept his manor. Our manor. Father said he'd never realized how much honor Grandfather had thrown away. That's when he decided that either Nicholas or Richard must become a lawyer, enter the king's service and regain our honor.

"Nicholas flatly refused. Richard was more sympathetic. He'd recently become a journeyman, but he agreed to do it. It was a mistake. You wait and see. He'll do those sketches. He can't help himself." She shook herself as if sloughing off her family problems. "Your family clearly sided with the right king for you to own a manor now."

"All I know of my mother's family is that she was the last," Jane said cautiously. She had too many secrets, too much hurt, to welcome questions. "Mother died when I was a child. But how did your mother come to own a goldsmith shop?"

"She inherited it from her first husband." Fortunately, Cecily appeared more interested in her own family. "He was quite old when they married. Mother made him sign a marriage contract giving her the house and shop when he died. After his funeral, his family contested it. Father won the suit for Mother. That's how they met. Grandfather Smith had worked for the old man as a journeyman for years. Once Mother got clear title to everything, she paid for Grandfather to be made a master craftsman. He had charge of the work, but the business belonged to Mother. I'd like to own a business some day."

The sound of feet loping down the stairs from above interrupted further conversation. Richard burst into the hall, eyes dancing. He rushed to the bow window.

"I thought it was her. Nicholas has a visitor."

"Blanche again?"

Cecily scurried across the room and peered out.

"He won't be pleased."

Brother and sister exchanged gleeful grins. A door slammed below. The two at the window straightened.

"She'll send her maid to fetch him," Richard said. "They'll come here."

"Hurry! Sit down." Cecily grabbed Jane's hand and dashed for the settle by the fireplace. Before she could think, Jane found herself wedged between sister and brother and listening to the sound of angry voices coming up the main staircase.

"How many times must I tell you? Don't come here while I'm working." The volume of Nicholas's voice ascended with him.

"I wouldn't have to if you called on me more often."

They came into the hall. When Nicholas saw the three by the fireplace, he stopped and frowned. Blanche breezed past him to greet Cecily and Richard and to be introduced to Jane. Blanche had an abundance of straw-yellow hair and a moon face set with small perfect features. Her mouth, round and red and moist, reminded Jane of an over-ripe cherry.

Nicholas caught Blanche by the elbow and steered her into the book room tucked between hall and dining parlor. He closed the door.

"When Nicholas is ranting at me about my life," Richard said, "he should think on the trouble he's made for himself."

"Nicholas and Blanche are contracted to marry," Cecily told Jane. "Father can't stand her. Naturally Nicholas was determined to wed her. Now he's found he can't stand her either."

"He'd like to withdraw from the contract," Richard added, unfolding himself from the settle. "But that would be admitting Father was right. He's currently caught between Blanche and his pride."

Cecily glanced toward the closed door.

"They could be there for some time. I need to speak to the housekeeper about tomorrow's meals."

Jane came to her feet.

"I'd best go. Lucy will be expecting me."

"I'll have a servant accompany you home."

"I can accompany Jane," Richard said.

For the third time that day Jane found herself walking with Richard. They left the house through the main entrance at the stair bottom. The courtyard bordering the house, side and back, was larger than Lucy's. Rather than flower pots, an orderly row of tangled, almost leafless shrubs was spaced along the walk and half-filled a garden square in the rear corner.

"Father's roses," Richard said. "They don't look like much now. I wish you could see them covered with bloom. Father has someone hired to tend them. Half the time he does the work himself anyway."

During the walk from Guthran Lane to the Vintry, Richard made no more conversation. Once again, Jane was acutely aware of the man at her elbow. When they arrived at Lucy's gate, she pulled the latch string. Richard remained gazing down at her. Jane hesitated, held at the gate by his presence.

"I'm glad to have met you, Jane. I hope -."

"Goodbye, Richard," she said quickly.

He made no move to depart. Jane edged through the entry.

"Yes ... well ... goodbye."

He was still standing in the street when Jane shut the gate. Doubtless he would wander away eventually.

In the days that followed, Richard appeared several times when Jane visited Cecily. He managed to be at her side when she accompanied Cecily and Hugh to the Lord Mayor's show at All Hallows tide. Soon everyone expected that he would be the one to accompany her home after an evening visit. Initially Jane attempted to unobtrusively avoid him. His patient persistence made that impossible. As time passed, she had to admit she enjoyed his undemanding companionship. His gentle uncertainty was such a contrast to Owen's single-mindedness. Each time they were alone, Jane braced herself, expecting him to declare his suit. That he made no such overtures was both a relief and a cause for growing bewilderment.

If Richard's behavior baffled Jane, it nonplused Cecily when she asked about it.

"Do you mean he hasn't poured forth any words of love at all?"

They were toasting themselves before the small fireplace in Cecily's chamber. The room, bright with cushions and wine-red bed hangings, was a marked contrast to the drab hall below.

"Don't be silly," Jane said, sure she was blushing. "We've barely known each other a month."

"Ah, but I've seen how he watches you when he thinks no one's looking. I wonder if Hugh ever looks at me like that?"

"I'm sure it doesn't mean a thing."

"Richard may want Father's approval before he declares himself," Cecily said. "We'll soon know. Father should be home any day."

CHAPTER 13 – DECEMBER, 1525
TO TWELFTH NIGHT

When Jane arrived to dine with the Denzils the following evening, the door opened almost before her hand left the knocker. A servant whisked her cloak away and informed her that Cecily was in the hall.

"Father's home," Cecily said. "You can tell by the way the servants scurry about."

Jane laughed.

"Where is he now?"

"In the book room with Richard. He inspected his roses and then took him off to examine him on his studies. They've been there for the last hour."

As Jane accompanied Cecily up to her chamber, her thoughts centered on the master of this household who, but for a twist of fate, would have been titled lord of five manors. Over the last weeks she had grown increasingly curious about Martin Denzil. Despite his physical absence he remained a dominant force in his children's lives. He was clearly a man to evoke strong and conflicting emotions in those around him. What emotion would he arouse in her?

When Jane later came down the stairs with Cecily, Martin Denzil was waiting at the bottom, one hand resting on the railing. He was a tall, square-shouldered man, his once-black hair now heavily laced with gray. This would be Richard in thirty years. Studying his face more closely as she reached the bottom, Jane corrected herself. Martin's hard black eyes held none of Richard's gentleness, nor was there humor in the set of his mouth. This was the face of justice untempered by mercy.

"You're nearly late for dinner."

He sounded so like Cecily that Jane smiled. Her smile dimmed when Martin acknowledged Cecily's introduction of her with little more than a curt nod. He turned to his daughter.

"Hugh and your brothers are already waiting at table."

He strode off, leaving them to follow. Jane slipped into her place and looked across at Richard. His face sagged. Evidently the session in the book room had been grueling.

"Hugh," Martin said as he helped himself to the mutton, "Richard must give more attention to writs. He's not progressing as quickly as I'd expected."

"Richard has been working hard."

Martin's shaggy brows drew down.

"Working hard and progressing in one's studies doesn't necessarily constitute the same thing."

A pained expression crossed Richard's face. Already she was beginning to dislike Martin Denzil. He also proved to be a poor host, dominating the table talk. Like a trial lawyer questioning a witness, he examined Hugh about recent cases at Westminster and activities at the Old Bailey. The rest of the table ate in silence.

Jane, knowing little of such matters, allowed her thoughts to drift. She was musing over Lucy's plans for the coming Christmas season when she had her attention abruptly called back. Martin was addressing her, or believed he was.

"Mistress Harris, pass the salt, please."

"Forgive me."

Jane reached for the silver saltcellar. Richard swiveled in his seat.

"It's Jane Horne, Father. Not Harris."

"Horne?" Martin looked at Cecily. "You said Harris."

"My tongue may have slipped," Cecily said with unexpected meekness.

"Jane's father was Sir Harry Horne of Essex," Richard continued.

"Sir Harry Horne?" Martin reached a hand toward his goblet. "I don't recognize the name."

"No doubt you've heard of the Stantons of Herefordshire," Cecily said. "Jane's mother, Eleanor Stanton, was of that family."

Cringing, Jane dropped her gaze. Who else in London beside Owen's mother knew Eleanor Stanton had given birth to a bastard?

"Fetch a cloth."

Martin's sharp command brought Jane's head up. A dark pool of wine was soaking into the white linen tablecloth beside his goblet. The nervous servingmaid scurried away to return almost immediately, rag in hand. Jane breathed a silent prayer of thanks for the distraction. By the time normal conversation resumed, Nicholas had turned it to London news.

At meal's end everyone gathered in the hall for an evening of music. Cecily took her seat at the harpsichord with Hugh on a stool beside her to shift the music. Soon Richard and Nicholas joined her, singing as she played. All three Denzils sang beautifully. Jane had enjoyed more than one evening listening to them. Evidently their father, sitting at the edge of the candlelight, appreciated music as well. Jane noticed his foot tapping.

The trio had barely launched into their second tune when Jane looked up to find Martin at her elbow.

"May I?" he asked gravely before folding himself down onto the bench beside her.

"They're very good," Jane said.

"They take their talent from their mother. She was an excellent musician. Do you sing?"

"Not that well. I do play the lute."

"You must entertain us some evening soon." He sank into silence. After some moments, "Have you been in London long?"

"Just over a month."

"Did your parents accompany you?"

"My parents are dead. My mother died when I was a child and my father a year-and-a-half ago. I'm visiting my half-sister."

"I didn't know. I'm sorry." Turning away, he gave his attention once again to the music.

Jane studied him from the corner of her eye. Seeing a more civil side of him tempered some of her earlier dislike.

When Cecily cried 'enough' Nicholas fetched a set of dice. As usual Hugh refused to toss for coins. Instead he chose kindling chips, a decision that exasperated Cecily. Nonetheless she grew heated over the game as her pile of chips waxed and waned.

Richard joined Jane and his father. Initially she tried to include him in their conversation. She was forced to give up. Once again Martin dominated the exchange, questioning Jane about her family and what activities she and Cecily had shared. Annoyed with Richard for allowing himself to be pushed out, she threw herself into the conversation with more enthusiasm than usual. At one point she found herself telling Martin how she and Cecily had gone wading. As she described Cecily's flight from the fish, Martin broke into a deep chuckle. When his laughter rolled out, the three at the dicing table looked around in astonishment.

All too soon the evening ended. When the servant appeared with Jane's cloak, Richard reached for it. Martin took it from him and slipped it over Jane's shoulders.

"I'll escort you home. Night isn't a safe time for young women to venture out alone."

As Martin steered her toward the stairs, Jane glanced over her shoulder. Richard stood looking after her, his hands hanging empty and on his face startled disbelief.

The dark, nearly-deserted streets were wet with misting rain as Jane and Martin passed along with their horn lantern. Bow Bell would be ringing curfew shortly. Approaching Lucy's gate, Jane broke the silence they had carried with them from the Denzil home.

"My sister lives here."

Martin banged a gloved fist on the portal. As they waited in the drizzle, he held the light up as if to see her face. His own remained dim.

"I enjoyed talking to you this evening, Jane. I think Cecily will benefit from your friendship. She takes matters too irresponsibly."

Jane heard the scraping sound of a bar being lifted. The gate creaked open.

"I hope we'll see much of you," he said. "Good night."

Unlike Richard, Martin strode away at once.

"I don't know how you managed it," Cecily said to Jane a few days later as they huddled close to the fire in Lucy's hall. Outside the glazed windows stray snowflakes drifted down to join the thick layer that had fallen during the night. "You've charmed Father. He practically ordered me to invite you to dine with us again. He even hinted that I should include you in some of our Twelfthtide celebrations."

Jane couldn't keep the bad news to herself any longer.

"George's sister wants us to join them for Twelfthtide. Her letter was quiet insistent."

"You aren't going, are you?"

"George and Lucy have been discussing it for two days," Jane said. 'Arguing' would have been more accurate a word. "George feels he owes his sister something because of Sybil. I think we'll go. Lucy is already talking about leaving shortly after St. Nicholas Day so she can visit friends on the way."

"But you can't."

"I've little choice."

"You can stay with us."

"Lucy will be gone at least a month. Your family wouldn't want me that long."

"Richard would."

"After Hugh and I are wed," Cecily said, "Father says we can have Hugh's old room for a small parlor."

Jane and Cecily were in Cecily's room while a maid unpacked Jane's belongings in the adjoining chamber.

"I didn't know Hugh had lived here."

"He came when he was nine in payment for a case." Cecily gave a short laugh. "Don't look so shocked. Father occasionally handles a case for some poor fellow without charge."

"How kind of him."

"Not really. He likes crossing swords with nobility. Hugh's father was a fisherman. His boat collided with a nobleman's barge. The nobleman had him thrown in prison and brought a suit for damages. Father got him out and won the case. The man was so grateful he insisted Father take one of his brood."

"How awful for Hugh."

"Why? He got more to eat here than he would have in that hovel. Father found out he had a sharp mind so sent him to school and made a lawyer out of him. When I was old enough, Father said I was to marry him. Becoming betrothed sounded exciting at the time. At least Hugh has never tried to run my life. He moved out afterward. He said he couldn't accept Father's charity any longer."

"But he's moving back again after you're married."

"Of course. I've no intention of living in that horrid little room he's got near the Leaden Hall. I don't understand why he stays there. He has a good income. If I didn't know better, I'd suspect him of wasting his monies on women or gambling."

"Could he be helping his family?"

"He'd better not be. Father made it clear to the fisherman that, if he took Hugh, they had no further claim on him."

At her first meal as a member of the Denzil household, Martin invited Jane to accompany him to Westminster the following day.

"You said you wanted to see the place. I've got business there that shouldn't take long."

"Richard," Cecily said quickly, "why don't you go along and show Jane around while Father is tending to his affairs?"

Jane glanced hopefully at Richard. She had seen little of him since his father's return. Either he was at Lincoln's Inn or pouring over his lessons in the book room. Nor did he any longer see her safely to Lucy's after dark. His father had preempted him on the few times she had needed an escort. Much as she appreciated Martin's courtesy and his approval of her friendship with Cecily, she missed Richard.

Before Richard could reply around the bite that lumped his jaw, Martin spoke.

"Richard has too much studying before Epiphany to waste a day." His terse tone softened. He turned to Jane. "We'll take a boat up. Dress warmly. The river is cold this time of year."

Hugging her fur-lined cloak, Jane scrambled into the tiltboat Martin had hailed from the river steps near Queenhythe. As soon as they were seated, the boatman shoved off, pointed his craft upriver and began rowing. The cold clear current flowed past them, a dark pewter gray. Gradually the city rising out of the north bank was replaced with winter-brown rushes and trees whose bare branches embroidered the leaden sky. Occasionally Jane saw teals or swans swimming among the reeds. She breathed deeply of the chill breeze that tugged at her hood, clearing London's stale odors from her lungs.

As the Thames curved south, Westminster, seat of government and home of royalty, floated into view, stretching, ribbon-like, along the north bank. They passed Whitehall Palace with its orchards, gardens and park and soon pulled up to the Old Palace stairs. The tiltman, his face wet with exertion, held his craft against the steps with a cloth-wrapped hand while they disembarked. On the landing, Jane cautiously shuffled her freezing feet to restore circulation.

"Take my arm," Martin said. "These steps can be treacherous."

They reached the top and started across the cobblestones. Buildings of stone, red brick and occasionally of half-timber edged the square. Martin turned left toward an arched gate flanked by towers.

"The Old Palace is this way. You can see Westminster Abbey beyond. We can hear mass later if you wish and see the tombs of the kings. I thought to take our noon meal at a cookshop by Westminster gate. You might even catch a glimpse of the King since we'll pass Whitehall on the way. But I must go to Westminster Hall first."

•

When they arrived, Martin left her in a long, paneled room filled with people. After he disappeared through a near door half hidden by a red-painted screen, Jane found an inconspicuous corner from which to watch the room's other occupants. Although their dress ranged from dark homespun woolens to peacock-bright silks and satins, they stood as one expectantly watching a tall yellow door at the far end.

After a time the door opened. The crowd surged forward. The door shut and the watchers receded to their previous places. An attractive auburn-haired man in a conservative black gown emerged from the throng and made his way toward the exit close to Jane. A stocky man in a black satin doublet hurried after, catching him as he neared the door.

"Thomas, have you seen Cardinal Wolsey?"

"I only now left him," Thomas said.

"What was his concern?"

"Cambridge. Lutheran heresies are spreading like hemlock throughout the university."

"Where aren't they rife?" Although the stocky man dropped his voice, Jane caught every word from her corner beyond the door frame. "If there wasn't so much truth in what that German monk says, people wouldn't be so quick to listen."

"Take care what you say, Percy," Thomas said.

"We both know the Church is filled with corruption. Look at any frocked priest and you'll see a thief or worse."

"I only know a man's guilt as it's proved in a court of law. If you know a religious who's a thief, report him to his bishop."

"Why must you be so literal?" Percy said. "You know quite well I'm talking of ideas."

"I thought you were speaking of thieves. As for ideas, they're like seeds. If we allow them to grow unchallenged, we'll find ourselves with the devil's own crop to harvest. Would you see the peace of England and the authority of God's Church destroyed here as they've been in Germany?"

Jane was so intent on the conversation she failed to notice Martin until he greeted the two men. He beckoned her to join them.

"Jane, may I introduce Sir Thomas More and Sir Percy Clay?"

After the introductions Jane stood listening as the three men chatted. When Sir Percy took his leave, Sir Thomas's look followed him. His pleasant face hardened.

"Men are absorbing these heinous ideas from the Continent without even realizing it. That frightens me."

"The Church has survived well over a thousand years," Martin said. "One devilish German monk won't bring its downfall."

"He may well do so in Germany."

"But this is England."

"England is changing."

As the tiltman returned them to London, more quickly this time since they were going with the Thames, Jane was preoccupied. Martin had given her an interesting day. Yet nothing held her thoughts as did the brief encounter with Sir Thomas More.

Howard Willcotte had cautioned her about choosing a husband. She'd intended to heed his advice and guard her heart well. She'd not expected Richard to slip into it so effortlessly. How easily she could find herself in love with him. The realization filled her with terror. To love meant to be vulnerable. She couldn't bear to be hurt again as Owen had hurt her. But the two men were so different. Owen had been so single-minded, so determined to follow his dream at the cost of all else. In the end he'd needed no one but God. Richard, torn between father and brother, unsure of his way, was the opposite. Richard would need the woman he married. And she wanted so badly to be needed.

But, first, she must know what he thought about the Church and, as Sir Thomas had put it, 'the devil's own crop' coming from the Continent.

Jane's opportunity came that very evening. After the meal, Richard disappeared into the book room to study. Once the rest of the family were occupied in the hall, Jane slipped away. She found Richard, his law books spread out on the writing table, busily at work with paper and ink. As the latch clicked shut behind her, he started and pulled a loose sheet over his work before looking up. Seeing her, his face sagged with relief.

"I thought you were Father."

Jane crossed to the table and picked up the paper on which he'd been working. A drawing of an engraved goblet, slightly smudged, met her eyes. Cecily had said Richard was an artist, not a lawyer. Sadness filled her as she looked at the proof in her hand.

"It's exquisite, Richard."

He made a small gesture of depreciation.

"Nicholas has an order for twenty goblets."

"Your mark should be on the finished ones, not his."

It angered her how readily Nicholas took his brother's designs without a word of thanks, almost as if they were his by right.

"I'm going to be a lawyer."

"Of course. I only meant ... shouldn't Nicholas make his own designs?"

Richard's stiff look eased.

"I'm always seeing ideas in my head. This way someone has the benefit of them. I enjoy seeing the finished object."

His wistful tone wrung her heart. She handed the paper back and pulled up a stool.

"I'm certain Nicholas will be pleased with your sketch."

"I could have been a good goldsmith if I'd chosen. My becoming a lawyer means so much to Father. All his life he's had to take second place to less able men because of his oath. I want his final years to be spent in hope for the future, not in regret over the past."

She looked down at the beautiful drawing. Richard was letting his father to do to him something far worse than his grandfather's oath had done to Martin. She could think of nothing to say. Or could she?

"Your father is hardly old. He might even marry again and have a second family."

A glint of anger flashed in Richard's eyes. He picked up his sketch and began folding it into increasingly smaller squares.

"Did you have a pleasant day with him?" He sounded resentful.

"Yes, I did. I wish you could have gone with us. I overheard a conversation today." Briefly she repeated the exchange between Sir Thomas and Sir Percy. "What do you think? Is there truth in what Martin Luther is saying?"

"Frankly, I try not to think about it."

The matter was far too important to allow him an evasive answer.

"Surely you've heard people talk."

"Of course. After all, this is London. You may be peaceful in the country but we're a hotbed of controversy here."

"I'm serious. Do you think the abuses in the Church can be corrected without destroying it?"

"Some of the worst offenders are the bishops themselves. If they were planning to correct the problems, why haven't they done it? On the other hand, if the Church were destroyed, who would care for the souls of the people? And what of the hospitals, alms houses and all the other charities the Church provides?"

"I don't know about the charities," Jane said cautiously. "As for the people's souls, couldn't they be given the scriptures in English so they wouldn't have to rely on a corrupt clergy?"

Richard eyed her.

"That's a radical thing to say."

"I heard it somewhere. Do you think it has merit?"

"No, I don't. You've only to look at Germany. The country is torn by war. No doubt problems existed before Luther. But his scriptures and flagrant disregard for the Church were the sparks that lit the blaze."

"Do you think the Church should punish people for reading Luther's writings?"

The corners of his mouth curved.

"Has someone given you a pamphlet? Is that the reason for all these questions?"

"No." Then, like a gauntlet being thrown, she added, "I do have Erasmus's Latin Testament. I'm not sure if the Church would approve."

"You're right. Many officials don't like it. Sir Thomas does, though, and has defended it. I'm not surprised that you have one." He swallowed visibly. "I'm glad your devotion hasn't led you to be a nun." He reached for her hand. "Surely you know how I admire you."

The touch of his fingers thrilled her and brought irrational alarm. She was not ready. Jane slipped her hand free and stood.

"I shouldn't keep you from your studies."

Ignoring his hurt look, she fled.

The Christmas season arrived with a flood of parties, plays and pageants. Cecily, riding the crest of the celebration, swept Jane from one entertainment to the next, accompanied by whichever man of the family could be gotten to escort them. Most often, Hugh squired them safely to and from. Sometimes Nicholas escaped Blanche and joined them. Even Martin, to Cecily's amazement, took his turn. Only Richard, struggling with torts, writs and litigations under his father's demanding eye, did not.

Jane was glad for Cecily's preoccupation with the season. But for that, she certainly would have noticed something amiss, not only with Richard but with Martin as well. Jane couldn't say exactly when Richard had changed toward her, perhaps from the evening in the book room. She was only sure that he had withdrawn his attention. At times he cleverly avoided her. When circumstances forced them together, he kept their conversation impersonal.

If Richard neglected her, his father made up for the deficiency. Martin might be short on smiles and an agreeable word for his children. He never lacked them for Jane. She had briefly considered that Martin might be courting her but had dismissed the idea. As genial toward her as he was, he made no attempt at a more intimate relationship. Nonetheless, she sensed that he saw her as something more than merely a good influence on Cecily. But what?

To her discomfort, she realized Richard was aware of his father's behavior. At odd times she would look up to catch Martin watching her and Richard watching him. Jane was conscience of being part of a drama she didn't comprehend. Thus the Christmas season passed.

By Twelfth Night Jane was exhausted. She sat picking at her midday meal, sated with the extravagances of the past fortnight.

"I wish I had a bowl of pease porridge," she said to the room at large.

Cecily wrinkled her nose.

"That's food for peasants."

"Peasants don't die of overeating. If I have one more bite of marchpane that's what I'll do."

Martin smiled.

"I'll see no one serves you any tonight at Sir Thomas's."

"Father," Cecily said, "must we always spend Twelfth Night with the More family?"

"Sir Thomas is a friend." Martin's tone brooked no argument. He turned to Jane. "You should find the evening entertaining. Sir Thomas has hired Welsh minstrels." His look sharpened as he switched back to his pouting daughter. "See you're prepared to leave on time this year."

When Jane learned that the whole family would be attending the festivity, she determined that Richard would be her escort. Surely during the boat ride to Chelsea, she could break through the wall he'd erected. She had merely to be at his elbow when Cecily appeared in the hall.

Cecily came down the stairs early. Jane herself had only arrived a moment before and had stopped to exchange a brief word with Hugh before joining Richard and Nicholas near the fireplace. When Martin, waiting with Hugh, saw Cecily he offered Jane his arm. As she reluctantly took it, she threw a despairing glance at Richard. For once she was in full agreement with Nicholas's attitude toward his domineering father.

The cold boat trip reduced Jane's mood to brooding resentment. When they arrived, she hobbled hurriedly across the frozen grass toward candle-lit windows reaching out a warm welcome through the gathering darkness. The long, high-roofed hall Jane entered swarmed with guests. Near the huge fireplace the Welsh minstrels were tuning their instruments. Tables along the paneled walls sagged with roasted fowl, stuffed whole fish, venison haunches, tender roast piglet and pastries and puddings of all kinds.

"No pease porridge," Martin said as Jane surveyed the feast. She laughed at his unexpected joke. Richard, who had been eying a huge fruit-laced pudding, disappeared abruptly from the edge of her vision. She looked round in time to see his retreating figure being swallowed up in the sea of celebrants. Frustration gripped her again.

"Martin, how good of you to come. And Mistress Horne."

Jane turned to see Sir Thomas approaching.

"Clement Wellington is here, fresh from the Continent, and asking after you," he said to Martin. Jane morosely followed the two men as they wove their way through the maze of guests to a lank man with the face of a sorrowful horse.

"Clement was telling me about the devastation the peasants' war has wreaked on Germany," Sir Thomas said.

Clement turned to Martin.

"Didn't you spend some time on the Continent?"

"About two years. Well before that German monk began stirring up trouble."

"How Frederick of Saxony can be so blind," Sir Thomas said, "as to protect that devil's spawn. Luther ought to be burned along with his Testament."

Made bold by the disappointments of the evening, Jane pushed into the conversation.

"Why should the holy scriptures be burned?"

"'Unholy' is a better label for Luther's mistranslations."

"Then why doesn't the Church make correct translations?"

"That wouldn't be wise," Sir Thomas said. "Common men haven't the training or the loyalty to Church doctrine to enable them to understand the scriptures correctly. If they're given a vernacular translation, they'll destroy England as surely as they've destroyed Germany."

Clement Wellington broke in.

"Peasants quoting scriptures and screeching for equality ravaged the southern German states. They torched churches, razed castles, killed priests and noblemen alike. They were put down at a ruinous cost." He shuttered. "The countryside I saw was a wasteland. Hardly a village remained standing. Peasants had to be slaughtered by the thousands. Some places have hardly enough left alive to serve their masters. That nightmare must not come to England."

Grim silence settled over them. Jane, thinking of Jack Weaver's desperate desire for the scriptures, spoke first.

"How can people be brought to God unless they're given his word?"

"As they are now," Sir Thomas said. "By the Church. After all, we had the Church before we had the written scriptures."

"Are you saying the Church is of more value than the scriptures?" Jane asked.

"Are you saying it isn't?" Sir Thomas countered with a smile.

Jane dared not answer. His smile faded. He continued.

"For the good of mankind the world must be united. Only under the Pope, through the Church and its teachings, can we be made one."

"But can't the scriptures accomplish that?"

"Germany is your answer. Give men the scriptures. Tell them they're equal to the Pope and the Church in their understanding. What do we have? As many interpretations as people. Where are the absolutes? What becomes of law, of peace and order, of unity?"

"But why doesn't the Pope rid the Church of corruption?" Jane persisted.

"Our churchmen are no more wicked than we laymen. We should first correct our own faults."

"When I was young," Martin said, laying a hand on Jane's arm, "I also was impatient with how the world was. Age has taught me that solutions don't come so easily. The Church's problems can't be solved in one evening. Let's put them aside and enjoy ourselves."

"You're right," Sir Thomas said, his pleasantness reasserting itself. "I shouldn't be disturbing my guests with talk of black deeds."

Not long after, he excused himself. Clement Wellington followed. Martin turned a somber face to Jane.

"Have a care what you say to Sir Thomas. He might misunderstand your concern. He's a brilliant scholar, a good lawyer and a valued friend. He's also a firm churchman."

CHAPTER 14 – WINTER, 1526

Cecily looked up from the harpsichord when Hugh arrived, closely bundled against the biting January cold. Near the fire Jane threaded another violet strand onto her needle. She was embroidering a pillow cover for Lucy, expected back in two days.

"Your father may be late for dinner." Hugh peeled off his outer garment and handed it to a servant. "Cardinal Wolsey sent for him."

"Cardinal Wolsey?" Cecily's eyes widened, and she turned from the keyboard. "Whatever does he want?"

"I've no idea."

Nicholas and Richard, coming in later, were equally mystified. Enlightenment waited for Martin. He appeared eventually, his face expressionless. His quick frown of warning cut short any questions before the servants.

The meal was served in pregnant silence. Not until the last blue-clad servingmaid had been dismissed did Martin speak of his meeting.

"Wolsey is growing concerned over the influx of heretical literature from the Continent. Too many people are taking an unholy interest in it. Some of the bishops want him to make a greater effort to stop it. Wolsey has appointed Sir Thomas to search for Lutheran heresies here in London."

Jane casually lowered her chin, hiding alertness. This was more than talk overheard at Westminster or debates at a Twelfth-night celebration. Cecily leaned forward.

"Where's Sir Thomas going to search?"

Martin ignored her question. Nicholas didn't.

"It doesn't concern you."

Cecily made a face at him.

"Why should the Cardinal tell you?" Richard asked Martin.

"Wolsey wants me to help Sir Thomas."

A chill brushed Jane's skin. Her vague apprehensions took on a new and more personal focus.

"You didn't agree, did you?" Richard said. "You'd be serving the King."

"The order didn't come from the King. It came from Wolsey."

Nicholas snorted.

"Wolsey thinks himself the king."

Martin shot Nicholas an exasperated look. He turned back to Richard.

"Your grandfather died twenty-five years ago. I've kept my oath. But I'm also indebted to Wolsey. He's never asked anything of me before. Besides, I'm a lawyer, and these heretics are criminals. They're disturbing the king's peace."

"If they keep their ideas to themselves -." Richard began.

"They don't." Martin's look raked their faces. "Listen, all of you. These ideas will fail. The Church is too powerful. With a king on the throne loyal to the Pope, a few rabble-rousing priests and illiterate Lollards will never stand against it. See that none of you become involved with these heresies." He cast a hard look at Cecily. "Not even out of idle curiosity. This family has already suffered enough over lost causes."

"You needn't worry about Nicholas," Cecily said. "Annulments come under Church jurisdiction. He'll stick to the Pope like a tick to a dog, at least until he's rid himself of Blanche."

"Hugh should take a switch to you after you're wed," Nicholas said. "You need to learn some manners."

Hugh spoke before Cecily could carry the bickering further. "You needn't be concerned for Cecily and me."

Martin turned to Richard.

"You'll be accompanying us on the searches."

Jane's breath caught.

"Father, I'd rather not."

"Nonsense. You have your future to consider. Wolsey will remember you and he has the King's ear."

"I ... I don't like it. Rather than arresting people for complaining, why can't the Church reform itself? If the accusations were groundless, no one would listen."

If only she dared cheer Richard.

"Don't be so naive," Martin said. "Men are more ready to believe a lie than the truth. As for reform, that's a matter for the Church. Our only concern rests with halting the influx."

"But are they lies? We aren't allowed to read the pamphlets."

"Are you in sympathy with the heretics?"

"Of course not. It's just that I'd like proof that they're wrong before I help arrest them."

"The Church has judged them so. That should be enough. When a client comes for legal advice, he doesn't expect to be taught the law first. He accepts my advice because I'm the authority. The Church is our authority in religious matters."

"I suppose you're right."

Jane looked away. She couldn't bear to see him in defeat. Willcotte's caution on choosing a husband echoed in her mind. Was this also the defeat of any hope that that person might be Richard?

"Then it's settled," Martin said.

"Sir Thomas is searching the Steelyard tomorrow at two o'clock," Cecily, eyes dancing, told Jane a week later. They were warming themselves by Lucy's hall fire, Jane having returned there on St. Hilary's day. "I heard Father tell Richard. Those German merchants must have a great amount of heretical writings in that building. Did you know women aren't allowed in? Not even a cook or a laundress. And every bedchamber has a suit of armor. Wouldn't it be exciting to dress as men and go?"

"Cecily!"

"Oh, Jane. Don't be so prim. We wouldn't succeed anyway. I've no chance of passing for a man. But I am going to watch outside the Steelyard tomorrow. You've got to come with me."

"Your father will see us."

"He'll be too busy. If he should, we can say we're shopping. That's why I need you."

"Oh, all right."

Jane felt as if she'd agreed to attend a wake.

That night she couldn't sleep. Her thoughts kept turning to the unsuspecting Hanse merchants. If only they could be warned. Bow Bell was tolling another hour when she suddenly remembered something. Throwing back the thick pile of covers, she shivered her way to the chest where she kept her Latin Testament. Her fingers quickly found the slip of paper, serving as a bookmark, on which Willcotte had written a name and an address. This Joseph Ansley might know how to warn the Germans.

The pale winter sun had been up for some time before Jane could slip away to Coleman Street. She found the narrow tenement squeezed between a merchant's tall house and a dank alley. The building needed paint and sagged from the peek of the thatched roof to the warped doors and leather-hinged shutters. The street entrance was locked. Jane started down the alley. Further along, an upper-story shutter banged open and slops rained down into the gutter ahead. She called quickly before the window closed.

"Is Joseph Ansley within?"

A wrinkled crone, her head half swallowed by a night cap, leaned out.

"He don't live here now."

The shutter slammed. Jane stood alone in the stench. Confounded, she retreated from the alley. She hadn't considered that Ansley might be gone.

Wandering aimlessly, she eventually found herself on Thames Street across from the Steelyard. The massive stone buildings behind their strong gray walls gave all the appearance of a fortress.

A fortress about to be breached.

Jane passed twice. The first time she walked down the steep street to the Thames, rippled by icy winds and filled with lighters ferrying goods between Queenhythe and the forest of ships tied below the bridge. She left the cries of sailors and creak of cranes and retraced her steps. An old gatekeeper stood shivering in the arched middle gate, the flaps of his woolen cap pulled over his ears. She stopped. If only she dared warn him. Even as the thought came, the man hobbled into a crude hut inside the courtyard. She could do nothing but return home.

Three hours later Jane again approached the German stronghold. Cecily rushed into the street and intercepted her.

"You're nearly late," she said, dragging Jane toward a dried-fish shop across from the Steelyard. "Father should be here any time. Pull your hood forward so he won't recognize us."

Jane readjusted her cloak, glad for the excuse to hide from Cecily's inquisitive eyes. The old porter from the morning huddled in the door of his hut. Cecily clutched Jane's arm.

"Here they come."

Jane looked up the street. A delivery man wheeling a cart of stock fish and ling hurried to the side as Sir Thomas and Martin strode past, Richard at their heels. They were followed by a double rank of city watch, pikes over their shoulders.

In the street, passers-by paused to gawk as the ominous procession marched through the Steelyard gates. The gatekeeper stumbled from his hut. Sir Thomas's brusque order rang out. The huge iron-studded doors crashed shut. The last thing Jane saw was the gatekeeper's grizzled face quivering with terror.

Mouth dry and heart thumping, she stared at the heavy gates, the echo of their closing ringing in her ears. The curious passers-by soon lost interest with the silence that followed and continued on their way. Even Cecily grew impatient as the minutes dragged and the portal remained shut. The tantalizing aromas wafting from cooked-food shops further up Thames Street began to distract her.

"Buy yourself a pasty if you want," Jane said. "I'm staying here." Nothing now would drag her away.

"You're right. They'd come out while I was gone. We'll eat later."

By the bells half-an-hour more had passed before the gates creaked open to spew out the unwelcome English visitors. Sir Thomas and Martin led the way, grim satisfaction marking their faces. Richard followed, a bulging sack over his shoulder, his expression a hard mask.

"They've arrested some of the German merchants," Cecily murmured as the double rank marched out.

Jane's heart ached. Four men, their arms bound tightly behind them, were being hustled along by the pikemen. One, barely more than a youth, had a bright blood stain on his temple. The gaping spectators parted with a ripple of whispers.

"Where will they take them?" she asked Cecily.

"Lollard's Tower most likely. Come on, let's eat. I'm starving."

"I've been home three weeks," Lucy said to Jane one afternoon in early February as they bent over their stitching, "and I've yet to see Richard Denzil. I was sure he was interested in you."

Jane caught another two inches of seam between thumb and forefinger.

"Having me in the same household for over a month seems to have changed his mind." The first acute pain had subsided to a dull bruise that only hurt when pressed, as now. "We're still friends."

"Much good that does when it's a husband you need. Stop wasting your time with the Denzils and let George and me find you one."

Jane refused to be drawn.

"I'd best hurry or I'll be late dining with them this evening."

Jane arrived with time to spare. The meal was delayed by Martin.

"Sir Thomas kept me," he said as the family gathered around the table. "A prisoner was brought down from Cambridge today, an Augustinian prior, Robert Barnes. His Christmas sermon was filled with heresy."

An icy finger brushed Jane's spine. Owen had known Robert Barnes. Martin continued.

"Wolsey ordered the university searched but nothing was found. Someone must have warned them."

Hugh spoke up.

"Where's the prior now?"

"In Lollard's Tower with the Germans."

"What will happen to him?" Jane asked with an effort at indifference.

"Wolsey will give him the same option the Germans had, recant or burn."

"Would Wolsey actually send him to the stake?" She was unable to completely hide her horror.

"He'd rather burn the writings than the readers," Martin said. "It's bishops like Tonstall and Fisher who are demanding this heretical business be stamped out, whatever the cost."

"And Sir Thomas More," Nicholas added.

Jane saw Richard flinch.

"Can't we talk of something else?"

Cecily immediately grabbed the opening.

"Do you know what that pinch-gut tailor planned to do with my wedding gown? He was going to give the work to someone other than Jem."

Jane had met Jem, according to Cecily the best journeyman tailor in London. He was a freckle-faced young man with pale skin from inferior food and not enough sun. Also, according to her, his employer kept him too poor to save the necessary monies to become a master and set up in business for himself.

"I'm not having my wedding gown ruined by some clumsy-handed dolt," Cecily said. "I told him if anyone but Jem sets a single stitch in it, I'll have Father and Hugh take him to court for breach of contract."

Hugh made a sympathetic sound. Cecily expanded on her complaint with vigor.

"Jem's employer has no skill at handling customers. His shop is a filthy disgrace, and he hasn't got enough business sense to fill a thimble. But for Jem...."

Martin lifted a sarcastic eyebrow.

"The tailor shop is untidy," Jane said to Martin as he accompanied her home through the foggy streets. "Every time I'm there I feel like sweeping the place."

"Cecily makes herself ridiculous pretending knowledge of commerce. Women have no place in business."

"I understand your wife was in business."

"That's precisely why I know." His bitter tone silenced Jane.

They were within sight of Lucy's home before Martin spoke again.

"I'd not meant to speak sharply. I find it difficult to talk of my wife." He laid a light hand on her arm. "I've missed seeing you at my table. Don't be so long in coming again."

Martin's gesture and confession threw Jane into confusion.

"I don't want to be a nuisance."

"Nonsense." His voice was itself again. He rapped on the gate. "You're always welcome. And if I can ever be of service...."

The cold February wind whistled down dirty frozen streets as Jane made her way to St. Paul's Cathedral. Today, Strove Sunday, the

German Lutherans and Robert Barnes were to recant publicly at Paul's Cross. Normally Cecily would have come with her. Now she was too busy staging her wedding to give thought to other entertainment. Jane was thankful. She couldn't have borne with Cecily's frivolous curiosity today.

She turned the corner into Bowier Row. Immediately she was caught in the stream of people jostling their way toward the Church's enclave. They carried her through the churchyard gates and across the cobbled courtyard toward the cross-adorned pulpit that gave the place its name. A large pile of brushwood waited between the pulpit and the observation gallery. Jane braced herself against the press of the crowds, against the icy wind that tugged at her cloak, against the distress that tore at her heart.

An enterprising hawker thrust hot roasted chestnuts under her nose. She jerked back in helpless anger. Her near neighbor exchanged a coin for the treat. Tearing open the soft shells with a work-blackened fingernail, he popped the nuts, one after another, between his bearded lips.

Brassy trumpets blared. People craned their necks. A wedge of stave-wielding city watch shoved into the milling masses and parted them with rough efficiency. When the crowds settled, Jane found herself at the forefront with a clear view past the human barricade ringing off the area before Paul's Cross. A second fanfare sounded. A murmur swept the audience. All eyes turned toward the breach in the spectators. Through the gap came marching all the might of the Catholic Church in England.

Cardinal Wolsey, like a ponderous scarlet mountain, led the way with measured step. In his wake marched an endless stream of prelates, coped and mitered, rich with crimson and purple and gold and pristine white. Carrying with them all the solemnity of a high mass, they took their place in the gallery far above the gaping public.

The five shackled prisoners, filthy from their imprisonment and bent under the weight of the faggots they carried, stumbled along at the rear. As they were prodded to the base of the gallery, the wind caught their stench. Jane pulled her hood close, less to shield herself from the odors than to hide her tears. If only she'd been able to warn the Germans. They, at least, might have escaped.

Her hands fisted as Bishop Fisher stepped to the pulpit. She tried unsuccessfully to blot out his scathing sermon on the consequences of sampling the devil's teaching. He finished with a thundering rebuke for the shivering captives waiting on the cobblestones.

The five wretches were pushed forward. Men plunged blazing torches into the woodpile. Fisher's voice rang out again.

"Heretic Barnes, kneel and ask forgiveness for your detestable heresies. Beg these good people to pray for your soul."

Barnes dropped to his knees. His unsteady voice could scarcely be heard over the fire's crackle. The German merchants knelt in turn. Finally, the five circled the blazing pile as ritual demanded then flung their faggots into its burning heart. As if by signal, men hurried out, loaded with bulging sacks and baskets brimming with books and pamphlets. These also were fed to the greedy flames. Soon the sharp clean smell of burning paper overpowered all other odors. While the last basketful was being reduced to fragile black ash, the prisoners knelt and were absolved of their sins.

Unable to look away, Jane watched, hand gripping hand, fighting despair.

Was Martin Denzil right that the Church, with all its corruption, would prevail? If even Steelyard merchants and Augustinian priors couldn't stand against its power, what hope had she?

She would have crept off, too sick at heart to stay longer. The press of bodies forced her to remain until the church officials took their magnificent departure. The wretched prisoners followed meekly after. The city watch holding the spectators in check broke rank and departed, their staves over their shoulders.

Jane trailed the dispersing crowds out the courtyard gate. Only once before, on an icy winter road, had she felt more alone.

Robert Barnes had saved himself from the stake. Now he sat in Fleet Prison waiting for Cardinal Wolsey to decide his future as, two weeks later, Jane and the Terrells took a Sunday stroll in the fields beyond London. The day was windless with a white sun shining faintly through cloud. The crisp air was a welcome change from the accumulated odors of past meals, smoky fires and unwashed bodies trapped behind doors tightly shut against winter.

Lucy's two boys dashed away across the snow-crusted grass to join their friends in a game of ball.

"I'm glad Cecily persuaded you to stay until after Lent," Lucy said to Jane as they ambled along.

"She's got no one else to make her wedding lists." Jane smiled. "She's discovered a use for reading and writing. I'd teach her if there were time. She's planned such a big wedding ... I don't know how she'll manage to get everything done."

"You should be planning your own wedding."

"Cecily can be organized when she wants to," Jane said, skirting a icy patch.

Lucy wasn't to be put off. She followed Jane around the patch.

"I also wish you'd quit wasting your time with Martin Denzil. Why you allow him to drag you off to Westminster ... or to visit the Mores...?"

"Don't be so hard on the girl, wife," George broke in. "Important people frequent Sir Thomas's board. Jane might come away with a nobleman for a husband. You'd like that."

"If only, " Lucy said. She turned back to Jane. "How you can abide Martin Denzil. He's such a difficult man."

"I admire him. I can't explain. Perhaps it's because he's kept that oath all these years. His intentions are good."

"I'd like to know his intentions toward you."

Jane shrugged off the uncomfortable memory of Martin's hand on her arm.

"Don't be silly, Lucy. He's old enough to be my father."

"You're the silly one if you think age has anything to do with it. You should be looking for someone with position and money. Martin Denzil has little wealth, no position, and three grown children."

As they talked, they drew near the butts on Moor field. On a summer day the place would have been alive with young men fulfilling their military obligations and producing an army of deadly long-bowmen that, in times past, had rained destruction on the French. Today only the hardiest souls were out with bow and arrow. George stopped to watch. Lucy and Jane halted with him.

"Isn't that one of the Denzil brothers?" Lucy asked pointing to another watcher.

Jane, having seen Nicholas earlier and swallowed disappointment that it wasn't Richard, nodded.

Nicholas must have spotted them, for he waved and strode over. Jane saw Lucy's eyes widen with interest as he took her off to buy some hot chicken feet from a nearby hawker. She sucked the first joint clean and spit the bone out onto the pale frozen grass.

"You look pleased," she said.

"I am." Nicholas broke into a grin. "Blanche came by yesterday. She's having our marriage contract annulled."

"You must be relieved."

"She's going to pay the costs," he said with a smug look. "I knew she would if I waited long enough."

Blanche might be as fortunate to be free of Nicholas as he was to be free of her.

"Now you won't have to hold to the Pope so firmly."

"Cecily was talking to hear herself. I'm all for reform. By the saints, something needs to be done. Wolsey and his blood-sucking priests want to tax us to the last penny to keep themselves and the Pope in pocket. But I'll have nothing to do with Barnes and his kind. They're preaching anarchy. A third of my orders comes from the Church. If the heretics had their way, why, it would ruin me."

Mid-March brought a fresh warm wind which broke winter's icy grip. Almost overnight London's hard, snow-packed fields were transformed into soft earth, puddles and soggy grass. Mid-March also brought Jane's twentieth birthday. Lucy acknowledged the day with a sigh and shake of her head.

Then Lent, with its tiresome diet of fish, ended. All over Christendom people were kneeling in confession in preparation for Easter communion. In previous months the priest had not examined Jane closely. He wouldn't be so lax with Easter duty. What if, under strenuous questioning, she let slip her Lollard beliefs? Since she no longer believed the priest had any power to grant forgiveness, she chose a simple and novel solution. Locking the chamber door, she knelt and confessed her sins directly to God. That done, she packed and moved to the Denzil home. With the wedding only days away Cecily had begged her presence. The Denzils would believe she had already made her confession. They would be right.

The following morning Jane joined them in the Easter service with a peaceful mind. Her single twinge of conscience came because she lacked the courage to tell the Denzils they also had no need of a priest.

CHAPTER 15 – SPRING, 1526

Two days before the wedding Jane sat at a table in the Denzil hall, quill in hand. Cecily's list lay before her. As Cecily paced feverishly about naming completed tasks, Jane ticked them. The bride chest was bursting with napery. The house, smelling of lye soap and scented rushes, was decked for celebration. The kitchen bustled with preparations for the wedding banquet. The bridal gloves waited in Cecily's chamber. The guests had been invited. The church was arranged and the priest would be waiting at the door.

"Have you marked that the cushions were delivered?" Cecily asked, peering at the list.

"Yes, right here." Jane glanced at the new padding on benches and settle. "The hall looks much more homey."

"It lacks one thing." Cecily straightened and her mouth set.

Curious, Jane followed as she took two menservants up to an attic storeroom and fetched down a large chest. Back in the hall Cecily threw open the lid. Jane watched in wonder as the servants lifted out and hung a large tapestry. The jewel-like colors of the vibrant hunting scene brought the room to life.

"My mother loved this," Cecily said. "Father took it down when she died. He'll probably be angry, I don't care. I'll not have my wedding banquet celebrated in a barn."

Jane was alone in the hall when Martin arrived home. His greeting smile froze when he saw the tapestry. He paled.

"Cecily wanted to brighten the hall for the banquet," Jane said.

"I gave that to Clare when Cecily was born." His voice was gruff. "She'd always wanted one. It seemed such a small thing after...." He cast a furtive glance at Jane.

"It's a beautiful picture."

"I took it down when she died. The memories were too painful." His eyes grew wet.

"You must have loved your wife," she said in surprise. She'd assumed that Martin's marriage had been one of convenience.

"Yes, I did, very much. But it's too late."

He stalked off. Baffled, Jane watched him go.

The tapestry stayed and Cecily did not receive the expected rebuke.

The day before the wedding began well with delicious aromas wafting up from the kitchen.

In midmorning Cecily's intricately sculpted wedding ring vanished. The house was turned upside down but to no avail. The next catastrophe arrived in the shape of a dozen scrawny chickens rather than plump geese. The cook boxed the delivery boy's ears. Cecily threatened to serve him up on a platter if the geese were not forthcoming. The hired minstrels provided the final blow. Their leader had caught the pox.

"All we lack," Cecily wailed, "is to hear that St. Michael's has burned to the ground."

Richard vowed to find minstrels if it took all night. Hugh arrived just in time to give Cecily the audience she needed. Jane and the old housekeeper began restoring the house to its original immaculate order.

They finished just as the boy returned with geese. Soon after, Nicholas arrived with the missing ring. He had spotted it in the shop mixed with the jewelry for sale. By the time the pale-gold wedding dress was delivered, Cecily's nerves had begun to calm. Shortly before Martin arrived home for the evening meal, Richard returned with news that he'd found other minstrels.

Relieved that the day was ending well, Jane slipped into her place at the dining table in a much happier mood. Judging from the light banter, the rest of the table felt the same.

Halfway through the meal Hugh, his look tender, turned to Cecily eating beside him.

"I've brought you a wedding present."

Cecily eyed the round leather bag he'd deposited on a corner stool.

"Is that it?"

"Wait and see."

Jane had never seen Cecily finish a meal so quickly.

"You can give me my present now."

Hugh laughed.

"All right. Go sit there, close your eyes, and hold out your hands."

Cecily perched on the edge of a bench while Hugh fetched the bag. Stopping beside her, he upended it over her cupped hands. Jane gasped as a cascade of coins overflowed Cecily's hands and fell clinking into her lap. Cecily's eyes popped open.

"It must be a fortune," she squeaked, gaping at the glittering pile.

"Fifty-six pounds, four shillings and a penny."

"Where did you get it?"

"I saved it."

"But what's it for, Hugh?"

"So you can go into business."

Jane heard Martin suck in his breath. Hugh continued.

"Only have a care you use it wisely. With a wife to support now, I'll never again be able to save so much."

Cecily glanced from the money filling her lap to Hugh, an empty bag dangling limply from his hands. A deep sob wrenched from her.

"No one has ever done such a wonderful thing for me. Oh, Hugh."

She lunged to her feet, sending coins flying, to throw her arms around his neck and weep noisily against his jerkin.

Gradually the tinging of falling coins and Cecily's joyful sobbing quieted. Jane heard the hard scrape of a chair being shoved back. Martin was standing.

"You're a fool, Hugh Peterman. She'll waste every penny."

Jane saw the quick hurt on Cecily's face. Hugh tightened his arms about her.

"It's my money and my decision."

"This could be the ruin of your marriage."

Face haggard, Martin turned and stumped from the room. Only when the sound of his heavy tread faded did Jane realize she'd been holding her breath.

Cecily wailed.

"My money! Oh, help me pick it up."

Tension slackened into laughter. Jane found herself scrambling after the money with Nicholas, Richard and Hugh. Eagerly they sifted through rushes and peered under furniture. As quickly as the coins were collected, Cecily stuffed them into the leather bag.

"Fifty-six pounds, four shillings," she announced at last.

"That's enough," Richard said from under the dining table.

"You can't quit until you find my penny."

A moment later Jane, walking the floor, spotted the missing coin inside a table leg. She dropped to her knees and reached for it just as Richard, under the table, also grabbed. One moment they were laughing and tussling over the coin, their heads behind the draping linen tablecloth. The next Richard's expression was intense. His face was close to hers, so close that.... Jane's heart contracted.

He's going to kiss me, right here under the table.

Then, inexplicably, his look hardened. Before she could do more than breath his name, he jerked away. Jane stumbled to her feet, the coin clutched in a hand warm with the touch of Richard's fingers. Mutely she returned the piece to Cecily.

"Richard," Cecily said, gazing from the last coin to Hugh, "I want a necklace made with this one."

She received no reply. Richard had disappeared.

After the wedding Jane returned to Lucy's. Cecily no longer needed her, and Richard was again clearly avoiding her. She realized, with a pang, that she'd stayed too long in London. Had Richard kissed her, and knowing he'd searched the Steelyard with reluctance, her visit might have turned out differently. He hadn't, and the lambs would be growing big at Wynnfield. At home a hundred activities would demand her time and counter her restlessness. She would go home. Nevertheless she delayed sending the message to Willcotte. She let day follow day, held by the hope that Richard might call. Martin visited once and Cecily came twice to speculate on how to use her money. Even Nicholas came.

"Why haven't you been to see us?" he said as he settled beside Jane in Lucy's hall. "The evenings are boring now. All Father and

Richard do is talk law. Cecily has got Hugh teaching her to read. I might as well be living in a school."

Unexpectedly he reached for her hand. His own, narrow and clean-fingered, was very like Richard's. But it wasn't Richard's. Jane let her hand lie passively in his.

"You have lovely fingers. You should let me craft you a ring."

She waited, saying nothing.

"Actually, I came to ask you to marry me. I've grown fond of you, and I should be free from Blanche any day now. With my goldsmith shop and your manor...."

Jane hoped her surprise, and disappointment, wasn't showing on her face. Already Nicholas smelled the profits. Regardless of the affection she did have for him, she couldn't abide his petty greed. She slipped her hand gently free.

"I'm honored, but I must refuse."

"I can give you more time."

Jane shook her head.

"When I wed it won't be for financial considerations or even friendship. I'm sure London has lots of young women who'd welcome a proposal from you."

"Well, yes." Nicholas reddened. "In fact, I recently met one, a stonemason's widow. Don't misunderstand, I wanted to ask you first. But I thought... that is...." He floundered to a halt.

So she was merely the first on his list. No doubt in a week's time he'd have conveniently forgotten he'd ever asked her. Jane swallowed her pique.

"Tell me about her."

Somewhat embarrassed, Nicholas complied.

"She's a fetching little thing with a mass of dark-honey hair. Her husband left her a tidy sum. She does have two daughters, but any sons would be mine."

Jane sat brooding after Nicholas left. Why couldn't it have been Richard? That same day she sent the message to Howard Willcotte which would end her time in London.

On the afternoon before her departure Jane set out to bid farewell to London. She'd come to love this bustling, vibrant city. There was an excitement, a challenge, a quickening of the blood and mind in living here. She would miss it.

Returning along Grasse Street, she spotted Hugh limping ahead. She called his name. Only as two people turned did she realize he wasn't alone. The plainly gowned young woman glanced up at Hugh.

"It's all right, Madge," he said. Then, to Jane, "This is my sister."

Jane recalled Cecily's ill humor at the suggestion that Hugh might have contact with his family. She smiled in an effort to reassure Madge. Hugh handed a coin to his sister.

"I'll see you next week."

Madge disappeared in the busy street. Hugh turned to Jane.

"Please don't mention her to the Denzils, including Cecily."

Jane fell into step with him.

"Is she your only sister?"

"I've one more living. And a brother. Madge is the only one I see regularly. She was a baby when I joined the Denzil household. I managed to apprentice her to a baker. She's doing well."

"You're making her a businesswoman too," Jane said. "You were so generous to give Cecily that money."

"Actually, my motives were purely selfish."

Jane shook her head in disbelief. He must had saved for years to pour that fortune into Cecily's lap.

"I've wanted but two things in life," Hugh said, "to be a lawyer and to wed Cecily. I've got them both now. Unfortunately, getting and keeping are different matters. I know she doesn't love me as I love her. Having a business will make her more content in our marriage."

She stared at him in astonishment.

"You refuse to gamble a few pence on a dice game. But you'll risk a fortune and your life's happiness on a frivolous girl."

He smiled.

"I do expect to win. Despite all her complaints, Cecily is loyal, a particular Denzil trait. She also has a lot of her mother in her."

Jane side-stepped a puddle.

"What was Clare Denzil like? Was owning a goldsmith shop worth the bitterness it created in Martin?"

"The fault was his as much as hers. Shortly after I joined the household, Martin accidentally killed a nobleman's son. He was acquitted, but the nobleman was powerful ... and vindictive. He got Martin exiled. Clare fought for two years to get the decision reversed. Eventually Wolsey intervened on their behalf. During his exile all Clare had to support herself and her babies was the shop."

They halted as two men carrying a massive roasted pig crossed their path.

"When Martin returned, he'd changed." Hugh said as they walked on. "He was moody, irascible. His attitude toward the shop had changed too. He'd always had the nobleman's disdain for trade. When they were first married, he'd tolerated it because it provided a good living while he established his practice. After he came back from Germany, he pressed Clare to sell. She was afraid to. She loved him, but she'd discovered a side of him she didn't know and couldn't trust. The shop was security for herself and her children."

"How very sad."

"You're fond of him, aren't you," Hugh said as they turned up Lucy's street.

Jane nodded.

"Do you plan to marry him?"

She halted abruptly.

"I do not."

"Richard will be relieved. He believes his father's courting you. It's been tormenting him for months."

"So that's why he avoids me. And I've been waiting...." Tears for the many wasted opportunities blurred Jane's vision. Because Richard wasn't in the narrow, shadowed street she rounded on Hugh. "You can tell that ... that idiot ... if he's got so little sense ... he deserves all the misery he's made for himself."

Hugh proved to be a prompt messenger. Jane and the Terrells had scarcely started their evening meal when Richard burst in, an agitated maidservant in pursuit.

"I tried to stop him, mum."

Lucy waved the servant away. Her look said that she had no intention of having Richard stopped. At sight of his eager, determined expression, Jane felt her face heat. She quickly bent her head over her food. Richard halted at her elbow.

"Jane, may I speak to you?"

Jane, heart thumping, kept her head down.

"Can't you see I'm eating?" She shoved a bite of meat into her mouth.

"Please, Jane." His voice was an agonized whisper.

She looked up. Richard's face was scarlet.

"What you told Hugh, was it true?"

"If it hadn't been I wouldn't have said it."

Richard's eyes blazed. He took a deep breath. All at once Jane was terrified of what he might say before her family. She dropped her spoon.

"We can talk in the hall."

Although the outside world was still wearing blue twilight, the hall was dressed in black when Jane, carrying a lighted candle, entered with Richard. She set the taper down on a side table and turned to face him. Surprisingly her voice sounded normal.

"What is so important that you rush in like a madman and interrupt my meal?"

Richard threw his cap onto a nearby chest and caught her hands.

"Jane, I love you."

"You're a dolt, Richard Denzil, and a fool and an idiot."

She jerked her hands free and moved away. Richard followed.

"I know. Can't you love me anyway?"

She halted, her back to the window. The dusky light reaching in across her shoulder lit his ardent expression.

"I could try."

Jane had time only to see joy flood his face before his arms were around her. Instinctively she nestled against his shoulder. When Owen had left, she had thought she'd never love again. Now, realizing how good the feel of another man's arms could be, she knew it was possible.

"Will you marry me, Jane?"

She stiffened and broke free to put the table and bright candle between them.

"I can't, Richard."

"I thought you cared for me."

"I do. But, I'm afraid." The words came without conscious thought.

"Afraid?"

"I loved a man once. I defied my father, everyone, to wed where my heart lay. When we at last gained permission, he left me to serve God." The flickering candle flame, Richard's tall attentive figure, the long room overfilled with dim furniture, all blurred before Jane's eyes. "I couldn't bear to be hurt like that again."

Richard was around the table and drawing her back into his arms.

"Please, sweeting, don't cry. I can't stand to see you unhappy."

She hid her face against his shoulder. She hadn't intended to tell him about Owen.

"It happened a long time ago," she said, trying to restore the seal of silence.

Richard tightened his hold on her.

"I'll never leave you."

"But I'm leaving." His muscles tensed. She looked up. "I planned to come later this evening and bid everyone farewell."

"Where are you going?"

"Home to Wynnfield."

"But you can't. Not now."

She slipped from his hold. Turning away from his pleading look, she picked up his cap and ran a fingertip around the enameled brooch pinning up the brim.

"I've already been away too long. The servant to accompany me home arrived today. We leave tomorrow."

"Will you come back?"

"I'll return after the harvests. I can't before."

"That will be an eternity."

Jane crossed to him, reached up, and put the cap on his dark head. On impulse, she pulled his face down and kissed him lightly.

"Write to me and the summer will speed more quickly."

CHAPTER 16 – SUMMER, 1526

Richard proved a more faithful correspondent than Owen had. Although the bailiff linked Jane's happier mood to the frequent arrival of letters all addressed in the same somewhat large, lacy script, he said nothing. That the correspondent was a man had been obvious. When he'd handed her the first letter, given him by the common carrier, her color had heightened. Despite this, he suspected that Jane's heart was not irrevocably committed to her London suitor. She had written regularly to Owen Alton. The flow of letters this young man received was far less steady.

For all his astute observations, Howard Willcotte couldn't know that, one night in late May, Jane lit her bedchamber fireplace and fed Owen's letters to the flames. She stirred the pages until the last one curled to ash. When she finished, she felt as empty as a house stripped of furnishings and swept out to await a new occupant.

The space in her chest where she had kept Owen's letters gradually filled with Richard's. He wrote of designs he'd sketched for Nicholas, of tedious trials he'd attended at Westminster, of Cecily's decision to use her money forming a partnership with her tailor Jem, of how he longed for Jane's return. In June he mentioned that Nicholas planned to wed a young widow before summer's end, that Sir Thomas had made no recent searches for Lutheran sympathizers, that Wolsey was noticing him as his father wanted.

At the end of the month, on St. Peter's and Paul's eve, an event happened which wiped Richard and all else from Jane's mind. On that day, she was spinning beside a window in the blue parlor when the bailiff strode in.

"Back from Hensford so soon?" Only after she spoke did she notice Willcotte's grim face. She straightened. "Is something amiss?"

He swept off his cap and ran a rough hand through his fading russet hair.

"Jack's been arrested."

Her thread snapped.

"On what charge?"

"Heresy." Willcotte bent onto a stool. "Walter the tiler told the priest that Jack said the font was a stinking tarn."

"Where's Jack now?"

"In Hensford jail. The priest is holding him there till the bishop arrives."

"Could he escape?"

"The place is too secure."

Jane sank back, fighting tears.

"They'll force him to recant like Robert Barnes and the Germans."

"They'll try."

"You think he won't?"

For the first time Jane noticed the hard spark in Willcotte's eyes.

"Jack's changed in the last year. Your scriptures put fire in his blood."

A new and very personal terror gripped her.

"What of the translations? Where are they?"

Willcotte's finger went to his lip.

"The priest found them."

For a moment she couldn't breath.

"Don't be afraid," he said hurriedly. "No one knows where Jack got them."

"What if they press him to tell?"

"He won't name you."

Jane looked out the window at the pleasance where bees and butterflies dipped over the colorful blossoms. She was ashamed that, with Jack in such danger, she should be thinking of herself. She dragged up a weak smile.

"Do you remember the night I waited while you dug the peddler out of the smoke house?"

"We succeeded."

"Yes, we did."

She knotted the broken thread with unsteady fingers and resumed spinning.

After Willcotte left Jane, he stopped on the dais and leaned weakly against a chair back. He'd lived with the danger of being a Lollard for so long he wore it with hardly more thought than he gave his hose or jerkin. He merely guarded his tongue, had little public contact with other true believers and, as much as possible, stayed clear of the priests. He'd even cleverly denied himself a family that the Church could hold hostage for his compliance. Even so, life had snared him.

On hearing of Jack's arrest he'd remembered the translations and turned cold with fear. All unthinking, through them, he'd brought his young mistress, as dear to him as a daughter, into peril. Only his trust in Jack provided reassurance. He fervently prayed that his trust would not prove groundless.

Three weeks passed before the bishop reached Hensford. Jane retained little memory of how she spent the days. Apart from attending mass at the village church, for this was no time to be absent, she barely left the manor, clinging to the familiar routine as an antidote to anxiety.

When word reached Wynnfield that the bishop had come, Willcotte rode into Hensford to hear the news. He returned in the afternoon. Jane was in the accounts room working on the books. He shut the door and bent onto a stool. Laying her nib aside, Jane braced herself.

"Gossip is flying like chaff at threshing time," Willcotte said.

"What's being said about the translations?"

"If you disregard that a demon in the shape of a black cat delivered them to Jack, the most common belief is that he got them from a passing Lollard. That's what he told the bishop. It's close enough to the truth."

Jane released her pent breath.

"How is Jack?"

"He preached to the bishop for two hours and called him a wolf in sheep's clothing." Willcotte's tone held admiration. "There's to be a full inquiry at the guildhall in two days."

An awful weight settled upon Jane. She had given Jack the scriptures and they'd led him to this.

"What will become of his wife and children?"

Willcotte gripped his knees, his look stolid.

"Pray he has the faith to leave them in God's hands."

Hensford's guildhall was second only in importance to St. Sebastian Church which it faced across Market Square. The impressive brick building with its tall clock tower loomed over Jane as she waited for the bailiff to return from stabling their mounts.

Normally the square of the small prosperous town would be alive with activity - shopkeepers and hawkers crying their wares, housewives strolling past with loaded market baskets, children playing tag across the hard-packed dirt, servants gossiping while they drew water from the town well, the resonant clanging of the blacksmith's hammer.

On this day, marketing was forgotten, water fetching could wait and silence hung over the smith's forge. The townsfolk were more interested in the trial being held in the guildhall. Not since two passing beggars had been hailed into court for stealing and mutilating one of the local children had a trial stirred up more attention. Seeking to increase their takings, the beggars had severed the child's hands, making her such a pitiable object that even the tightest purses would be opened. When they received a well-deserved death sentence, the packed courtroom had cheered.

Jane shuddered with foreboding at the thought of today's judgment. She glanced back through the stragglers hurrying toward the guildhall, searching for Willcotte. He was just coming. The hour hand in the clock tower moved. Chimes began to ring. Hensford's first heresy trial began.

She followed Willcotte as he shouldered his way through the rabble clustered at the guildhall entrance. The long magnificent hall was crowded. The bailiff ejected an apprentice from the end of a bench not far from the entry so Jane could sit. He might have secured a better seat near the dais but, given the heresy trials he'd mentioned witnessing as a youth, she sensed he felt safer with the door at his back. Jane also was content to remain at a distance. But for her sense of responsibility, she wouldn't have come. All around her waited the same curious, casual crowd she'd experienced at Paul's Cross.

The bishop, fat as a Michaelmas pig, sat in a high-backed chair, dominating the dais. His gouty foot was propped before him on a purple cushion.

Beside the dais Jack towered over the guards to which he was chained. Jane had expected him to be as broken as Robert Barnes. Instead he stood squarely, head lifted, eyes closed, black-bearded face intense. She couldn't tear her gaze away. Here was Samson, hands on the pillars of the Philistines, preparing to die. The revelation buoyed her up. She sat more straightly, better prepared for the tiler's damning testimony and that of other witnesses which followed. She was completely unprepared for Elizabeth Weaver's testimony.

From her single meeting with Jack's wife, Jane had retained an image of a perfectly groomed woman. Now, standing before the bishop, Elizabeth exhibited carelessness in a strand of escaping hair, an unknotted tie, a cap that didn't match her gown. In a flat voice she described how Jack had taught their children the Lord's prayer in English, how he'd demanded she listen as he read from his scriptures, how he'd kept her from confession saying the priest had no power over sins.

The bishop put one final question.

"Where did your husband get the translations?"

The query came so unexpectedly, Jane's heart stopped. Her muscles bunched for running. Willcotte's hand caught her shoulder, holding her firmly in her seat. She waited without breathing to hear her name.

"He was sent them by a Lollard preacher."

Jane's eyelids slid shut. Now Willcotte's grip was bracing her up. When she grew strong again, his hand lifted. She glanced up to see him unobtrusively wiping his brow.

"How could Elizabeth Weaver do such a thing?" Jane said in horror as she jogged home beside the bailiff.

"My mother turned on my father like that," Willcotte said. "He recanted. Afterward he died of prison fever. My mother hanged herself in remorse. The priest gave him a Christian burial. He wouldn't touch her. I buried her myself. I sat by the grave, shovel in my hand, and laughed till I cried for the irony of it."

Jack's burning was set for August second. Jane found black humor in the date. The day before, the Church would be celebrating Lammas, commemorating St. Peter's miraculous delivery from prison. Jack the Weaver could count on no such release.

"You needn't attend," Willcotte said to Jane as they talked in the courtyard.

Jane squinted against the sun as she looked up at him.

"Will you go?"

Willcotte nodded, short, somber.

"Then I'm going. If Jack has the courage to die, at least I can be there."

The day following Lammas, Jane and Willcotte rode into Hensford to witness Jack's execution. Already a crowd marked the spot outside the town's west gate. Willcotte reined up some distance short and helped her dismount. He stepped off the track and tied their horses to the low branch of an oak. All around, fields of ripening barley bent under the effects of last night's rain. The ground underfoot was soft, and the grass soaked Jane's skirt tail as she waited on the verge.

She took note of the pitch barrel and great pile of rain-darkened faggots stacked at the edge of the road between where they stood and the gathering townsfolk. Jane glanced around for a stake. Willcotte, joining her, must have read her thought. He spoke in a low, matter-of-fact voice.

"Likely he'll be stood in the barrel. Setting a stake is a lot of trouble for one."

Jane's stomach lurched.

Gradually the crowd increased. Jane and the bailiff had been standing beside the road for some time when a white-haired old man on a piebald nag came shambling up. Willcotte stepped out to intercept him. The newcomer dismounted stiffly.

"I wasn't sure you'd come." Willcotte's quiet words reached Jane.

"I couldn't let him go alone."

"I'll tie your horse with ours."

The man glanced at Jane as if noticing her for the first time. She returned his look, held by his amber eyes. His soul shown out of them, pure and warm. All at once Jane knew who the old man was. Had the sun been shining to turn his hair to silver, she would have recognized him instantly. He'd been the fifth man at the stream, the Lollard weaver from Newmarket to whom Jack had been apprenticed.

"I'll see to his horse," she said.

She took the reins and moved away before the bailiff could protest. She had no wish to stand exchanging names and pleasantries at such a time.

Willcotte and the old Lollard were talking softly, their heads bent close, when Jane noticed several men bustle out of the city gate. They attacked the pile of faggots, sorting the rain-soaked sticks from the usable ones. Jane approached the bailiff and his companion. Almost she couldn't speak the words.

"I think it's time."

Both men looked past her toward the increasing activity. The old weaver turned his amber gaze on Jane.

"I'm Benedict Shore, Mistress Horne. Howard tells me you've never seen a burning. Are you sure you want to stay?"

The compassion in his lined face canceled out the presumption of his question.

"I have to."

The procession that brought Jack to his death was a disorderly affair. The constable's man led the way, shouting for people to stand back and swinging his staff to send a passing dog in yelping retreat. Next came the Hensford constable. Four liveried town watch followed him herding Jack like a giant tame bear. The bishop hobbled after, leaning for support on the Hensford priest and wincing with pain at every step. Lastly, two hastily recruited laborers tramped along swinging a large, low-backed chair between them while a wide-eyed baker's apprentice trotted at their heels, a stool gripped in one hand and the bishop's purple cushion in the other.

As the bishop took his seat, Jack was clumsily hefted into the barrel. The crowd settled. Jane found herself between Willcotte and Benedict Shore at the fringe. Her stomach twisted more tightly every moment. Jack stood without moving, his face white as his linen shirt, while men stacked the drier faggots around his barrel. The usable pieces barely reached midway.

Jane's nails dug into her palms.

How much wood was needed to end a man's life?

After much conferring and a fresh search through the previously discarded pile, one of the watch scuttled into Hensford. More waiting.

Jane noticed Jack had opened his eyes. She also realized that Benedict Shore had unobtrusively moved to stand directly across from him. What was Jack thinking? Very likely he was trying not to think. Jane willed her own mind to blankness, to estimating how many days of drying sun would be needed before the surrounding fields could be harvested.

The constable's man returned with a hunchbacked wood seller and his cart of firewood. After a brief exchange, the cart was unloaded and the bundles stacked high about Jack. Straw was stuffed between the faggots and a blazing torch brought up. The bishop, obviously thinking more of the responsibility of his office than the pain in his toe joints, heaved himself up. A hush fell over the gathering.

"Heretic Weaver, consider your peril. Recant while you can. Return to the Church and save your soul."

Jack turned his eyes to the bishop. His brow glistened with sweat.

"My soul is already in God's hands. I pray God to forgive you ... and to lead everyone here to the truth that I've found."

Jack continued, his voice growing stronger. Jane knew his words would be unfamiliar to the bulk of the crowd, laymen and churchmen alike. But she recognized them. She herself had translated those verses from Latin into English.

From the edge of her vision Jane saw the bishop jerk a hand. The torch bearer plunged the fiery end into the waiting straw. She focused on Jack's face, trying desperately to stop time, to shut out thought. The crackle of flames and the sight and smell of drifting smoke broke through her defenses. The moment had come. She froze in horror, her skin running with chill sweat. Unable to move, she watched the flames lick at the wood, lick at the barrel, leap up in devilish, devouring tongues to lick at Jack's white shirt. The air filled with smoke, with the odor of singed hair and roasting meat. The scriptures on Jack's lips were replaced with gasps, groans and then deep, choking screams. He was clothed in a yellow dancing cloak of flames.

Jane whipped round and pushed blindly through the people behind her. She stumbled across the uneven ground toward her horse. Her stomach jerked. She swallowed frantically, tasting acid.

Even as she struggled to free the reins, Jack's cries faded and died. Jane heard them still. Then Willcotte was there and the reins were free. She felt his hands under her foot and then found herself in the saddle. Jamming her feet into the stirrups, she jerked her horse's head around and sent him galloping for home.

A quarter-of-a-mile down the track, just after it entered the forest, Jane pulled her horse to a halt and dismounted. When Willcotte and Benedict Shore caught up with her, she was braced against an oak tree, retching.

Jane took a final sip of ale from Master Shore's clay bottle before handing it back to the old man seated on the fallen log beside her. Willcotte leaned against a nearby ash tree.

"I'm all right now."

She brushed another tear away. If only she could stop crying. The air around her was scented with wild flowers and bird song filled the silence. Jane still smelled scorched flesh and heard Jack's screams. The weight of her guilt was smothering her. She swung to face the old Lollard.

"Did Master Willcotte tell you I gave Jack those scriptures? But for me, he'd be alive today."

Benedict Shore shook his head.

"Jack was arrested because of what I'd taught him years ago. Only after that did they find your scriptures. The translations didn't bring him to his death. The Church did. It will be the one to answer in the final judgment. Your scriptures gave him the strength to face death courageously."

She desperately wanted to believe Master Shore. But Jack was dead, hideously and forever dead. Benedict Shore continued.

"Suppose you hadn't given Jack the scriptures. Tomorrow he might have died of a sickness or been killed by a falling tree or struck down by robbers. This way Jack made his death count. People will remember why he died. They'll be forced to question. Nothing the Church can do will change that. Be proud you helped him win."

The rain that fell the night before Jack died was the last August saw. In the sunny days that followed, the fields turned from mottled-green to yellow-brown and golden-white. Harvesters swarmed over the countryside, sickles in hand, cutting and tying and gathering. At Wynnfield, Jane worked as hard as any, pathetically eager for distraction. Gradually, pondering Benedict Shore's words, she realized he was right. She'd not been to blame for Jack's death. Nevertheless, his words did little to rid her of nightmares or lighten the weight of responsibility she felt toward Jack's children.

The very day Jack died, the Church confiscated his property. Elizabeth Weaver, witnessing her cherished possessions being tossed carelessly into the yard, ranted and clawed at the constable's men. When they tried to evict her, she clung to the door post with a grip of iron. The men were forced to tear her fingers loose before they could lock the cottage against her. Immediately she fell into a fit, oblivious to the terrified cries of her son and daughter.

Willcotte, riding over the next day, found her sitting in a daze beside the feather mattress, cooking pots and spinning wheel. With the help of the children and a Wynnfield cart, he moved Elizabeth and her belongings into a hut just outside of Hensford. Jane paid half-a-year's rent and provided them with a goat and a few hens. She also, from time to time, sent a small sack of oats or peas or a round of cheese. The gifts eased her conscience. The news she received in return was disquieting.

The eviction had unsettled Elizabeth's mind. She appeared to have only two realities in her collapsed world. One was her spinning wheel. She would sit by the hour lulled into a near trance by the soothing monotony of the work, oblivious even to her hunger or that of her children. The other reality, which sent her cowering with terror into the nearest corner, was the specter that she alone could see hovering behind her left shoulder.

August drifted toward September and Elizabeth remained unchanged.

"The townsfolk are calling her half-witted," Willcotte told Jane one afternoon on his return from Hensford. "At least the children have their wits about them."

Jane looked around at her comfortable hall. She pictured again the dark bare hut in which Jack's family now lived.

"How will they manage through the winter? Little Jack is barely nine and his sister even younger." She pressed a hand wearily to her temple. "They might stay here during the worst months."

Inwardly Jane shrank from the thought of having Elizabeth Weaver under her roof. Yet, for the children's sake....

"I doubt her mind could stand another move." Willcotte said. He stroked his upper lip. "You need to get away from your worries, not bring them into your household. Having Lucy at Horne Hall for a time will give you something new to think on. You might even consider spending Nativity in London with her."

"I couldn't do that. What if I'm needed here?"

When Lucy arrived a few days later, she took one look at Jane and decided she was pining for Richard. She immediately insisted Jane return to London with her after Michaelmas. Jane was too emotionally exhausted to resist long. With twinges of guilt about leaving Jack's children, she gave in.

Jane had given Richard little thought in the last two months. She always received a letter from him with mild surprise. Answering them was nearly impossible. He belonged to another existence. His letters were filled with his attempts to juggle Nicholas's demands for designs and his father's expectations in the law, with news of Nicholas's recent marriage and Cecily's dress-making business. In comparison to her storm-tossed life, Richard's appeared as peaceful as a quiet cove. Then, a letter she received in mid-September reminded her that even his calm inlet contained treacherous shoals for her. Wolsey was growing concerned over a new and more dangerous flood of heretical literature from the Continent.

This particular letter arrived the day she agreed to return to London with Lucy. That night the dream came again.

As on other nights since Jack's death, she found herself standing beside the Hensford road watching the flames lick at his white shirt. She saw him lift his hands in supplication as he had when he'd begged for the scripture translations. As before, Elizabeth Weaver drifted through the smoke toward her husband, her finger pointed accusingly.

Then Jane's dream took a different shape. For the first time, she noticed that Elizabeth was dragging a shovel. Jane suddenly found herself looking out of Jack's eyes. In terror, she stared at the face of the approaching woman. It was Richard's face! He smiled tenderly at her from above his voluptuous woman's body. His lips parted.

"It'll soon be over, sweeting. I'll take care of you. See, I've even brought a shovel."

Jane struggled against the engulfing smoke, fighting for breath, a scream welling up in her throat.

She awoke sitting upright in bed, drenched in cold sweat, gasping and shaking violently. From the onset of the nightmares, she'd taken to sleeping with the bed curtains thrown open to the moonlight. She forced herself to concentrate on the dark, reassuring furniture-shapes in her chamber, the shapes of reality. Gradually the pounding of her heart lessened and her shivering stopped. She lay back against her pillows, willing her mind to forget the terror. But try as she would, she couldn't completely blot out the image of Richard's face or the echo of his words.

CHAPTER 17 – AUTUMN, 1526

A week after Michaelmas, Jane rode into London at Lucy's side. She had purposely not told Richard she was coming. She didn't want to find him waiting at Lucy's door. He would expect to pick up their relationship where she'd dropped it six months earlier. That wasn't possible. Too much had happened in the interim. She needed a few days' grace in which to resolve her ambivalent feelings before facing him.

After three days she could delay visiting the Denzils no longer. In midmorning, confident that Richard would be absent, she walked over to Guthran Lane. She entered the courtyard to find Martin Denzil on his knees packing straw around a rosebush. She stopped behind him.

"I'll have to visit in summer and see your roses in bloom."

His grizzled head twisted up, glad surprise on his face.

"I didn't know you were in London." Martin came stiffly to his feet, dusted his knees and hands "Are you wintering with your sister again?"

"Part of it." She looked at the bare bushes. "What colors are they?"

"These are various pinks," he said, waving at the bushes he'd just mulched. "Those beyond are dark red. That bush produces scarlet flowers."

"What of the ones on the trellis?"

"White as fresh milk, my father's favorite." He bent to retrieve his basket of mulching. "I've no favorite color. They're all beautiful, with thorns that can draw blood if I'm careless."

As Martin started toward the small shed in the back corner, Jane recalled that the white rose had been a Plantagenet emblem.

"What was your father like?" she asked as she trailed him.

"He was a simple man." Martin put the basket in the shed. "And a fanatic. He sacrificed everything for a king past caring. I'll never understand why. 'What difference does it make who's king,' I used to ask him, 'as long as we have the law? Even kings can't transgress it with immunity. Our first loyalty should be to the law.' He never took the point. His world was made up of things he could see and touch and bend a knee to."

He settled himself onto a bench near the high wall that separated courtyard from street.

"But he was a good father to me. He sold everything we had so I could study law. If he could see me today," Martin said, eying his dirt-stained hands with a wry look. "I hated having to slave in the fields like a commoner. Now I grub in the dirt willingly."

Jane joined him on the bench. The muted cries of hawkers floated over the wall and the cold October breeze brushed her cheek.

"Is Cecily at home?"

"She's gone this morning. She's entered into business with her tailor. I expect she's out spreading discontent among all her acquaintances over the state of their gowns."

Jane laughed.

"Would you tell her I've returned? Also Richard and Nicholas."

"Richard's at Oxford. He's serving as temporary secretary to one of Wolsey's officials. He'll be back after All Hallows eve."

Jane couldn't say whether relief or disappointment was stronger. She'd dreaded facing him, her feelings as yet unresolved. Now that meeting would be delayed for at least three weeks.

"Nicholas married a month ago," Martin continued. "A widow with two daughters. She's managing the household now." He smiled at her, his hard black eyes softening. "Dine with us tomorrow evening."

As usual it came out sounding like an order.

"Will Nicholas's wife mind?"

"I'm master of this house."

"What do you think of my business?" Cecily asked Jane as they stood in Threadneedle Street the following afternoon.

Jane studied the shop in the tall half-timbered building, its entry overhung by a gilt thimble. Its bright-rose front and shiny glazed windows stood in flamboyant contrast to its sedate limewashed neighbors.

"Who chose pink?"

"I did. Jem was skeptical. I told him we must catch peoples' attention if we're to attract their business. He's had to admit I was right. Already the shop is known as 'The Pink Thimble'." She laughed and started on along the street. "Jem is annoyed, though he's too much the man to admit it."

Cecily was momentarily distracted by an unusually colorful display of silks in a shop they were passing. After a moment she continued.

"The old widow who leased us the shop is moving next summer. She's agreed to let the upper floors to Hugh and me. Jem will continue to live behind the shop. I'd move now if I could. Nicholas's wife and I don't get on."

"Your father said she's managing the household."

"Do you know what she did the moment I handed her the keys? She dismissed two of the servants and Mistress Hobb. Old Hobb has been housekeeper for me since Mother died. Did Isabel care? No. She said she could do a better job and save five pounds a year in the bargain. Of course Nicholas agreed with her. He's got a cashbox for a heart. I expect they snuggle up in bed at night to count their pennies."

"Mistress Hobb seems happy looking after Jem."

"I wasn't about to see her turned out in the street. She's too old to find a new position." Then, with a smug glint, "Isabel hasn't won her way in everything. She wanted your room for her daughters. Father refused. He said you'll need it when next you stayed."

"I don't want to cause conflict -."

"Don't worry. I waved your ancestry in Isabel's face and told her that some day, when you're married to a duke, she can brag how you and she were intimate friends. You should have seen her eyes light."

"What did Richard think of my marrying a duke?" The question was out before Jane could catch herself.

"He didn't look pleased. He wrote to you all summer, didn't he? Were they ardent love letters?" She laughed. "They must have been. Your face is the same color as my shop front. I tried to peek now I can read. Richard never gave me the opportunity. When are you getting married?"

"You're placing too much importance on a few letters. Richard has his career to establish."

Cecily threw her an exasperated look.

"If you're delaying till Richard becomes a barrister, you may have a long wait. I think Father has realized he'll never pass the exams. That may be why he wants to bring Richard to Wolsey's notice. If Richard can't rise in the world as a barrister, he may yet gain advancement as a heretic hunter."

Jane felt as if the street had opened beneath her.

"Is that why he went to Oxford?"

"I don't know."

"Well, Jane, have you boiled the boil?"

George Terrell followed the question with a shout of laughter as he entered his bedchamber some days later.

"See for yourself."

Jane stepped to the bed where Lucy lay propped up with pillows, faded brown braids hanging past her heavy face like twin bell pulls, and lifted the wet cloth. George examined the huge scarlet-and-yellow pimple on Lucy's ample calf which had kept her home from early mass.

"Looks ready to burst."

Jane crossed to the pan of steaming water on a nearby stool to refresh the cloth.

"Well, wife," George said, settling his bulk on the edge of the bed, "the priest said something of interest. The Church is having a book burning next Sunday at Paul's Cross. Seems some fellow on the Continent has printed a lot of English Testaments and smuggled them in. Anybody with one has till then to surrender it or face arrest."

George's words caught Jane as she was lifting the rag from the hot water. She remained motionless over the pan, her heart pounding. An English Testament. Could it be?

"I'd be interested in seeing one," Lucy said.

George shook his bald head.

"Not me. With the Church banning it, I'll not take the risk."

To Jane, Paul's Cross the following Sunday seemed a repeat of the day nine months ago when Robert Barnes and the Germans had recanted. The churchyard was filled with a similar noisy inquisitive crowd held back by the city watch. The gallery overflowed with an equally brilliant display of the English arm of Rome. Even the crackling fire, its yellow tongues licking out in ravenous anticipation of the feast to come, appeared the same.

For one sickening moment, as Jane looked into the flames, Jack Weaver's image floated before her. Her stomach lurched.

In a frantic effort to block the picture, she began studying the disorderly jumble of overflowing baskets. The variety in book sizes and bindings said that more than the English testament was destined for the flames. Some of the books lay open, their white pages fluttering like helpless hands in the chill autumn wind.

Bishop Tonstall mounted the high wooden pulpit and launched into a tirade against all writers of heresy. Jane clung to his every word, praying for him to speak the name she'd come to hear. Tonstall did not fail her. The translator of the blasphemous English testament was William Tyndale. The bishop concluded his sermon. Men heaved the contents of the baskets into the leaping flames. Others, armed with long poles, stirred the fire, determined that not a single page escape.

Jane stood, hands fisted, and watched the destruction of the books that had cost her so dearly. If only Jack had lived to hold an English Testament. How much better it would have fed his spiritual hunger than had her own poor efforts. For the first time, she comprehended the power of William Tyndale's dream and the compulsion that had driven Owen to follow it. Between one heartbeat and the next, the griefs she had borne, her losses and guilts, took on meaning.

As the Church dignitaries departed, she stared at the pile of glowing ash that had been books. Already the wind was scattering the blackened cinders. She squared her shoulders defiantly. Let the Church ban what it would. She must get an English Testament.

Had Richard arrived immediately after the book burning, Jane might have blurted out everything from the pedlar's escape to her part in Jack Weaver's death. As it was, she had almost a week to regain her caution before he came. She remained determined on one point only. If they were to have any future together, he must be told where her true sympathies lay.

Richard appeared one crisp November morning. He caught Jane in his arms and kissed her the moment Lucy left them alone in the hall.

"A servant could come in any moment," she said, pushing him gently away.

"Let them. I was so afraid you wouldn't come back. When I arrived last night and Cecily told me you were here, I slept well for the first time in weeks."

"If you'd stayed home, you'd have seen me sooner." Then, casually, "What business took you to Oxford? More heretic hunting?"

"A lawsuit involving church property. I spent my time scribbling notes on some real arguments. It was nerve-wracking. Father would have loved it."

"You're not finding the law so entertaining?"

A shadow crossed his features. Then he grinned.

"I must be more peace-loving than Father. At least my dearest aspirations are different. Will you wed me now?"

Jane wandered over to the pot of thyme Lucy kept near a window and pinched off a leaf.

"We've not seen each other for half-a-year."

"But you came back to me."

"I came back to London. I do have a sister here and other friends besides you."

"Did you give them as warm a greeting?"

"Don't be silly." Nervously she stripped another sprig. "Did you help collect the English testaments they burned at Paul's Cross?"

Richard's brow creased.

"What's that got to do with us?"

"I just want to know, that's all. Did you?"

"I'd already left for Oxford. I heard they made a merry blaze. But for them I'd have been here two hours earlier. I had to attend a meeting with Sir Thomas and some of the bishops. This priest, Tyndale, has caused an uproar with his testament. The bishops say it's got over two thousand errors."

Jane's mouth dried with excitement, all else momentarily forgotten.

"Have you seen a copy?"

"No. It's forbidden reading."

She studied Richard in exasperation. How ironic that he would likely have easy access to the testaments and was too compliant to open them.

"If all those books went to the fire unread, who counted the errors?"

He flashed a brief, appreciative smile.

"You reason like a defense lawyer. Were you at the burning?"

The room held tension that, a moment ago, had not been there.

"Yes. I was also at another burning at Lammastide. A man. Someone I knew."

Surprise and then pity swept Richard's face.

"You never mentioned that in your letters."

"You could have been the one who stacked the wood around him. You're part of the burnings."

"Only of books, sweeting ... not of men," Richard said, horrified.

"What of Barnes and the Germans? If they hadn't recanted -."

"But they did. Is that why your letters changed? And today you seem so.... Do you see me as someone who'd send a man to the flames?"

"I don't know how I see you. If we're ever to have a life together -."

"You do want us to have a future, then."

The alarm on Richard's face evaporated like mist. He reached out for her. This time she didn't draw back. She leaned against him, marshaling her courage to tell him that, if he continued hunting heretics, he might have to arrest her. She lifted her head and froze. His face held the same tender expression she'd seen in her worst nightmare.

She dropped her gaze quickly.

"Why, sweeting, you're trembling."

Hiding her face against his velvet sleeve, she fought to draw a steady breath. When her knees could support her, she slipped from his grasp.

"His death upset me." She spoke over her shoulder, afraid to look at him. "Afterward the Church took his property and left his little children to starve."

"You know the law. The Church always confiscates the property of heretics."

Jane spun, anger wiping out fear.

"Wasn't it enough that they took his life? Hasn't the Church wealth aplenty? Why must it grow fatter at the expense of babes?"

"Hush, Jane." He cast a nervous glance at the hall door. "Someone might overhear. Who was the man? A close friend?"

"I'd met him only twice," she said evasively. "But I owed him a debt. My horse fell on a winter road. If not for his help, I would have frozen."

"Little wonder his death upset you. He could have recanted. No, hear me out," Richard said with unexpected firmness. "I'm sorry he died. I don't like this heretic hunting any better than you. For now I have to involve myself to gain Wolsey's favor. The truth is ... I'll never make a barrister. Father thinks I should become an attorney. With the Cardinal's influence even an attorney could climb high."

"Is that what you want?"

"You know what I want."

She looked away, unable to face his passion. After a moment he continued more calmly.

"I have to do this to secure a proper future for us. The instant I'm established, I'll get out of it. Until then, I need your understanding."

Jane did understand, much more than he knew. The time had passed for telling him that, could the Church read her mind, it would send her to the stake like Jack. Already Richard was being pulled to pieces by the conflicting demands of father and brother, by his determination to be a lawyer and his soul's craving to create beauty. To tell him now would merely add one more impossible demand.

Overwhelmed by melancholy, Jane looked down at Richard's nimble, narrow hands. They could sketch such beautiful designs. Now they nervously fingered a fold in his gown. For his own sake, she hoped he'd break free from his father and brother and choose his own path. For her sake, she prayed he would soon part with Sir Thomas More. Until he did, she must keep him at arm's length.

Reaching up, she kissed Richard's cheek, an action as tender and free of passion as comforting a child.

"You would have made an excellent goldsmith."

Richard's fingers tightened on the gown fold.

"At this moment I wish I'd stayed one."

CHAPTER 18 – WINTER, 1526 TO SPRING, 1527

Winter arrived a few days after Richard returned. Now, when Jane woke in the mornings, frost decorated her chamber windows. Bone-chilling winds whistled down streets and standing water formed a crust of ice overnight. Increasingly, thoughts of Jack's children and their dark drafty hut disturbed Jane. She knew Willcotte would attempt to watch over them. But, because she took her ease here, he carried the work of two. One thing only kept her in London. She wanted an English Testament.

Richard's association with the books drew her like a needle to lodestone. Eager for news of them, she encouraged him to talk about his meetings with Sir Thomas. He willingly complied.

According to him, Wolsey's spies on the Continent confirmed that the book burning hadn't brought an end to Tyndale's testaments. Too late the church agents would hear of a large number changing hands at some book fair and disappearing again. Following their trail was like tracing an underground stream with no knowledge of its source or likely route. The one certainty was that England would be their destination. How the testaments were smuggled in and distributed remained a puzzle.

As winter's grip tightened on London, Jane would see a shivering beggar child, recall Jack's children and resolve to return home. Richard would talk of Tyndale's testaments and revive her hopes that he would somehow lead her to one. Twice she wandered past Coleman Street wistfully thinking of Willcotte's departed Lollard friend.

Inadvertently Nicholas's wife, Isabel, solved Jane's dilemma.

As Jane had hoped when she'd first met Isabel, the present of a fragrant ham kindled a welcome in the new wife's pale-blue eyes and brought a smile to her pretty, sharp-nosed face. Whether as a result of several such gifts, a mutual liking for needlework or Cecily's inflated description of Jane's wealth and position, Isabel soon accepted her completely.

When, near the end of November, Isabel voiced her desire for a side of venison for Nativity, Jane knew what Christmas gift to give her. The following day she wrote to Willcotte. She expected Dickon Carter to bring the meat. Instead, Howard Willcotte himself arrived. Once over her surprise, Jane realized his coming was exactly what she needed. The moment he was sufficiently warmed at Lucy's hall fire, Jane drew the bailiff into a private corner.

"How are Jack's children coping?"

Willcotte pulled on his lip.

"Elizabeth took to wandering soon after you left. Mostly she went one place."

"Jack's cottage?"

He nodded.

"I stopped by their hut the morning the first ice formed. She was missing. Little Jack said she'd not come home all night. I rode to the cottage. The Church hasn't got tenants for it yet. I found her in the woods behind. She'd come out in nothing but her kirtle." His hands spread in a futile gesture. "She was long past doing for. I left her and went back for the children. I wanted to get them away before the Hensford priest could stop me. They're with Benedict Shore's daughter and husband. Jack would have wanted that."

"I'm sure you did right."

She was too stunned by the unexpected news to cry. Pity was her strongest emotion. Unlike Jack, Elizabeth had lost everything and gained nothing. And the children? They were no longer her responsibility. They'd be all right with Master Shore. She breathed a sigh of relief. The bailiff continued.

"A woodsman found Elizabeth the next day. The priest laid claim to her belongings for burial fees." Willcotte smiled faintly. "He didn't get the goat or chickens. I'd had Dickon fetch them. He took them to Little Jack later. The family will need them this winter with two extra mouths to feed. Come spring, they'll have two more to work."

Jane returned the bailiff's smile. Spring would come. The children, a goat and half-a-dozen chickens were little enough to salvage from the wreckage. Nevertheless, even a small amount can be an accomplishment when accompanied by hope.

She leaned close and told Willcotte about the Testaments. His eyes blazed.

"An English scripture. Mistress, do your best to get copies for Benedict and me."

Richard stopped to see Jane three days after the venison was delivered. Leaving Lucy by the fire, Jane, embroidery in hand, led Richard to a seat where they could talk more privately.

"I'm on my way to Westminster," he said, bending onto the bench. "I may not be free to attend the minstrel show with you this evening. Sir Thomas and I are meeting with Archbishop Warham."

"Warham?" Jane's needle paused. In years past the Archbishop of Canterbury, William Warham, had led persecutions against the Lollards and sent several to the stake. Now he had joined Sir Thomas and Bishop Tonstall in the fight against Tyndale's testament.

"Yes," Richard said with more optimism than Jane had seen in weeks. "We've news for him. A sailor told one of Sir Thomas's informants about a shipment of English testaments hidden in a load of cloth from Antwerp."

Jane quickly looked down at her sewing, hiding her excitement. Richard continued.

"If his information is true, we may at last discover how the smuggling is done and put a stop to it."

Her mind was as sharp as the needle in her sweating hands.

"What is Sir Thomas planning?"

Richard glanced around. Near the fire, Lucy was mending a garment. Beyond, a servant rubbed a table leg with beeswax and turpentine. He leaned close.

"We're going to Greene's shop in the morning and search the place."

"Greene?"

"Yes. He's got a shop on Candlewick Street."

Jane sat staring at her stitching after Richard left. She knew what to do. She had only to wait until he was safely gone. When the bells of St. Thomas chimed the hour, she got up, fetched her cloak and left the house.

Jane had pictured Master Greene's shop the moment Richard spoke his name. She always passed it on her way to the Pink Thimble. Now it lay a hundred paces ahead. Her feet dragged as fear fluttered in her stomach. What if Sir Thomas had posted a watch? She should have questioned Richard more fully. She pulled the hood of her cloak close about her face and sauntered past the shop looking for loiterers. A second pass satisfied her that there were none. Ignoring her fluttering stomach, she pushed the door open and entered.

With one sweeping glance, she took in shelves piled with cloth, a long table near the window and two people bent over it. A brown-clad clerk was carefully cutting a length of black velvet for a woman customer. Jane stepped to the nearest shelf and pretended to examine the bright satins stacked there. When the woman left, the clerk approached her.

"I wish to speak to Master Greene about a cloth order," she said, keeping her face averted.

Her voice sounded unnecessarily loud.

An eternity passed before the clerk returned with his employer. Master Greene had the gray hair and narrow, long-nosed face of a greyhound. The clerk left to put the bolt of velvet away.

"Could we speak in private?" she said.

Master Greene lifted a questioning eyebrow but obligingly led her to a small back room where a table was spread with account books. He stopped by the table and twisted his head as if trying to see her face. She halted just inside the door, her hood pulled close.

"You mentioned a cloth order?"

"Actually I didn't come about cloth."

"Why did you come?"

"To warn you. Sir Thomas More plans to search your shop tomorrow. You must move the testaments immediately."

Master Greene blinked his large dog's eyes.

"I deal in cloth, Mistress, not books. If you're interested, we have a new selection of silks from the Continent."

Jane's clammy skin heated in mortification. Could there be two merchants with the same name, and she had come to the wrong one? She fumbled for the door latch.

"I'm sorry. I must be mistaken."

She was out the door and flying through the shop before Master Greene could reply. Once in the street, she hurried away, heedless of her direction. She'd been a fool to think she could help.

When Jane dined with the Denzils the following evening, the conversation turned to the morning's search. Hot with remembered shame, she kept her eyes focused on her plate.

"Greene had nothing," Richard said to Hugh. "Not a book, not even a pamphlet. I think the sailor was lying."

"Why would he do that?"Cecily asked.

"For revenge. The first mate caught him tampering with some of the consignments and threw him in irons for pilfering. When the ship docked here, the captain discharged him without pay."

Martin frowned.

"Why lay the book smuggling to the cloth merchant? I grant you the sailor probably was pilfering. That damages his credibility. Nevertheless, I believe he found something."

Richard said no more and the talk drifted to other topics. Jane ate in silence. Could Master Greene actually have had the books? She'd never know. She also was no closer to getting a Testament than she'd been last autumn.

The day after Twelfth-night, London awoke to a pristine snowfall. The knife-sharp wind, capable of piercing the thickest woolens, had died. The silvery chimes of a hundred bells peeled out over the city. Even the sun appeared, glowing dimly through the thin cloud cover. All who could flocked to the white fields and frozen marshes beyond London for a few hours of fun.

In midmorning Jane set out for a walk. Beyond Moorgate she stopped to watch a group of noisy youths sliding over the ice on bone skates. Behind her a man spoke her name.

She turned to find herself staring into Master Greene's long-nosed face. She flushed with embarrassment. The cloth merchant spoke quickly.

"Mistress Horne, I owe you gratitude and an apology. You saved me from the bishop's prison."

"You did have the books. Why did you play me for a fool?"

"We'll draw less attention if we're strolling."

Grudgingly she fell in at his side.

"You might have been sent to trick us."

"What decided you I wasn't?"

"My clerk followed you when you left the shop. Had you been sent, you would have reported to someone. When you didn't, we decided to trust your warning. We moved the books that night."

Jane stopped abruptly.

"How did you know my name?"

"We made a few discrete inquiries."

"You've been spying on me."

Master Greene had the grace to appear uncomfortable.

"I want a New Testament," she said.

"I'd be honored to give you one."

"I prefer to pay." She started off again. "How much are they?"

Jane knew she was acting churlish. But she'd betrayed Richard's trust to warn this man, and he'd made a fool of her.

"Four shillings."

"I want three copies."

Master Greene's gray brow lifted in surprise.

"Most people require only one."

"How soon can you have them for me?"

"In two days, unless Sir Thomas arrests me first. We don't know who informed on us."

Whatever his fault, he didn't deserve to be left in fear. Briefly she told him about the sailor. His sigh of relief came out in a cloud of white vapor.

"So the discovery was an isolated incident. Again we're in your debt. May I ask how you knew?"

Jane walked on several steps, the snow crunching beneath her feet.

"I overheard it at a friend's table."

"The Denzils?" Then, delicately, "You brought us valuable information. We had to know more than your name."

Jane remained silent.

"If I've given offense, I apologize. We had our reasons."

"You keep saying 'we'. Who are 'we'?"

"Others like myself who want to see the Church reformed and the scriptures in English. We hope you feel the same." Jane was aware that Master Greene was studying her keenly. "I came today to thank you, and to ask your help. We need to know Sir Thomas More's plans."

"You want me to play informer," Jane said, aghast.

"You'd be protecting lives, and the testaments."

"I'd be deceiving friends."

They had nearly circled the field. Master Greene focused on Jane like a dog on its quarry.

"If I'm not mistaken, you've been doing that already."

"You have a hard way of putting it."

"I've little choice. Will you help us?"

Jane looked across the field at the young men sliding on the ice.

"Do you know the priest who did the translating?"

"Sir William Tyndale? He's said to be an excellent scholar."

"What of those with him?"

"I've heard of one, William Roye. He helped in checking the translations. Tyndale parted with him the moment he could. Roye's loose tongue almost got the churchmen onto them."

"And the ones who smuggle the books?"

Master Greene eyed her warily.

"The fewer names you know, the safer."

Making no attempt to hide her irritation, Jane glanced at the low clouds scudding by. The wind had come up and was whipping the edges of her cloak.

"Where shall I come for the testaments?"

"Lombard Street by the Stocks Market. Ten o'clock tomorrow morning. With regard to helping us -."

"You'll have my answer when I have the books. Good day."

Turning on her heel, Jane stalked off.

"Here they are," Master Greene said as Jane met him the following day among the housewives buying meat at the Stocks Market. The cloth merchant slipped a wrapped bundle adroitly out of his gown and into her basket. Quickly Jane covered it, her gloved fingers caressing the hardness of book edges. Master Greene tucked the payment into his purse.

"Will you help us?"

Jane had wrestled with heart and conscience since yesterday.

"Yes."

"You'll not regret it."

That's easy for you to say.

"How do I get information to you?"

"There's a tiny apothecary shop near your sister's house. Leave written messages there. They'll see I get them. Should I need to contact you, I'll send the son Wat with a bag of sweets. His mother makes some of the best in London. Come, I'll introduce you."

Jane accompanied the cloth dealer on leaden feet. She'd made the right decision and should be feeling noble. Instead, she felt sullied. Had she liked Master Greene more, her conscience might have troubled her less.

By Lent, Jane's dislike for Master Greene had reached a new level. Previously, she'd been free to tell Richard of her Lollard leanings when the time was right and accept a proposal of marriage. With the safety of the Bible smugglers to consider, she no longer could do that. The true responsibility for her impasse lay with the Church. That knowledge didn't help when Richard's wistful look followed her or she passed on information from him. The value of her help was brought home to her uneasy conscience by his despondent reports of failed searches.

Richard also lived with tension. His blue eyes were dark-smudged and his long hands moved restlessly as he talked. Her insistence that she was not ready to wed was partly responsible. The pressure of working with his father in an ill-suited occupation and his failed hopes of advancement accounted for the remainder. Preferment might have come if efforts to stem the illegal book trade had been more successful. This was one more weight of blame that Jane had to shoulder.

"We've faced enough problems with Tyndale's books," Richard said one afternoon in late April as he sat with her in Lucy's hall. "Now pirated copies from Dutch printers are arriving. Selling English testaments is a lucrative business."

"Someone will always sell what others will buy."

"Archbishop Warham is the one buying now. He's instructed his agents on the Continent to purchase all they can find and burn the lot."

"Won't more be printed?"

"He'll gain time. One of these days we'll learn how the books are smuggled in. Then we can stop the whole business."

Jane idly fingered a fold in her skirt.

"Are you certain it can be stopped?"

Richard flushed.

"I know we haven't shown ourselves successful...."

"I didn't mean that," she said gently, guiltily. "What if you're fighting against God? You're putting the holy scriptures to the torch. I know we're told it contains errors. But if the priests can claim authority over our souls in spite of their faults...."

She let the sentence hang. Richard swept his cap off and crumpled it in his hands.

"Father and Sir Thomas think we have an informant."

Jane started.

"Is that what you think?"

"I think I should have stayed with goldsmithing. When I worked a piece of gold, I knew what I was doing. Being a lawyer is like floundering in a quagmire. The harder I try, the deeper I sink. You were there the other night when Father laid into me for getting the wrong writ. If Hugh hadn't caught my error, we'd have lost the case."

The misery on his face tore at Jane's heart.

"Anyone can make a mistake."

"Not that kind. Not if you're a proper lawyer. That was sheer carelessness. I had my mind on a necklace design. When I was studying, I found time to put my ideas on paper. Now they sit in my head and interfere with my work. Did you know I've become a thief?" He gave a brittle laugh. "I steal candles so I can sketch when I should be sleeping."

"Go back to being a goldsmith."

"Father would be too hurt. Despite his criticism, he's proud to have a lawyer son." Richard caught her hands. "If you're truly concerned, marry me. Nothing else would matter if I had you."

Richard's image blurred.

"I can't," she whispered. "Not yet."

"I don't even know the man and I still hate him. He broke your heart and left me nothing but pieces."

Jane remained silent, unable to meet his eyes. From the day of the book burning, when she'd discovered meaning in tragedy, her heart had begun to heal. Now it was whole again. She dared not tell him that. She must allow him to blame Owen for the wall growing between them. She could safely give him no other explanation.

CHAPTER 19 – SUMMER, 1527, GERMANY

O wen Alton reined his tired roan to a halt at the forest edge and reached for the clay bottle hanging from his saddle. Had he been in England and with Midsummer's eve a week away, the woods through which he'd ridden all morning would have prompted thoughts of dancing and bonfires. But this was Germany. In a country recently torn by war, the forests had become the haunt of rogue peasants and robber bands.

He took a swallow of the tepid liquid then looked across the patchwork fields of the flat Rhine valley toward the small city of Worms, its welcoming spires marking journey's end. Once again he'd made the long trip to Antwerp and back. Soon he'd be home, if two rooms shared with William and the remaining testaments could be called home. Behind him a robin trilled, proof that this piece of forest was currently free of danger. He remained wary. Vigilance had become second nature in the three years since he'd arrived at Hamburg trailing William Tyndale.

Owen had caught William in Wittenburg. He stayed with the priest a week, laying plans, before taking the road to Antwerp. The Christian Brethren in London had given him the name of an English merchant there, one Richard Herman. The merchant would arrange to have the testaments smuggled into England. All that was needed, once the books were printed, was to get them to Antwerp. That was the task Owen set for himself. For the next year, while William translated at Wittenburg, Owen traveled throughout Germany as a buyer for Master Herman. He carefully mapped every highway and byway, every navigable river, noting the places where government and church officials were most diligently opposed to Luther. To insure anonymity Owen had, from the first, passed as German.

On this day, as he shoved the cork back into the bottle's mouth, he looked like a much-traveled petty German merchant. Under his black felt cap his sacking-brown hair hung nearly to his shoulders. His short linen blouse, green vest and brown trousers tucked into dusty high-topped boots were travel-stained. The fur-edged coat tied behind his saddle showed signs of having been used as bedding. He sat confidently, no longer the priest-to-be who dreaded even one day's ride. Now he thought nothing of spending a week in the saddle. During the last three years he'd often done that, first for Richard Herman and more recently smuggling testaments for William.

William had intended to print them in Cologne. Despite the city being a Church stronghold, transporting the books over the great road to Antwerp would have been easy. That was before William Roye. The Augustinian friar knew Greek, which William Tyndale needed to check his translation. Roye also possessed a wagging tongue. The friar's bragging of the storm about to break upon England caught the Church's attention. William barely had time to grab the pages already printed and flee to the safety of Worms. There he completed the printing and got rid of Roye.

From Worms, Owen boldly smuggled the first six hundred down the Rhine in a corn shipment, slipping them right under the noses of the Cologne churchmen and on to Master Herman. Two times during the last eighteen months he and William sold a thousand copies at the Frankfurt book fair, letting the buyers deal with the dangers of transporting the books past Wolsey's hunting dogs sent over from England. After that first daring trip through Cologne, Owen delivered three more loads to Richard Herman. Once he took several hundred books hidden in a cargo of clocks and accompanied by a handful of staunch Mainz Lutherans. Another time he again smuggled a hundred through Cologne in a barge load of wine. He arrived in Antwerp to news that Wolsey had ordered the Low Countries ambassador to arrest all printers and sellers of English testaments. Christopher van Endhoven, an Antwerp printer, had been caught.

On this most recent trip, Owen and the Mainz men had taken five hundred books, first by barge and then by packhorse. In the forest, a militant peasant band set upon them. Owen and his companions, being better armed, beat them off in short order, leaving one dead. They themselves suffered only minor injuries. His gashed left arm had healed cleanly. Now, with Worms in sight, a red scar and a carefully mended sleeve were all that remained from the attack.

Owen turned his gaze from the distant town to squint at the overhead sun. He sleeved sweat from his whiskered face. He'd not shed these clothes for a week. They, and he, stank. Around him, insects rasped and the robin sang. Behind these sounds, he caught the soft rumble of water gurgling over rock. The thought of being clean was irresistible. He turned the roan's head toward the forest brook. The bad news he was bringing could wait a few hours more.

The sun was sinking low over the rooftops of Worms when Owen rode through the city gate. A short while later, his horse stabled, he wearily pushed open the door to the rooms William rented over a haberdasher's shop. When the hinge creaked, the dark-robed priest looked up from his small writing table.

"You're back." William jammed his quill into the ink pot and came to his feet. "I've prayed for you every day of this last month-and-a-half."

Owen slumped onto the single hard bench. All the fatigue the stream had earlier washed away flooded over him again.

"Did you get the books safely to Master Herman?"

"Yes." Owen let his head loll against the wall. "I'll tell you everything after I've eaten. I've had nothing since morning but a bread crust and some moldy cheese."

William cast a look of surprise at the fading daylight slanting through the window.

"I'd not realized it was so late. I'll fetch something from the cookshops."

"I want a very large meat pasty and at least a quart of ale."

"How did you manage at the Frankfurt book fair?" Owen asked after he'd reduced his supper to crumbs and described his own trip briefly.

"I sold all one thousand. Doesn't that speak well of my salesmanship? To be honest, I'd almost have given them away rather than see them sitting here unread."

"You'd never make a businessman with that attitude."

"Fortunately, I didn't have to worry. Now we can pay our debts, and have money for rent and food for some months to come."

"Who bought the books? Some of our old customers?"

"New ones this time. Scotsmen."

"That's good. The news from Antwerp isn't."

William's plain face grew grave. He waited for Owen to continue.

"I heard in Antwerp that Archbishop Warham's agents were at Frankfurt buying all the English testaments they could, with plans to burn them. Rumor said they got a thousand, the same number you'd taken."

"They'd burn the Lord himself if he were here today," William said. He lifted the candle that had lighted their meal and crossed to throw open the inner door. His high-held stub cast a wavering light on the tall piles of testaments within. "A thousand copies in flames. How many did I unwittingly sell them?"

"The Church didn't get those the Scots bought. Ambassador Hackett got to Zealand one day too late to confiscate them. The Scotsmen had already sailed for Edinburgh."

William returned to the table, his face grim.

"Are any of the books getting into the right hands? I only hear of burnings."

"I've been wondering the same. We've only got another fifteen hundred, a thousand for you to sell at the autumn book fair and five hundred for me to take to Antwerp. After that, I'm going to England."

"You'll be walking into danger."

"I don't think so. Since I've avoided Antwerp's English community, any churchman who's stumbled across my trail here can only know me as Frederick Steiner. If I cut my hair and let my beard grow, I should be safe making a short trip."

William picked at a pasty crumb.

"You'd come back?"

"Of course. There's nothing for me in England. Besides, you'll soon have a revised edition to smuggle."

"While you've been gone, I've also been thinking. I'm becoming too well known here, and Wolsey's arm is getting longer. It might be wise if I disappeared for a time."

"Where would you go?"

"Probably Marburg. The city is small enough to be overlooked by church agents but close to Frankfurt for the book fairs. I may also have future printing done in Antwerp. That would eliminate your transport problems. If I did, you'd be of more use as a legitimate English merchant like Richard Herman."

"The thought of a roof over my head and a decent bed at night does sound inviting," Owen said with a tired grin. "Are you sure you won't need me with you at Marburg?"

"I'd like you settled in Antwerp, with a wife and children."

"If you're wanting a little house frau of your own now that Martin Luther's taken a wife, you've picked a poor way of telling me." Owen's words came out sharp-edged with anger.

"I'd never expose a wife to my dangers," William said, refusing to take offense. "Your situation is different. If you can become a legitimate merchant again, why not have the joys of a family? You've taken numerous risks for me during these last three years. I'd be a poor friend to hold my tongue now. I believe one reason you've driven yourself so hard is to keep from thinking of the maid you left."

Owen turned away, his hand on the tiny lump under his shirt. Behind him, William continued relentlessly.

"I know you still carry her ring."

He swung to face his friend turned tormentor.

"She's a wife and mother by now. And her ring reminds me that I'm a fool. I was so sure I had to forsake everything to serve God I wouldn't even listen. She would have come with me. After my first time in Antwerp, I saw it might have been possible. I left her ... threw her away as a sacrifice that wasn't even required."

CHAPTER 20 – SUMMER, 1527

With the passing of April, Jane knew the time was fast approaching when she could no longer put Richard off. Her only safe course lay in returning to Wynnfield. Nevertheless, she dared not leave. Master Greene needed the information she provided. Fortunately Cecily provided Jane with an innocuous excuse to stay. Having at last taken possession of the home over the tailor shop, she insisted Jane help oversee its cleaning and furnishing. All she actually wanted was a listening ear as she argued with craftsmen, haggled over prices of material and gave orders to cleaning maids. Half of June was gone before Hugh and Cecily moved in.

By then Jane had another excuse. Soon Isabel would be presenting Nicholas with an heir. As a close friend of the family, she must stay for the christening. Efficient in her timing, Isabel completed the transformation of Cecily's vacated chambers into rooms for her children and, the following day, delivered a healthy boy. A week later, Jane accompanied the Denzil family as Nicholas proudly carried his son Charles to the baptismal font.

Now, in mid-July, with the christening almost a fortnight ago, all her excuses for remaining were exhausted. Already Lucy was laying plans for her annual flight to the countryside. Jane knew with dread certainty that, should she remain after Lucy left, Richard would be put off no longer.

"Which of these brooch designs do you like best?" Richard asked.

Jane was staring out the book-room window at the blaze of colors below where Martin Denzil worked among his roses. Today, St. Swithin's Day, was a holiday. The flower-scented breeze floating through the open window was a welcome change from the fishy smells that drifted into Lucy's house. She crossed to study the sketches on the table then arbitrarily selected one.

"I've also drawn some rings," he said, glancing at her. "I'll craft your favorite for a wedding ring."

Jane drew a sharp breath. The room was suddenly too small and Richard too close. She retreated to the window. He'd not asked outright. She could smile and say nothing. But to do that would be tantamount to lying. In his lawyer world silence meant consent. For months, torn by conflicting loyalties, she'd struggled between integrity and deceit. She already felt dragged down into a mire. To mislead him now was to befoul the last remnants of her honor.

She braced herself against the window frame.

"I'm sorry, Richard. Don't make rings for me. I can't wed you ... ever."

The color drained from his face.

"You don't mean that. A year ago you said you loved me."

"You're my dearest friend." She saw him flinch. "Once I thought I could give you more. But now I know I can't. You deserve better."

"I won't pretend I hadn't hoped for more, sweeting. But I'm still going to marry you. I can be satisfied with your friendship."

"You shouldn't be. It isn't right. Your whole life is unfair. Nicholas takes your designs. You're in an occupation that makes you miserable. I've failed you."

Richard crossed the room and reached for her hand.

"As long as you're being honest with me...."

At his words, the magnitude of her deceit washed over her like dirty water. She turned away, unable to meet his eyes. His hand tightened unexpectedly, uncomfortably on hers. She glanced up. He was looking past her down at the garden below, his expression hard. He pulled her roughly around to face him.

"Are you in love with my father?"

She gaped at him.

"How can you think that?"

He flushed and loosened his grip.

"Forgive me. It's just ... you've always seemed fond of him. If he ever came between us, I could learn to hate him."

"Please give me up. I make you unhappy."

"And I say you don't. You're the brightest part of my life. It's just ... we're both tired. London in summer isn't pleasant. Whatever your reason, I'm glad you've stayed."

Jane looked away. Perhaps his patient persistence would, in the end, breach the wall her actions had built between them. But he was speaking again. That part of her committed to a life-or-death cause grew alert at his words.

"Tomorrow I'll not be here to bother you. I'll be closeted with Sir Thomas and the bishops."

"What are they planning?"

"They're searching the booksellers along Paternoster Row in the next day or so."

Jane moved away from the window. She must get a warning to Master Greene today.

Jane climbed into bed that night confident that the note she'd given Wat had already reached Master Greene. In spite of that, or perhaps because of it, she slept poorly and awoke with a pounding head.

"I need a day away from London," she told Lucy at breakfast. "I'm taking the barge up to Westminster."

"Don't be late returning. We're having guests and you'll want to look your best."

Jane sighed. That meant Lucy had invited another marriage prospect to dinner. She was too weary to argue.

"I'll not forget."

The talkative widower Lucy seated beside Jane brought back the headache the river ride had dispelled. For Lucy's sake, she kept a smile on her face but did nothing more to encourage the draper, bidding him a cool farewell at evening's end. Reading all the signs of a frustrated matchmaker in Lucy's blazing eye, Jane escaped to bed.

"Lucy's still angry about last night," George said when Jane saw him in the hall the following morning.

"I know. We talked earlier. If only she had better taste in men."

"Lucy's taste is excellent."

"When she was choosing for herself. Now that you're taken, who's left for me?"

George grinned.

"You can have a sugar tongue when you choose. That reminds me. A lad came by yesterday with your order of sweets. What with company and Lucy being upset, I forgot."

George rummaged in a wall cupboard and returned with a fat twist of cloth. After he left to open the wine shop, Jane climbed the stairs with the small bundle. Master Greene seldom sent a message. Was something amiss?

Behind her locked chamber door, she dumped the yellow sweets onto the bed searching for a note. There was none. Wat would have it. Only after she'd placated Lucy by going with her to call on friends would she be free to collect it. Whatever Master Greene wanted had better not be urgent.

The church bells had chimed two o'clock before Jane arrived at the apothecary shop. A short while later, back in her chamber, she unfolded the paper to read Master Greene's message. She froze. This was not the cloth merchant's writing. It was Owen's!

The room spun as Jane fought for breath. The note slipped from her fingers and fluttered to the floor. How dare he come back into her life! She closed her eyes, her heart pounding, willing the sheet to be gone when she looked again. It wasn't. She sank down and reached for it with a hand that shook

'I'll be in England only briefly. May I see you? I'll wait tomorrow at the fallen tree beside Finsbury field at two o'clock. Owen.'

How could he ask?! And at the fallen tree of all places. Didn't he remember how they'd sat there on the day he'd learned of her betrothal to Francis Grady? On the day she'd defied everyone for him? Later he'd walked out the pleasance door ... left her to bear all the pain and suffering of the last years alone.

She crumpled the message and flung it across the room. Her head sank onto her updrawn knees. He'd said he'd be waiting. He was too late, three years too late.

The church bells chiming the hour called Jane out of her stupor. She tottered to the washstand and splashed her face with water. Tomorrow Owen would wait in vain.

But tomorrow was today!

Her heart stopped with shock. It had been yesterday when Wat brought the sweets. Owen was waiting today, at two o'clock. And the bells had already rung three. Jane scrambled for the note, spread it flat and stared at the words. She tried to think. It was too late for thought, too late, perhaps, for anything.

She grabbed her purse and jammed the note inside. Probably he was already gone. He wasn't like Richard. He'd not seek her out a second time. A horse hired from a stable would be the fastest way. Even so, how much time would pass before she reached the spot? Clutching her purse in one hand and dragging her skirts up with the other, she rushed out.

Insects rasped as Jane walked her horse toward the distant man in the brown doublet slumped on the fallen tree. Mouth dry and heart thudding, she rode closer. He seemed not to hear her approaching, her horse's hooves treading softly on the springing grass, until she reined up. Only then did he lift his head.

Jane looked down at Owen, at the tears in his gray eyes, on his tanned cheeks and wetting his short beard. She'd never before seen him cry. He stood slowly, cautiously.

"I thought you weren't coming."

His voice, husky with emotion, was barely audible above the insects' song. She continued gazing at him, her heart full to bursting.

"Please help me down." Her voice was as rough as his.

The hands that reached up to her were no longer the pale soft ones of a priest. They were hard-palmed and brown. Her feet touched the ground and she was face to face with him. With a muffled cry, she threw herself into his arms.

Jane's horse, tied in the shady forest edge, switched his tail at a persistent fly while she sat nearby on a weathered tree trunk, held close in the circle of Owen's arms. She gazed into his face with untiring eyes. A smile touched her lips. His sacking-brown hair could use a trim.

"How did you find me?" she asked.

"Howard Willcotte. I rode up to see him the moment I reached England. I thought you'd be wed. Instead, he told me about Sir Harry's death, the peddler's escape and Jack Weaver."

"But how did you know about Wat?"

"I was there when Master Greene got your message. Seeing your writing.... He must have thought me daft. He told me what you'd been doing."

Jane's eyes misted. Of course Owen would have discovered it all. When had they not known everything about each other?

"Master Greene said Richard Denzil wants to wed you." Gruffly, "Will you?"

"I'm marrying you. And this time," she said, kissing him, "if you leave for the Continent, I'll follow you."

"I was wrong to leave you before."

"No, you did right. Otherwise, I might never have come to understand." She looked down at their linked hands. "I now also understand something else. Your mother came after you left. She told me why she was against our marriage."

"I'm sorry."

"You've known all these years," she said, her chin trembling. "Why didn't you tell me?"

"Sir Harry wouldn't allow it. Besides, it didn't matter to me."

"It did to Francis."

"He was a fool, thank God."

A tear wet Jane's cheek. Owen brushed it away.

"My prospects aren't nearly as good as when I asked to wed you four years ago. I do have a position with an English merchant in Antwerp. It won't be as grand a living as you'd have here."

"I don't need a grand living. I only need you. And we'll have Wynnfield's revenues." She remained silent for a long moment. "Did you sell my ring?"

"I couldn't."

Owen pulled the small bag from his shirt and poured the ring into her hand. The oval ruby glowed warmly in the afternoon sun.

"Father said this ring came from my true father."

"He must have been wealthy," Owen said, eying the ring with interest. "Also, your mother must have loved him to have kept it."

Jane's hand fisted around the ring.

"Little good that wealth or love has done me. Between them, I've no name."

"You'll have mine as soon as I find a priest to wed us."

Joy overwhelmed bitterness.

"How soon?"

"Two, three days. I've yet to see my parents or my half-brother. I'll need to get a wedding ring and some clothes." He cast a grimace over his worn garments. "I don't want to come to our wedding in these."

Jane opened her hand.

"This can be my wedding ring."

"Because it came from your parents?"

"No." She laid a palm against his beating heart. "Because you carried it here all this time."

She tucked it back into its bag and snuggled her head on his shoulder. His arms tightened around her.

"I want you to stop seeing the Denzils."

Startled, Jane leaned back in his arms.

"Why?"

"They're a danger to you. Especially Richard Denzil."

"But he's the gentlest, The most patient.... If you knew him you'd have to like him."

"I doubt it."

Jane stood and moved away, putting distance between them as she fought anger and uncertainty. This was Owen, who had come back to her. But to stop seeing the Denzils.... She faced him.

"They're my friends."

He frowned slightly with the familiar determined look. Her heart sank.

"You're playing informer on them."

"What else can I do?" Hand twisted on hand. "Their information is keeping your friend's testaments out of Church hands. It may even save men from the stake." Her voice choked. She fought on, tears beginning to wet her face.

"Everything was so horrible after you left. My whole world fell apart. You've no idea. Then I met Cecily. She made me laugh again. They've all been kind to me. I feel so guilty betraying their trust, but I've no choice. I watched Jack Weaver die."

Jane was sobbing by the time she finished. Owen left the log and wrapped her in his arms.

"I'm sorry, love. I wasn't thinking. At least not with my head. Of course you can go on seeing the Denzils. I'm frightened for you ... and jealous of Richard Denzil."

"I've never loved anyone as I love you. In a few days I'll be your wife."

"If only I could tell him that. In fact, you mustn't tell anyone. Not even Lucy. She'd have too many questions I can't answer."

"Have you put yourself at risk by coming back?"

He shrugged indifferently.

"I was thinking of you." He lifted a hand to caress her cheek. "The next two months will see the last of this printing smuggled in. If I'm caught, I don't want you involved. You can go on to Antwerp. I'll come after Michaelmas."

"No. If I left, who would warn you of danger?"

Her troubles crowded in on her with increased intensity. She dared not tell Owen that Martin suspected an informant. He'd never allow her to stay, and stay she must. This time it was his life that she was protecting.

In the hot July afternoon, Jane shivered.

Owen rode behind Jane to Bishopsgate where they reluctantly parted. When she rode away, he would have given his right arm to call her back. He clamped his jaw against the words.

When he'd heard her story from Willcotte, its suffering had been overshadowed by his joy at finding her unwed and committed to the path he followed. But listening earlier to her broken confessions, to her forlorn weeping, his own heart had wrenched at her pain. He'd begun to comprehend the crucible through which she'd passed, the intolerable burden which she currently carried. Watching her ride back into danger, he wondered, with pangs of conscience, to what degree he was responsible for changing her from an innocent-eyed, hopeful girl into this worn and wary woman.

The sooner he could get her away to Antwerp, the better.

The long afternoon shadows had swallowed up the narrow streets before Owen turned up Bucklersbury Lane. He loitered unobtrusively near the mouth of an alley, watching his father's business being locked up for the day. A few minutes after the front windows were shuttered and the door closed, he spotted his half-brother, Dick Bolt, come out the courtyard gate and start down the street. Dick's expensive velvet doublet and jeweled hat-pin said that the last years had been good to him. Clearly Humphrey Alton had carried out his threat to disinherit Owen in favor of Dick. His half-brother would scarcely welcome his return. Nevertheless, every instinct said he should see Dick before trying to see his parents.

He trailed Dick until he turned up a lane of thatch-roofed cottages. Owen quickened his pace and called his name. Dick turned and his jaw dropped.

"Where did you spring from?" He broke into a smile. "So you've come back."

"Not to stay," Owen said, warmed by the unexpected welcome. "I wanted to see you and get news of my parents."

Dick lowered his voice.

"I've been hearing rumors of an English testament and remembered what you said before you left. Are you involved in that?"

"Don't ask questions."

"I see." Dick's eyes narrowed and he glanced at the passers-by. "No need to talk in the street. Come eat with us."

He drew Owen toward a cottage with a bright-blue door and hustled him in.

"Nan," Dick said, leading Owen into a small dining parlor, "look who's come."

The hot-tempered maid who'd once toppled Owen, her body now swollen with child, looked up from feeding a sandy-haired toddler. Her welcoming smile froze.

"What do you want?"

Dick forced a laugh.

"Wife, I vow, in your surprise, you've forgotten your manners. Owen will only be in England a short time. He wants news of his parents."

Nan's antagonistic look faded.

"I'll set another place."

Handing Dick the feeding spoon, she steered her expanding belly toward the kitchen. Owen settled down to watch Dick feed his small son. After seeing the child return a bite to his chin three times, Owen chuckled.

"You've become domesticated." He hitched his stool nearer to the table. "How are my parents?"

The spoon halted. Dick glanced at his wife who had returned with a wheaten loaf.

"Nan sees your mother often."

"She's taken a fancy to Little Ned." Nan set the loaf on the table. "She wants us to move to the big house after this next babe comes. She's lonely by herself."

"Where's my father?"

Nan cast an appealing look at Dick.

"I'm sorry. Our father died within a year of you leaving."

The room blurred as Owen absorbed this unexpected blow. He had so hoped to make peace with his father. And, now, to find him more than two years dead....

Dick resumed feeding his son. The little kitchen-maid scurried in with a bowl of pears and set a third place. Nan sliced the bread before fetching a mutton roast from the kitchen. Owen spoke past the tightness in his throat.

"Who's managing the business?"

"I am." The feeding spoon halted as Dick looked at Owen. Here again was the crafty, defensive man Owen had known three years previous. "He left a portion of the yearly profits to Frederick and your mother. She also got the house and courtyard. He left me the warehouse, store and the merchandise. It's all there in his will. I've earned that business, and I'm good at it. I've also seen to your mother as you asked."

Owen laid a hand on his half-brother's rigid arm.

"I didn't come back for the business. All I wanted was Father's understanding. Didn't he have any word for me before he died?"

Dick's hostile look faded and he shook his head.

"If it's any consolation, I understand. I think you're daft, but it's your life. I'll help you any way I can, provided it doesn't endanger my family or my business. I owe you that."

"Would you ask my mother if she'll see me?"

The following afternoon, Owen stepped into Dick's little hall where a black-gowned woman sat gazing out the window. Catherine Alton must have heard his footfall for she looked around. Sight of her shocked Owen. The trim shape she'd fought so hard to retain had ballooned into a well-stuffed pudding bag. Something, perhaps the added flesh, had softened her expression. Owen stopped before her. She studied him in silence.

"Have you no greeting for me, Mother?"

"How does one greet a rebellious son?"

"Say whether you're glad to see me or not."

"I'm glad you've come to your senses and returned. The house is so empty."

Owen pulled a stool close and covered her plump hand.

"Dick told me about Father."

"At least now I know where he sleeps at night." She pulled her hand free and cast a critical eye over Owen. "You'll need to see the tailor. You can't take your place in the business dressed worse than a clerk."

"I'm not staying in England."

"Of course you're staying. Your place is here."

"Have you forgotten why I left? If I stay long, I'll end in Lollard's Tower."

"That was three years ago. You're home now. You can put that Lutheran business behind you."

Owen shook his head. Weak tears began to drizzle down Catherine's soft wrinkled cheeks.

"Someone once told me you had a vocation. I didn't want to believe her."

"I'm sorry, Mother."

"Sorry!" She heaved herself up. "What of your duty to me? While you're running after heresy, I'm left to the care of strangers. Not even your father had such a hard unfeeling heart."

Owen winced. He'd forgotten how sharp her tongue could be.

"Dick and Nan are hardly strangers."

"If you can't stay, why come back at all?"

"Matters of business. Also I wanted news of you ... and of Jane Horne."

His mother's mouth set.

"How is the woman?"

"We're to be married tomorrow, here at Dick's. We'd be pleased if you'd come."

"I can't." Her eyes brimmed with fresh tears. "You'll make a fine bridegroom, your life in forfeit and no living."

"It isn't quite that grim. I've a position waiting for me in Antwerp with an English merchant."

Owen saw his mother's eyes narrow.

"You can tell him to find someone else. You're going to be our agent in Antwerp. If Dick argues with me, he can do his loading and unloading from the street. He'll never use my courtyard again."

CHAPTER 21 – JULY TO SEPTEMBER, 1527

hoped he'd break free from his father and brother and choose his

Jane knocked on Dick Bolt's blue door. Over her arm she carried a basket holding her toilet items and prettiest nightdress. Today was her wedding day. This would not be the wedding she'd pictured four years ago. She would have no grand procession, no gathering of family and friends, no elaborate wedding banquet, no bedding ceremony after. She was merely stepping out in a pretty yellow gown to spend a few days with a new friend and returning a married woman.

The door opened on a small, copper-haired mother-to-be who eyed her with unveiled sympathy.

"Is Owen Alton here?" Jane asked, looking past Nan's head.

"Is that Owen?" The male voice came from within.

"No, Dick," Nan called. "It's the other half of the wedding."

"Hasn't Owen come?" She trailed Nan into the hall where two men, one in priest's garb, waited. Catching sight of Dick, she stared momentarily, amazed at his resemblance to Owen.

"I'm sure there's a good reason he's late," Nan said.

Jane's breath stopped. She'd seen little of the Denzils in the last few days. What if Sir Thomas had laid a trap and Owen had been caught?

"A message came for him as we were setting out," the priest said. "He'll be along shortly."

She began to breath again.

"Let's leave the men to wait," Nan said. "I've laid out a wedding feast in the dining parlor."

When Jane saw the array of roast duck, meat pies, cakes and candied fruit that filled the table, her heart swelled with gratitude.

"A wedding's not a wedding without a banquet," Nan said. "Now to get your hair down."

She followed Nan up the narrow stairs to the bridal chamber where a myrtle wreath waited on the bed. Nan removed Jane's coif and began loosing the ribbons binding her hair. After a few minutes' work, Nan set the wreath on Jane's long hair and handed her a bronze mirror.

"Now you look like a proper bride."

They were interrupted by a sharp knock on the chamber door followed by Owen's urgent voice.

"Jane? I need to see you."

Jane started toward the door. Laughing, Nan beat her there and spoke through the crack.

"Owen, you know it's bad luck to see the bride before the ceremony."

"Our luck couldn't be worse. I'm coming in."

The door opened, and Owen stepped through.

"Why aren't you changing into your wedding clothes?" Nan demanded.

"Nan," Owen said, his gaze locked on Jane, "please go away."

Clicking her tongue, she left.

They were alone, just she and Owen in the garden of Eden. Then Jane noticed his frustrated look.

"What is it, Owen? What's wrong?"

Clasping her hands in his, he drew her down onto the edge of the bed.

"Master Greene heard from Antwerp this morning. Wolsey's men are getting too close. Richard Herman is sending the next shipment early. If I'm to be ready for them, I've got to leave for the north today."

"You can't do this to me." She began to cry. "You promised we'd marry. You promised."

"Of course we're going to wed," Owen said fiercely, pulling her close. "I'm not playing the fool twice. This isn't the way I wanted to start our marriage but I don't know what else to do."

"It's all right," Jane said, fighting for control. "No matter how bad this wedding is, I can stand it. I can stand anything if I know I'm your wife and you'll come back to me."

Although all her joy had flown, Jane came down the stairs dry-eyed and calm. She purposely closed her mind to everything but this moment and the man at her side. Owen couldn't spare the time to change from his worn brown doublet. That, also, she wouldn't dwell on.

Time ceased as they faced the priest across the table with its white cloth, sprig of rosemary and glass of wine. She gave her full attention to the short sermon. Their exchange of vows sounded distant in her ears. Owen slipped her mother's ruby ring onto her finger. They drained the wine glass. She was wed.

The distant wail of a small child broke over the wedding party.

"At least Little Ned slept through the ceremony," Nan said as she started up the stairs.

Dick turned to Owen.

"Nan has food laid out in the dining parlor."

"Our plans have changed. I can't stay."

Jane stiffened within the circle of his arm and slipped free. Fighting tears, she hurried for the staircase.

"You can celebrate without me," she heard Owen say.

"A bridal feast without the bridegroom," Dick said. "You're in the wrong business."

Owen pushed the bedchamber door open. Jane was standing at the window, her back to him. The myrtle wreath lay discarded on the floor between them. He picked it up and laid it on the dressing table. She made no sign that she heard. He stopped behind her.

"Good day, wife."

Jane swung round, her eyes bright with unshed tears, her face for one moment as rosy with happiness as he could have wished for any bride. She melted against him. Her long dark hair was like crumpled silk under his hands.

"Say it again."

"My wife." He kissed her. "My dearest wife, Jane Alton."

A single tear escaped. She brushed it away.

"I promised myself I'd not cry again. This is a tear of joy."

Owen pressed her close. She smelt of lavender and her skin was soft under his lips. Desire for this woman stirred in his loins and threatened to overwhelm him. He must break the spell else resolve would fail and duty be forgotten. He forced his tongue to speech.

"I want you to leave for Wynnfield immediately. You're not safe in London. I'll come there when my work's done."

She stirred.

"I'm safer than you. I'll go ... but only after Master Greene tells me the books are away and you with them."

Fear for her tore Owen's heart like talons and anger at her stubbornness roiled up within him. He started to protest but caught back the words. Her invaluable service to Master Greene was part of who she was now, and becoming that person had brought her back into his arms. Until they were safely in Antwerp, he must hold his tongue. He must allow her to follow her conscience as he'd followed his.

"I'll pray for you every moment."

"And I for you."

Owen released her and stepped back.

"I have to go."

"Wait." Jane twisted the ruby from her finger. "I sent this with you before. Bring it to me at Wynnfield and we'll have our wedding night. Leave now before I try to stop you."

He hesitated for a moment to fix her image in his mind, then he turned and went out the door.

Jane was sitting on a stool struggling unsuccessfully to rebind her hair when Nan bustled in.

"It's disgraceful," she said. "I leave for just a moment and look what happens. I come back to find Dick and that priest gorging themselves on the wedding banquet. Owen's gone, you're forgotten."

"I seem to be clumsy today," Jane said, fumbling with the yellow ribbons.

"It's little wonder. Were I you, I'd be in a rage of tears." Nan stopped behind her. "Here, let me. I used to do Madam's hair regularly before Dick and I was wed."

Jane buried her trembling hands in her lap and withdrew into her own thoughts.

One thought she must not entertain. That marked the path to tears. Instead she must plan. The next shipment would be arriving within a week. She didn't know how long it would be before the books left London. She must remain until they did. That meant having an innocent reason to stay after Lucy left next week.

"What? What did you say?" Jane said, called back by Nan's voice.

"I said you're welcome to stay a few days."

"I can't." To sleep alone in this room she'd thought to share with Owen would be more than she could bear. "I've business to attend to."

Her coif again covering her hair, her basket repacked, Jane glanced about the room a final time. Only the cast-off myrtle wreath bore witness to the wedding. Both her ring and her husband were gone. She, also, must be on her way.

Jane arrived back at the Terrell house just as Lucy herself returned with a maidservant carrying a full market basket.

"Weren't you staying the night?" Lucy asked as she followed Jane into the hall.

"I'm not feeling well."

Lucy lay a hand against her cheek.

"You don't feel hot. But your color is poor. Go to bed. I'll send up a tonic."

In her chamber, Jane stripped off her yellow gown, climbed into bed and pulled the sheet over her. She dutifully drank the mixture the maid brought and later picked at the white fish and sodden bread carried up for her dinner.

As night fell the house quieted and street noises faded. Jane lay on her back listening to Bow Bell ring curfew. This was her wedding night. Images of Owen, held at bay earlier, flooded her thoughts. Longing, hot as fever and turbulent as a tide race, throbbed with each pulse beat. Where was he? Were his thoughts reaching across the miles to her as hers reached for him? She rolled over, buried her face in her pillow and wept.

In the morning, Jane declared herself recovered and left to visit the Denzils. Her stomach knotted as she entered their courtyard. She'd not spoken to Richard since St. Swithin's day when she'd refused his proposal. Only six days. It could easily have been a year. The shape of her whole life had changed. No longer the person she was a week ago, she'd not yet learned who she'd become. Only Owen could teach her that. But it was Richard she must face today.

Jane stopped to sniff Martin's pink roses while she gathered calmness. Her path between integrity and deceit had narrowed to the taunt rope of a fair acrobat where one false step would bring her crashing down, Owen and Richard with her.

And upper-window hinge squeaked, and she heard Richard calling her name. His words fell like a weight. Jane forced a smile and then looked up just as his head disappeared within. She entered the house and climbed the stairs to the hall with dragging feet.

The following fortnight was fraught with tensions that must be concealed with a cloak of normalcy. Jane paid for her daylight deception with the coin of sleepless nights.

But for her forebodings, the days would have passed pleasantly enough. Once again, long-suffering Richard confined his passions behind the face of friendship. Sir Thomas's spies made no new discoveries. And, as if by a miracle from God, Jane had a plausible excuse for remaining.

George would rather have blamed the devil. Two days before Lucy's departure, his gout flared. A servant was sent running to the apothecary for meadow saffron, but Lucy herself could not postpone her leave-taking. George's sister, that thorn in Lucy's ample flesh, had scheduled a visit to Horne Hall within days and would demand a hostess. Jane, grasping her opportunity, offered to remain to brew George's tonic and fuss over him. A week later, with George much improved, Jane received the longed-for message from Master Greene.

She departed London as the sun's first rays lit the horizon. After a day's hard riding, she arrived at Wynnfield feeling as light and burden-free as a soap bubble.

In the blue parlor the candles cast a pool of mellow light over Jane's homecoming meal. When the servant left, she looked at Willcotte across the table.

"Owen Alton and I were wed in London two-and-a-half weeks ago."

"I wondered," Willcotte said with a smile. "He came asking after you. He's a good man."

"Owen is carrying a load of testaments north to Cambridge and beyond. When he's finished, he'll come here. After Michaelmas, we're going to Antwerp." Her deepest fear surfaced. "If he were caught ... would you hear of it?"

Willcotte stroked his lip.

"Benedict would. He hears everything. I'll ride up to see him in the morning. Don't think on it now. Use your time arranging affairs against your departure."

As the days passed with no word from Owen, Jane forced herself to follow the bailiff's advice. She filled her time with ledgers and tenants, crops and wool prices. One day she rode over to visit Lucy and the unwelcome sister-in-law.

More than a fortnight after her arrival, Willcotte, returning from Newmarket, caught her in the hall. He glanced around. The servants were busy setting up tables for the evening meal.

"You'll be having a visitor tonight," he said quietly.

Clad in her nightdress, Jane sat at her dressing table combing her hair. Her bedchamber shone bright with candles. The hearthstone's cheery blaze dispelled the autumn chill. Freshly baked manchet bread, two roast pigeons and a jug of apple juice waited on a large chest.

She crossed to the window. Where was he? Would he come by the road and slip around? Was he even now crossing the meadow from the far woods? Or, after meeting Willcotte today, had he been caught by churchmen? Where could he be?

A hinge protested behind her. She spun. Owen stood in the doorway, his white shirt in sharp contrast to the blackness beyond. With a muffled cry, she raced across the room. He shoved the door shut and tossed his doublet aside. Catching her in his arms, he began to kiss her.

"Your hair's wet," she said when his mouth momentarily lifted from hers.

"I washed in the stream. I could hardly come to my wedding night smelling of horses." Then, "I've brought you something."

He pulled the small bag from the neck of his shirt. Lifting Jane's left hand, he slipped the ruby ring onto her finger.

Jane would have preferred to live openly with Owen. Lucy being three miles away, she dared not. The family must not learn of her marriage until she and Owen were safely in Antwerp. His presence must remain a secret, at least outwardly.

If the stable-hands wondered about the strange horse they boarded, or the cook and indoor servants puzzled over the unseen guest who dined with their mistress, they knew enough not to ask. Clearly the bailiff knew what was afoot and expected them to keep their counsel. They did.

Jane and Owen had over a week together. They spent two days at Stourbridge fair wandering hand in hand through the rows of booths, stopping to enjoy jugglers, wrestlers and dancing bears. On several occasions, they spent their day beside the stream at Wynnfield where they had met so often in past years, catching and cooking a fish for their nooning. Afterward, they lay in each other's arms talking through the lazy afternoons or listening to the rustle of dying leaves in the trees overhead, their tranquil hearts beating as one. Each night of that all-too-short, blissful time, Jane fell asleep to Owen's peaceful breathing and awoke with him stretched warmly at her side.

Too soon came the time for parting. Even now Dick Bolt was securing the king's permission that would allow Owen to legally embark for Antwerp. Dick did not know that Owen would be returning secretly a week or so later bringing the final shipment of testaments. That task completed, Jane would follow him to Antwerp, for her name also would be on the permission Dick was obtaining, Jane Alton, wife of Owen.

To delay the moment of separation, Jane rode to London with him. They took two leisurely days for the trip, avoiding, as if by common consent, all mention of their imminent parting or the hazards ahead. Staying their final brief night in Nan's second bedchamber, they could no longer keep their anxieties at bay.

"Promise you'll take extra care," Owen said, drawing Jane close beneath the bed covers. "At the slightest hint of danger, I want you on the first ship for the Continent."

"I'll be safe enough," she said, burying her face against his neck. "Only three weeks until Michaelmas."

Neither of them added, "What possibly could go wrong in such a short time?" Experience had taught them the futility of that thought.

Owen sailed down the Thames under a pale-blue sky. Jane stood on the quay watching the ship, her shoulders braced, a determined smile on her face. As the watery expanse between them widened, she felt as if she were being ripped in two. Only her very real fear that Sir Thomas would stumble onto Owen when he returned with the final load made it possible for her to remain behind on the cobbled pier while the jaunty little merchantman carried her husband away. At the rail, Owen lifted an arm in farewell. Before she could answer, his ship slid behind a Venetian galley. He was gone.

CHAPTER 22 – SEPTEMBER, 1527

Jane remained with Nan and Dick for two days fortifying herself for the ordeal ahead. On the third day, she arrived at the Denzil home, ready with an explanation for her early return. That day was the seventh birthday of Nicholas's younger stepdaughter, Alyce. During the previous months, she and the child had become friends. Alyce, and her older sister Emma, had been willing recipients of sweets from Wat's shop while Alyce's warm little body had allayed some of the emptiness in Jane's heart and arms she dared fill no other way.

Jane presented Isabel with an enormous pike. To Alyce and Emma she gave dolls she'd stitched. Isabel, with enough fish to feed a company and no doubt shrewdly hopeful of a free lace cap for Alyce, promptly invited Cecily and Hugh to a birthday celebration.

To Jane's intense relief, Richard was absent. Owen's re-entry into her life, far from raveling out her conflicting loyalties, had for the moment created further entanglements. Although she was Owen's wife in every sense, with her heart and mind fixed on him as surely as a compass needle pulls north, she couldn't easily dismiss Richard from her affections.

After admiring baby Charles, Jane passed the afternoon helping Isabel reduce a pile of mending and sympathizing with her over the cost of living. Now and again she cast an encouraging smile at Emma, struggling to set a line of neat stitches in a cloth scrap under her mother's demanding eye. Although Alyce was two years Emma's junior, her needle gave her no such trouble. Jane marveled that two children with the same parents could be so different. Alyce was a plump cherub, all sunshine and smiles. Emma, thick-bodied and clumsy, consisted of sulks and shadows.

As usual, Alyce finished first and held her sewing out for her mother's approval. All Emma's untidy stitches earned was a sharp rebuke before Isabel left for the kitchen. While Emma struggled to complete her piece, Alyce snuggled up in Jane's lap with the new doll.

They were selecting its name when voices, Martin's disapproving, Richard's wearily apologetic, drifted up from the entry. As Jane braced herself, Alyce slid down and tripped across the floor. Skipping cautiously around Martin, she waylaid Richard.

"You're looking as fresh as a spring day," Martin said to Jane. "A month in the country suited you."

"Yes, it did."

Jane smiled, her thoughts on Owen. She was abruptly aware of Richard's puzzled look as he approached, Alyce clinging to his hand. A moment later, Emma, angry over a snarled thread, demanded her attention. Jane was glad for the excuse to avoid Richard's eyes.

By the time she had Emma's sewing sorted out, Richard was dutifully admiring Alyce's doll. Then Cecily breezed in with a rustle of lavender satin. Hugh, in black velvet, limped shadow-like behind. Nicholas joined them soon after.

When they gathered in the dining parlor, Jane took her place across from Richard at the dimly-lit table. Whereas Cecily would have squandered at least a dozen tall tapers on the meal, Isabel considered half that many sufficient. Between the mixed-meat pasty and stuffed pike, Jane causally turned the conversation to her most pressing concern.

"Have Sir Thomas and the bishops made any progress lately?"

Her question, directed at Richard, was answered by Martin.

"Matters are much the same. Have some pear preserves, Richard."

Jane's face warmed. Had she been rebuffed?

"We've a dearth of news in the country."

"Then you can't have heard." Cecily's eyes sparkled. "King Hal has picked himself a new queen ... provided the Pope grants him an annulment. Her name is Ann Bolyn. They say her sister Mary was the King's mistress."

Isabel gasped.

"Wherever did you hear that?"

"Probably from one of her less-reputable customers," Nicholas said.

"I did hear it from a customer," Cecily said haughtily. "A baron's wife."

"What about Queen Catherine?" Richard asked, frowning. "She's a good queen and a faithful wife, before God, his lawful wife."

"She's failed to give the King an heir," Nicholas said reaching for the bread.

"She gave him Princess Mary," Cecily said. "Or don't girls count?"

"They're useful for strengthening alliances. But as for ruling.... A woman could never hold England in peace."

Even in the dim light Jane saw Cecily's eyes flash.

"I suppose next you'll be saying you can order your business better than I can mine."

"Enough of this bickering," Martin said. "Tudor problems are no concern of ours. Let the Church give the King a solution."

"Wolsey will have that task," Hugh said.

"At least I can afford enough candles to see my food," Cecily muttered.

Isabel, starting to speak, evidently missed her comment.

"Father Denzil is right. We have our own problems. As I was telling Jane, the price of fresh eels...."

Jane looked from one dimly-lit face to the next. What would Owen make of this family? Thinking of him, the room and its occupants slipped away. She was once again beside the stream close held in his arms. She came to herself to find Richard studying her quizzically. Quickly she tucked her chin and resumed eating.

"What did you do at Wynnfield?" Richard asked Jane as the family sat enjoying Cecily's lively harpsichord music. Jane shifted on the bench they were sharing. Something in his tone prickled her neck hairs.

"Manor accounts," she whispered. "And you? Were you closeted with Sir Thomas and Bishop Warham?"

"Father's been attending Sir Thomas alone. He thinks I should give my time to clients until plans are laid."

"What's being planned?" She held her breath. This was what she desperately needed to know.

"Father hasn't said."

"You've no idea? You could always ask."

"I'd rather know what you did besides manor accounts."

Alarmed that she suddenly had no easy access to Sir Thomas's plans, Jane answered at random.

"I went to the fair ... and riding and fishing."

"I wish I'd been there."

Richard reached for her hand. She snatched it away.

"Not here. Not now."

Cecily finished her piece. Jane sprang up and crossed to the harpsichord.

"That was lovely, Cecily. Play another and I'll turn the pages."

"Another time. Hugh and I must be off home."

"Isabel," Jane said, inspired by desperation. "Play us a tune. Nicholas and Richard can sing."

Isabel, not to be outdone by her sister-in-law, willingly obliged. She played the harpsichord, as she did everything, with efficient thoroughness. Her performances were technically faultless - and flat as consecrated bread. Once Richard and Nicholas were well into their song, Jane approached Martin by the fireplace. Pleading travel weariness, she bade him good night and escaped to bed.

For the next two days, Jane somehow managed never to be alone with Richard. At the same time she tried frantically to discover what Sir Thomas was planning. Gradually the joy she'd brought back to London faded as apprehension for Owen grew. Only Martin could provide her with information now. Forced to give all her attention to avoiding Richard, she was unable to draw Martin out.

On the third evening, after the meal, rather than joining the family in the hall, Richard excused himself. Grabbing her chance, Jane settled beside Martin near the fireplace.

"Richard isn't helping Sir Thomas as much now," she said. "Has his career taken a change of direction?"

"Not at all. He'll be busy soon enough."

"You're planning something?"

"Our informant would give much to know that."

Jane's stomach knotted. She would learn nothing tonight. How many more nights did she have?

When the lantern clock on the mantel marked nine, Nicholas banked the fire while Isabel snuffed candles. Martin bade Jane good night and left. Jane, frustrated and anxious, was in no mood to retire.

"I'll leave a candle for you," Isabel said when Jane remained sitting by the fireplace.

The sounds of footsteps climbing the stairs faded. Only the ticking of the clock filled the silence. Jane glanced at the single small flame waiting for her on the mantle. The candle was as short as her thumb.

Why must Isabel be so close-handed?

She collected her stub and started for the stairs. Richard stepped from the book room.

"I've been waiting for you ... for a very long time."

Jane's fingers tightened on the candlestick. She should have remembered how patient he could be. He must have sat in there all evening on the chance of catching her alone. Now he had.

"I only have a stub. I can't stay."

She took a step on her way. He cut her off.

"I've got candles. I'm still stealing them, you know. You know everything. I'm the one who doesn't. Tonight I'm going to find out."

His hard, desperate tone shook her. She'd never seen him like this. Her muscles bunched, preparing to push past him.

"Why have you been avoiding me? What happened at Wynnfield?"

Jane looked away quickly before he could see startled fear on her face. How swiftly and accurately he'd read the change in her. A chill ran through her tensed sinews. Danger had joined them in the dark.

"We can talk in the morning."

She started around him. He caught her wrist in a hard grip.

"We'll talk now. What happened? Why have you changed?"

She swallowed past tightness. She must answer. She forced herself to meet his eyes.

"All right. The truth is ... I'd left Wynnfield to escape memories. When I went back this time, I found the contentment I'd lost. I don't need to run away any longer. After Michaelmas, I'm going home for good."

Richard stared down at her. The light of the single candle, dim though it was in the circling darkness, lit the anguish on his face.

"This is your home ... here with me."

She shook her head.

"You begged for time," Richard said, his voice breaking. "I've given it. I've forced myself to wait ... to be patient."

"I told you two months ago I couldn't wed you."

"In spite of what you said, you were mine then." His bitter words wrung her heart. "But not now. I've truly lost you, and I don't understand."

Silently, she brushed past him; this time, he let her go.

Part way up the staircase, Jane faltered. Another lighted taper shown out of the darkness. Martin stood in the bend of the stairs. She continued on past him without comment.

How long had he been there, and how much had he heard?

After a restless night, Jane dragged from bed when the maid brought in a pitcher of hot water. In fairness to Richard she should move to Lucy's immediately. Owen's safety compelled her to remain. She must discover what Sir Thomas planned. She'd try again with Martin. A casual question put to the maid revealed that she had seen Martin and Richard leave together earlier.

Jane knew Martin could well be gone the whole day. She passed the morning helping Isabel with the household chores. In the afternoon, unable to hide her anxiety any longer, she strolled out into the chill gray day. Returning an hour later, Jane recognized Sir Thomas More's russet head and dark robe disappear through the Denzil courtyard door. If she could get him talking.... She dashed for the gate.

"Sir Thomas," she said coming up behind him on the walk.

"Ah, Jane. How was the country?"

"Rather dull after London." She hoped Owen would forgive her that answer. "We had no interesting guests stopping in for a meal."

They were almost at the door.

"I can't stay. I've just come to see Martin."

"More Bible smugglers?"

They began climbing the stairs.

"We should know soon enough."

"What have you heard?"

"Thomas."

Jane started at the sound Martin's voice. He stood on the landing. Sir Thomas's attention shifted even as his look sharpened.

"Have you news?" Martin said. "Come in the book room."

Jane stood trembling outside the closed door. Something was happening. But, what?

When they emerged an hour later, Jane sprang up from the hall seat where she'd been pretending to read. She quickly approached, desperate to catch a stray word. Her mouth set. They were discussing roses.

After Sir Thomas left, Martin turned to Jane, the hard lines of his face softening.

"We should have a talk soon."

He excused himself and returned to the book room. Jane looked after him with foreboding. His eyes had held a look she could only describe as calculating.

Sitting across the dining table from Richard was even more difficult than she'd feared. Keeping her eyes focused on her plate, she made no effort to join the table talk. Rather she plotted how she could draw Martin out. Halfway through the meal, she glanced up to find Richard watching her with an expectant look. She dismissed it with only half a thought. She had more pressing problems.

After the meal, Jane hung back to avoid Richard. Only when the rest of the family had drifted into the hall did she notice Martin was waiting for her by the book room.

"I'd like that talk now."

At his tone, Jane's foreboding returned. Nonetheless, she accepted with a smile. This could be her opportunity to question him about his meeting with Sir Thomas.

She followed Martin into the room then wandered over to look out the night-black windows while he lit the tapers in the wooden chandelier. Isabel might keep the rest of the house dim, but the book room was his domain.

"I've a confession to make," he said with a smile. "I overheard your conversation with Richard last night. Nothing would please me more than to see you two wed."

Jane's stomach knotted. She'd been mistaken in thinking the battle over. Tonight she must fight it again, and with a much more aggressive opponent.

"Then you know I've refused him. That's the end of the matter."

"Of course it's not the end. He gives way too easily."

"I wouldn't make him happy."

"On the contrary, when I questioned him, he said nothing would make him happier. Richard has good blood, at least on my side. In a few more years, he'll be well established in his career. We aren't a poor family. You already have some affection for each other. What could be better?"

"But I don't want to wed him."

"What do young people know of their own minds? At first, I resisted my father when he chose Clare for me, but he was right. I'm going to approach your family about a match tomorrow."

Jane swallowed alarm. Between Martin Denzil and Lucy, she could find herself betrothed to Richard by week's end.

"I can't."

"And why not? Give me one sensible reason."

As Martin waited with a confident smile, Jane knew that events were fast moving beyond her control. She felt trapped, unable to use her only weapon. Or was it her only one?

She'd never told Richard of the stigma of her birth, partly from shame, partly because she doubted it would have mattered to him any more than it had to Owen. But it certainly had mattered to some. If it caused Martin to pause just for a few weeks, just until Michaelmas. She drew a steadying breath.

"I can't wed Richard because I'm a bastard."

The room was abruptly, deathly silent. Martin gaped at her, his look stricken, confused, almost ill. His expression hurt her far more than she'd been hurt by Francis's look of revulsion.

"Don't look at me like that." she said, grieved. "I didn't choose to be born without a father's name."

"I thought Sir Harry Horne was your father."

"I wish he had been. He married my mother only weeks before my birth. For love of her, he let me wear his name."

"But if not him, then who?"

"All I know of my real father is the ruby ring he gave my mother."

"Holy Mother of God!"

Martin's eyes started out of his head; he collapsed onto a stool. Alarm overriding her distress, Jane hurried around the table to bend over him.

"Master Denzil, what's wrong? Are you ill?"

His lips moved, but no words formed. She sped across the room to the livery cabinet and slopped ale into a cup. He took it with a shaky hand. Gradually, as he sipped, his color improved. He set the empty cup down and studied her face in the bright candlelight as if she were a stranger.

"All this time ... searching for Eleanor in you and finding so little. How could I have been so blind. It's not your mother you favor."

Jane started.

"What do you mean?"

"The man who gave her the ring," he said hesitantly. "It was I."

"That's not possible. You never even knew my mother."

"Oh, yes, I knew her, a lifetime ago." He stood. "It's time you sat and I got the ale."

She watched, dumbfounded, as he fetched another cup and poured them both a generous portion.

The hard-metal feel of the cup against her palm helped restore reality.

"If it's true, I have to know how it happened."

"Yes, I suppose you do." He gave a short sigh. "You've heard the stories of my father. How his loyalty to a dead king lost our fortunes. I was nine. When I reached fourteen, my mother insisted I be sent away. She was willing to sacrifice herself for my father's stubborn loyalties but not her only child. Relatives secured me a place in Lord Stanton's household. My mother hoped I'd better my position."

His mouth thinned. Jane's attention was riveted on his abstracted face.

"Did you?"

"No. I had too many fights with the other pages. The Stantons were Tudor and my father Plantagenet. I was big for my age, and strong. They learned to leave me alone.

"I could have left after my mother died. I remained because of Eleanor. I'd never have come to her notice except I could read. The ladies often had me read to them during the long winter days. Eleanor was always there, her gaze meeting mine over the book edge. I was never allowed to speak to her.

"I was eighteen and she fifteen when, during a hunt, we became separated from the rest. In that half-hour, I learned she carried my image in her heart just as I carried hers in mine. I should have seen the gulf my father's loyalties had put between us. But impossible hopes filled me completely. She'd kissed me that day, and I'd given her my mother's ruby ring."

Jane studied the face before her, trying to see past the graying hair, deep lines and somber gaze to the hopeful youth he'd once been.

"What dreams we dreamed, and what fragile paper castles we built during those summer months. They all came to naught. Lord Stanton married her to Lionel Radcott in the autumn. I'd pled with her to stand against the marriage. When we parted that last time, I didn't know whether she would. She knew how ruthless her father was. She must have tried, in spite of her fear, because of what happened."

Martin gulped a mouthful of ale. His tone, when he began again, was as bitter as gall.

"Lord Stanton had me dragged out in the dead of night, whipped me unconscious and threw me and my ring into a stinking little room to wait for my father. I didn't see Eleanor again for over ten years. And I'll carry the scars of that beating till I die.

"I hated them all after that, even my own father. But for his useless allegiance, I would have had the lands and titles I needed to wed Eleanor. I returned home and worked like a peasant till I could stand it no longer. One day, all the hatred and despair burst like a boil. When Father learned how I felt, he sold the manor and brought me here to study law."

Martin lapsed into another lengthy silence.

"But what of me?"

He took another swallow of ale, glanced at her and then looked away.

"I was a lawyer, married to Clare, Richard a baby. A nobleman employed me to handle a dispute over a will. We traveled north to look over the property. On our return trip, my client stopped to visit a friend, Lionel Radcott. Lord Radcott was gone, had been for a month or so. Only Eleanor was there. I could see in her face that her life hadn't been easy. Lord Radcott was expected the following week, so we waited for him. I saw Eleanor every day, but I could never talk with her. I felt like a page again with her the carefully guarded daughter of the house."

Martin passed a trembling hand over his face.

"One day, I went out to admire the roses. She was alone in the summerhouse. In all these years it never occurred to me that a child might have come from that brief moment of passion."

His voice faded. He sat, eyes closed and lips pressed into a straight line.

"What did you do after?"

Martin opened his eyes.

"I killed Lord Radcott."

Jane gasped.

"You killed him?"

A stray story slipped into place, like gears meshing.

"The nobleman's son you accidentally killed ... your two-year exile ... that was Lionel Radcott?"

He nodded shortly.

"Only it wasn't an accident. You must understand. I wasn't quite myself that week. Meeting Eleanor so unexpectedly, seeing what he'd done to her, the moments in the summerhouse. And afterward, she refused to go away with me. She decided to retire to a convent. Then he came home."

Martin's face darkened. Jane found herself holding her breath.

"We were in the courtyard. The servants were loading Eleanor's chests onto a packhorse. She had her traveling cloak around her shoulders. Lord Radcott rode in. He demanded to know what she was doing. When she told him, he struck her. I grabbed his arm. He wasn't accustomed to having someone interfere. He drew his knife. We struggled. The blade stood between us, the point at his breast."

Sweat glistened on Martin's forehead, and his fingers curled as if gripping a knife.

"All my hates and sufferings flooded me, and my shame. When I'd held Eleanor in the summerhouse, I'd called her 'Clare'. For that hurt, if for no other, I had to set her free. From a youth I'd been strong. I merely pushed.

"We fell together, and I arose red with his blood. The witnesses called it an accident. They couldn't see into my mind."

He uncurled his fingers and spread them wide on the table. It was a moment before Jane could find her voice.

"What did your wife say when you told her?"

Martin carried the jug back to the livery cupboard and closed the door with a snap.

"I never told Clare."

"You killed a man, spent two years in exile and never explained?"

He swung around, his face twisted in torment.

"What could I say? That I'd committed adultery and then murdered the woman's husband? I know the law. I've served it all my life. In its eyes, and those of the Church, I stood condemned. That knowledge was burden enough without reading condemnation in Clare's eyes also." He began pacing like a caged animal. "In the summerhouse, Eleanor saw what my ten-year-long obsession had blinded me to. I'd come to love Clare as dearly as I'd once loved her. That's why she refused to leave with me. She only took my ring as a pledge of help in need. I couldn't tell Clare. She might have hated me."

"Or she might have forgiven you."

"I couldn't take the chance. But my silence cost me her trust."

"So you destroyed your marriage as completely as your father destroyed your inheritance."

He halted and ran a shaky hand over his face.

"You're right. I'm not so different from my father after all."

One of the candles, shorter than the rest, guttered and died. Jane waited. Eventually, Martin brushed his hand across his eyes. He turned to gaze at her.

"My daughter. I've never seen you with the ring. Where is it?"

Jane tensed, alert, cautious.

"I don't have it with me."

"So many secrets." For one chilling moment she thought his words were aimed at her. "Let's have an end to those we can. You're my daughter. It's time I claimed you as such."

Jane's heart warmed as she looked up at the man whose blood she shared. Then another thought hit her.

"No! You mustn't. Richard wants to wed me. You can't tell him I'm his sister."

"But, Jane, I owe it to you," Martin said, taking her hand.

She jerked free and backed away.

"What about Richard? Do you own him nothing? I had another father. Richard has no one but you."

"Granted, it will be a shock. He'll recover."

"As you did when my mother was forced to marry elsewhere? You hated your father because of what his loyalty cost you. Imagine

Richard's reaction when you tell him your adultery has turned his love for me into vile filth."

Martin's determined look wavered. She rushed on.

"You've forced your will on him regarding his profession. Don't destroy him further."

"You believe I'm destroying him because I want him to be a lawyer?"

"Richard loves two things, goldsmithing and me. You've already denied him the one. He will never forgive you if you deny him the other."

His face crumpled.

"You're more cruel with me than your mother was."

"I'm doing it to save Richard," she said, fighting tears.

Martin dropped wearily onto a stool.

"He knows I planned to speak to you. What do I tell him?"

Jane's head throbbed, her emotions in turmoil. Thought was nearly impossible.

"Tell him ... tell him I admitted to loving someone else."

"That's no good. He hasn't seen you with another man."

"Say that I met someone at Wynnfield."

Jane felt her hands begin to tremble. She hid them behind her back. Martin peered curiously at her.

"You were unusually happy when you returned. Have you met someone?"

Danger's light fingers brushed her skin as concern for Richard fast turned to fear for Owen.

"It's merely an answer for Richard."

"I hope that's all it is."

CHAPTER 23 – SEPTEMBER, 1527

J ane lay on her hard, hot pillow staring into the darkness. Her head pounded at the slightest movement, and her eyes grated in their sockets. The scene with Martin Denzil revolved like a mill wheel in her mind. She had always longed for a brother or sister. Suddenly she had three, and a father eager to acknowledge her. She should be ecstatic. Instead, guilt was her bedfellow. Before tonight, in helping the Bible smugglers, she had betrayed dear friends. Now she was playing Judas with her own family. The tortuous tangled strands of her relationship with this household had, in the last few hours, taken on the terrifying proportions of a gordian knot.

A longing for Owen's strong arms and comforting shoulder overwhelmed her. Clamping her hand over her mouth, she began to weep.

Holy Cross Day dawned dark and sulky. The calling bells reverberating through the damp cold awakened Jane. Her mouth tasted foul, and her body ached. The family and most of the servants would shortly be leaving for Matins. Normally she would have joined them. Not today. She couldn't face Richard. When the maid arrived with hot water, Jane sent her off with word that she'd attend mass later. Her toilet complete, she went down to the dining parlor. Too late, she noticed Richard, haggard-faced, sprawled on a bench in the corner. He looked up. Jane halted in confusion.

"Good morning, Richard."

"Is it? I hadn't noticed."

Avoiding his eyes, she started toward the food on the sideboard. He blocked her way.

"Why didn't you tell me you loved someone else?"

"I wanted to save you hurt."

"So you've been deceiving me all these months to save me hurt."

"Not months, only weeks. Since I went home."

"I've courted you for two years. You go to Essex for a month and meet a stranger."

"He's not a stranger," Jane cried, caution forgotten. "I've loved him all my life. Until he came back a few weeks ago, I thought never to see him again."

"Is he the one who left you before?"

She nodded.

"He could desert you again."

"Not this time."

Thinking of Owen, every fiber in her weary body warmed with love. Her thoughts must have shown on her face because Richard winced.

"Am I to have the privilege of meeting him?"

"Do you want to?" Weariness overwhelmed her again.

"No. I thought you cared for me."

"I do," Jane said, tears gathering in her eyes. "But as a friend. I've never pretended otherwise."

She sat down at the table, dropped her head on her crossed arms and let the tears come. She heard him approach and stop at her elbow.

"Please don't cry, sweeting."

For his sake, she must curb her tears. She straightened and scrubbed her wet face with her sleeve.

"We'd not meant to tell anyone yet that he's returned. Please don't say anything, not even to your father."

"Why can't he court you openly like an honest man?"

"We want a few weeks to ourselves. Just until Michaelmas."

"As you wish."

"I feel horrible."

"You look horrible."

Richard fetched a cup of cow's milk and a piece of fish from the sideboard. He plunked the food down at her elbow.

"Eat and you'll feel better." He gave her one last despairing look. "I would have made you a good husband."

He turned and walked out of the room.

Jane shoved her barely touched food away. Isabel, Nicholas and the children would soon be returning from St. Michael's. She wondered if Hugh had managed to prize Cecily from her bed for mass. Probably not. At thought of Cecily, Jane had an overpowering urge to see her. She wanted to sit and look at her, to say in her mind what she couldn't confess aloud. You are my sister, my own true sister.

She fetched her cloak and started down the main stairs. At the bottom, she heard the high sharp ringing of a mallet on metal coming from the workshop. Who was breaking both guild and Church laws by working today? Tiptoeing to the door, she peeked in. One of the wooden shutters had been thrown back, and a fuzzy band of light fell across both workbench and craftsman. Richard.

He was sending the hammer around the lip of a shining cup with unerring precision. She'd often seen Nicholas and the journeyman at work. Never had their faces contained such intense concentration, such deep contentment, as she now read on his. Quietly Jane backed away and left him to the craft he loved.

The morning mists had melted by the time Jane returned from Cecily's. She entered the courtyard and glanced at the workshop window. The shutter was still open. Further along, and with his back to her, Martin was mulching his roses. Ambivalent, she remained standing on the walk. Last night he'd bared his guilt-ridden soul to her. What if, today, he resented her knowledge and drew away?

Bracing her shoulders, she started toward him.

"Good morning."

He twisted around. Sagging face and heavy eyes said he'd also spent a restless night. His look brightened. Something within her loosened. He came clumsily to his feet, brushing dried grass and soil from his knees. He searched her face for a moment then smiled.

"How are you today ... daughter?"

Warmth filled her.

"I'm fine."

"Does 'Father' come so hard to you?"

"I'm fine, Father."

He was studying her again.

"Now that I know where to look.... You're so like my mother. Your eyes, your mouth, even your expressions."

"Tell me about her."

"Not here. We'll be interrupted. Let's escape London for the day."

Jane and Martin arrived home in the late afternoon to be met in the hall by Bishop Tonstall's impatient clerk.

"My lord wants to see you within the quarter-hour."

Jane panicked. She'd forgotten her desperate need to discover the Bishop's plot.

"I'll come straight away," Martin said. "Has Sir Thomas been called?"

The clerk nodded. "I'll tell the Bishop you're on your way." He bounded down the stairs.

"More business about the Bible smugglers?" Jane asked quickly before Martin could follow the messenger.

"Very likely."

He started down the stairs. Jane hurried after, her mind racing.

"Will you need Richard? I think he's in the workshop."

"I'll send for him if he's wanted."

She had to stop him, to discover what they schemed. Frantic, she tried again.

"Shall I ask Isabel to wait dinner for you?"

"No."

He disappeared out the door. Trembling, Jane sank onto the bottom step. Something was fast coming to a head, and she'd learned nothing. In desperation she looked toward the workshop. Even if she dared disturb Richard, what could he tell her?

As the family gathered for the evening meal, Martin walked in. Jane's knees wobbled with relief. Richard hadn't been sent for, and her father had returned. Nothing had happened yet. She might still have time to discover what was afoot.

The dinner talk was unusually lackluster. Richard ate in brooding silence, avoiding Jane's eyes. Martin remained almost as quiet as his younger son. Several times Jane caught him studying Richard, his expression unreadable. Jane ate sluggishly while Isabel's and Nicholas's casual conversation washed over her. Having slept badly for two nights, her head felt stuffed with wool.

Several times before the meal's end, Martin yawned.

"You must have had a tiring day, Father Denzil," Isabel said. "A man of your age should rest more."

Martin threw her a baleful look. Rather than heed the warning, she continued.

"Growing old is nothing to cause shame. It happens to everyone."

"To women faster than men, or so I'm told." He pushed up from the table. "I'd best retire before I grow too feeble to climb the stairs."

"I was merely trying to show concern," Isabel said.

Richard soon also disappeared up the stairs. Jane had planned to try again to draw her father out about his meeting with Sir Thomas and Bishop Tonstall. With no hope of that now, she pleaded a very real headache and took herself off to bed.

Sleep overtook her the moment her head touched the pillow, and she slept undisturbed until the maid threw back the bed curtains to let in the dawn. Jane yawned and stretched. No urgency accompanied rising on a Sunday morning. The Denzils always breakfasted late and took their ease until time for high mass. Once she was dressed, she would seek her father out and try again to learn what Sir Thomas was planning.

The maid was securing a last lock of Jane's hair when knuckles rapped sharply on her door. Before Jane could turn on her dressing stool, the door burst open. Martin strode in, his face carved from stone.

"Get out," he barked to the maid.

With a frightened squeak, the servant dropped the ribbon and fled. Martin shut the door and slammed the bolt home. His eyes were black ice. The thought came to Jane that he'd once murdered a man. She tried to rise, but her legs refused. He stopped beside her.

"I believe this is yours."

He opened one fist over her lap. Something small and shining dropped onto her green skirt. Jane looked down. The ruby ring! She stared up at Martin, wondering why his figure swam before her eyes, why the room was growing dark.

"You will not faint!"

His words stabbed through the swirling blackness, through the roaring in her ears. Hands gripped her shoulders, forcing her head down. Gradually the dimness passed. The rush mat beneath her feet came into focus again. She struggled free from the iron hold and caught the ring in shaking fingers.

"Where did you find it?"

"On a Bible smuggler. A bearded, gray-eyed fellow."

Jane threw herself on Martin.

"Where is he? What have you done to him?"

Martin tore her hands loose.

"He's in the Tower."

Jane shuddered. The Tower. Where people went in, but never came out. Only their severed heads were displayed on spikes from London Bridge until time and the ravens had reduced them to bare grinning skulls. She collapsed back onto her dressing stool.

Martin continued, his voice cold.

"Tonstall heard rumors of testaments to be delivered by boat at the Old Swan an hour before dawn. This time, Sir Thomas and I were taking no risk of someone learning our plans. Even Richard knew nothing until I woke him. We had men waiting by the river steps. We'd have caught them both, but one of the watch showed himself too soon. They tried to shoot the bridge. The boat smashed on a pillar. We lost one. We fished the other out near Billingsgate."

"Was he hurt?"

Martin's unrelenting look bored into her.

"He has a nasty bump on his head. He swallowed too much water to be questioned immediately. He'll be fit enough to face Tonstall. Sir Thomas left me to deliver him to jail. When the guard found the ring around his neck...." Martin's voice shook with rage. "How did he get that ring? What is he to you?"

Jane's hand tightened on the ruby. Owen was alive and relatively uninjured. Her head lifted defiantly.

"I gave it to him. He's my husband."

Martin blanched.

"You're the informant. I knew when I saw the ring, but I didn't want to believe. My own daughter."

His bitter cry cut Jane to the heart.

"I had to do it."

"Your husband made you?" Hope brushed his face.

Jane came to her feet. The truth was out. The worst that could happen, had. She'd nothing more to fear.

"I did it because people have a right to the scriptures."

"You're breaking the law."

"Whose law? Man's or God's?"

"Man's law backed by the Church, God's representative on earth."

"The scriptures don't give them that authority. The Church bans God's word to keep people enslaved to their own lies and deceit."

"You're speaking heresy. That man has corrupted your mind. He put you to spying."

"Owen knew nothing of what I was doing. When he learned, he wanted me to stop because of the danger."

"He was right. You are in danger, grave danger. If Tonstall or Sir Thomas discovers you...."

"Aren't you going to tell them?"

Martin sucked in his breath. His hand fisted.

"I can't. Whatever you've done, you're my daughter. You must leave for Ipswich today. Tonstall isn't likely to question him before tomorrow. If he mentions you, I'll send word. You can take the first ship to the Continent."

"I won't leave until he's free."

"You don't understand. They caught him in the act. No court alive would find him innocent, especially not the Church. If you stay, you could well find yourself in prison with him."

"At least I'd see him."

Martin caught her shoulders and shook her like a rag doll.

"Be sensible, girl. Wolsey isn't the one who's got him. It's Tonstall. You must go now, while you can."

"Not without Owen." Jane angrily brushed a tear away. This was no time for weeping. "You put him in the Tower. You know where he is. Could he escape?"

Martin staggered back.

"No! Don't even speak to me of escape. Have you forgotten my position? Because you're my daughter, I won't see you in prison as well. Let that be enough."

Martin stumbled into his bedchamber and dropped the ruby ring onto a side table. In the slanting window light, the jewel shown as red as a rose, as red as blood gushing from Lionel Radcott's breast, as red as that which flowed through Jane. His blood.

"I have no further need of it," she'd said, shoving the ring at him as he left. For one terrifying moment, he'd seen his father's face in the set chin and determined brow of his daughter.

Cold sweat broke over his skin. He'd failed utterly. Jane wouldn't leave, and he had no way of forcing her. Where was his sharp lawyer's mind now? He lacked the energy even to lift his hand. An intense longing for his wife swept him. Clare would have known what to do, how to convince this stubborn child of his.

Life had played the ultimate trick on him. For twenty years he had demanded others obey the law, and all the while he had evaded its judgment. He'd forgotten the higher law. He had not escaped from that. God had passed sentence, making him the instrument for his own punishment. His own actions had alienated the wife he loved. Now he had set in motion the destruction of his daughter.

Gradually, like an ancient fortress crumbling before siege weapons, his face broke into a thousand pieces. Scalding tears poured down his lined cheeks and splattered on his tightly gripped hands. His body shook with hoarse sobs.

"Clare, forgive me. God, forgive me."

Richard had been in the jailer's room when the guard, delivering the prisoner to his cell, had discovered the ring and showed it to Martin. Preoccupied with thoughts of bed, he had little thought for his father's stark expression as they strode home through the black streets. Back in his own chamber, Richard kicked off his shoes, tossed his outer clothing aside and fell into bed. He didn't waken until midmorning. When he at last ventured out, he found Jane waiting for him, her face calm but pale, her eyes resolute. Only her trembling hands testified to the strength of her suppressed emotions.

She pushed him back inside and shut the door.

"Richard, for months I've owed you an explanation. Your father already knows. The man you took from the Thames this morning ... he's my husband."

When Richard burst into the book room, Martin was staring out the window.

"Father, what are we going to do?"

Martin turned slowly, his face gaunt. Richard was momentarily shocked out of his immediate concern.

Why, he's an old man.

"Do? About what?"

Richard's thoughts jumped back to his urgent errand.

"About Jane. I only now left her. She told me everything. She intends to go to the Tower tomorrow. She wants to see her...." His tongue stumbled. "To see the prisoner. If she tries, Sir Thomas will surely hear. He'll know who's been the informant. We've got to stop her."

"It's useless. Once Tonstall examines her husband.... She'll be discovered in the end."

"We must do something."

"I wanted her to leave London, if necessary to flee to the Continent. She refused. She won't go without him."

"Couldn't you reason with her?"

"Don't you think I tried? Do you know what her response was? She wanted me to help him escape. Me."

Richard studied his father thoughtfully. He'd wanted to shower Jane with all the artistry at his fingertips. Now he could give her nothing except, perhaps, the man she loved.

"Could he escape?"

"Have you taken leave of your senses also? He's broken the law."

"The law." Richard ground his teeth. "How I've come to loath that word. I should never have gotten involved in this wretched business. Let people have the scriptures if they want them. The Church might look to its own faults more."

Martin opened his mouth then closed it again.

"Father, let's leave this business before it gets worse. Let's see Jane safe and then get out. I could go back to goldsmithing and you -."

"She's been a traitor in our own house."

"I don't care what she's been. I'll not see her end at the stake. Since she refuses to go without that man, we must help him escape."

Martin's eyes narrowed.

"There is another way. We could pretend to help. If he were killed in the attempt, she'd be safe. She'd also no longer be married."

Richard stepped back in shock.

"You'd have us commit murder? What kind of man do you take me for?"

A hopeful look stole over Martin's features. Gradually, his clenching fingers relaxed.

"A better one than I," he said softly.

The face he lifted to Richard contained new life.

"All right. If a way can be found, he must escape. Tell Jane."

Martin returned from the Bishop's palace in late afternoon. Jane and Richard followed him into the book room. Leaving Richard leaning against the door, Jane focused her anxious attention on Martin.

"Tonstall is having your husband transferred to Lollard's Tower in the morning for questioning," he said. "I see no way he can be delivered from either prison. As yet nothing is known about him. He must escape while that remains true."

"But if he can't be gotten out...." Jane's voice caught.

"He'll be out while he's being moved. And more easily reached on the street. That will be our only opportunity."

"What if they move him by river?" Richard asked, joining them at the table.

"They won't. I offered to transfer him. I'll take him through the streets with a minimum escort." He turned his attention back to Jane. "You'll need half-a-dozen men, several carts and a cutpurse. Can you get them?"

Jane wiped damp palms on her skirt. Would Master Greene help? He'd have to.

"Yes."

"One thing." Martin's shaggy brows drew down. "In making the arrangements, you must under no circumstances mention our part. I also want your promise to leave London if we fail."

Jane stiffened. If this effort miscarried, she must try again.

"Unless I have your word, I won't help. Or would your husband wish you to die with him?"

Tears blurred her vision.

"No."

"Have I your word?"

She nodded.

Martin reached for writing materials. The sound of a quill scratching paper filled the room. He drew the last line of a crude map and wiped the nib.

"This is how we'll try."

CHAPTER 24 – SEPTEMBER, 1527

Half-an-hour later, Jane arrived at Master Greene's home. He hurried her into a private chamber.

"Owen Alton's been caught," Jane said without preamble.

"I know. His companion escaped and brought word. We also lost the shipment."

Jane bit back an angry retort. What did books matter?

"He's in the Tower," she said. "He'll be transferred to Bishop Tonstall's prison tomorrow at ten. Master Denzil plans to take him through the streets with only a small guard. He must escape. I've a plan."

When she finished drawing Martin's crude map, explaining as she sketched, she searched Master Green's face, her life hanging on his decision.

"It might be possible," he said. Jane's knees wobbled. He continued. "The timing will be crucial. If Master Denzil should take a different route, or discover the key missing...."

"We have to take that chance. Get Owen on the first ship to the Continent. I'll be going also."

Standing near the Tower-of-London's wide gates, Jane pulled her cloak more closely about her face. Martin had strictly forbidden her to come.

She craned her neck, greedy for a glimpse of Owen. Yesterday, with Master Greene, she'd been confident that the plan would work. Time had been the soil for growing doubt. Suppose Sir Thomas accompanied her father? Or a much larger guard was forced on him? What if a guardsman spotted the cutpurse? Or the carts didn't appear in time? During the long night a thousand nightmare possibilities had sprung up like poisonous weeds. With Owen's life hanging by such a slender chain of events, she couldn't bear to wait at home.

The raucous congestion of Tower Street swirled around her. Carts and barrows, hawkers and delivery boys, horseback travelers and nobility, long strings of laden packhorses, housewives and servants on their way to market, all fought for space. The habitual press was such that even King Henry himself had been forced on more than one occasion to wait for the way to clear. Today, the teeming throng should provide the cutpurse opportunity to lift Owen's fetter key from her father's belt.

Her father's black gown came into view. He strode out Tower gate, a single guardsman at his elbow. Two more guards followed with Owen, shackled, between them.

Jane's look fixed on her husband. Owen, shivering, leaned into the cutting wind without cap or gown. His rust-colored jerkin and black hose were begrimed with muck. Tears blinded her. Even as she blinked them away, the crowds swallowed him up.

Jane started up Tower Street after them. At times, she could see the top of Owen's tousled head, her father's black velvet cap, the stave ends of the guards. At other times, the crush blocked her view.

Any moment now a cart should lurch out from a side lane to provide the delay the cutpurse needed. A string of packhorses turning from Minchen Lane blocked her. When she broke clear, Owen and his guards had again disappeared in the crowd. By the time she sighted them, they were nearing East Cheap. Already the congestion grew less. Had the cart halted Martin or not? Jane's mouth dried.

They marched along East Cheap. The thinner crowds forced Jane to fall back. She shielded behind a mounted rider. Across the city, and growing ever nearer, she could see the dark roof and looming spire of St. Paul's that marked their destination. Her body ran with cold sweat as she walked on.

They left East Cheap behind. The horseman turned off. Jane slipped behind a fish cart. They were entering Candlewick Street. Ahead, through the parade of market-bound housewives, noisy apprentices and the occasional cart, lay London stone. What it marked had long been forgotten. Only the marker remained, wrapped in protective iron bars. The stone, claiming the center of the street, was a curse to carters.

Today, London stone was a marker for Owen. If her father's plan succeeded, Owen would be free before reaching it. If he passed the stone still shackled, he'd be walking to his death. They were almost upon it.

A cart traveling twenty paces ahead of her father attempted to overtake an offal barrow and ran a wheel onto the marker. The cart tipped. Its load of empty wine tuns spilled, rumbling over the cobblestones like a long run of thunder. Passers-by leaped for safety, filling the air with angry protests. The carter met their objections with curses for the barrow pusher. The pusher answered the abuse with simple effectiveness. He grabbed a bucket of his odorous load and heaved.

The wet slippery entrails arched through the air like a shower of curling pink ribbons.

Pandemonium broke loose. Women screamed. Men swore. An offal-decorated merchant lunged at the barrow pusher and knocked into a laborer. The carter cursed all comers until he was felled by a furious tiler. A gleeful apprentice grabbed the bucket to finish what the offal pusher had started. A free-for-all broke loose in the midst of entrails and rolling tuns.

The fish cart ahead of Jane prudently pulled to one side. Spectators, drawn by the uproar, ringed the area. Over the head of an excited servingmaid, Jane saw her father speak to two of the guardsmen and point to the fray. The men moved forward, their staves held in readiness. The remaining guard, chained to his prisoner, gave full attention to the brawl. Jane spotted a small, wiry man step close to Owen.

Between one heartbeat and the next, Owen was free and spinning. He raced through the crowd, pelting down the street in her direction, running for his life. The wiry man followed hard on his heels. The guard shouted and started after them, the empty shackle chain swinging in his hand.

The three men came barreling toward her. The fleet-footed guard closed on the small man and sent him sprawling. Owen was nearly upon Jane. She quickly ducked her head. He mustn't recognize her and break stride. He flashed past. She looked up to see him sprinting for a side street. Behind her the guard shouted. She turned and purposely stepped directly into his path. She only had time to grab his arm before they crashed down in a tangled heap on the dirty cobblestones. She lay gasping for breath.

My cloak is ruined and probably my gown as well.

The guard staggered to his feet, head swinging, searching for his fleeing prisoner. Owen had vanished. Jane saw the guard glance over his shoulder. The small man also had disappeared. The guard glared down at her. With an angry growl, he yanked her to her feet. Leaving her staggering unsteadily, he returned to his companions.

The city watch swept in a moment later to restore order. Jane hobbled away, aching with every step. She would be covered with bruises. What did it matter? Owen was free.

"What do you mean you lost him?!"

Jane stared incredulously at Master Greene in the back room of his shop three hours later.

"My man lost Owen when the guard knocked him down," he said.

"So he's out there all alone. He doesn't know about the ship tonight, and he hasn't even a gown to keep him warm."

Jane set her jaw, fighting tears. She was acting like an hysterical child, but she didn't care. She'd expected to find Owen here. His absence left her desolate.

"No doubt he'll contact me," Master Greene said.

Jane buried her fists in her cloak. She would enjoy hitting this man.

"Should I see him first, when and where are we to meet the ship?"

Jane embroidered in the hall, her fingers moving automatically, every muscle tense, as the hours dragged past with no word of Owen. Only a part of her was in the Denzil home. Most of her was wandering in limbo with her husband. Once during the long afternoon, she heard the outer door slam and steps coming up the stairs. She sprang up, heart pounding. Richard appeared on the landing. He gazed at her for a moment then continued up the first-floor stairs. Jane saw no more of him until mealtime.

Martin arrived home as the servants were setting the table. Jane drew him into the book room and told him that Owen was missing.

"He's likely made contact by now and is in hiding till his ship leaves," Martin said.

"If he had, I'd have been told."

Cecily and Hugh's unexpected arrival prevented further discussion. Isabel had invited them. After the meal was served, Isabel turned to Cecily with a smug look.

"Father Denzil lost his prisoner today." She was obviously enjoying having news of which Cecily knew nothing. "The fellow ran off faster than the king's post."

Martin's mouth set in irritation.

"Did Tonstall fall into a rage when you told him?" Cecily asked Martin after Isabel had completed her version of the day's excitement.

"Naturally he was disappointed. I took full responsibility."

Jane looked up, startled. She'd not considered the repercussions to him.

"Will you be in trouble?" she asked.

Martin's mouth gentled.

"Not in the way you mean. Wolsey has decided my services are no longer needed. After today, I'm nothing more than a simple attorney again."

Richard swung to stare at his father. Jane saw a light flicker in his eyes.

Hugh spoke up.

"Isn't the Bishop mounting a search?"

"Yes," Cecily said. "They may catch him again."

Jane's heart stopped. Richard turned.

"Shut up, Cecily."

"Tonstall is making an effort," Martin said. "I doubt he'll succeed. We weren't able to learn the fellow's name or even his nationality. As I told Tonstall, he looked German."

Martin's attempts to reassure her did little to ease Jane's growing fears. His reluctant reply said clearly that Tonstall was making an all-out search for Owen. Only a handful of hours remained until they were to meet the ship. Where was he?

Sir Thomas arrived as the family was gathering in the hall to listen to Cecily play the harpsichord. Martin waved their visitor to a seat near the fireplace. Jane moved close enough to eavesdrop. After a few pleasantries, Sir Thomas came to the point of his visit.

"Martin, I think you've been hasty in requesting to be dismissed. You're not to blame for the prisoner's escape. Clearly the informant discovered when you were moving him."

"I lost the man, and that makes me responsible. You'll do better without me."

"But what about Richard's career?"

"He took to the law at my insistence. If he wishes to continue, I have a few influential friends I hope would recommend him." Martin smiled briefly at Sir Thomas. "If he wishes to return to goldsmithing...."

A maidservant appeared at Jane's elbow.

"There's a messenger from your sister at the door."

A message from Lucy? She was still at Horne Hall.

Jane's mouth went dry at another possibility. She jumped to her feet. Curbing her impatience, she followed the servant down the stairs.

Of the four wall sconces set to light the main staircase, Isabel kept candles burning in two. The meager light revealed a muffled figure in the darkest corner of the entry. The moment the servant disappeared toward the kitchen, the man straightened and looked up. Jane's heart leaped. This was not a messenger from Master Greene. This was Owen himself! She flew down the last steps and into his arms.

For two heartbeats, he was all that existed. Then, in the hall above, Cecily launched into a new tune. Pans clattered beyond the half-open kitchen door at her elbow. Reality broke through Jane's fever of relief and ecstasy. Any moment they could be discovered. She tore herself from Owen's embrace and hurried him into the workshop.

"Wait while I light a candle," she whispered.

She made her cautious way to the forge and started a taper from a banked coal. Owen stripped the cloth wrappings from his head, dropped them on the workbench and reached for Jane.

"You're safe," she said. "I was so frightened."

"You weren't the only one. Master Denzil found your ring. I saw his face. He knows something. We're leaving now, this moment."

Jane heard the sound of feet on the stairs.

"Hush," she murmured. "Someone's coming."

Jane felt Owen tense. Quickly, quietly, he put her behind him and snuffed the candle. In the near blackness, she heard the soft silken rip of a sword being drawn. Scarcely breathing, she focused her whole being on the sound of footsteps. They stopped at the stair bottom.

"Jane?" Richard called.

Her taut muscles relaxed.

"It's only Richard," she whispered close to Owen's ear. "I'll go to him."

"No."

The footsteps neared. Richard, flickering candle in hand, appeared in the doorway. He halted and lifted his taper. In the entrapping circle of light, Owen's blade flashed, its point at Richard's throat.

"Owen, no!" Jane grabbed his free arm. "You don't understand. He helped you escape, he and his father."

She looked frantically from Owen's disbelieving face to Richard's antagonistic one. She'd momentarily forgotten that they had been rivals for her hand. They had not.

"Why would they help me?"

Jane bit her lip. How could she explain with Richard standing there?

"They saved you for my sake. Please believe me and put your sword away. Richard, come in quickly before we're discovered."

With a dubious expression, Owen lowered his weapon and stepped back. Richard pulled the door shut and set his candle on the workbench. She gave him a grateful smile.

"Your father said Owen should hide in a safe place until time to meet the ship. What safer place than here?"

"I didn't come to be hidden," Owen said. "I came to fetch you."

With his sword gripped in one hand and catching Jane's fingers in the other, he started toward the door.

"Owen, wait." Jane pulled back. "Richard, please. I must speak to him alone."

For one desperate moment, she feared he would refuse. Then, lips thinning, Richard left.

Owen studied her.

"Do you trust the Denzils that much?"

"Yes." Jane spoke softly, hurriedly. "Master Denzil recognized the ring because he gave it to my mother. He's my father, Owen. That's why he helped us, why you're safe here. Richard doesn't know. Please, Owen. I want to stay until time to meet the ship. I need to stay. Martin Denzil is my father. I may never see him again."

The house slept around Jane and, beyond the house, London slept. Jane knelt to lock her three chests. The smallest would go tonight, the others Dick Bolt would send later. On the dressing table the candle flickered. Soon it would be gone. She would be gone first.

Isabel would quickly take over this chamber which had been hers for two years. That didn't matter. Long before the room gained a new identity, she would be settled with Owen in their own home in Antwerp. She hoped Owen and Richard had survived being closeted together these last hours while she packed and spent one final night with her father. At least now Owen had no cause to fear her affection for Richard.

A soft tap interrupted her musings. Owen strode in, clearly impatient to be on their way. She flew to him, ablaze with love. Only when he released her did she notice Richard and her father behind him. She reached her cloak down from the peg.

"I've left notes for Cecily and Lucy telling them I've eloped," she told Martin. "Please send the rest of my chests to Owen's half-brother in the morning."

She glanced around the room one final time, her eyes misting.

"We'd best go," Owen said, hoisting her smallest chest to his shoulder.

Jane nodded. Stepping to her dressing table, she picked up a book. She stopped before Richard, standing pale and withdrawn beside the bed.

"Thank you for all your kindness. I want you to have this. You've seen enough of them go to the flames. I hope you'll find a better use for this one."

She shoved her English Testament into his hands and fled.

In the silent, empty room, misery washed over Richard like the tide over the rocks beneath London Bridge. So many different images of Jane filled his mind and tore at his heart, images that would gradually fade over the passing years. One picture, though, he would never be able to forget: her look of ecstasy when she had gone running into her husband's arms. Richard seated himself at the dressing table. Tyndale's testament lay in the pool of flickering light before him. He studied the plain cover for a moment. After lighting a fresh candle, he opened the book and began to read.

Fog filled the streets that Jane, Owen and her father followed on their way to the Thames. It blotted out the stars, turned the round, brilliant moon into a wan hazy plate and reduced the surroundings to a small circle lit by her father's torch. Buildings and street corners materialized only when they were upon them. Even as mist blotted out London, Jane blocked thought of past and future from her mind. For this brief time, the dark streets and the men with her were all that existed. One man she'd found, now only to lose again. The other she'd lost to find again. For this short precious time, she had them both.

All too soon, they reached the river. She could hear the creaking of ships at anchor below the bridge. Owen halted at the end of a darkened warehouse near the river steps.

"Wait here."

He disappeared into the drifting mist, her chest balanced on his shoulder. Martin shifted the torch and reached into his purse.

"Take the ring," he said quietly, pressing the familiar ornament into her palm, "proof that you're my daughter. Someday I'll tell them all, even Richard."

Jane's fingers curled around her father's gift. Martin's hand tightened on hers. His words came haltingly.

"Will I ever see you again?"

"Oh, yes." Jane threw her arms about his neck, unable to keep the tears back. "We're part of each other now."

Soft steps padded on the cobblestones. Owen reappeared without her chest.

"The boat's waiting."

Jane clung to Martin for one moment longer.

"Thank you for my husband's life. Goodbye, Father."

She was gone. Martin continued to peer into the night long after the sounds of their footsteps faded. Gradually, his shoulders lifted. She'd said they would meet again. He must believe that. But now Richard waited at home to hear they'd gotten away safely, waited in pain and desolation as he himself had once waited for his father. He must go to his son. Martin turned and hurried toward home.

The End.

... here and it had [...]own [...]
caused Martin to pause just for a [...]
She drew a steadying breath.

"I can't wed Richard because I'm a bastard."